By Nicole Edwards

The Alluring Indulgence Series
Kaleb

Zane

Travis

Holidays with the Walker Brothers

Ethan

Braydon

Sawyer

Brendon

The Club Destiny Series
Conviction

Temptation

Addicted

Seduction

Infatuation

Captivated

Devotion

Perception

Entrusted

Adored

The Coyote Ridge Series
Curtis

The Dead Heat Ranch Series
Boots Optional

Betting on Grace

Overnight Love

By Nicole Edwards (cont.)

The Devil's Bend Series

Chasing Dreams

Vanishing Dreams

The Devil's Playground Series

Without Regret

The Pier 70 Series

Reckless

Fearless

Speechless

The Sniper 1 Security Series

Wait for Morning

Never Say Never

The Southern Boy Mafia Series

Beautifully Brutal

Beautifully Loyal

Standalone Novels

A Million Tiny Pieces

Inked on Paper

Writing as Timberlyn Scott

Unhinged

Unraveling

Chaos

Naughty Holiday Editions

2015

Speechless

A Pier 70 Novel
Book 3

Nicole Edwards

Nicole Edwards Limited
PO Box 806
Hutto, Texas 78634
www.NicoleEdwardsLimited.com
www.slipublishing.com

Speechless – A Pier 70 Novel is a work of fiction. Names, characters, businesses, places, events and incidents either are the products of the author's imagination or used in a fictitious manner. Any resemblance to actual persons, living or dead, or actual events is purely coincidental.

Cover Image: © Pavlo Vakhrushev | 123rf.com (front cover image - 35248917); © carther | 123rf.com (back cover image - 17825407)

Ebook Image: © magenta10 | 123rf.com (formatting image - 14284060)

Cover Design: © Nicole Edwards Limited

Editing: Blue Otter Editing **www.BlueOtterEditing.com**

ISBN (ebook): 978-1-939786-63-0
ISBN (print): 978-1-939786-64-7

Gay Romance
M/M interactions
Mature Audience

Dedication

This book is dedicated to anyone who suffers from depression, who knows someone who suffers from depression, who has lost someone to this illness, who works to eliminate the stigma associated with suicide, and who helps to raise awareness for this disease. We are the voice and we need to be heard.

Dear Reader,

This book touches on some very sensitive subjects, including suicide and depression, all of which should not be taken lightly.

If you or someone that you know suffers from depression or has thoughts of suicide, please, I encourage you to seek professional help.

If you are in crisis, call 1-800-273-TALK (8255)

National Suicide Prevention Lifeline

http://www.suicidepreventionlifeline.org

For more information or resources on suicide prevention:

American Foundation for Suicide Prevention

http://www.afsp.org

Table of Contents

Prologue

Thursday, June 2nd

TEAGUE CARTER TRIED to ignore Hudson Ballard. Hell, he'd tried to ignore the bastard for the past … what? Two years now? Maybe three? *Who freaking knows and who really cares.* Regardless, it was getting more and more difficult as each day passed, but he wanted to think he'd done a pretty decent job all this time.

Until now.

Until today.

Until this fucking cruise, where he'd seen more of Hudson than he cared to.

Yup, Teague had mastered the art of avoidance or so he'd thought. But here on this stupid cruise ship, with the way Hudson was watching him, avoiding the man was damn near impossible. To the point that Teague simply wanted to punch him. In the mouth.

But he hadn't.

No, he had settled for drinking himself into oblivion and it'd worked. He could no longer feel his fingers or toes, and his tongue had long ago gone numb thanks to the whiskey he'd been drinking like water. Chasing it with beer helped, too. It'd been the only way he could handle watching Hudson talk to the guy he'd brought on the ship with him. Stupid asshole.

He peered over his shoulder at Hudson, noticing the big guy was watching him intently. Teague had the sudden urge to stick out his tongue, but he knew that was petty and childish, and he was doing his best not to give in to those impulses. Shit, he was twenty-five years old, for fuck's sake. He could act like a grown-up when need be.

Still didn't mean he liked the fact that Hudson had brought along a plus one on this trip. Teague was pretty sure someone had said the guy's name was AJ, but he wasn't positive. Nor did he give a fuck. What the hell kind of name was that, anyway?

"A. J." Teague smiled to himself as he began saying the letters faster. "A. J. A. J. A. J. Age. Age. Age. Age. Age." He laughed because they now sounded funny and made his tongue tingle.

He rolled his eyes and lifted his empty glass. Too bad the bar was closed already. Then again, the reception was over, which meant the private room would probably be closing soon, too. The alcohol was definitely helping to keep him from thinking about Hudson. In fact, he'd done everything in his power not to pay attention to Hudson and his new boy toy. The boy toy who had been signing to Hudson earlier and was now talking to Milly.

Did anyone else find that strange?

Gay guy. Straight girl. No matter how you calculated it, the math didn't add up.

Speechless

Damn. He'd obviously had far too much to drink, because it sure as shit looked like Milly and the guy were flirting it up. But that couldn't be the case. The asshole was here with Hudson.

Hudson the Prick.

Mmm-hmm, that was what Teague had started calling him. It was a good name for him, too.

When his head started spinning again, Teague knew it was time to get to his cabin. He wasn't sure how he was going to make that happen, but he figured he'd get there eventually. If not, he could always lie down on the floor and take a nap. It wasn't like anyone would be worried about where he was or who he was with. Unlike everyone else on this stupid cruise, he didn't have a plus one. He was rolling solo, like always.

Oh, wait. Roan was, too.

Whatever.

Roan wasn't important right now.

"Son of a fucking bitch," he muttered, holding his empty glass. No more whiskey and no more bartender meant heading back to his room was a definite must.

He managed to twist in his chair and get his feet firmly on the floor, but when he went to stand, the room started spinning again. He had to sit back down. Luckily, no one had moved the chair or he would've been on his ass on the floor, and he was seriously questioning whether or not he could've gotten up from that point.

Okay, one more try.

Again, Teague pushed to his feet, this time remaining upright long enough to get away from the table. He started in the direction of the door, hoping he would make it. Right foot. Left foot. Right foot.

Wait, which foot was he on?

He looked up at the door. That was a long-ass way from where he was, but...

Shit.

He stumbled again and grabbed the nearest chair. "If the ship would stop rocking, I'd be fine." He wasn't sure who he was talking to, but the words helped his tongue not feel so numb, so he continued to ramble as he pushed away from the chair and made another go at getting to the door.

Unfortunately, the door disappeared from view when a giant body stepped in front of him.

Fucking great.

Now he had to deal with Hudson the Prick.

Teague instantly looked at Hudson's hands as he signed. He had absolutely no fucking idea what Hudson said, but if he knew Hudson, it was going to be something that involved telling Teague what to do. So he replied in kind. "Thanks for the bit of advice, Dad."

The next thing Teague knew, he tripped on his own foot, and the world tilted sideways. Just as he was gearing up to kiss the floor, Hudson's enormous arms wrapped around him, keeping him from face-planting. Because he was too drunk to do otherwise, he allowed Hudson to get him to his feet by putting his arm around his back.

Hmm. The guy smelled good.

Then again, he always smelled good.

Something dark and woodsy...

Had to be cologne. The expensive shit, at that.

Speechless

While Hudson guided him toward the door, Teague tried to ignore the heat that seared him from Hudson's touch. He hated how fucking good it felt for someone to be touching him like this. He wasn't sure anyone had ever attempted to take care of him or given a flying fuck whether or not he made it where he needed to go, but it seemed Hudson was doing just that. Sure, Teague had friends, kind of, but most of them would've laughed their ass off once Teague hit the ground. They wouldn't have helped him by any means. And since he had no family...

Teague was distracted by Hudson's scent.

"Why the fuck do you have to smell so good?" He tried to peer up at Hudson, wanting to look into those emerald-green eyes. "And why the hell aren't you with your boyfriend?"

He knew better than to expect an answer from Hudson. The guy was mute; he couldn't speak. If he signed a response, Teague wouldn't understand, anyway. And truthfully, he didn't want an answer to that. He'd done his best not to think about Hudson and that guy sharing a room, sharing a bed...

He shook his head, trying to dislodge the stupidity that was bouncing around inside his brain.

Hudson helped him onto the elevator, then pointed to the panel by the door.

Teague reached out and hit a button. Seven was a good number. It was random, sure, but that was because he couldn't remember what floor he was on.

When they got to the floor, Hudson helped him out, still holding him upright as he led him down the hall. For some reason, this didn't look like the right one, but Teague really didn't know. His vision was blurry, so he couldn't tell for sure. The carpet was different, maybe?

"Not my floor," he mumbled, trying to remember what floor he actually was on. "Room number doesn't have a seven."

Or did it?

He felt Hudson's arm tighten around him, and he got the sense Hudson wasn't pleased with him, but he didn't give much of a fuck. No, he didn't give a fuck at all. The thought made him chuckle.

No fuck at all.

It seemed like forever before they finally made it to the right floor. It had only taken another detour on the wrong one before he got lucky. This one looked like the right place. And this—he reached out his arm and pointed—was the right door. Maybe. When they stopped, he noticed Hudson's hands moving, but he didn't know what Hudson was saying, so he frowned back at him.

Not wanting to touch Hudson any more than he had to, Teague attempted to stand up on his own. "Fuck. Why's the room spinning so damn much?" And who stretched it? The last part he kept to himself because his lips felt funny.

He peered up at Hudson at the same time those penetrating green eyes glared back at him. He was tempted to ask him what his problem was, but then…

Son of a bitch.

Hudson's hand dove into Teague's pocket, dangerously close to… Oh, fuck. Just a little to the left…

No, wait. Not to the left. He wasn't supposed to want Hudson touching him.

He tried to jerk away. "I didn't say you could touch me." Teague shifted his hips, trying to keep Hudson's hand from brushing against his dick.

Unfortunately—*or was it fortunately?*—Hudson's hand disappeared as quickly as it had appeared.

Speechless

Everything seemed to be happening in slow motion. Hudson unlocking the door, pushing it open with his foot, then maneuvering Teague forward until the door was pushing against his shoulder. While he let Hudson do all the work, his brain started conjuring up images of a naked Hudson in the room with him.

Mmm. He liked that idea. "I knew one day I'd get you to my room. Didn't think it'd be so soon." It was true. He'd had a million fantasies over the years about Hudson. He'd used those fantasies when he jacked off, in fact.

As they neared the bed, Teague found himself staring up at Hudson, his eyes trained on the guy's mouth. He wanted to know what those lips would feel like, what his tongue tasted like... Mmm. Those lips looked good. They'd look really good wrapped around his dick.

He quickly looked into Hudson's eyes. They didn't look happy. They never looked happy.

When Hudson nodded toward the bed, Teague once again focused on Hudson's mouth.

"Fuck, I've wanted to kiss you for so goddamn long." He didn't mean for the words to come out, but so help him, he couldn't stop talking. "Sometimes I wish I could hate you as much as I pretend to."

That was also true. He would prefer the hatred to these overwhelming cravings he had for the man. He hated that he wanted him so fucking much.

Hudson once again urged him closer to the bed, using his bigger body to shift Teague backward, but before he hit the mattress, Teague gave in to his desires. He reached for Hudson, latching on to his neck and pulling him down until their mouths were crushed together. Warmth penetrated him, but Hudson seemed to resist, but only for a second.

If he hadn't been drunk and so fucking horny, he would've questioned why the hell he had instigated this kiss. He didn't do the kissing thing. Ever.

But he couldn't bring himself to care right now.

And then Teague experienced an earth-moving lip-lock that rocked him to his very soul. The way Hudson took control, gripping his chin as he fucked his mouth with his tongue... Oh, shit. He never wanted it to end. He wanted to climb this man's giant body, to devour him whole, to take everything Hudson was willing to give him.

The room began to spin again, but Teague didn't let go, clinging to Hudson while their tongues dueled. His dick was swelling and throbbing, desperate to feel Hudson's touch. The arm around his waist tightened as Hudson deepened the kiss, making Teague see stars. It was fucking fabulous.

And then it was over.

Hudson's warmth disappeared as Teague fell onto the bed. Lifting his head, he saw a blurry form, but it didn't seem to be getting closer.

"Where're you goin'?" he called out to Hudson, not wanting him to leave.

But then Hudson was gone, and Teague's eyes opened, the sun blinding him, making his head pound from the hangover that wreaked havoc on his brain and his stomach in equal measure. He closed his eyes, willing the dream to return. He wanted to see what happened next. He wanted Hudson to come back, to join him on the bed...

Son of a bitch.

As he felt the ship rock beneath him, Teague sighed. His mind was once again playing cruel tricks on him. It was morning, he was still dressed in the stupid tuxedo, lying on the bed, trying to recall that dream...

Yep, his mind was definitely playing cruel, cruel tricks.

One

Friday, July 1ˢᵗ

"GIANT ASSHOLE!" TEAGUE kicked a box out of his way as he pretended to be looking for something.

He wasn't.

Looking.

More like, he was trying to cool the fuck off because he couldn't deal with being in the same room with Hudson for one minute longer. The man made him...

"Son of a— Stupid, motherfu— Giant fucking asshole!" Teague kicked the box again, then thrust his hands through his hair and tugged. It was a wonder he had any hair at all, what with Hudson irritating him to the point he wanted to yank it all out.

Teague growled, gritting his teeth.

Hudson frustrated him to the point of insanity. And for no apparent reason, either, which, yes, Teague knew was stupid on his part. Still, he couldn't stop his reaction to the man. It wasn't that he liked the guy. No way. Definitely not that.

Sometimes he could tolerate Hudson.

Sometimes he could even handle working alongside him.

Once in a while he didn't mind looking at him, but that was only because he found him mildly attractive. Okay, *devastatingly* attractive. That was all. But a lot of people did. It wasn't hard to figure out why. The guy was a freaking giant mass of muscle. Six foot two … long and lean, with beefed-up arms, smoldering emerald eyes and thick, dark hair, which he kept cut shorter on the sides, a little longer on the top. The strong jaw was a nice touch, too. Plus, the cheekbones… And maybe his fantastic lips…

Teague growled again.

He wasn't the only person in the world who found the guy attractive, jeezus. A lot of men did, apparently, since it seemed Hudson had a long list of them coming by to see him, talk to him, flirt with him.

"Giant, stupid asshole."

Teague kicked another box, trying to get the image of Hudson smiling at that guy out of his head. The one who had stopped by a little while ago to chat it up. Teague had seen him come around before, all buddy-buddy with Hudson. They'd looked all cozy and shit, and for some insane reason, Teague had lost his shit watching the spectacle. It reminded him of the anger he'd felt for Hudson before he found out the hot guy who'd accompanied him on that stupid cruise had been Hudson's brother.

It would've been nice if someone would've just told him.

Speechless

His reactions were irrational, he'd be the first to admit that, and with each passing day, he seemed to be getting more and more incensed by everything Hudson did. For whatever reason, Teague couldn't stop thinking about the giant asshole. The sad thing was, he could even pinpoint the exact moment when he'd taken a turn for the worse. It was the night of Cam and Gannon's wedding, when he'd had too much to drink. Somehow, he'd managed to make it back to his cabin and passed out on his bed. The stupid alcohol had played cruel tricks on his brain, and he'd dreamed that Hudson had been the one to get him safely into his bed.

Oh, and then there was the part where he and Hudson had kissed.

Stupid dream.

A whole goddamn *month* had passed since they'd returned from the cruise when Cam and Gannon had pledged their eternal love for one another—the same cruise Teague had been on when he'd had that crazy fucking dream. He should be over this shit by now, not allowing it to drive him stark raving mad.

For the most part, everything had gotten back to normal, yet Teague couldn't stop thinking about that damn dream. The reason he knew it was a dream was because he was directly opposed to kissing, yet there had been a few rare instances, but *never* had it been like that. Never had one man had the ability to steal his sanity with one simple kiss. Though, if he were being honest, the kiss from that dream hadn't been simple by any means. It had been hot. Smoking hot. Turn-up-the-fucking-air-conditioner hot.

Which meant it couldn't possibly have happened and his subconscious was likely on crack.

However, sometimes, when he caught Hudson looking at him—which, yes, the giant asshole did from time to time—Teague wondered if maybe it had been real. If at some point on that cruise he had crushed his mouth to Hudson's and allowed the man to kiss him senseless.

"No way did I kiss him." Teague wasn't that stupid. "I wouldn't kiss that giant asshole if my dick depended on it."

Speaking of his dick.

Teague adjusted himself, righting the freaking steel rod in his shorts so as not to scare half the lake with the boner he was sporting. All thanks to Hudson and those stupid memories of that stupid dream.

"Giant asshole."

The sound of a wrench tapping against metal had Teague spinning around to find Hudson staring at him. Although Hudson was mute, he could hear, which meant he had probably listened to Teague's tirade. Since he couldn't take back the last few minutes, Teague decided to pretend they'd never happened.

He was getting good at the pretending thing. He pretended he didn't like Hudson. He pretended that he didn't wish that dream had been real and he'd actually had the opportunity to kiss the guy. He pretended he didn't want to feel the man's body covering his in every possible way, owning him in a way no man had ever done before.

Yes, sir, Hudson Ballard was a giant fucking asshole, and Teague couldn't stop thinking about him. He was crazy fucked-up for sure.

Speechless

Since they had to work together, that magnified Teague's problems tenfold. He spent most of the day alongside Hudson, helping out with the boat repairs, rubbing elbows with the guy while doing his best to ignore him. Since it was the middle of the summer, it seemed all they did was work on engines and fiberglass repairs, and Teague's assistance was needed more than ever because of the workload. It wasn't quite so bad in the fall and winter because most people stored their boats and didn't require so much maintenance.

Not the case right now.

Which meant there wasn't going to be any relief in sight.

"What?" Teague snapped at Hudson, noticing the giant asshole was still watching him closely. "Take a picture, it'll last longer."

Yes, he sounded like a fucking twelve-year-old. So fucking what?

Right now, he was too pissed to care. It bothered him that he had this reaction to Hudson, more so because he didn't know why. They'd worked together for a long time now. In the beginning, Teague hadn't had a problem, other than the mild attraction that was easy enough to ignore. As time went on and he'd gotten to know Hudson a little better, it was possible that he might've developed a tiny little crush. And it should've been fleeting, but for some reason, it had dug its claws into his brain and was hanging on for dear life.

But he was strong enough to ignore it. Strong enough that he shouldn't allow one man to get to him like this. There was no way he should be letting Hudson derail him from what needed to be done. Yet, for the past month, Teague's frustration had only intensified.

He needed to get laid. That's what his problem was. It would be in his best interest to take his ass to the club tonight, find some guy—or two—he could pass the time with, get down and dirty for a little while, and then get back to the world of the living. That was how he'd handled it in the past.

Until that fucking dream.

Now, no matter how much he wanted to go out and tie one on, have a brief, one-night fling, Teague was having a damn hard time following through.

All because of the giant asshole staring at him now.

And that was what pissed Teague off the most.

HUDSON WATCHED TEAGUE throw another fit, stomping around, kicking shit, and most of all, acting like a five-year-old who didn't get his way—the very reason Hudson had started referring to him as a kid. At some point, the nickname had simply caught on.

For the past few minutes, he'd caught glimpses of the kid as he passed by his office, muttering to himself. Like usual, Hudson had no idea what Teague was going on and on about, nor did he really care. With Teague, it usually had something to do with him since, for some inexplicable reason, Hudson managed to rub him the wrong way.

The tantrums weren't new, but they seemed to be intensifying as time went by. Rather than kick something once, Teague now did so repeatedly. However, he had stopped throwing wrenches, which was a good thing. They'd had to do a little extra repair on a couple of boats thanks to those fits.

Speechless

As for his creative commentary, Teague always had a way of expressing himself using mostly four-letter words, but now, it seemed he was getting more imaginative. And if Hudson had to guess, his new nickname was *giant fucking asshole*. He liked that one, actually. Better than Hudson the Prick, which had been what Teague called him for the entire month of June.

The kid had been doing this nonstop ever since they had returned from the cruise, and for the life of him, Hudson didn't know why. Well, other than the fact that Teague didn't like him, but that was nothing new.

Since the day Hudson had started working at Pier 70 Marina a little more than two years ago, he and Teague had been on the outs. His best assumption was that there was an undeniable attraction between them that both of them were denying—which, now that he thought about it, was a complete contradiction. Not to mention, it was a dumb-ass excuse for Teague to be such a dickhead.

Hudson couldn't speak for Teague, but he knew that he'd been pretending not to find the guy utterly fuckable, and based on the rage-filled grumblings, Teague was, too. That sort of inexplicable draw tended to make people a little irritable, sure. Especially when they were ignoring it.

Fortunately, Hudson knew how to hide his emotions far better than Teague. He'd had more years of practice.

One thing Hudson had noticed lately was that any time he had a visitor, Teague got more irritable. Whether it was when his brother, AJ, stopped by—which hadn't been until recently—or one of his buddies whom he'd known most of his life ... seemed any time a *man* was there to see him, Teague's frown deepened. Since his brother and his friends had taken to giving Hudson a hard time about the kid, he could only imagine how it looked. But in his defense, not one of the men who had visited him as of late was he romantically involved with. If Teague would act like a grown-up and *ask*, he would know that.

As he'd done several times before, when it was clear Teague's tantrum wasn't going to end anytime in the near future, Hudson had picked up a wrench and tapped on the side of a metal can he kept on his toolbox for this very reason. Because he was mute—had been since birth—Hudson couldn't announce his presence any other way. Well, unless he wanted to happen upon the kid and tap him on the shoulder, but that would likely get him sucker punched. Teague was nothing if not prone to violence.

Realizing he was still staring at Teague, he turned away and headed back into the tiny boat repair office, allowing the kid some privacy to pull himself together. It would've been a hell of a lot easier if Teague would simply tell Hudson what his issue with him was, but that wasn't the way Teague worked. The kid kept everything bottled up, and from what Hudson could tell, he let loose by having casual sex with the losers he encountered at the clubs he frequented.

Speechless

Although he'd been tempted to do a little investigating of his own, Hudson didn't know this firsthand. He'd never followed Teague to one of these infamous clubs, had never seen him actually go home with a guy. Until recently, he wouldn't have had the opportunity. But now that he and Teague lived across the hall from one another, each of them renting the apartments above the Pier 70 Marina office, Hudson wouldn't be so lucky. He prayed he never had to encounter that because, honestly, he wasn't sure how he would react.

Yes, he fucking wanted that man. All five-foot-nine inches, with his steel-blue eyes, shaggy blond hair, and surfer-boy good looks. Teague definitely did it for him in many ways. He'd had plenty of fantasies about getting him on his knees, watching as he…

Oh, hell, now he was going to be thinking about that shit.

No, he never intended to act on his insane attraction to the kid.

For one, Teague was almost ten years younger than he was. At thirty-five, Hudson was far too old to be interested in someone as emotionally immature as Teague. He could've said that Teague was immature in every way, but despite the tantrums and the foul language, Hudson got the impression Teague used that as his armor, shielding himself from ever getting close to someone. Why, Hudson didn't know. And he never intended to pry in order to find out, either.

Nope, they were all better off if Hudson focused his desires elsewhere.

As he was sitting at his desk, feet propped up, tossing the wrench high in the air and catching it, Hudson heard Teague's cell phone ring.

"'Lo?"

Hudson rolled his eyes.

"Hell yeah, man. I'll meet you at the club tonight. What time?" Teague's tone was far more cheerful than two minutes ago, when he'd been cursing a blue streak.

Hudson dropped his feet to the floor but kept his ass planted in his chair.

Not your business.

Not your business.

Not your—

"Cool." *Pause.* "Yeah." *Pause.* "Fuck yeah. I'm game." *Pause.* "Threesome, baby. Haven't done that in a while." *Pause.* "Hey, I got a better idea. Why don't y'all come over to my place." *Pause.* "Yeah. Got my own digs now. Nice little apartment by the lake." Teague chuckled. "You bring the condoms; I'll get the beer."

Oh, fuck no.

Every muscle in Hudson's body tensed from the effort it took to stay seated. This wasn't his business; he had no right to interfere, yet…

There was no way in hell he was going to sit back, knowing that Teague and his gang-bang buddies were getting their freak on. Ever since that damn kiss they'd shared on the cruise ship, Hudson had been lucky Teague hadn't brought any guys around. When he thought about some asshole putting his hands (or other various body parts) on Teague, he got pissed off. *Insanely* pissed off.

And the mere thought of actually knowing it was happening right across the hall from him…

Nope. No way.

"Cool, man. See you tonight."

No, not cool. Not fucking cool at all.

Sitting up straight, Hudson clenched the wrench in his hand until it was painful. He wasn't sure he was capable of letting Teague go through with this.

Actually, he was fucking positive he couldn't.

Speechless

Shit.

Two

AT FIVE O'CLOCK, Teague cut out for the day. After cleaning up his tools, he headed up to his apartment, took a quick shower, then hopped in his truck and headed to the beer store. Ever since he'd talked to Jason—one of his past fuck-buddies—on the phone, he'd been trying to psych himself up for tonight, trying to get into the partying mood, but he was having a difficult time, which was doing little to help his attitude.

Seriously, a month ago, he would've been all over going out and getting fucked by some stranger because it was how he'd learned to cope with all the shit in his life. No, perhaps it wasn't the safe way to process his emotions, but he honestly didn't give a flying fuck. He was safe, first and foremost. Hell, he should own stock in Trojan for how many condoms he'd bought over the years. In fact, he was regularly tested, because even though he couldn't seem to stop his destructive behavior, he wasn't a fucking idiot.

And quite frankly, sex was the perfect outlet. It had a way of calming him down for a bit. Who didn't enjoy a fucking orgasm or two? It was all in good fun. A few beers, a few laughs, a fantastic blow job… The perfect ending to a shitty week.

If he could just relax, that was.

Speechless

Now, he needed to loosen up, take a breather, and chill. It was one night with two guys he'd known for a long time. They were safe and familiar, so why he was still debating whether he should call them back and cancel, he didn't know.

He forced his shoulders to relax, then took a deep breath. Once Jason and Benny got there, he doubted he'd have much of an issue getting in the spirit of things. After all, his dick was in desperate need of attention, and the one thing he'd learned over the years ... sex was a surefire way to get your mind off shit for a little while.

And sex with *two* guys... Yep. It increased the chances of him actually getting off, which was a definite plus. Teague damn sure didn't mind being sandwiched between two hot men who wanted nothing more than to make him blow his load. It was a win-win situation.

Tonight wouldn't be an exception.

When he got to the beer store, he grabbed a case, then snatched a bottle of whiskey for good measure. Being good and wasted was the way he wanted this night to end. Maybe by morning, he wouldn't remember anything that happened.

Shaking his head as he loaded the booze in the passenger seat of his truck, he ignored his subconscious, which had become a real pain in the ass lately. That little voice in his head that whispered what a bad idea this was could go fuck itself. Teague hadn't been with a guy in ... at least two months. No, wait. Make it three.

Not that he would admit that to anyone.

And he needed to get laid. A hell of a lot more often than four times a year, that was for damn sure. At the rate he was going, that was about all he would get.

Which was why he fully intended to change that tonight.

When he pulled into the parking lot of the marina a little while later, Teague noticed they had already closed the office for the evening. There was only one other vehicle in the parking lot, and that was Hudson's beefed-up, black Chevy truck. That meant Hudson was home. Probably. The guy didn't go out much. Not that he'd seen in the couple of months since he'd moved into the apartment across from Hudson, anyway.

Of course, Hudson could've gone out with one of the many guys who had been stopping by to visit lately. Teague didn't know who they were or what they were to Hudson, nor did he care. He'd made a point not to get into Hudson's business. The fact that Teague didn't know much sign language helped to keep him in the dark, as well. The guys who did stop by to visit Hudson usually spoke ASL, rather than talking to Hudson, although everyone knew Hudson could hear. Not that it bothered him. He didn't give a shit if they wanted to cut him out of the conversation. In fact, he preferred it. Because he wanted to remain oblivious, unlike Dare, Cam, and Roan, Teague hadn't embraced the whole sign language thing.

And he didn't intend to.

It took him two trips to get the beer up to his apartment. He shoved one of the twelve packs in the refrigerator, left the other on the floor beside it, and grabbed the bottle of whiskey before planting his ass on the couch.

As he cracked open the bottle, he took a deep breath for what felt like the first time that day.

This was where he could find a little solace.

Speechless

Ever since Roan had decided he needed to move in with his drug-addicted sister, the apartment Roan had been living in had been available. Since Teague had been living with friends—sleeping on couches or sometimes the floor, even in his truck from time to time—ever since he graduated from high school, he'd jumped on the opportunity when Cam had offered the place to him.

He'd never had a place of his own. In fact, he'd never had a bedroom of his own. Not one that he remembered, anyway. When he was placed with foster families, he always shared a room with one of the other kids, which had sucked because the only thing he'd ever wanted in life was to have a place to call his own.

His single mother had taken her own life, setting the dominoes in motion by leaving him with nothing and no one at the age of three. She'd even been so kind as to do so when he would find her—something he had apparently blocked out, according to the stories he'd been told. What the fuck a three-year-old was supposed to do when his mother was dead on her bed, he had yet to figure out. From the details that had been shared with him, it had taken two days before her boss at the grocery store she had worked for finally showed up to check on her. Teague had been living off crackers and water from the sink in the bathroom, or so they'd said.

From that point forward, he'd been a ward of the state. The longest he'd stayed with one family was two years, right after he had been taken into the system. Of course, he didn't remember that. Being in foster care, Teague had been passed around from one family to the next, no one capable of taking care of a wild, out-of-control kid like him. He'd hated school and had started rebelling at an early age, which pretty much made him unlovable. To put it simply, he'd been unwanted.

Sure, he'd probably made it more difficult by acting out, but he didn't feel bad about that. He'd been dealt a shitty hand; why should he have to make nice with everyone else? Fuck them.

He was sure there was some psychiatrist somewhere who would say that he used sex to feel close to people, but that couldn't be further from the truth. He didn't want to feel close to people. He wanted to get his dick sucked and his ass fucked. It wasn't sexy, it wasn't intimate. It was a means to an end. There was no psychological bullshit attached to his motives. If anything, Teague didn't want love at all. He'd survived all these years without it; he damn sure didn't need it now.

However, he had established a great friendship with the three guys who owned Pier 70. If it weren't for them, he didn't know where he'd be today. Cam Strickland had given Teague a job when he was sixteen years old, letting him help out in the repair shop, and over time, he'd proven himself. So much so that four years ago, Cam had offered him a stake in the business. Him. A broke-ass twenty-one-year-old with a high school diploma and a beat-up old truck that got him from point A to point B, was now part owner of one of the most successful marinas in the area. He hadn't had a dime to contribute, but Cam said that wasn't the reason they wanted to bring him on board. It'd been the nicest thing anyone had ever done for him. Ever.

Which was the very reason that Pier 70 was the only thing that mattered to him. He would do anything for the three people who had taken a chance on him, and the business they all held near and dear. No matter what happened, Teague would never let them down. That was his only motive in life.

A knock sounded on the door, and he took another long swig on the bottle in his hand before pushing to his feet.

It was time to get this party started, and time to stop thinking about all the bullshit.

Speechless

HUDSON HIT THE button on the remote to change the channel. He continued to click past all the nonsense, finally settling on baseball. He turned it up another notch, trying to drown out the noise coming from across the hall.

For the past hour, Hudson had attempted to ignore the ruckus coming from Teague's apartment. Between the music and the loud laughter, he'd been hell-bent on sitting on his couch and not going to put a stop to it. Despite what Teague thought about him, Hudson wasn't an old man. He didn't get his rocks off by being grumpy or interfering in other people's lives.

What Teague did wasn't his damn business, and he had somehow managed to talk himself out of interfering tonight although it had been touch and go there for a little while. If it hadn't been for the hour he'd spent at the gym, followed by a cold shower and the pizza he'd devoured when he got home, he could've still been holding on to that irritation. Some people turned to drugs or alcohol to relieve stress; Hudson turned to weights. He didn't drink. Maybe the occasional beer with his brother, but never more than that.

So, rather than go over there and tell the gang-bang boys to turn that shit down, he had turned on the television and tried to ignore them.

It was getting harder to do the louder they got.

As he watched the TV, trying to feign interest in a game with two teams he couldn't care less about, he heard something crash across the hall, and he was immediately on his feet. Someone yelled, someone else laughed, and before he knew it, he was knocking on Teague's door.

A young, attractive black guy pulled the door open. He was half-dressed, missing a shirt, with his jeans unbuttoned, showing off the bright red briefs beneath. In his hands, he was holding what appeared to be a broken bottle—likely the reason for the noise.

Knowing he shouldn't, Hudson's gaze swept the room, and he felt rage boil up inside him when he found Teague on the couch, his dick stuffed into some skinny white guy's mouth. His hands balled into fists, and a tremor of unrestrained violence coursed just beneath his skin. Telling himself this wasn't his business was no longer working. Not by a long shot.

"That's it, Jason." Teague groaned, his head falling back, his eyes closed. "Suck my dick... Oh, fuck, yes. Such a good cocksucker." He pumped his hips, his dick tunneling in and out of the guy's mouth while he held his head in place. It seemed oddly disconnected, as though Teague didn't give a shit whose mouth his dick was in, as long as it was wet and warm. The fact that Teague was wearing a condom only added to the emotional detachment.

Interesting.

"What the fuck you want, man?" the punk kid in front of Hudson asked.

Hudson ripped his attention away from Teague and peered down at the other guy. He nodded toward the stereo and signed for him to turn it down.

"What the fuck, man? You stupid or what? I don't know what this"—the asshole had the audacity to flail his hands around—"even means. You're gonna have to use your words." The kid slowly enunciated the next sentence, as though Hudson was ignorant. "You know, with ... your ... mouth."

Speechless

Hudson was tempted to knock the little shithead out, but he refrained. He'd heard every lame-ass insult he could hear in the thirty-five years he'd been on this Earth. They had started when he was in kindergarten, and strangely enough, there were even assholes who still tried to push his buttons with their stupidity to this day. The most recent … the little bitch in front of him.

"Come on, Benny!" Teague hollered, tightening his grip on the cocksucker's hair. "Come put your mouth on my nuts. They ain't gonna suck themselves."

As Teague yelled, he turned and Hudson captured his gaze from across the room.

"What the fuck?" Teague glared at him. "Go the fuck home, Hudson. You ain't invited to this party."

Well, that explained a little bit. Teague was slurring his words, and there was an empty fifth of Crown sitting on the coffee table. Knowing Teague, he'd downed that shit all by himself.

Hudson shook his head. He wasn't going anywhere. Not until they turned this shit down.

"Dude, this guy's whack," Benny, the little bitch, announced. "Can't even talk. What kind of freak can't talk?"

Never once did Hudson look away from Teague.

"Man, Benny, shut the fuck up. Get over here and suck me, you asshole." Teague laughed, but Hudson didn't hear any humor in his tone.

Benny never looked away from Hudson. "Not until the retard goes away."

Funny how the guy felt ten feet tall and bulletproof with a little alcohol running through his veins. He didn't know the first damn thing about Hudson, yet he'd already resorted to firing ignorant remarks. Being that Hudson was six two and this little punk was even shorter than Teague, he towered over him by roughly half a foot, outweighed him by probably thirty pounds of muscle to boot. He could've laid him out with a thump on the nose.

Hudson turned his attention to Benny, making sure the little punk saw the fury burning in his eyes. He wasn't angry about the adolescent name-calling. He'd long ago learned to let that shit roll right off him. No, his ire was directly related to Teague lying on that couch, his dick in some asshole's mouth.

When Benny attempted to close the door in Hudson's face, he took a step forward, keeping the door from shutting. He put his hand on the wood and shoved it open, sending it slamming into the wall behind it, causing Benny to stumble backward.

"Dude. What the fuck's your problem?" This time the cocksucker was the one asking questions, kneeling between Teague's legs.

Hudson pointed toward the hallway.

"What the fuck does that mean?" Benny asked, laughing like a hyena. "This fucktard can't even talk. How stupid is that?" Again, the shit-fuck started flailing his hands, mocking Hudson.

"It means get the fuck out," Teague called out, anger flashing in his eyes.

Hudson watched as Teague pushed the cocksucker away, knocking him onto the floor. Teague huffed, yanking off the condom before pulling up his jeans and getting to his feet.

Speechless

"Yeah!" Benny yelled, moving closer to Hudson. "Get the fuck out!"

"I'm talkin' to you, asshole." Teague blasted Benny with a hateful glare. "Grow the fuck up, man. Get outta my fuckin' apartment." Teague turned back to the cocksucker. "You, too. This is over."

"What the hell is wrong with you?" Benny turned his attention to Teague. "We were just getting to the good part."

"Like I said… This. Is. Over." Teague pointed to the door.

Benny grabbed his shirt from the floor while the cocksucker grabbed his clothes. Neither of them said a word, but if looks could kill, Hudson would've been laid out on the floor in need of a body bag. Not wanting to halt their progress, Hudson took a step back and let them leave, ignoring the urge to shove them along.

When they were out of sight, he turned back to Teague.

"You, too!" Teague yelled. "Get the fuck out."

Hudson shook his head. He wasn't going anywhere.

"You're a giant fucking asshole, you know that?" Teague pinned him with a glare. "Why the fuck do you hafta interfere with my fucking life? I haven't been laid in three goddamn months, and I simply wanna get off. There was a damn good chance that woulda happened if you didn't stick your fucking nose where it doesn't belong."

Although he seemed to have sobered somewhat, Teague was still slurring his words. Hudson snatched Teague's phone from the coffee table and shoved it at him before retrieving his own from his pocket. He pulled up Teague's contact info and typed out a message:

What the fuck are you doing with those assholes?

Teague's phone vibrated and the kid looked down at it.

"I was getting my goddamn dick sucked. What the fuck did it look like?"

Hudson typed out another message: *Two?*

Teague appeared confused when the message showed up on his phone. He looked up at Hudson. "Two what?"

Hudson nodded toward the hallway, cocking an eyebrow.

"Ahh." Teague went to the refrigerator and grabbed a beer. "You don't like the fact that it takes two to please me, huh? What? Are you jealous? Or just a prude?"

Hudson typed again: *If it takes two, you haven't been with the right man.*

Teague scowled at his phone when the message popped up. He set his phone on the counter, opened his beer, and lifted his eyes to meet Hudson's. The kid laughed. "What? You think you're man enough?"

Hudson didn't think, he knew.

He had no idea what compelled him to do what he did next, but whatever it was, he wasn't strong enough to resist it.

Three

FUCK.

Fuck. Fuck. Fuck.

The second he said those words, Teague noticed the determined gleam in Hudson's eyes. Rather than their usual brilliant emerald color, they were darker, more intense.

Teague wasn't nearly as drunk as he was pretending to be. Sure, he had been at some point tonight, but his buzz had quickly been dampened when that jackass Benny had started talking shit to Hudson. It was a wonder the guy could walk out of here. Had he been in Hudson's shoes, Teague would've laid the fucker out for talking shit like that.

Maybe Teague wasn't Hudson's biggest fan, but he damn sure wasn't going to sit back and let someone talk shit to him like that. Only now, he kind of wished Benny and Jason were still there, because Hudson was stalking him from across the room, and that glint in his eyes was dangerous.

Teague swallowed hard as he backed up against the refrigerator. He ran out of room before Hudson got to him, but his reflexes were dulled by the alcohol, so he didn't manage to dodge him in time.

Hudson planted his hands on the refrigerator—one on each side of Teague's head—with a thud, shaking the glass bottles inside. For the longest minute in the history of time, Hudson didn't move, simply stared, their noses practically touching. Teague tried to come up with some smartass thing to say, something that would get Hudson to back off, but he couldn't formulate words with Hudson so damn close.

Fucking hell, Hudson smelled good. That enticing scent of expensive cologne was like a bolt of lust straight to the nuts.

And because of that delicious scent, the heat of Hudson's body, and the softness of his lips, Teague found himself practically climbing the man as Hudson kissed him hard.

Oh, fuck.

Warmth infused him, trickling down his spine, right through his balls, and down to his toes. He was assaulted by a sense of need so overwhelming his knees threatened to give out. He'd only been kissed like this once before and that had been a fucking dream.

There was no question who was in charge here, and it damn sure wasn't Teague.

Trying to gain some semblance of control, Teague fumbled behind him, managing to set his beer on the counter before he grabbed on to Hudson and held him, thrusting his tongue into the big man's mouth, taking what Hudson was clearly offering. Under normal circumstances, he would've refused the kiss, choosing for that wicked mouth to do other things, but this was Hudson and...

Fuck.

No one had ever kissed him like this. No one had ever even tried.

Speechless

The guy was so damn big, his chest solid against Teague's. At five nine, Teague wasn't a big guy by any means, more like average. But up against Hudson, he felt small. And he fucking liked it.

The memory of that dream flooded him. This felt like déjà vu.

Hudson cupped Teague's jaw with one hand, his grip bordering on painful, holding him in place while he plundered his mouth. Their tongues dueled, teeth clashing together as they both tried to inhale the other. Teague shouldn't have enjoyed it, he shouldn't have wanted more, but he did.

Hudson pulled back before Teague was ready, but he didn't sign anything or go for his phone. They stood there, eyes locked, panting as they fought for breath. Teague mentally willed Hudson to kiss him again, but he didn't. Instead, Hudson took a step back, grabbed Teague's phone from the counter, and tossed it toward him. He managed to catch it, though he wasn't sure how. Not only was the alcohol making his brain fuzzy, that damn kiss had intensified the sensation.

Hudson typed something on his phone while Teague willed his dick to chill the fuck out.

You want someone to fuck you the right way, I'm your guy.

Teague's eyes widened in disbelief as he read the message, then read it again. When he looked up, he noticed Hudson was walking out his front door, pulling it closed behind him.

What the hell had just happened?

Teague tapped out a reply: *You make an offer like that and you walk out? What the fuck?*

A few seconds later, another message came in. *The offer stands. You want to be fucked the right way, you simply have to ask. Think about it. In the meantime, don't let me see your dick in anyone's mouth. You're lucky I didn't lose my shit. When you're ready, you know where to find me.*

Shit. Teague was ready now. He messaged Hudson and told him as much.

The response he got back was not one he wanted.

Two things you should know. One, I'm in charge, and two, you have to be sober. You make that happen and I'll show you exactly what you've been missing. No strings.

Teague dropped onto the couch and stared at his phone. He didn't know how much time passed, but he never moved, still trying to process what Hudson was telling him. Or more accurately, what Hudson was propositioning.

Could he be serious?

Sex with no strings.

He could only imagine what sex with Hudson would be like. The man would no doubt dominate him in every fucking way. Even the thought made his dick throb with anticipation. Sure, he'd had plenty of sex in his life, but never had he been truly dominated by a guy. Then again, he'd never wanted to be.

It was the very reason Teague went for guys his size, not bigger. Keeping things cool and on an even keel was what always worked best for Teague.

Right?

No strings. With Hudson.

Holy. Fuck.

Speechless

HUDSON DIDN'T EXPECT Teague to respond to him after that. In fact, he didn't want the kid to. He wanted Teague to think about what he was telling him, about what he was offering.

Granted, Hudson had no fucking idea how things had gotten that far, but when he'd had his tongue in Teague's mouth, when he'd felt the way Teague was trying to devour him, the only thing Hudson could think about was owning him in every possible way. He wanted to show Teague exactly what he was missing when he ventured into these bullshit orgies that he claimed to find satisfaction in. If the kid wanted someone to satisfy him, Hudson would be more than willing to oblige.

He replayed what had happened in his head. Knocking on the door, seeing Teague face-fucking some little pussy while he kept his eyes closed. Had he been thinking about someone else? He damn sure hadn't been focused on the mouth that was on him. Hudson wouldn't have put up with that shit. He would've insisted Teague watch him while he swallowed his cock.

He willed his dick to relax.

He should've known better than to make the offer in the first place, but now that it was out there, he didn't want to take it back. This had been a long time coming. And since he'd done it via text message, it wasn't like Teague would forget. Unlike the kiss on that cruise. Luckily, Teague had been too intoxicated that night to remember, which had worked in Hudson's favor.

Until now.

For so long, the two of them had been doing this dance, and quite frankly, Hudson was tired. He was tired of jacking off every damn night to thoughts of Teague on his knees or Teague beneath him. If he was ever going to get the kid out of his system, he knew they had to take this step.

As it was, Hudson had been suffering through a dry spell. The last time he'd been with a man... Well, if his memory served him correctly, it'd been back in November of last year. Two dates, fairly decent fuck, then Hudson had known it wasn't going to work. He didn't hide the fact that he was a dominant lover, and some men couldn't handle that fact. He was a top and he preferred his bottoms to desire that. Unfortunately, that guy had been hoping to dominate Hudson.

Wasn't going to happen.

He didn't think he'd have that same issue with Teague. The kid was a natural bottom, and from the stories he'd heard Teague tell, he enjoyed it.

Since neither of them were looking for anything serious, he figured no harm, no foul.

And okay, yes, maybe he'd purposely put the proposition in a text message. That way Teague *couldn't* use alcohol as his excuse. Hudson wanted him to remember what had happened, the way he'd felt when they'd shared that damn kiss. This way, Teague wouldn't be able to deny it. Not this time.

No, Hudson wanted Teague to relive every single second of what had transpired between them tonight. He wanted that memory to replace any Teague might have of the cocksucker trying to get him off. In fact, he wanted to make Teague forget any fucking man from his past and think only of Hudson. He didn't want Teague to have the option of pretending Hudson hadn't offered to fuck him with no strings attached.

He dropped his head back on the cushion and stared up at the ceiling. He took a deep breath and exhaled slowly.

Speechless

Well, part of him did. Part of him wished he had never gotten up off his couch and gone over there. He couldn't unsee that shit, and it pissed him off even now as he remembered the way that cock-sucker had been slobbering all fucking over Teague's dick. In fact, that bothered him far more than all the bullshit that had come out of the other guy's face. Hudson didn't want anyone's mouth on Teague. Or their hands. Or their dick. No one other than him.

And yes, he knew exactly how ludicrous this all was. Teague was nothing more than a punk kid who hadn't yet come to terms with himself. How he was going to embrace something like this, Hudson didn't know.

But it was worth a try.

For one thing, Hudson didn't want Teague going around fucking anything with a dick. The kid drank way too damn much, and that kind of shit led to stupid mistakes. Who even knew if Teague had been safe all this time? Sure, the kid had been wearing a condom for oral sex, so that was a good sign, but didn't mean Teague had always had the forethought.

Should Teague take him up on his offer, that was the first thing they would deal with. He would have Teague get tested, make sure he was clean. Hell, Hudson would do one, too, so the kid didn't think it was all on him. Once the results came back…

Shit.

He was getting way ahead of himself. Teague hadn't even accepted his offer yet.

Maybe he wouldn't.

Which would probably be for the best.

With his head still leaned back, Hudson closed his eyes. He needed to sleep, needed to stop thinking about Teague. The damn kid had been on his mind for far too long as it was.

He heard the sound of glass shattering, followed by Teague's irritated yell. "Giant fucking asshole!"

Hudson couldn't help but smile. Looked as though he was right, that was Teague's new nickname for him. And since he was so irate, it was clear Teague was once again thinking about him. He couldn't say he was disappointed.

One way or the other, Hudson fully intended to get the kid out of his system. A couple of weeks of fucking him until neither of them could walk should certainly do the trick.

Now it was up to Teague on how that would play out. And when.

Speechless

Four

Monday, July 4th

TEAGUE MANAGED TO ignore Hudson all day on Saturday. Not once did he leave his apartment, for fear of running into the giant asshole. At one point, when he saw Hudson leave, he'd been tempted but then feared he would run into the man when he came back, so he had nixed that idea.

Yep, safe to say he was acting like a big fucking chickenshit.

On top of that, he hadn't had a single thing to drink since the two swallows of beer he'd had two seconds before Hudson had kissed the ever-loving fuck out of him.

He wanted to say his resistance to alcohol wasn't because of what Hudson was offering, but he wasn't sure that was the case. However, pretending he didn't want what Hudson was offering was a hell of a lot more difficult than not drinking. He'd managed to push away the urge to drink by dumping the rest of the beer one by one down the sink. Ten seconds after that, the regret had sunk in.

Then, when the urge struck him again, he'd started jacking off. That had helped three times. After that, he'd feared he would have calluses on his dick, and that wouldn't help him in any way. So, he'd had a porn marathon last night. And yes, it was possible to watch porn without jerking off. Mostly. And it also helped to keep his mind off Hudson.

Okay, that part was a lie. No matter how hard he tried, whether his eyes were opened or closed, whether the TV was on or off, he thought about Hudson. He thought about that kiss; he thought about what Hudson was offering him. And he was slowly going insane.

Sunday had gone much the same way except he had managed to help Cam with a couple of appointments due to how busy they were because of the holiday weekend traffic. Which was why he was thankful it was now Monday and that was almost over. He was spending the day working, and no doubt they would be slammed. They always were on the Fourth of July.

Rather than going straight to the boat repair shop, he headed for the main office.

The sun was up and shining brightly, the breeze warm. They were in for record heat today, which wasn't at all surprising. As he walked around the building to the front door, Teague took a deep breath of humid air, let it out slowly, and steeled himself for a busy day.

He opened the door and...

"Oh, shit," Cam said by way of greeting, a huge smile on his face. "I thought you avoided this place like the plague?"

It was true, Teague hated anything that involved paperwork, so he did whatever was necessary to avoid it. Which usually meant he didn't make an appearance in the office unless it was to grab keys or check on an appointment.

"I try," he replied, forcing a smile.

"What's up? How was your weekend?" Cam leaned his elbows on the counter, looking interested in what Teague had to say.

"Good."

"Anything exciting happen?"

Exciting? Was that how he would describe what had happened between him and Hudson? Nah. Probably not.

Teague shook his head. Now that he was standing there, he felt like an idiot. He didn't know what to say to Cam, or anyone for that matter. He should've expected the questions, but he'd been too caught up in his own issues to prepare himself. He'd actually stopped in as a way to avoid Hudson for a little while longer—another chickenshit move.

"Got any appointments today?" he asked, hoping Cam would take the hint.

"As a matter of fact..." Cam peered down at the appointment book in front of him. "Dare's out today, so if you're interested in taking a couple, that'll be great."

"Absolutely." Shit. He was pretty sure he said that with far too much enthusiasm.

Since Cam was quite perceptive, Teague figured he'd noted it, as well.

"Awesome." There was a hint of curiosity in Cam's blue eyes, but thankfully, he didn't put voice to it. "We've got one coming in at ten and another at three. You want to take those and I'll divvy out the others between me and Roan?"

"Sounds like a plan."

"I'll hit you up on the radio when they get here."

Teague nodded, knowing he needed to go back outside and head down to the shop. It was only eight, so he had a couple of hours to kill before the first appointment.

"You okay?" Cam's tone lacked the lightheartedness it'd had a minute ago. He actually sounded concerned.

"Fantastic," Teague lied.

"The apartment good? No issues?"

Smiling a true smile for the first time in a couple of days, Teague nodded. "It's great, man. Really great. And thanks again for letting me have it."

"Glad it all worked out."

Teague wasn't about to tell Cam that this was the first place he'd had of his own. The first place he'd ever lived where he didn't have to worry about being tossed out the next day for whatever reason. Whether it was a foster family who decided he was too much trouble or one of his buddies who had a better offer and needed him to get lost, he always found himself waiting for someone to send him on his way. But not anymore. As long as he paid the rent and utilities, he could probably live there forever if he was so inclined.

The back door opened and Roan walked in, which was Teague's signal to leave. It wasn't that he didn't want to chat it up with Roan, but he knew the guy would likely start tossing out personal questions. Unlike Cam, he was prone to speak his mind when he was curious. Which was fairly often. Even though Teague had noticed that Roan was the master of avoidance when it came to answering personal questions, he didn't have a problem dishing them out.

"Hey, hit me up when the appointment's here."

Cam nodded. "Oh, and if you're not busy, you can check out the Jet Skis, make sure they're not having any issues. We're gonna be slammed because it's the Fourth. Everyone'll want to be out on the water."

Teague knew that Cam would usually handle that when Dare wasn't available, so it was obvious Cam was giving him an out this morning. He briefly wondered whether or not he had a sign on his forehead that said *I don't want to be around Hudson if at all possible*. Then again, maybe he had that on his forehead every damn day.

"I'll take care of it," he told Cam before spinning around and heading for the door. The risk of paperwork magnified when Roan showed up, and Teague could already feel the hives coming on.

"Hey!" Roan called after him.

Reluctantly, Teague turned back around, his hand on the door as he geared up to make his exit.

"Could you give me a hand with the fireworks later?"

Oh, shit. He'd forgotten about that. Every year the marina put on a huge pyrotechnic show. Roan usually managed everything from buying the fireworks to setting up, even making sure the music was in sync. Teague had been so caught up in thoughts of... Never mind. He'd been otherwise preoccupied, and he hadn't been paying much attention to the festivities that would take place.

For him it was just another day.

"Sure."

"Cool. Thanks, man."

Without wasting another breath, Teague pushed open the door—ignoring the irritating dog growls that sounded thanks to Dare's tweak on the door sensor—and headed down to the pier. He had shit to do, and the best part about it, he wouldn't have any time to think about Hudson.

And that would ultimately make for a great fucking day.

BY FOUR O'CLOCK, it was clear Teague was avoiding him.

Not that Hudson hadn't expected it. There were days, sometimes a solid week, when Hudson wouldn't see Teague at all. The kid had the ability to keep busy and avoid the repair shop like no one else. Only a few times had it actually impacted business, because no matter how he tried to play it, Hudson couldn't handle all the work all the time.

But Teague's disappearing act didn't bother him in the least. Not today, anyway. After spending all weekend wondering if Teague would send a message or knock on his door, telling him he was ready to take him up on his offer, Hudson was a little out of sorts.

He wasn't complaining, actually. For the first time in a really long time, he felt something inside him. Something a hell of a lot like anticipation. It'd been years since he'd felt like this. Years since he'd wanted something enough that he held out hope.

The whole reason he was working today—technically a holiday for the repair shop—was proof that he was having difficulty sitting still. Now that he was all caught up for the next two days, he wasn't sure what he would do with himself tomorrow, but he'd have plenty of time to figure that out then. Right now, he was ready to hit the gym, take a shower, have some dinner, then hang with the guys out on the lake to watch the fireworks.

As he made his way toward the main office, he saw Teague tying up one of the Jet Skis. He stopped for a second, watching the kid work, admiring the sleek lines of his well-defined body. It wasn't unusual to see Teague strutting around without a shirt on—temperatures in Texas required less clothing, for the most part—but it wasn't often that Hudson had a chance to watch him without being caught.

Speechless

The kid was all golden hair and sun-bronzed skin, his face hidden behind his sunglasses. Teague reminded him of a surfer, lean and muscular but not bulky. His blond hair was a little shaggier than normal, and because he'd been working out in the sun so much this summer, his skin had tanned to perfection.

As though he sensed someone watching him, Teague stopped what he was doing, his head popping up as he peered around. Hudson didn't bother moving, didn't try to hide the fact that he was ogling him. He would've been busted either way, and he wasn't about to let Teague think he was backing down from the challenge he'd offered. Whether or not Teague accepted was all on him now. It didn't matter to Hudson one way or the other.

Liar.

He could practically hear his brother giving him shit. AJ had always called Hudson to the carpet, never letting him get away with anything, especially when it came to things he denied himself, of which there were many. Relationships and alcohol, for example. It'd become somewhat of a game between them. AJ would attempt to predict what Hudson was avoiding at the time, and Hudson would pretend he was wrong. Truth was, the guy was pretty damn good at guessing.

When it came to Teague, Hudson figured his attraction was obvious. Well, to everyone except Teague, but that was due to the fact he'd worked hard to hide it from the kid. Despite his inability to ignore his intense desire for the guy, he had been successfully avoiding Teague for two solid years. Until recently.

Sometimes temptation was too great to ignore.

He watched as Teague turned away, giving Hudson his back. The sight made his mouth water as his brain was suddenly overwhelmed by carnal thoughts. He imagined what Teague would feel like beneath him, Hudson's hands gripping those sexy shoulders as he plowed into him from behind…

"Yo, man. What's up?"

Hudson spun around, his lewd thoughts rattling right out of his head at the sound of his brother's voice. Fuck, he hoped his face wasn't as red as it felt.

Smiling, Hudson jerked his chin at AJ in greeting, then followed by signing his question: *What brings you by?*

"You invited me, remember? Fireworks and shit?"

Right. He remembered now.

AJ's gaze slid past Hudson, and he knew that his brother noticed who he'd been looking at. Luckily, AJ didn't say anything, which was a first.

"You wanna hit the gym, then grab some dinner?"

AJ knew him so well. Hudson nodded, then replied with his hands: *Just need to change first.*

Falling into step with his brother, Hudson ignored the urge to glance back at Teague one more time. He was being an idiot. Based on the way Teague was ignoring him, he should've taken the hint by now. It appeared the kid was turning him down on his offer, and that should've brought some relief, but it didn't. Not at all.

"Hey, you heard from Milly lately?" AJ inquired as they made their way up the stairs to the second-floor apartment.

Hudson shook his head.

Speechless

Ever since they'd returned from the cruise, AJ had mentioned Milly's name at least a few dozen times. What his brother had thought was a good thing on the cruise had halted the instant they'd hit dry land. Not that Hudson knew all the details—he didn't *want* to know all the details. Looked as though his big brother was infatuated with the woman.

Figuring he would ease his brother's mind, Hudson paused before stepping into his apartment. *Honest, she hasn't been here since the cruise.*

That seemed to pacify AJ for the moment, so Hudson opened the door and stepped inside.

Five minutes later, Hudson was behind the wheel of his truck, AJ in the passenger seat as they headed for the gym. Maybe a solid hour on the weights would get his mind off things better left alone.

He cast a quick sideways glance at his brother, who appeared to be lost in thought as he stared out the window.

Then again, if AJ was going to spend the rest of the night moping over Milly, perhaps thinking about Teague was going to be unavoidable.

Five

TEAGUE DIDN'T WANT to admit that he'd spent the better part of the last hour wondering whether or not Hudson would show up for the fireworks show. He'd caught the man watching him while he worked, and even across the distance that spanned between them, he'd felt the heat of Hudson's gaze. Then, AJ had showed up and whisked Hudson away, and they still weren't back although it was now dark and the show was about to begin.

He was a little disappointed, although he hated even acknowledging that fact. It was so much easier when he didn't give a shit about anyone or anything. Then, he didn't have to worry about being let down. Like now.

"Beer?" Cam offered as he joined Teague on the private pier behind the marina. He was carrying a cooler in one hand, a cold one in the other.

Teague was tempted but managed to resist. For whatever stupid reason, he did not want Hudson to catch him drinking, even if it looked as though Hudson's lascivious proposal was no longer on the table. The guy had told him he needed to be sober, and no way would one beer hurt, but until he decided whether or not he was going to accept what Hudson was offering, he didn't want to risk it.

"I'm good, thanks."

"In the cooler if you change your mind."

Speechless

He nodded, watching as Cam headed down to the end of the pier and sat next to his husband, Gannon, his feet sliding over the edge to dangle in the water. Teague felt a little out of sorts standing there by himself. Not for the first time, he wondered where Dare was. The guy had been acting a little off lately, and Teague had to assume that was due to the man from his past making a reappearance in his life. He remembered Dare sharing the sordid details of what had happened between him and Noah all those years ago, and he had to wonder if there was any way to come back from that sort of heartache.

Then again, he didn't ever want to find out. The reason he'd never experienced heartache—other than what he'd been born into—was because he'd kept himself closed off from everyone. Far better than he'd ever thought possible. He'd learned his lesson after the second foster family had sent him back during the middle of first grade. He'd gotten into one too many fights, and they'd come out and said they couldn't deal with the violence. He'd been six. Apparently, he'd been too much to handle for the couple.

Whatever.

He had learned over the years not to get attached to anyone or anything. In his experience, nothing lasted. Once the newness wore off and reality set in, people moved on. So, he had learned to, as well.

Not once in his twenty-five years had he fallen in love, either, and if he was lucky, it would never be something he would have to deal with. He'd seen what it had done to his mother. She'd taken her own life because of a man.

Stupid.

"What're you doing over here all by yourself?"

Teague turned at the sound of Roan's voice coming from behind him. He didn't want to answer the question, so he deflected with one of his own. "They get it all set up?"

Turned out, Roan had hired a company to handle the pyrotechnics show this year, and the only thing he and Roan had to do was help them get the stuff down to the lake. It had taken all of fifteen minutes since there were four of them, so his distraction from Hudson hadn't lasted as long as he'd hoped it would.

"They did." Roan glanced at his watch. "About to start." Roan nodded toward the end of the pier, where Cam and Gannon were sitting. "You coming?"

Teague shook his head. He wasn't planning to stay long, so he figured he'd stand there for a few minutes before heading in for the night. Today had been a brutally busy day, and he was wiped out. The lake would likely be slammed with boaters again tomorrow because it always worked that way, and he knew he'd be working from sunup to sundown since Cam had taken him up on his offer to help with the appointments.

Not that he'd ever cared about that before, but tonight, he was going with that excuse.

"I'm gonna head up in a minute."

Roan nodded, a hint of a frown forming between his brows as his gaze swept over Teague's face. Luckily, the guy didn't bombard him with questions; instead, he turned and made his way down to Cam.

Teague stood there, staring out at the water, listening to the hushed conversation from the people all around him. They were lining the banks of the lake, lawn chairs and blankets as far as the eye could see, everyone gearing up for the show. Rather than hang out on the pier, he decided to sneak down to the dock so he could watch the show from the boat that they all shared for recreational activities.

Speechless

When the first boom sounded, Teague felt his heart skip a beat, the exhilaration slamming into him as he stood there, his hands thrust in his pockets. He wasn't sure what it was about the Fourth of July, but it had always been his favorite holiday. Maybe it was the fireworks that drew him or perhaps because it didn't carry the stigma of family along with it. Sure, there were families who spent the day together, but it wasn't a requirement like Thanksgiving and Christmas—both of which he'd spent by himself every year for as long as he could remember. Since he didn't have any family, the Fourth of July was one of the few holidays that didn't make him feel completely alone.

As he watched the colors brighten the night sky, he must've gotten caught up in the brilliance of it, because he didn't register the person joining him on the boat. He felt the slight shift as the boat rocked on the water from the weight, but he didn't bother looking over.

He remained perfectly still, pretending he wasn't interested in knowing who it was, until he felt the warmth of a body at his back. He didn't need to turn around to know that heat belonged to Hudson. He could smell him. A sexy, musky scent that he'd gotten all too familiar with surrounded him, and he swayed a little on his feet.

For the longest time, they both stood there, neither moving as they watched the lights in the sky.

A million things ran through Teague's mind in that moment, but he was too scared to move, not wanting to break the spell.

DURING HUDSON'S WORKOUT, he had somehow ended up remembering the night he'd interrupted Teague's little orgy. That had stimulated a spark of anger that powered him through the weightlifting, making him work harder than he had in months. When it was over, he'd felt anxious and on edge, something he wasn't particularly fond of. As a means of punishing himself, he had refused to jack off during his shower, although by then, thoughts of Teague were overwhelming him.

It was as though he couldn't think of anything else, and that was unacceptable.

Although he had considered staying in his apartment for the night, he'd given in when AJ started giving him shit. It was that or knock AJ out. Hudson wasn't keen on the idea of hitting his brother, no matter how irritating he could get, so here he was.

When AJ had decided he wanted to go hang with Cam and Gannon, Hudson had used that as his excuse to slip away, heading down to the dock. On occasion, he would come down to the boat and simply sit, enjoying the way it gently rocked on the water when no one was out here. He hadn't seen Teague on the boat at first, although it had been a nice surprise. He'd simply been coming down to get a better look, to have a few minutes away from everyone else to enjoy the show without constant chatter.

His first clue that something was up was when Teague didn't say anything. He didn't even look his way. Not even when Hudson came to stand directly behind him. That might've been a first. Usually Teague was prone to making a scene and getting away as fast as he could. Not tonight.

Speechless

Now, as Hudson stood behind Teague, he couldn't resist the urge to take a step closer, to eliminate the space between their bodies. He wasn't surprised when Teague flinched, but he felt immeasurable relief when he didn't move away. Not for the first time in his life, Hudson wished he could speak. Wished he had the ability to say something, to relay what was on his mind. He'd learned long ago to quell that urge because it wasn't something he could change. He didn't have a voice, he couldn't verbally relay his thoughts, but he could do so by touch.

It was a risk he was fearful of taking, but after a few tense moments when his breath was lodged in his throat, he finally moved his hands, placing them on Teague's sides, then sliding them down to his hips. Teague was still without his shirt, so the warm, smooth skin of his torso slid beneath Hudson's palms, heat infusing him. He wasn't asking for anything, his touch wasn't even sexual—okay, maybe a little— but he wanted Teague to know he was there. He wanted Teague to feel him because that was how he spoke—through his hands.

Closing his eyes, Hudson drank in the feeling through his fingertips, enjoying the warmth of Teague, smooth skin covering firm muscle. Forcing his eyes open, he reminded himself this was not going to go further. He was simply letting Teague know he was there.

He heard Teague's sharp intake of breath, felt the way Teague lightly swayed on his feet. He liked that he made the kid feel off-balance. He had noticed that the first time they kissed on the cruise ship, and again the other night. Although Teague had been drunk both times, Hudson could tell that he affected Teague. Teague might not like that he did, but he did nonetheless.

For someone as self-assured as Teague pretended to be, Hudson knew that was a façade. He didn't know what had happened in Teague's life to make him the way that he was, but he couldn't deny that he wanted to know. Not that he would ask; that would be inviting too much intimacy between them. Hudson might've offered to show Teague an unobstructed world of passion, but he wasn't asking for anything more. He wasn't *offering* anything more. He knew better.

Teague leaned back and Hudson wasn't even sure he realized he was doing it. As they stood on the darkened boat, Hudson's chest against Teague's back, his hands firmly gripping Teague's hips, the move the only way he could keep from touching more of him, they simply stood there as the night sky burst with color.

Hudson was tempted to slide his hand down the front of Teague's shorts, grip the smooth, warm length of him in his hand. He was desperate to learn Teague's body, to find out what made him sigh and moan. This would've been the perfect opportunity, and he would've probably jumped on it had Teague agreed to his proposition.

Unfortunately, for both of them, Teague had been hiding from him, so they had yet to settle how this would play out. Until that time came, Hudson wasn't going to pursue him. He would have to settle for feeling the warmth of Teague's body, the slight shift of his muscles beneath his hands while they stood there alone in the night.

He wasn't sure what he was feeling, doubted Teague knew what he was feeling, either, but it was nice. It was a moment between them, one Hudson didn't expect to last, nor did he ever expect it would happen again, but he was grateful for this. Right here. Right now. No anger, no masks, nothing between them but the warm breeze and the brilliant lights in the sky.

Speechless

Some might even call it progress.

"WHERE'S HUDSON?" ROAN asked AJ when Hudson's brother joined them down by the water.

AJ shrugged, glancing behind him. "I saw him walking down toward the boat slips."

Roan nodded. That made sense. The marina's boat was down there, and it would offer an unobstructed view of the lake without anyone around to interrupt. Not that Roan knew anything about that. Okay, maybe a little.

"What's up, man?" Gannon called out to AJ, turning to look up at him, a smile on his face. "Haven't seen you since the cruise. You doing all right?"

AJ grinned and Roan watched as the man moved closer to Gannon. "Can't complain. And you? I see you survived jumping out of an airplane."

Gannon's smile was awkward, as though he were reliving that moment and he didn't much care to. It made Roan chuckle. He'd heard the story about that incident, and for the life of him, he couldn't understand how Cam had gotten Gannon to jump out of a plane. Then again, it seemed Cam and Gannon pushed one another's boundaries in ways that defied logic.

"I survived. If I didn't love this guy"—Gannon nodded toward Cam—"I can tell you, I would've been really pissed that day."

A rumble of laughter ensued. Roan didn't doubt that one bit.

"It's good to get you out of your comfort zone," Cam teased.

That was Cam. He'd always been the reckless one. As a way of rebelling against his underlying fears—traveling and relationships—Cam had opted for taking things to the extreme. Sometimes Roan wished he'd been born with that trait. Unfortunately, that hadn't happened. Hell, he was scared of every damn thing. Although he wouldn't admit that out loud. He tried to be the tough one, the strong one, the rebellious one. Instead, most of the time he simply felt like the third wheel.

"So, you think you'll do it again?" AJ asked, chuckling.

"Not a chance." The definitiveness in Gannon's response made them all laugh.

"Figured as much." AJ sat down on the pier beside Gannon. "How's Milly?"

Roan glanced over at AJ, noting the hesitancy in his voice when he directed his question at Gannon. He knew why AJ was asking, because, during the cruise, AJ and Milly had spent quite a bit of time together. Roan knew this firsthand because he'd been helping Milly with the wedding preparations—he'd been Cam's best man and Milly had been Gannon's maid of honor—so he'd witnessed quite a bit of their interactions.

Now that he thought about it, Milly had been happier than he'd ever seen her. That was saying something because the woman always had a smile on her face.

"She's good." Gannon looked confused as he stared back at Hudson's brother. "You haven't talked to her?"

AJ shook his head. "I've tried a couple of times, but she won't return my calls."

That was interesting. Roan hadn't seen Milly since the cruise, either, but he had talked to her on the flight back to Texas, and she'd been quite excited about her little rendezvous with AJ. He wondered what had happened that she was avoiding the man now.

Speechless

Gannon looked as baffled as Roan felt. "Sorry to hear that. But yeah, she's doing good. She took a couple of days off last week. She hasn't been feeling well. I tried to get her to come tonight, but she's pretty sure she has the flu."

The flu? Now Roan wasn't a doctor, but he didn't think it was flu season.

"Sorry to hear that."

Roan turned his attention toward the sky, watching the colors light up the night, the acrid scent of sulfur drifting on the breeze. He wished his sister would've joined him. He had invited her, but of course, she'd turned him down. If he had to guess, she was trying to find a way to get her next fix. Roan probably should've stayed with her, but he had needed a break. A break from her anger, a break from the fighting, a break from the constant bitching … a break from *her*.

He wouldn't pretend to know what she was going through, but he felt as though he did put forth enough effort to help her that she should've recognized that by now. Hell, he'd given up his apartment to move in with her. Not that she'd been happy about that, but truthfully, he didn't give a shit. She was heading down a dark and dangerous path, and his biggest fear was finding her dead somewhere from an overdose. Not that he could stop her from doing what she was doing, but he was damn sure making an effort to interfere as much and as often as he could.

She was on her own tonight, though.

For a few minutes, Roan was going to stand here on the pier, watching the fireworks and pretending that his life hadn't become a full-time babysitting gig. And then, when it was all over, he'd get back to it.

Six

Friday, July 8th

"ARE YOU FUCKING serious?" Cam's laughter boomed, slipping out through the open door as Teague headed inside the main office. "Congrats, man."

Teague watched the bro-hugs taking place as Cam smacked Dare on the back hard enough to rattle the guy's teeth. Cam was a big guy. There was a lot of power in that arm, sometimes more than he even realized, apparently.

Dare and Cam turned to look at Teague, matching smiles plastered on their faces. It was a little creepy, quite frankly.

"What's going on?" he asked, hesitant to get in the middle of this love fest.

"I'm gettin' married," Dare announced.

And now he had the creepy smile going on as he stared back at Dare. He knew he looked as dumb as he felt, but he couldn't have erased it if he'd wanted to. He was truly happy for his friend. Teague had known Dare for a long time, and he was a good guy. Something had always been a little off about him, in the sense that Dare had never been interested in love—very similar to Teague—but it looked as though that streak had come to an end.

"Congratulations, bro."

Dare's grin widened. "Thanks. And we're buyin' a house."

"A house? Really?" Well, that was fast. Then again, Dare and Noah had been together fifteen years ago, so maybe it wasn't as fast as it seemed. "That's great. Somewhere close?"

Dare nodded. "In Cam's neighborhood. Noah and I put an offer in a couple of days ago, and the sellers accepted it. We should close in early August."

Teague didn't know what to make of all that. It seemed that things were changing around Pier 70. Between Cam and Gannon getting married and now Dare and Noah. Even Roan was different since he'd been dealing with his sister's issues... What the hell was this world coming to? Everyone seemed to be ... growing up.

"I'm gonna go tell Hudson," Dare noted, glancing between Cam and Teague. "Be back in a bit."

Teague watched as Dare practically skipped out the back door, whistling as he did.

Cam was still laughing when he turned back. "Crazy shit, huh?"

That was one way to put it. Teague had no idea what to say to that, so he simply stared at the door where Dare had exited.

"Did you need something?"

Oh, right. Nodding, he looked back at Cam. "Wanted to see if you had any appointments I could help with today."

Cam glanced down at the appointment book. "We've actually got it covered." Cam lifted his head and met Teague's gaze. "Unless that's what you want to do. You can take mine. I'm sure I can find a way to keep myself busy."

Teague could see the concern in Cam's eyes. "No, I'm cool. I can help Hudson. I'm sure he's got too much on his plate as it is."

He'd actually been hoping to avoid Hudson today, but since he'd managed to pretty much keep his distance all week, he figured he had to suck it up at some point. Ever since the night of the fireworks, when Hudson had stood behind him, his hands on Teague's hips, holding him there but not doing anything more than that, he'd felt a little out of his element. For the most part, aside from that little moment they'd shared, things weren't weird between him and Hudson, although neither of them had brought up Hudson's offer again. Yet.

Granted, Teague still wasn't sure how he felt about that. Nor did he know how he wanted to handle it. For the first time in his life, Teague wasn't jumping feetfirst into something. He got the eerie feeling that giving in to Hudson could very well alter his life in ways he wasn't ready for. Didn't mean he would actually like the guy, but he could see himself getting addicted to the sex.

Maybe.

Then again, Hudson could very well be a huge snore-fest in the sack and Teague would get bored.

Doubtful but possible.

"If we get any more appointments, you'll be the first one I call." Cam's gruff voice interrupted Teague's thoughts, pulling him back to the moment.

"Awesome. Thanks."

Shaking himself out of his weird mood, Teague left Cam and took his time as he made his way down to the dock. He wanted to give Dare a few minutes to share his news with Hudson. Standing around and watching Dare's excitement would've made Teague a little uncomfortable.

Speechless

He'd managed to keep busy stacking rope for a good ten minutes when he saw Dare walking back to the main office. At that point, Teague headed over to the boat repair shop. With every step, he felt his tension increase. He wasn't excited about having to see Hudson face-to-face, or talk to him, or work with him, either. Sometimes the shop didn't feel big enough to house them both safely. And the place was actually pretty big.

It was nothing more than a giant steel building with one huge bay door that faced the water, allowing them to bring boats right in when necessary, or for customers to pull them around via the parking lot. On the left side of the building, a paint booth had been installed. Hudson's little side business of painting boats was evidently doing pretty well. Inside the building were tools galore, along with several industrial-sized fans, lifts, racks, engine stands, and all the other equipment used to repair motors and fiberglass.

At some point last year, Hudson had divided the shop more evenly so that Teague had his own space, which allowed them to divvy up the jobs. He wasn't as adept as Hudson in everything, but he was a quick learner, so generally, it only took him studying Hudson for a bit to catch on to something. All in all, he loved the work; it was the company he had some issues with.

When he stepped into the building, Teague glanced around, searching for Hudson as was normal for him. He was always aware of the guy. Always. And ever since that night on the boat… God, he had such a hard time thinking about that night without a foreign sense of anticipation filling him. He had yet to broach the subject with Hudson, and at this point, with a week having passed since the offer, he wasn't even sure if he could accept now. The only good thing—if it could even be considered that—was that he hadn't had a single drink in almost seven full days.

Now, he wouldn't go so far as to say he was an alcoholic, but he couldn't deny that he used alcohol to numb himself. It'd been a crutch for a long time, one that wasn't easy to kick, but he'd managed.

Hudson stepped out of the small office, his gaze zeroing in on Teague instantly. He felt the intensity radiating from Hudson, something that wasn't new, nor was it unfamiliar, but it hit him the same as it always did. Whenever they were in the same room—especially when they were alone—Teague felt like Hudson was a jungle cat and he was the prey. As though any second now, he was going to be pounced on. Only that had never happened.

And when Hudson turned around and returned to the office, effectively brushing him off, Teague didn't think today was going to be any different.

Except maybe it was, because for the first time all week, he felt the anger begin to bubble up from within. And it looked as though Hudson was about to be his outlet.

HUDSON HAD HEARD someone enter the shop, which was the reason he stepped out of the office to check it out. Sometimes customers wandered in, and he made a point to keep an eye out for them, although greeting them was sometimes uncomfortable. There was a white board on the wall near the office, which he used from time to time to communicate. It stated that Hudson could hear but couldn't speak, because that seemed to be the easiest way to get the news out there. No sense in trying to pretend otherwise.

Speechless

Most of the time, Teague dealt directly with the people when they arrived, but there were the one-off instances when Hudson had no choice. Since these days most people had a cell phone, it was easier for Hudson to explain via text message. For the most part, the people who came into the shop were receptive to that. Although, there had been a couple of jackasses who refused, and in those cases, Hudson would seek out one of the guys so they could relay what he needed to say.

However, this time the newcomer wasn't a customer, so rather than have a confrontation with Teague, he decided to go back to his office to take care of the paperwork he'd been working on.

"Are you purposely ignoring me?" Teague blurted as he stepped into the office a few seconds later.

Keeping his expression neutral, Hudson glanced up at him. He'd been waiting for Teague to come to him, to tell him whether or not he was going to take him up on his offer, only that hadn't happened. Even after the night of the fireworks, when they'd shared a moment—and yes, no matter what either of them wanted to say, they had shared a moment—Teague hadn't confronted him. Possibly a record for the kid.

Rather than answer, Hudson gave Teague his undivided attention, watching him closely.

"I don't know what you want from me," Teague grumbled, his hands going to his hips. "One night you barge into my apartment, kiss the fuck out of me, offer to fuck my brains out, and then..."

And then?

Teague stared at Hudson's hands as he signed the two words, but the expression on his face didn't change. Sometimes, he wished Teague would've learned sign language like the others. Admittedly, Hudson had been floored when Dare insisted that they were going to learn sign language so that they could overcome the communication barrier between them. It had taken him completely by surprise, and in a way, it had made him feel more welcome at the marina than he'd felt anywhere in his life.

Only Teague had purposely avoided learning, which meant the only way they could communicate was if Hudson wrote out the words or sent them via text. He opted for the latter, grabbing his phone as he leaned back in his chair and propped his feet up on the desk.

He typed out the same words: *And then?*

Teague peered down at his phone when the message came in. "I fucking hate this shit," he mumbled under his breath.

Hate what shit?

"That I can't fucking talk to you."

You're doing a good job now.

Hudson knew it was uncomfortable for a lot of people that he couldn't talk. He'd experienced so many strange situations over the years because he was mute. Some people assumed he was also deaf, so they chose not to talk to him at all. A couple of people had made that assumption and then spoken aloud their real feelings, which had both amused and infuriated Hudson at the same time. He'd put many people in their place when he responded to what they said via writing down his thoughts or typing them out. When he was younger, he would often call them on it, which made things even more awkward. These days, Hudson pretended not to notice most of the time.

Speechless

"What do you want from me?" Teague dropped his hands and stared directly at him. Hudson could see the frustration in the kid's steel-blue eyes.

I gave you my offer.

"But you haven't acted on it," Teague retorted after he read the text.

Not my place. I told you what you needed to do.

Hudson watched Teague closely.

"I quit drinking. What fucking more do you want?"

I'm proud of you.

He didn't mean it as condescension—he was really fucking proud of him; it couldn't be easy—but clearly Teague took it that way. That was one of the major issues with "talking" through text messages. People assumed what they wanted to when they read the message. They could "hear" emotions that weren't there.

"Fuck you."

Hudson smiled. He couldn't help himself. For the past week, Teague had been a little off. Not quite as combative as Hudson was used to. And during the two years they'd worked together, Hudson had experienced a gamut of emotions from Teague. His mood swings could take you out at the knees if you weren't careful.

He didn't know why Teague had been extra prickly until now. Seemed he'd knocked the kid off his game with the offer.

The offer still stands.

Teague stared at his phone for longer than was necessary to read the message, so Hudson waited for a response. Regrettably, the sound of voices in the shop brought their conversation to an abrupt halt. Teague glanced out the door, then back to Hudson. "I'll take care of this."

Hudson nodded, dropped his feet to the floor, put his phone on his desk, and got back to his paperwork. Well, he tried to, anyway. The only thing he could do was think about Teague. The kid had said he'd quit drinking, and from what Hudson could tell, he wasn't lying. Not once had he caught him with so much as a beer, and Teague wasn't the type to try to hide it. He was ornery by nature, so he would've felt the need to rub it in Hudson's face if he was still drinking.

So, technically, Teague had taken the first step. Now he needed to agree to be all in for the duration of their ... arrangement.

Although he should probably lay out the rules first and let Teague decide from there what he could or could not handle. The longer they allowed this to simmer between them, the more intense his craving for Teague became. He had no doubt he could satisfy the kid in ways he'd never imagined; he only hoped he could keep himself in check. The guy drove him fucking crazy, made his balls ache no matter how many times he jacked off in a given day.

Yeah, it was safe to say the kid deserved to know what he was in for if he did accept; otherwise, he might not be able to handle it.

Hudson picked up his phone and started tapping out another message.

Seven

NORMALLY TEAGUE WOULD welcome a distraction that kept him from having to deal with Hudson, but this one irritated him. Still, he managed to have a lengthy conversation with the two guys who were buying a boat from a friend and wanted to know how much it would cost to fix it. Considering they had no idea what was wrong with it, there was little Teague could tell them, yet they'd managed to chat him up for a full half hour.

Now, as he headed outside to clear his head and refocus, he remembered his phone had buzzed in his pocket a short while ago. As he leaned against the steel wall, propping one foot flat against it, he pulled up the text message he had received. It was from Hudson, which wasn't a big shocker. Not many people texted him. Or called, for that matter.

Rules we have yet to discuss:

Great. Just what Teague wanted, more rules in his life. He'd had enough of that shit when he was younger. Every damn person he'd ever encountered had rules for him. After his mother had died, it seemed he'd had to deal with one rule after another. Whether it was from a foster family, a school, a counselor, a social worker … they all wanted to lay out what Teague could and could not do. Mostly the latter.

Needless to say, he wasn't fond of rules.

He continued reading.

1. No getting intoxicated for the duration of our agreement.

Well, that one seemed easy enough and he wasn't blindsided by it. Hudson had already mentioned that he needed to be sober, which he was, thank you very fucking much. However, he didn't see a problem with having a beer from time to time, and he intended to tell Hudson that.

2. Testing for STDs required. I've got my results to give you.

Okay, so that made sense. Teague had his test results from two months ago. Since he hadn't had sex since, that should suffice. If it didn't, then … whatever. Safety was crucial, even he couldn't deny that. But it did make him wonder whether Hudson thought that meant they wouldn't be using condoms. Teague had never had sex without a condom. Hell, he'd never given or received a blow job without a condom. He was rebellious, yeah, but he wasn't fucking stupid. No way was he having sex with anyone unless condoms were involved.

3. No time limit. You can end this whenever you want. As can I.

For whatever reason, Teague had thought this was going to be a one-and-done type deal. At the most, twice in one night. Based on that rule, it sure as shit sounded like Hudson expected this to be ongoing. He wasn't sure how he felt about that.

4. During the time we're together, we will be exclusive. Period.

Again, that one made sense. No reason to take risks. Then again, if Hudson was as good as he claimed he was, Teague wouldn't need to stray. Not that he believed Hudson could hold his interest for more than one night, but whatever.

Speechless

Teague stared at the screen, rereading the rules over and over again. He was partly taken aback that Hudson had the audacity to pin rules to his offer, but in the same sense, they weren't completely unreasonable. Maybe the drinking part. That seemed to be a stickler for Hudson, and Teague briefly wondered why. Still, Teague found himself battling back the urge to rebel against them. That was how he'd spent his entire life; he didn't feel the need to change that now. If Hudson wanted rules, Hudson could go fuck himself.

It didn't take long for the calm to morph into a firestorm of frustration. It was a familiar feeling, something he was used to dealing with. He rarely knew what caused the rage to start boiling, but it never failed to appear.

As the anger burned hotter, he typed in a response: *Take your rules and shove them up your ass.*

Before he could hit send, he stopped himself, staring back at the words he'd typed. The resentment was prevalent, as it always was, but there was something else bubbling up inside him, something that was almost stronger than the anger. He just didn't know what it was or what it meant.

Deciding he needed time to process that, he deleted the words he'd written, dropped the phone in his pocket, and headed back inside. He had a job to do. Confronting Hudson had been a huge mistake. He didn't need this kind of bullshit in his life; he had enough of that.

So, rather than accept or decline, Teague did what he did best. He ignored it, pretended it never happened, and decided to move on with his life.

AFTER GOING TO the gym, then stopping by the sub shop and grabbing two foot-long turkey sandwiches and devouring them before hopping in the shower, Hudson found himself sitting on his couch, reading some crime novel his brother had recommended.

The psychopathic serial killer was almost good enough to keep Hudson's mind from wandering, but it appeared his thoughts of Teague were overpowering his ability to stay focused. When he found himself rereading the same page for the third time, he knew it was time to give it up. Tossing the book onto the couch, he dropped his head back and stared at the ceiling.

He'd been trying to figure out what had happened to Teague after their conversation in his office. While Teague had been busy helping the customer, Hudson had outlined his rules and sent them over. He'd never gotten a response from Teague one way or the other, and for the rest of the afternoon, they had worked side by side with Teague acting as though nothing had ever happened.

Looked as though the kid was back to hating him once more.

He wasn't surprised, to say the least. It seemed one second they were making strides—more like baby steps, really—and the next, Teague was pushing him away, treating him as though he were the shit on the bottom of his shoe that he couldn't seem to get away from.

Not that he cared. Okay, maybe a little. But only because he'd started anticipating what would happen when Teague finally gave in to him.

Speechless

Closing his eyes, Hudson recalled the kiss he'd shared with Teague after he'd barged in and chased off the orgy crew. Just like the kiss on the cruise, Hudson had been leveled by it. The way Teague responded... *Fuck.* He'd been done for the first time, and now it appeared he wouldn't be getting the opportunity again.

A loud pounding sounded on his front door, but before he could get to his feet to answer it, the door flew open and Teague stormed in, glaring at him.

"I don't know what the fuck you're doing to me, but you've got to stop."

No inside voice there. Teague was clearly angry.

Hudson stared back at the kid, confused.

"I can't stop thinking about you. About your stupid fucking offer, your stupid fucking rules, your stupid fucking kiss, your stupid fucking ... everything. I don't want to think about you, goddammit!"

Hudson was on his feet, moving toward Teague before he knew what he was doing. He stopped in front of him, cupped his face, and stared down into those stormy blue eyes that sparked with an odd mix of anger and anticipation. Teague was breathing hard, as though he'd just run a mile; his eyes were wide, his mouth hanging open. There wasn't a hint of alcohol on his breath, so Hudson knew he wasn't intoxicated.

No, it looked as though Teague was finally giving in. And relaying it in the way he knew how.

"Don't look at me like that," Teague protested, most of his bravado fading from his voice. "I don't want to think about you."

Hudson knew better.

"Why me?" Teague asked, a hint of vulnerability in his tone. "Why the fuck did this have to happen to me? Couldn't you find someone else to fuck with?"

Hudson didn't want anyone else.

As for the rest of it, Hudson wasn't exactly sure what Teague was talking about, but he had a good idea. Teague was referring to the attraction that was blazing between them. Maybe neither of them were looking for anything more than sex, but they couldn't deny the need that was building, swirling, suffocating them both.

Still holding Teague's face in his hands, Hudson brushed his thumbs over Teague's smooth cheeks. He wasn't gentle with his touch, making sure Teague knew who was in charge. This wasn't about romance; it was about pure, unadulterated desire. The need to fuck, the need to claim, the need to...

Hudson watched as Teague swallowed hard, before the sweetest words came out of his mouth. "I accept your offer."

Fuck.

It took all of his willpower not to slam his mouth down on Teague's, not to bruise his lips with a kiss so punishing neither of them would survive it. Instead, he continued to stare at him, waiting to see what Teague would say next. He wasn't disappointed.

"I wanted to tell you to go fuck your rules."

Hudson cocked an eyebrow, interested in Teague's reasoning.

"I don't like rules."

Everyone knew that.

"I don't like you."

Now, that was a lie, but Hudson knew Teague believed it.

"But, so help me, I want you to fuck my brains out."

Hudson's cock was rock hard, straining against his shorts, desperate to get out, but he ignored it.

"I only have one condition," Teague muttered.

Speechless

Hudson lifted an eyebrow, encouraging him to continue.

"No fucking in a bed. I don't do beds."

Interesting. Hudson wasn't sure how he felt about that, but he opted to agree. If Teague could compromise, so could he.

Hudson nodded.

Something passed over Teague's face, something that looked a hell of a lot like submission, and fuck if that didn't make him want to rip Teague's shorts down, spin him around, pin him to the door, and drive his dick right into Teague's ass, claiming him, showing him just who he was submitting to.

Again, he didn't.

"Tell me what you want from me," Teague pleaded.

Hudson couldn't tell him, but Teague already knew that.

However, he could show him.

Yes, he could definitely do that.

So he did.

Eight

ONE MINUTE TEAGUE was sitting on his couch, watching television, the next he was staring up at Hudson, watching as desire contorted the man's absurdly handsome face into something that captivated him unlike anything he'd ever known. He had spilled his guts to Hudson, hating that he'd been worked up enough to do so, but he got the feeling the result was going to be so worth it.

Hudson's callused hands cupped his face, holding him in place, making him lift up on his toes as their lips brushed. He felt light-headed, all the blood draining south, making his dick swell. His mind registered the sound of a door shutting, then something hard against his back before he realized that Hudson had him up against the door, their mouths fused together. The kiss ignited, the same as the last one. Hungry and desperate.

Fuck. Maybe this was it. Maybe Hudson was going to give him what he'd been dying for. A quick, brutal fuck that would set his world to rights and make him forget all about the giant fucking asshole who had plagued his mind for far too long.

Speechless

Teague gripped the waistband of Hudson's shorts, pulling him closer, trying to feel his body flush against him. The man's bare chest was right there, rippling muscle beneath the intricate scrollwork tattooed just below his collarbone. There were no words, simply designs. Sexy was what they were.

Teague wished he'd gone without a shirt because then he could've felt the heat of Hudson's powerful body on his. It was rare that Teague ever saw Hudson without a shirt, but when he did, he couldn't take his eyes off him. Unfortunately, he couldn't even admire him now because his eyes were closed and Hudson was feasting on his mouth, but he couldn't complain too much. Instead, he used his hands to *see*, feeling his way over the hard, tense muscle of Hudson's washboard stomach, the surprisingly soft hair on his chest, the firm planes of his pecs...

When their lips broke apart and Hudson's mouth trailed over his neck, Teague cried out, the sensations overwhelming him. He wasn't used to this. He had always limited his sexual encounters to blow jobs and fucking, no need to bring kissing or any of that other shit into the mix. Now he remembered why. His brain was fried from the intensity consuming him.

Teague tried to pull away, not wanting to send the wrong message. Rather than stop, Hudson's grip tightened on him, his mouth working more furiously against Teague's hypersensitive skin.

Oh, fucking shit. It was too much.

Hudson's tongue slid over his skin, warm lips skimming, teeth nibbling. The sensation bordered on pain, the pleasure so overwhelming he couldn't think straight. Teague tilted his head more, giving Hudson better access, allowing the man to drive him higher and higher. He used the excuse that he was too worked up. He needed to find release, and he didn't give a shit how it came about, as long as this man was the one delivering.

Unable to help himself, Teague rocked his hips forward, grinding his cock against the hard ridge of Hudson's.

Oh, fuck.

That felt good.

Too good.

Teague did it again, dry humping Hudson's leg, when the big man adjusted their positions, shoving his thigh between Teague's legs. He ground his hips forward, sliding his dick against the hard muscle separated by their clothing.

It was too much. Too fucking much.

"Hudson..." He tried to hold on, tried not to lose his shit, but Hudson was furiously nibbling on his neck, sucking his skin into his mouth and... "Fuck!"

Teague wrapped his arm around Hudson's head, holding him tightly as his body shuddered, an orgasm slamming into him right then and there, fully clothed, plastered against the door, Hudson's lips suctioned to his neck.

Embarrassment slapped him hard and fast, causing him to try to pull away, but Hudson held him in place. Teague couldn't believe he had come in his fucking shorts like a stupid horny teenager. He hadn't dry humped a guy since... It'd been years.

Speechless

He looked up to see Hudson studying him, fully expecting to see a smirk on Hudson's mouth, but there was none. There was a tremendous amount of heat swirling in his emerald gaze, but not an ounce of triumph.

Teague swallowed hard but relaxed into Hudson's hold. He couldn't fight him off, even if he'd wanted to. Hudson's giant body still loomed over him, pinning him to the door, unmovable. And for some stupid fucking reason, Teague didn't care. He was satisfied with remaining upright for now.

When he managed to get control of his breathing, Hudson's mouth found his again. This time the kiss was less urgent but just as intense. Their tongues moved together, Hudson's hands continuing to keep Teague's head in place, while Teague explored Hudson's rock-hard body with his hands. This was something else he wasn't used to. Sex was all about give and take as far as he was concerned. He'd gotten his rocks off, so now it should've been Hudson's turn. Only Hudson didn't seem to be moving that direction; he seemed to be slowing things down.

A whirlwind of emotions swamped him, making it hard to think. Desire, confusion, anxiety, maybe even a hint of desperation … they consumed him, made him unable to think rational thoughts. It seemed Hudson understood, because he didn't push for more. Hudson continued to kiss him, gently, softly, until Teague felt the world shift back into position. He was more in control, less panicked. Only then did Hudson pull back and stare down at him.

He wished Hudson could say something. To tell him what the fuck was supposed to happen next.

Only he couldn't.

And if Teague hadn't been so stupid, so damn rebellious, he would've taken the time to learn sign language and wouldn't be in this predicament.

THE KID HAD come un-fucking-done and it had been so damn beautiful. Holding Teague while he shuddered and came apart in his arms had been unlike anything else Hudson had experienced. He wanted to make him do it again and again, yet Hudson knew he had to pull back, to put the brakes on before he freaked Teague out.

There was no doubt Teague was as fragile as a live grenade. Only he could blow at any second, with or without the pin being pulled.

Not to mention, they still had a few things to discuss before they went full steam ahead.

"I'm … uh … I'm just gonna go," Teague mumbled, staring up at him.

Hudson wasn't sure if Teague wanted him to convince him to stay, but he figured letting him go for now was the best plan. For one, Hudson couldn't speak, couldn't say what was on his mind, and that wasn't fair to either of them. So he simply nodded, then pressed his lips to Teague's once more. The kid held on to him, and it felt oddly reassuring.

Once Hudson stepped back, he let Teague figure it out from there. With one last glance back, as though he was still confused over what had happened, Teague then turned, opened the door, and walked out, closing it behind him. With weak legs, Hudson managed to make it back to the couch, where he plopped his ass down and took a deep breath.

Wow.

Like, seriously. Holy. Fucking. Wow.

Speechless

He reached for his phone, tempted to send Teague a message to check on him, but decided to hold off for a few minutes. He needed to get his bearings, figure out what his next step was going to be. Teague had accepted his offer, which meant...

Well, he didn't really know what it meant, because other than offering to fuck Teague senseless in order to keep him from doing the destructive shit he'd been doing, Hudson wasn't sure how this was going to work. Sure, they could have sex. And it would likely be mind-blowing, possibly bordering on earth-shattering, but he had to put some structure around it. Even if only in his head. He had been purposely avoiding Teague for so long, the idea of giving in to him scared him a little.

What if Teague ended up wanting more?

Hell, what if *he* wanted more?

How were they supposed to handle that?

And was it possible to keep that from happening?

Maybe they should make a rule about no sleepovers. He shook his head. No, that was stupid. When Hudson invited Teague into his... Well, technically it wouldn't be a bed since that was Teague's one condition. Okay, so when Hudson lodged himself deep inside Teague the first time, he fully intended to stay there for a while. That could very well roll over into the morning, so that was out.

They definitely wouldn't date. It wasn't like Teague would expect Hudson to take him to dinner or a movie, so that was a given. He didn't need to outline that.

He was sure he didn't have to worry about Teague telling people about them. Teague didn't tell anyone anything. As a matter of fact, Hudson knew absolutely nothing about the guy's family. In the two years he'd been working at the marina, he had never once heard Teague talk about someone he was close to. And the dumb asses Teague had fucked in the past couple of years damn sure didn't count.

Where were his parents? Did he have any brothers or sisters? Grandparents?

Those were questions he doubted Teague would answer. But would the kid want to know about Hudson's family? He'd already met AJ, and there really wasn't anyone else to meet at this point. His father had bailed on them right after Hudson was born. And their mother had suffered from mental illness. She'd taken her own life when Hudson was sixteen. AJ had been eighteen at the time, and with help from their aunt, they'd kept Hudson from being sucked into foster care. Unfortunately, they didn't have a good relationship with their mother's sister, so his family was limited.

His phone buzzed, pulling him from his thoughts. Picking it up, he glanced at the screen and smiled.

I have my test results. It was done two months ago, but I haven't been with anyone since. If you want me to get it done again, I will.

This kid was no doubt going to get under his skin, he could feel it.

He typed out a response: *No need. Those results will do.*

The next thing he saw was a file downloading on his phone. He clicked on it and saw the test results. Looked as though Teague had been given a clean bill of health.

Good to know.

Another text came almost immediately: *But we're still going to use condoms with intercourse. No condoms, no deal.*

Speechless

That made Hudson smile, for the simple fact that Teague was adamant about safety. And maybe it brought forth a little measure of relief, as well.

He replied with: *No issue with condoms.*

Although the thought of going bare with Teague...

Hudson reached down and palmed his dick through his shorts. He was coming to life once again, and he needed to give it some attention or he'd be hurting come tomorrow. Tossing his phone onto the cushion, he unbuttoned and unzipped, then pushed his shorts down his thighs before getting comfortable again. He took his cock in his hand, stroking slow and easy while he stared at the door. The memory of making Teague come from a few well-placed kisses brought his dick roaring to life.

Shifting his position, Hudson kicked off his shorts and reclined on the couch, propping up on pillows while he fisted his cock, tugging it slow and easy, teasing the head, cupping his balls. He wasn't in a rush, enjoying the thoughts of Teague playing like a slideshow behind his eyelids.

It would've been better if he had Teague's mouth on him. That warm, sexy, smartass mouth... sucking, licking. Hudson continued to tease his iron-hard length as he debated whether or not he would allow himself to come. If he held off, it would spike his anticipation. Then again, if he held off, his balls would be aching by morning.

He wanted to see Teague's face, wanted to listen to those breathy moans.

Reaching for his phone, he shot a text to Teague: *Come over here and watch me jack off.*

While he continued to stroke his dick, he waited for a response, half expecting Teague to ignore him. The message came back within a minute.

Serious?

As a heart attack.

Hudson set his phone down on the table and resumed his hand job. When his front door opened and Teague stepped inside, he had to admit, he was surprised. He'd taken the chance to offer up a command, expecting Teague to rebel. But Teague had heeded it. Hudson wondered if the kid even realized he had. Since Teague wasn't fond of being told what to do and all, it was a little odd to see him respond so easily.

Hudson nodded toward the end of the couch where his feet were. He paused long enough to sign for Teague to sit, then pointed just in case. Whether he understood or it merely made sense, Teague propped his ass on the arm of the sofa, put his bare feet on the cushion between Hudson's legs, and watched.

Resuming his pace, Hudson never took his eyes off Teague's face. There were so many things he wanted to do to this man, so many ways he wanted to make him come undone. This was hot as fuck, something he'd never imagined doing, but he wanted so much more.

Teague's eyes lifted to meet Hudson's, and when he spoke, a tremor raced straight down Hudson's spine.

"Watching you makes my dick hard."

Oh, fuck. He liked that Teague was verbal. Nodding, he hoped to encourage him to continue.

"You're fucking huge."

Well, he was a big guy; it was to be expected.

"So fucking big." Teague's tone was laced with wonder, his eyes once again fixated between Hudson's legs.

Hudson continued stroking, tightening his grip on his dick while he kneaded his balls with his other hand. He lifted one leg up as he battled down the urge to come too quickly. He was enjoying Teague's eyes on him too damn much.

"Do you wish my mouth was on you?" Teague asked.

Speechless

It didn't sound like an offer, more like casual conversation, so Hudson nodded. As much as he wanted Teague's lips wrapped around his dick, he wasn't ready for that yet. More importantly, Teague wasn't ready for that yet.

"Fuck, that's beautiful."

Hudson noticed Teague was rubbing against his own crotch. He wanted to see, but he knew not to push this right now. Mostly because he didn't trust himself.

Teague's eyes lifted to Hudson's face again. "I wanna watch you come all over that fucking gorgeous chest. You wanna come while I watch you?"

Hudson was too lost in the pleasure to respond. He couldn't even nod his head, so he continued to roughly tug on his dick while Teague sat at his feet. He felt the spark ignite, knew he was going to come. He watched Teague's face as he stroked faster, as his cock jerked in his hand, spurting all over his chest, emptying his balls. He noticed the way Teague bit his bottom lip, captivated by the sight.

It caused another tremor to shoot through him.

Nine

Saturday, July 9th

TEAGUE WAS EXHAUSTED.

He had hardly slept last night, and it only had a little to do with the fact that Hudson had summoned him over so he could watch him masturbate (which, by the way, was hot as fuck). No, after that, when Teague had gone back to his apartment and attempted to sleep, he continued to think about Hudson. The man had captured his every thought and all of his dreams. He had tossed and turned, waking up with his dick in his hand because he was so turned on it fucking hurt.

So, suffice it to say, he needed a nap, but he had agreed to help out with some of the appointments today. And that's how he found himself sitting behind the wheel on the boat while a group of girls flirted it up with a group of guys on the pontoon they'd rented for the afternoon.

He was actually used to this type of outing. He'd even had women ask for him specifically, though he doubted they knew he was gay. Not surprising, since he didn't bother to tell them. What was the fun in that? He'd never so much as touched a woman in his life, and he had no desire to do so, either.

Speechless

From the time he was old enough to figure out what his dick was intended for, Teague knew he wasn't interested in boobs and pussy. Nope. It'd always been dick for him.

He'd experimented early on, topping a couple of times, but quickly learned that he preferred to be fucked, to be taken hard and fast, drilled into… Bottoming was certainly what he wanted. The whole top thing … required too much control, and that was one thing he lacked. Even he knew that.

And women … they didn't have the parts that would please him.

But he could definitely flirt when necessary because it was good for business.

His phone buzzed in his pocket, and he retrieved it while making sure no one was around him. After Hudson's text last night, he had no idea what the guy might send over, and he damn sure didn't want anyone else to see it. Still, he remembered the commanding message for him to come over and watch. At first, he'd thought it had been some sort of test. Without hesitating, he had gone over and… Holy fuck. If he'd been concerned about whether or not it had been wise to accept Hudson's proposal, he was no longer worried. The guy was hung like a fucking horse, and he was dominating when it came to sex. No way could Teague go wrong there.

You cool?

The message was from Hudson, and it was the first time he'd heard from him today, so it made him smile. Hudson was checking on him.

Not that he would put too much thought into that.

Yep. All good. You?

I'd be better if you were in the shop today.

Teague's mind conjured up a million ideas about what they could do if he was in Hudson's tiny little office, or even out in the shop.

Figuring it was his turn to tease a little, he responded with: *And what would you do if I was?*

What would you want me to do?

Of course Hudson would answer the question with a question. Still, he responded honestly: *Whatever you wanted.*

A minute passed, and Teague figured Hudson wasn't going to respond, but as he was putting his phone back in his pocket, it vibrated. He took a deep breath as he pulled up the text and stared at the screen.

You would be okay if I sit you on my desk and suck you off right here?

Alrighty then.

Teague was fairly certain he'd just had a hot flash.

Like, seriously.

He peered over at the people on the boat, making sure they weren't paying any attention to him. On a normal outing, he would've been hanging out with them, enjoying the party, but he was too tired today. Or he had been right up until he'd imagined sitting on Hudson's desk while Hudson sucked him off.

Fuck.

He tapped out a response with shaky hands: *I think I could handle that.*

We'll see about that. Come find me when you get back. As soon as you get back.

Thankfully, Teague had his sunglasses on, because it gave him some privacy for his thoughts. He knew he was easy to read, and the last damn thing he wanted was for these people to see the intense lust burning in his eyes.

He glanced at his phone to check the time. Still at least an hour and a half before they would be heading back to shore.

Surely he could wait that long.

Speechless

HUDSON HAD BUSIED himself by working on the boat that had been brought in that morning. The minor engine problem had taken no time at all to fix, so he'd opted to reorganize some of his tools and had been doing so when Teague wandered into the building a little before four.

Their eyes met from across the room, and he knew right then that Teague was still thinking about his offer. The one where he'd mentioned sitting Teague on his desk and blowing him…

Yep, that one.

Good thing, too, because Hudson had thought about little else since he'd sent the text to Teague a little more than two hours ago.

Nodding toward the bay door, he signaled for Teague to close it. Teague made an immediate U-turn and hit the button that would bring the door down. As he neared, Hudson went into his office. Because he'd used the place to sleep from time to time before he had moved into the apartment above the main building, there was a black curtain covering the window, which allowed him the privacy he needed for what he was about to do.

When Teague stepped into the office, there was a hint of uncertainty in his eyes. It was oddly endearing.

Again, Hudson motioned for him to close the door. Without being told, Teague also flipped the lock.

Taking a seat at his desk, Hudson moved the chair back enough so that Teague could stand between him and the desk. He opened the drawer, snagged the sheet of paper he'd tucked in there earlier, then motioned for him to come over while he kept his eyes locked on the kid. He got the feeling Teague was a little nervous, which belied everything Hudson knew about him. Then again, in recent days, he'd seen a different side of Teague, one he obviously didn't show most of the world.

No doubt about it, Teague was wild. He was impulsive and defiant. But he was also curious.

When Teague approached, Hudson held out the paper for him to take. Since Teague had given him his test results last night, Hudson had made a point to get his.

He watched as Teague glanced at the paper, his eyes skimming before he looked up and met Hudson's gaze once more. When Teague put it down, Hudson took that as his agreement.

Before Teague could hop up on the desk, Hudson reached for him, gripping the backs of his thighs and pulling him toward him. Once Teague straddled his lap, legs hanging over the armrests, Hudson cupped his face and pulled him closer. He allowed their breaths to pass between them for only an instant before he couldn't resist the urge to kiss Teague anymore. The soft moan that escaped the man's mouth made his dick jerk to attention. While he held Teague in place, Hudson feasted on him, making sure he showed him just how much he wanted him, how much he wanted this.

Although he could've easily made this about the blow job and nothing else, Hudson wanted more. A little bit of a connection, something to show Teague that there was more to life than quick, casual encounters. Now, he wasn't looking for too much, but a little kissing, some heavy petting … there was nothing wrong with that.

Speechless

Long minutes passed before Hudson worked his hand into Teague's shorts, fisting Teague's cock in one hand while he cupped the back of Teague's head with his other hand. This was the first time he'd actually touched Teague intimately, and he savored the moment, memorizing the heft and weight of his thick cock, the silkiness of his shaft against his palm. The guy was so damned sexy, so eager … it was hard to maintain his control, but he managed. Hudson didn't want Teague pulling away just yet, so he stroked him in rhythm with their tongues, enjoying the grunts and groans and erratic thrusts of Teague's hips.

Knowing he had to maintain control, he urged Teague to his feet, then helped him out of his shorts while Teague pulled off his shirt. Ahh, yes. Just as impressive as always. For a moment, Hudson took the time to admire the gorgeous, naked man standing before him. His skin was smooth and sun-kissed, not a single thing marring it. No tattoos, no piercings, nothing that would reinforce some of that rebellious nature.

In a word, Teague was perfect, and Hudson wanted to spend hours learning every contour with his tongue, but he knew this wasn't the time or the place for that.

Scooting his chair forward, he forced Teague to step back until his ass bumped the edge of the desk. Hudson reached around and patted the top with his hand, his signal for Teague to take a seat. Teague hopped up on the desk, legs spread wide, offering Hudson an unobstructed view of his cock and balls. It was evident the kid manscaped, which was a pleasant discovery, as well.

Teague's dick was long and thick, with a slight curve in it. The head was wide, definitely a mouthful.

"Condom," Teague muttered.

Hudson met Teague's gaze as he shook his head. He would gladly use a condom to fuck, but for this … he wanted Teague to feel everything without the barrier of a rubber between them.

"I never do this without a condom," Teague argued.

Rather than respond, Hudson simply stared back at him. He wasn't going to blow him with a condom. He appreciated Teague's need to be safe, but they'd shared their test results, so as far as oral sex went, it wasn't necessary. He wasn't going to compromise on this, either.

"Fine," Teague finally huffed, obviously too worked up to put up a fight.

Hudson needed to touch him, to feel the silky length against his palm again. After lifting Teague's feet and planting them on the armrests of the chair, forcing his legs wider, Hudson moved in closer, allowing his breath to fan the swollen head of Teague's impressive cock. Hudson watched it twitch, bobbing upward as though beckoning him to come closer. The man's dick made Hudson's mouth water with the need to taste him.

Taking his time, he used his tongue, grazing the smooth skin, brushing the head lightly, teasing his glans, curling around the crest. He didn't take Teague into his mouth at first, rather sliding his tongue down his shaft while Teague leaned back on his hands, watching him. Teague's breaths became more rapid the more Hudson tormented him, which only spurred Hudson on.

"Fuck," Teague panted. "You're too fucking good at that. I want to feel your mouth on me."

Speechless

Hudson wanted to tell him to beg, but he decided now wasn't the time. They would have to work on a few words in sign language to make this easier on them both. But for now, he gave Teague what he needed, wrapping his lips around the engorged head and lapping at the pre-cum that had formed there.

Teague sucked in a breath at the same time Hudson stretched his mouth wide and took him all the way to the root.

"Oh, fuck." Teague's moan was loud in the small room.

Hudson looked up to see that Teague had closed his eyes. He instantly pulled back, allowing Teague's cock to fall out of his mouth. The kid's eyes flew open, meeting Hudson's gaze. He shook his head, then pointed to Teague's eyes and signed: *keep them open.*

Teague nodded, but Hudson wasn't sure he understood. He resumed feasting on Teague's cock, stroking every inch with his tongue, lightly scraping his teeth along the sensitive underside, keeping his eyes on Teague's face the entire time. When the kid's eyes closed again, Hudson stopped.

It only took two more times before Teague clearly understood what Hudson wanted. He kept his eyes open, and Hudson gave him what he needed. He sucked him deep, bobbing his head, taking Teague to the back of his throat over and over until Teague was rambling incoherently, begging Hudson to finish him off.

Although he was enjoying the shit out of this, got off on driving Teague higher and higher, he finally gave Teague what he needed, using his hand to stroke Teague's dick roughly while he sucked him harder, faster.

"Oh, fuck... Hudson... Fuck..." Teague reached for Hudson's head, but he dodged him, not allowing the kid to take control.

He sucked harder, faster, stroking him urgently as he cupped Teague's balls with his other hand, kneading them until he knew Teague was hovering on the razor-sharp edge of release.

"Gonna come..." Teague groaned. "Wanna come in your mouth... Please let me come in your fucking mouth... Hudson... Oh, fuck."

Teague's hips jerked as his dick pulsed in Hudson's mouth, his salty taste splashing over Hudson's tongue as Teague came with a strangled cry and a jerk of his hips.

It was so fucking beautiful; Hudson wasn't sure how he managed not to come in his shorts.

Somehow he did.

Barely.

Ten

ALTHOUGH TEAGUE SPENT all day Sunday helping out with tours, he knew that Hudson had taken the day off. Part of him wished he hadn't volunteered, but he would never go back on his offer to assist, so he had gone in at eight and spent the entire day trying not to wonder what Hudson was doing.

The marina was unusually busy, so much so that he'd had to make an unscheduled run to the store in order to pick up hot dogs and ground beef because the restaurant had run out completely. That alone had kept his mind off Hudson for at least an hour.

By the end of the day, Teague was exhausted physically, but he couldn't get his brain to shut down. He continued to think about yesterday, about the blow job Hudson had given him in the repair shop office.

Holy. Fuck.

He could practically feel the warm heat of Hudson's mouth on his dick. Never before had he had a man's mouth on him without a rubber between them and … it was a wonder Teague had held off as long as he had. It had been incredible.

And now the only thing he could think about was how he was hoping for a replay, only this time he wanted to be the one with Hudson's dick in *his* mouth.

Except Hudson wasn't home, which piqued his curiosity and pissed him off that he cared. Teague should've been happy that he was home alone—something he had wanted for a long time. However, he'd soon learned after he moved in that he didn't enjoy it as much as he'd thought he would. Not to mention, he was spending too damn much time thinking.

He blamed Hudson for that. He blamed the sex, and Hudson's apparent need to maintain a slow pace with whatever this was that they were doing. If he'd had a say, Teague would've been fucked already, and they could've gone their separate ways. That was the way he did things. No strings, and repeats were rare, only with the guys who knew he would never be serious.

That didn't explain why he couldn't stop thinking about Hudson. The only rational answer he had was that he was caught up in the chase. Surely once Hudson fucked him, Teague would be content to move on with his life.

He fucking hoped so, anyway.

After taking a shower, Teague flopped onto his bed and propped up his phone so he could see the screen. He had Googled sign language, and ever since yesterday, he had been attempting to teach himself a few things. Nothing major, just some words he'd jotted down during one of the times he'd thought about his interactions with Hudson. Words like: *door, eyes, open, close, sit, stand, my, yours.* Easy things. Then, of course, he'd ventured down another path entirely. He'd looked up other words, like: *penis, mouth, ass, swallow, fuck.*

Speechless

Needless to say, his lesson hadn't gone in the direction he had originally intended. So, now he was hoping to get back on track.

Before he could pull up the website that provided video clip demonstrations, a text message notification came across the screen.

Teague sat up instantly, pulling up the text from Hudson.

Just got home. Taking a shower. I'm coming over in ten. Be naked and sitting on your couch. Make sure the door is unlocked.

Okay, wait.

Teague read the text one more time. Then again. And one more time for good measure.

Yep, he had read it right.

Bossy asshole.

He looked up at the clock, noting the time before hopping off the bed. He should've been taken aback by Hudson's command, not yanking off his fucking shorts, yet that was exactly what he was doing. Once he was naked, Teague scaled the back of the couch and landed on his ass on the cushion. He squinted to see the numbers on his alarm clock across the room.

Shit.

He had nine minutes to wait.

With some of his excitement fading, he got to his feet, went over to the bed, and grabbed his phone before returning to the couch. He pushed one of the pillows against the arm and leaned back. That lasted all of a second before he was sitting up. He propped one foot on the couch, exposing his junk. He put it down, shifted, crossed his legs, uncrossed them. Nothing was working, so he tried the same thing at the other end.

Teague glanced at the clock, then looked at his front door. It was unlocked, so he didn't need to do that.

Another glance at the clock.

Shit. Still five more minutes.

Maybe he should get some water.

Or a condom.

What about lube?

Two condoms?

He crossed his legs again, uncrossed them, propped one ankle over the opposite knee, and leaned back, trying to appear casual. His nuts were getting couch burn, so he dropped his phone on the cushion and got to his feet.

The sound of the doorknob snagged his attention, and he flew back against the couch, lying down, his phone stabbing him in the ass.

Shit. The pillow was on the other end.

Quickly, he tossed his phone to the floor, then flopped to the other end just as the door opened.

And Hudson walked in.

HUDSON HAD TAKEN the fastest shower in the history of showers. He hadn't bothered to shave, although he had noted that the scruff on his jaw was getting a little thick. While he'd considered busting out the razor, he'd finally decided against it. His mind had already wandered across the hall to Teague's apartment long before his body had, and he had no desire to waste time.

But now that he was both mentally and physically here...

He wasn't quite sure what he intended to do.

However, that quickly changed the second he saw Teague sitting on the couch, gloriously naked, just as Hudson had instructed.

Fuck, he looked good like that. So submissive. Hudson could practically see his dick tunneling in and out of that sweet fucking mouth.

He smiled at Teague before closing and locking the door—no way was he going to risk one of those goofy pussy boys coming over and interrupting what he had in mind for Teague tonight—then venturing over and taking a seat at the opposite end of the couch. He tapped out a message on his phone and hit send.

Something buzzed on the floor, and Hudson looked down to see Teague's phone. When he looked back at Teague, he noticed a pink tinge to the guy's cheeks. What in the world had he been doing before Hudson got there?

Teague leaned down and snatched up his phone, then sat back down to read it.

I like you just like that.

More color rose on Teague's face as he blushed.

Hudson typed again: *But I think I want to see more of you. Lean back against the arm, put one leg over the back of the couch, one foot on the floor.*

When he hit send, Hudson turned so that he was casually reclining as he waited for Teague to follow his instructions.

Something that looked a hell of a lot like defiance ignited in Teague's turbulent gaze. Unexpectedly, Teague did what Hudson asked. The position he moved to had Teague looking very much like an offering.

Very, very nice.

Teague read the message, then met Hudson's eyes.

Not planning to rush this, Hudson decided to make some casual conversation.

How was work? Busy?

While he waited for Teague to respond, Hudson allowed his gaze to rake over the beautiful body laid out before him. Teague was lean and muscled, probably not an ounce of fat on his body. He wasn't bulky, but when he moved, the definition of his abs was prominent, as well as his nicely sculpted arms. His shaggy hair was wet, which meant he'd taken a shower.

His phone vibrated and he glanced down at it. *Do you want me to answer you verbally or type my response?*

Hmm. That was a good question. He pretended to consider this while he let his gaze caress Teague's cock. He wasn't fully hard, but Hudson knew it wouldn't take much to get him there.

He responded with: *Up to you. Whatever you prefer.*

After Teague read the message, he met Hudson's gaze. "I prefer your dick in my ass. That's what I prefer."

Hudson smirked. *We'll get to that. I promise.* He waited until Teague read the message before he added: *Eventually.*

He had absolutely no intention of fucking Teague tonight, although it was the best fucking idea he'd ever had. But he knew better than to give Teague that much so quickly. The kid already used sex as a weapon; Hudson had no intention of ending this before he got his fill. He wanted Teague coming back for more, and as far as he was concerned, holding back was the only way to make that happen.

"So what *is* your plan?"

Right now? I'm quite content looking at your beautiful cock.

That beautiful cock twitched when Teague read the message.

"And later?" Teague's hand slowly moved down his stomach, reaching for his dick.

Speechless

Hudson sent another message. *Don't you dare touch yourself unless I specifically tell you to.*

Teague's hand moved back when he glanced at his phone, and Hudson saw heat flash in his eyes. The kid liked that he was being dominated. If Hudson had to guess, he'd never actually given up the reins, even if he was a clear bottom. They'd coined the phrase topping from the bottom because of men like Teague. Hudson had no desire to be topped from any direction.

Deciding on a slightly different tack, Hudson sent another message.

Question time.

Teague groaned, clearly not happy about that. Hudson didn't much care. He wanted to know some things about Teague, and in order to get that information, he had to ask questions because it was clear Teague wasn't going to voluntarily share the details.

Answer out loud.

Teague nodded, but he seemed reluctant.

Hudson moved a little closer to Teague so that he was within arm's reach of his now swelling dick. Based on the look in Teague's eyes, he knew what Hudson was up to.

Or he thought he did, anyway.

Only time would tell.

Eleven

TEAGUE ALREADY KNEW he was not going to like whatever Hudson thought he was doing here, but he was sort of at the man's mercy. He was, after all, very, very naked. The way those eyes raked over him, he found himself mesmerized, willing to do any damn thing Hudson wanted as long as he promised to touch him. Well, everything except the stupid questions thing, but whatever.

At first, Teague thought Hudson was simply getting his rocks off watching him lying there in the buff, but now that Hudson had moved a little closer, Teague's anticipation was growing.

His phone buzzed and he looked at the screen.

Have you ever slept with a woman?

The trepidation he felt over the personal questions he knew were coming grew, but he managed to force the answer past his lips. "No. Have you?"

Hudson smiled, then shook his head.

Good to know.

Have you ever topped?

"Yes. Have you ever bottomed?" He already knew the answer to that, but he still wanted Hudson to respond.

Hudson shook his head again.

Wow. The guy had never been fucked by another guy. "Do you plan to?"

Speechless

As he expected, Hudson shook his head, but then he shrugged and gave Teague a sinful smirk. That wasn't the answer he was expecting, but okay.

Hudson typed again.

For the right guy, I might consider it. One day.

Another hot flash.

Shit.

Hudson leaned forward and reached for Teague's free hand. Confused, Teague lifted it and allowed Hudson to take his wrist. Hudson guided his hand down and placed it on Teague's cock. Remembering Hudson's insistence that he not touch himself, he didn't move.

Stroke yourself slowly.

Teague swallowed hard. He couldn't count the number of times he had jacked off last week, but he could count how many times he'd done so for someone else like this. Never. He had to admit, this was pretty fucking hot, and if the way Hudson's Adam's apple bobbed in his throat was any indication, he thought so, too.

Teague started working his dick, tugging gently, not trying to work himself up but providing enough stimulation to make it enjoyable while he waited for Hudson to make his next move.

Did you graduate from high school?

As soon as he read the question, he felt the anger bubble up inside him. This wasn't the deal. He hadn't signed on to answer these types of questions, and he damn sure didn't want to play along. Before he could let loose with a string of curse words that would tell Hudson just what he thought, his phone vibrated again.

I'm going to ask ten more questions. You can say pass to two of them without penalty. If you answer eight, I'll let you fuck my mouth. If you answer five–seven, I'll suck you off. If you say pass to any more than that, or you call off the game completely, I decide what happens next.

Teague didn't need to ask what the difference was between fucking Hudson's mouth or Teague sucking him off. Based on yesterday's blow job, Teague knew that Hudson didn't allow anyone else to be in control. When he had reached for Hudson's head, wanting to hold on to him, Hudson had moved away, not allowing him to. So for him to allow Teague to fuck his mouth … that would be worth it. As for the last part…

"You're already deciding, so how's that fair?" he blurted, meeting Hudson's gaze.

His answer was a simple lift of Hudson's dark eyebrow. Clearly, Hudson had set the rules and Teague had two options: pass or play.

Fuck.

This was stupid.

"Yes, I graduated from high school. But only because Cam and Roan rode my ass to make me finish school."

One question down.

Hudson's smile was slow and sexy, not at all triumphant, which didn't make a damn bit of sense.

Do you have any brothers or sisters?

The man was already treading too close to his limit, but Teague still managed to answer with a curt, "No."

Two down.

Keep stroking yourself.

Teague hadn't realized he had stopped. Then again, the line of questioning wasn't conducive to a session with his hand. Hudson remained calm and cool, staring back at him until Teague began teasing his dick again.

Speechless

Are you opposed to being tied up?

Okay, this was definitely a better line of questioning. "Yes," he said truthfully. "I don't trust anyone enough to let them tie me up."

That was number three.

Hudson watched him, but there didn't appear to be any judgment in his eyes. The man certainly confused the fuck out of him. What was the point of the questions?

Have you ever been in love?

Teague snorted. "Nope. Never."

Awesome, four down.

Again, Hudson smiled. The guy had to be up to something.

Do you have a problem with me using toys on you?

That one was easy. "Bring it on. Just don't fucking use a toy on me that you used on someone else."

Five. That meant … Teague would get his dick sucked. Not a bad way to end the night.

I can assure you that'll never happen.

"Good."

When Hudson's gaze dropped to Teague's cock again, he continued to tug. His dick was coming to life nicely, but he doubted he'd get fully hard if Hudson kept this shit up. Teague didn't care if the questions were all about sex, this wasn't doing a damn thing for him.

Do you have a relationship with your parents?

Game time was officially over!

Teague's hand fell to his side and he started to get up, but Hudson was on top of him before that could happen.

HUDSON HAD KNOWN before he asked the question that Teague was going to bail out. He'd seen it in his eyes, but he'd tried anyway.

"I don't want to play this bullshit game," Teague snarled, trying to push Hudson off.

Standing his ground, he covered Teague's body with his own, kneeling between his legs before sliding his lips over Teague's. Teague resisted initially, but it only took a few seconds before he relaxed beneath him. Hudson didn't want to piss him off; he simply wanted to know more about him. He'd purposely mixed the questions about sex with a few more personal ones, and now he knew that when it came to his family, Teague wasn't going to talk.

When they broke for air, Hudson stared down at Teague, willing him to say what was on his mind. He knew the kid wouldn't be able to hold off for long.

"Don't make me answer these stupid questions," Teague whispered, his eyes pleading.

Hudson nodded his agreement, then eased backward, still kneeling between Teague's spread thighs while he typed up another message.

If you want to quit now, you can undress me, then let me fuck your mouth. Or we continue and I'll use my mouth on you. Your choice.

Teague read the message, and Hudson saw the flash of heat that ignited in Teague's eyes. The next thing he knew, Teague was tossing both phones onto the table and reaching for Hudson's shirt.

Apparently that was his answer. Honestly, Hudson was a little surprised by the unselfish move on Teague's part. He'd already answered five questions, which, according to the rules, meant Hudson owed him a blow job. Unless, of course, Teague quit.

Which he was apparently doing.

Speechless

Hudson moved back, allowing Teague to remove his shirt. He took the opportunity to touch Teague continuously as he did. He would concede when it came to giving Teague this for now, but he still insisted that they maintain the connection, even if Teague wasn't aware that they'd made one.

"Ever since I watched you jack off, I've wanted to put my mouth on you."

Hudson's dick thickened at Teague's words. When Teague went to pull his shorts down, Hudson pulled him closer, crushing their mouths together and stealing another kiss. He could tell Teague wasn't used to the whole kissing thing because it seemed to take him off guard every time, and maybe that's why Hudson liked it so much. Kissing Teague... It was fantastic.

He allowed Teague to work his shorts down his legs until Hudson was as naked as Teague was, but that was where he changed his strategy. Using his body, with his lips still sealed to Teague's, he urged Teague back until he was lying flat on the couch. When he was right where Hudson wanted him, Hudson pried his mouth away and got to his knees.

He was desperate to feel that sweet mouth on him.

Planting his hands on the arm of the couch, he straddled Teague's head, his balls brushing against Teague's chin. Thankfully, he didn't need to give any instructions. Teague opened wide and took Hudson's balls in his mouth, laving them with his tongue, moaning softly, the vibrations sending shock waves of pleasure up Hudson's spine. Teague's hands curled around his thighs, but Hudson could tell he wasn't attempting to hold him down, simply holding on. That was something else he liked about Teague. The touching.

The heat of Teague's mouth encompassed one of his balls, then the other. Teague worked them both in, using his tongue to tease his sac. Hudson's hands clenched on the cushion, enjoying the glorious suction on his nuts.

After a few minutes, Hudson moved back and fed the tip of his cock past Teague's soft lips, watching his beautiful face as he did. Teague was definitely working him harder than Hudson had expected, his eagerness apparent. Hudson shifted again, putting one foot on the floor, the other beside Teague's head as he squatted over Teague's face, pushing his cock into the warm haven of his mouth. If he could've groaned, he would have, because it felt so fucking good.

When Teague looked up at him, their eyes locking, Hudson slid his hand into Teague's silky blond hair as he began pushing his dick deeper. He had to lean forward for a better angle, which made it impossible to see Teague's face, and he wanted to see him, wanted to watch. Since this wasn't only about him, Hudson pulled out of Teague's mouth and started moving back so that he could sit at the opposite end of the couch. With his hand still fisted in Teague's hair, he tugged him forward. Teague moved quickly, as though he knew exactly what Hudson needed.

Then Teague's mouth was on his dick once again, and Hudson was pushing his hips up, driving deep into Teague's throat while he watched his face. Not once did Teague close his eyes, which made Hudson feel oddly proud that the kid knew what he wanted from him. His breaths rushed in and out of his lungs as he face-fucked Teague, his balls drawing up tight to his body. He couldn't hold back, needed to come, wanted to come deep in Teague's throat. He had fantasized about this daily, and now that it was happening, he wasn't able to hold off. With one last punishing thrust, he let go, filling Teague's mouth and holding his head so he swallowed every drop.

When his dick slipped free of Teague's lips, he pulled the kid onto him, holding him while he kissed him, licking the inside of his mouth, tasting himself on Teague's tongue.

Speechless

"Hudson," Teague groaned. "I need you to fuck me. I need you to make me come."

Hudson shook his head. He wasn't going to take Teague tonight. As much as he wanted to be inside him, to claim this man, to show him how good it would feel when they were one, he knew he had to put the brakes on. At least for tonight.

"Are you fucking kidding me?" Teague pulled back, glaring down at him. "You get me all worked up and you're not gonna fuck me?"

Hudson shook his head, then signed: *Not yet.*

He definitely would, but not tonight.

When Teague attempted to jerk away from him, Hudson grabbed him, then flipped their positions so that he was covering half of Teague's body while they lay together on the couch, skin to skin. He stared down at Teague, unwilling to let him run from him. He could understand Teague's frustration, couldn't even blame him for being pissed, but he needed Teague to know this wasn't always about him. The same way it wasn't always about Hudson. They were in this together and when the time was right...

The kid had to learn to compromise, and he definitely needed a lesson in patience.

When Teague stopped fighting him, Hudson kissed him again, slowly, gently, working his tongue into Teague's mouth. He maintained a leisurely pace until Teague was moaning and grinding against Hudson's thigh. He slid his hand down and fisted Teague's cock, allowing him to fuck his fist. Never did Hudson stop kissing him while Teague drove into his hand, getting himself off. Before long, Teague's fingers were digging into Hudson's back, as he shuddered and moaned, and finally, he was coming in Hudson's hand.

Twelve

Thursday, July 14th

"GOT IT!" TEAGUE called out to Cam as he headed back out the door. No way was he sticking around to see if there was anything else they wanted from him. He'd noticed that gleam in Roan's eye, which usually meant paperwork was going to be tossed his way. It was too damn close to closing time to be thinking about that shit.

He wasn't in the mood for paperwork. He was *never* in the mood for paperwork.

So, he would gladly take the pile of messages back to the repair shop and return the phone calls from people who were looking for repairs. That was something he was more than happy to take care of. Due to the fact that Hudson couldn't call people directly, Teague had always managed those when necessary. Certainly wasn't his favorite thing to do, but it came with the job, so he didn't bitch about it.

When he rounded the corner into the repair shop a couple of minutes later, he saw Hudson talking to two guys. More accurately, two guys Teague had seen come around before.

Speechless

One was a light-skinned black guy with a shiny bald head. He was a big guy, built similar to Hudson with muscles bulging throughout his upper body. The other guy was a tall redhead with buzzed hair and a quick smile.

Teague watched them as he passed by, going straight for Hudson's office. These two weren't customers, he knew that much. They'd stopped by to chat it up with Hudson on more than one occasion, although Teague had never questioned who they were. Right now, he wanted to know, and he knew that was stupid.

It was almost as though he were jealous, but there was no damn way that was the case. He couldn't give less of a fuck who Hudson spent his time with.

"Cool," one of the guys said. "Sounds like a plan. We'll run out and grab some food and bring it back. Meet you at your place in an hour?"

Hudson nodded, smiling.

Teague felt the anger burst in his gut. Who the fuck were they, and what the fuck was Hudson going to be doing with them in his apartment?

Fuck.

Don't care.

Don't care.

Don't care.

He repeated that over and over until he was in Hudson's office. He slammed the door a little harder than necessary, then dropped into Hudson's leather chair, pulling the phone toward him. A memory of last Saturday plowed into him. The day Hudson had blown him right here in this very office. On *this* desk. With his feet on *this* chair.

His dick jerked, but he ignored it.

Fuck Hudson.

Whatever he was doing with those guys was none of Teague's business. If Hudson wanted to get naked and screw them both, Teague didn't give a fuck.

Liar.

His chest ached from the fury that was building up. Why would Hudson want to flaunt that shit in front of him? They were barely a week into this stupid arrangement, Hudson hadn't bothered to even get down to business and fuck Teague yet, and now he was already moving on?

Bastard.

Teague grabbed the phone receiver and punched out the number, taking a deep breath. When the customer answered, Teague managed a civil conversation, getting the details of the problem. Ten minutes later, he hung up the phone and was moving on to the next one. The fury was still simmering, but the distraction was working. Teague knew how to be civil when necessary.

And right now, it was definitely necessary.

Two hours later, Teague decided to give up for the day. Hudson had left an hour ago without so much as a word. It was as though he was ignoring Teague, and that shit pissed him off. He was tempted to barge into Hudson's apartment to see what the fuck he was doing, but it was none of his damn business.

Instead, he stopped by the lakeside restaurant and grabbed a burger, then took it back up to his apartment to eat it. He heard sounds coming from across the hall. Voices— which had to belong to those two guys—as well as what was likely the television. His mind conjured up all kinds of shit that could be taking place behind that closed door. None of it was good.

Speechless

He reminded himself that he didn't care, that Hudson hadn't agreed to spend all his time with Teague, and that he didn't want to see Hudson today anyway. After downing his burger, he took a quick shower, pulled on a pair of shorts, grabbed a glass of water, and was back on his couch in front of the television once again.

Staring at the screen, he tried to ignore the mumbled sounds coming from across the hall.

Hudson had said they had to be exclusive during this arrangement, yet he had two guys over there. *Two.* That was bullshit.

The more he thought about it, the more pissed off he got.

"Fuck you, Hudson," he whispered, flopping back on the couch, trying to get comfortable.

"Oh, hell yeah!" someone hollered.

That did it.

Teague was on his feet and over at Hudson's door before he knew what the fuck he was doing. He rationalized it by telling himself it was okay, Hudson had already barged in on him, so he was simply returning the favor.

He knocked on the door and waited.

Ready to rip Hudson a new one and tell him to go fuck himself.

Just as soon as the giant fucking asshole opened the damn door.

"SOMEONE'S AT YOUR door, man. Want me to answer it?" Calvin asked, glancing over at Hudson.

Hudson shook his head. He knew who it was, and he could already picture Teague's angry face standing on the other side, practically burning a hole in the wood with the fury burning in his eyes.

He really wasn't looking forward to this confrontation, but he'd known it was coming since he'd seen Teague in the repair shop after Calvin and Shawn left to grab food so they could sit back and watch the baseball game together. They'd been giving Hudson a hard time because they hadn't seen him for most of the summer. Between the cruise and the workload, Hudson had been keeping busy. By this time of the year, they would've gone camping and fishing at least twice. It was what they did. Been a tradition since they were in high school.

Hell, for almost all four years of high school, the three of them had been inseparable. Thanks to football, they'd sort of stumbled upon an easy friendship, and they'd continued even after that stage of their lives was over.

Not that Teague would understand any of that. Hudson could only imagine what was going through the kid's head. Nothing good, he knew that much.

I'll be back in a minute. Don't eat my damn food.

"No promises," Calvin muttered, his eyes flipping back to the television.

Because he didn't want to subject Shawn and Calvin to Teague's tirade, he quickly opened the door and stepped out into the hall before Teague could get a good look inside.

"What the fuck are you doing in there?" Teague blasted him when he stepped into the hall.

Speechless

It probably didn't look good that Hudson was wearing a pair of shorts and nothing else. He'd taken a shower when he got home, and it'd been too damn hot to put on anything else. His buddies didn't give a shit what he was or wasn't wearing, so he hadn't thought anything of it. Calvin and Shawn were both straight as an arrow. Based on the way Teague's eyes raked over him, the kid was going to have an issue with it.

In a way, Hudson liked that he did.

"You're an asshole," Teague seethed. "You said we had to fucking be exclusive if we were doing this shit." He pointed toward Hudson's apartment. "Who are those guys? Are you fucking them?"

Knowing that Teague was loud enough for half the lake to hear, Hudson grabbed him by the shoulder, turned him around, and walked him back into his own apartment before shutting the door. Before Teague could scream at him some more, Hudson backed him against the door and crushed his mouth over Teague's.

Teague groaned, but he didn't push Hudson away, so Hudson deepened the kiss, trying to calm Teague down. Communication was damn near impossible because Hudson had left his phone in his apartment and Teague didn't know sign language, so this was about as good as it got. If Teague asked yes-or-no questions, Hudson could oblige, otherwise, he would have to do his communications with his hands.

And Hudson knew exactly how to talk to Teague.

"Are you fucking them?" Teague growled when Hudson pulled back to look at him.

Hudson shook his head, meeting Teague's eyes.

"Have you ever fucked them?"

Again, he shook his head.

"Do you *want* to fuck them?"

Hudson gave Teague a *don't be absurd* look.

Apparently that was the wrong thing to do because it sparked Teague's temper again. When Teague finally managed to work up enough anger to push Hudson back, he spun the kid around and pressed him against the door, his chest to Teague's back.

The kid was warm, his skin smooth. Hudson had begun craving this, feeling Teague's body against his. It had only been four days since the night they'd made out right there on Teague's couch, and Hudson had been aching to do it again ever since. The only reason he was holding out was because he knew he couldn't give in to Teague completely. The kid was irrational when it came to certain things, and sex was one of those things. The fact that he was jealous that Hudson had friends over was proof that Teague was looking for more than just sex, though he doubted Teague would admit that.

"Get off of me." Teague was breathing hard, his cheek pressed against the door.

Hudson leaned down and kissed Teague's shoulder, then sucked his skin into his mouth.

Teague moaned, still trying to buck Hudson off.

Not this time.

Hudson was not going to let Teague get away with making these assumptions. The kid had to learn a little control. He needed to have patience. And above all else, he had to trust Hudson. Otherwise, this was pointless. They would never get anywhere.

"Why are you doing this?" Teague questioned on a breathy moan.

Hudson pressed into Teague, grinding his rigid dick against Teague's ass while reaching around and flattening his palms on Teague's chest, holding him tight, pinching his nipples as he continued to suck the skin on his shoulder and neck.

Speechless

Teague stopped trying to resist, just as Hudson expected.

"Oh ... fuck..." Teague tilted his head, giving Hudson better access to his neck. "You're such a fucking asshole."

Hudson smiled. Those were the words he expected, but for the first time, there wasn't much conviction behind them.

In a few minutes, he figured Teague would be giving up the fight completely.

Or that was Hudson's plan, anyway.

Thirteen

TEAGUE REALLY, REALLY hated Hudson.

He hated that he wanted the giant fucking asshole so damn much.

He hated that he didn't mind being pinned to the door by Hudson's giant fucking body.

He hated that he wanted Hudson to finish what he was starting, and he didn't even care how that fucking played out.

As long as Hudson didn't go back to his apartment with those other fucking assholes.

Oh, and he hated that he'd been so weak that he'd blurted out his thoughts. He didn't give a shit if Hudson had fucked those guys before. Or even if he wanted to. As long as he wasn't doing it now, when they had a fucking arrangement.

The arrangement was the only thing he cared about.

Really.

Breathing roughly, Teague tried to slow his pounding heart. Hudson's mouth felt so damn good on him. And the way Hudson held him, his arms wrapped tightly, gripping Teague's chest while he sent sparks of pleasure-pain darting through his nipples … for a moment, he felt grounded. As though maybe he wouldn't fly apart in a fit of rage.

Speechless

Usually, when the rage took over, Teague would succumb to it, incapable of forcing it away, unable to calm himself down. He didn't know why that was, but it'd been the way things were since he was young. He craved the anger, fed off of it.

"I hate you," Teague ground out, the words bursting out of his mouth. As much as he enjoyed this, he hated it just the same. He did not want to be Hudson's plaything, but that was what he seemed to be.

Hudson's hand slid down into his shorts and...

"Aww, hell...Yes."

Teague's hips jerked wildly. The heat of Hudson's hands brushed the length of his dick, urging it to life, although he was half-hard already.

"Fuck... Oh, God, yes... Touch me."

Teague's eyes rolled back in his head as Hudson's big, callused hand wrapped around his dick. When Hudson's other hand dropped from his chest, he had about a second to breathe before his shorts were being ripped down his legs, puddling on the floor at his feet.

Oh, fuck. This was exactly what he needed. Hudson's big body once again pressing him against the door, his warm mouth on Teague's neck, and his hand stroking Teague's throbbing dick.

Teague didn't want to want him so damn much, but he did. He so fucking did.

"Hudson... Goddamn you... Aww, yes..."

Closing his eyes, Teague let the sensations take over. His body had come to life, and he felt every damn thing Hudson was doing to him. He was hypersensitive and keenly aware of every touch of Hudson's mouth, his hand, his chest.

Once again Hudson was shifting and then...

"Oh, fuck!"

Teague felt the smooth flesh of Hudson's dick against his back. It wasn't where Teague wanted it, but it was more than he'd ever had, so he would take it.

Hudson jerked Teague off while he pushed his hips forward, grinding his cock against him. Teague wanted to beg him to fuck him, but he wasn't going to tell Hudson as much. Not yet. He didn't want to risk Hudson stopping. Teague was already coming apart, the anger being overridden by something entirely different.

Teague flattened his palms on the door when Hudson's mouth began trailing down his back. He hadn't realized how sensitive that part of him was until this moment. The way Hudson's tongue slid down his spine... Teague's ass clenched, desperate for Hudson to fill him, to fuck him until all thoughts were obliterated.

"Yes ... yes..." Teague chanted the word as Hudson moved lower, his hand releasing Teague's cock and then separating Teague's ass cheeks before his warm tongue speared him. "Fuck!"

Teague went up on his toes, trying to urge Hudson right where he wanted him. His ankles were trapped in his shorts, so he couldn't spread his legs farther, but Hudson didn't seem to care. He was doing all the work, holding Teague open while he rimmed him.

Teague needed more, but when he reached down to stroke his dick, Hudson slapped his hand away, making him groan in frustration. He had no idea how much time passed while Hudson fucked his ass with his tongue. He felt the pressure building inside him, knew if Hudson kept that up, he would likely be able to come. Even without friction on his dick. It was that damn good, and Teague had always enjoyed having his ass played with.

Hudson bit Teague's butt cheek, then spun him around.

Speechless

Off-balance, Teague nearly fell, but Hudson's arm went across his stomach, holding him against the wall. Teague looked down his body to see Hudson kneeling before him. He held his breath when Hudson began kissing his stomach, licking his abs as he moved lower. When the furnace of Hudson's mouth slid over his cock, Teague nearly came.

He couldn't look away, mesmerized by how hot it was to see Hudson on his knees before him. Teague was still pinned to the door, unable to thrust his hips forward, unable to force himself deeper into Hudson's throat, but he didn't care. As long as Hudson continued working him like that, he wasn't going to last, anyway.

He watched Hudson's face, noticing the way Hudson's eyes locked with his while he sucked Teague's dick. He was controlling everything, but Teague hardly noticed. It felt so damn good, all the attention on his dick.

"Oh, yeah…"

Hudson lifted Teague's dick, pressing it against his stomach before taking Teague's nuts in his mouth. He sucked them so exquisitely Teague cried out, his dick pulsing.

"You're gonna make me come," he warned. "Fuck, Hudson. I'm gonna…"

Hudson's mouth wrapped around Teague's shaft once more as he took Teague all the way to the root. His tongue swirled over the head before he began sucking in earnest. Teague couldn't hold back any longer.

And when Hudson gripped his balls, kneading them roughly, Teague slammed his head back against the door and shot straight down Hudson's throat, spasms racking his body as he came. Hard.

HUDSON SWALLOWED TEAGUE'S cum down, then bolted to his feet, pressed his body against the kid, and devoured his mouth. Teague's hands flew around Hudson's neck, his fingers linking into Hudson's hair. It was as though Teague was trying to keep himself together.

Which had been the plan.

As much as Hudson wanted to push away, to walk right out that door and leave Teague to his thoughts, he couldn't seem to do it.

Not yet.

When Teague finally relaxed somewhat, Hudson pulled his mouth back, placed his hand on top of Teague's head, and roughly pushed him down to his knees. The throaty noise that came from Teague told him the kid didn't mind one bit.

Staring down at Teague, Hudson fed his cock into Teague's mouth, then planted one hand on the door, the other on Teague's head. He wasn't going to take his time, and he wasn't going to be gentle. Instead, he began fucking Teague's face, tugging on his hair, enjoying the way Teague's moans sent vibrations up his shaft, straight to his balls.

Hudson focused on finding his release, not willing to draw this out any longer. He'd given Teague what he needed, and now it was his turn. He wasn't usually this selfish, but he couldn't deny that he was pissed at Teague for pushing him this far. He shouldn't have given in when he got here, but he couldn't help it. He found too damn much pleasure in Teague's body, in making him cry out as he came.

So, it was only fair that Hudson get his.

He punched his hips forward rapidly, driving his dick into Teague's mouth while he held the kid's head still with one hand in his hair. Teague was slobbering as he tried to take more of him, but never did he try to pull away. When Teague's eyes lifted and met Hudson's, he was done for.

Speechless

He gripped Teague's face with both hands, thrusting deep and fast until his thigh muscles burned and his dick was exploding on Teague's raspy tongue. He watched Teague swallow before he released him. Hudson didn't give Teague time to think before he was pulling him to his feet and once again slamming his mouth on Teague's. The kiss was possessive, reflecting every ounce of his frustration. He doubted Teague would even notice, but he didn't care if he did.

Hudson would have to have a talk with Teague about this type of shit. The kid shouldn't be reacting so violently, but more than that, Hudson shouldn't have given in.

But it was too late for regrets now.

Softening the kiss, Hudson licked the inside of Teague's mouth a few more times before pulling back and pressing his forehead to Teague's. He had so many things he wanted to say, but the communication barrier made that impossible. If they were going to make this work—even for the short term—Teague was going to have to learn some sign language. Enough to have a fairly basic conversation.

"Why didn't you fuck me?"

Hudson shrugged. He could've signed to Teague, told him that he wasn't ready for that yet, but it wouldn't matter. Teague wouldn't understand.

When his heart rate returned to normal, Hudson pulled up his shorts, kissed Teague softly once more, and made the hard decision to walk out the door. He didn't know how Teague would react, but he didn't care. He needed some time to think.

Considering Calvin and Shawn were still in his apartment, he knew he would be ridiculed, but again, that didn't concern him right now. He needed to figure out how the fuck he'd lost control, how Teague had played him so easily, and how to ensure that it didn't happen again.

When he walked in his door, Shawn and Calvin peered up at him, both of them smirking. He shook his head and signed for them to keep their mouths shut. They both laughed, as he'd expected.

"Can't seem to stay away from that kid, can you?" Calvin asked.

Hudson glared at his friend.

Calvin held his hands up in mock surrender. "I'm not judging, man. I'm happy for you. You've been fighting this one for a long damn time."

Shut up and watch the game.

Shawn chuckled. "He was kinda pissed, huh?"

Calvin followed suit. "You tell him we came to watch the game?"

Hudson shook his head.

"Why the hell not? Probably would've made him feel better," Shawn noted.

"Or you coulda invited him over," Calvin added. "That would've eased his mind."

Probably.

"Probably, nothin'." Calvin snorted.

"So I take it y'all are a little more than friends now?" Shawn laughed, finding his statement far too amusing.

Hudson turned his attention to the television, trying to fight his smile. He lost the battle, grinning like a fool. Yeah, it was safe to say they were a little more than friends. Granted, Teague could be planning how he was going to kill Hudson in his sleep for walking out on him.

But that was something he would worry about later.

Right now, he simply wanted to eat some wings, watch the game, and try not to think about what the fuck had just happened a few minutes ago.

He had a feeling he could accomplish the first two things, but the latter would be damn near impossible.

Fourteen

Saturday, July 16th

TEAGUE FINISHED HELPING Dare look at one of the Jet Skis that was giving him problems, then headed back to the repair shop to tell Hudson he was done for the day. It was still early, but it was Saturday, and quite frankly, he was in desperate need of something a little more relaxing than work.

He fished his phone out of his pocket as he went inside the shop and shot Hudson a quick message.

Want to go out on the boat?

Before he made it to the office, his phone buzzed in his hand.

Absolutely.

Well, then. He hadn't expected such a quick response, nor had he really expected Hudson to agree, so... Shit. He didn't even know what to think about that, so he wiped the smile off his face and stopped at the doorway to Hudson's small office.

"Well, come on then," Teague announced when he found Hudson sitting at his desk, leaned back in his chair with his feet propped up. He looked as bored as Teague felt.

Hudson popped up out of the chair, but before Teague could turn around and lead him out of the office, Hudson grabbed his arm and pulled him back. The next thing he knew, Hudson was kissing him full on the mouth, making him moan and … yes, sigh.

He hadn't been expecting the kiss. It was sweet but hot. Hudson didn't touch him other than to cup his jaw and hold him in place. The touch was dominating, something Teague had become familiar with. Not to mention, he liked it.

Still holding his phone, Teague dropped his arms and relaxed against Hudson. This wasn't the first time Hudson had thrown him off course by spontaneously kissing him. It'd happened several times in the last week and it was… Shit, Teague didn't know what it was, and he damn sure wasn't going to think too hard on it. If Hudson wanted to kiss him, more power to him.

Teague was definitely getting used to it. Although he'd been adamantly against it in the beginning, there was no way he could resist this man. He simply wasn't sure whether that was a good thing or a bad thing.

But he wasn't going to think about that now. He wanted to spend some time out on the water. If he was lucky, he'd get to spend a little time *in* the water, as well.

Hudson pulled back, then nodded toward the door, grinning.

Teague pulled himself together and led the way out of the repair shop, hitting the button to close the door, then past the main office and down to the boat dock. There weren't many boats in the slips because it was a beautiful Saturday afternoon and no sane person was sitting at home when they could be out on the water. Sure, it was a little hot, somewhere around 103, but that was what the water was for. To cool off.

Speechless

Fifteen minutes later, Hudson was at the wheel, steering them out to open water while Teague stood beside him, enjoying the view. And he wasn't talking about the lake.

Most of the time, Teague only saw Hudson when they were working. The guy looked sexy as fuck when he worked, no doubt about it. He was usually sporting khaki cargo shorts and a plain dark T-shirt, along with steel-toed work boots. Today he had on athletic shorts, a white Pier 70 shirt, and Nikes, which he looked equally good in. Combined with his thick, dark hair blowing back, his sunglasses on, his shirt being pulled off and tossed somewhere on the seats behind them, all those sexy tattoos, and the damned muscles on display ... he'd never looked better. While Hudson drove, Teague studied the ink across Hudson's back. As with his chest, there were no words, simply designs, many of them tribal and all of the ink black or gray.

When Hudson peered over at him, Teague motioned to a spot, and Hudson turned the boat in that direction. Several minutes later, Hudson cut the engine and they were floating.

Without warning, Hudson tossed his cell phone onto the chair, toed off his shoes, pulled off his socks, then dove into the water, leaving Teague to stare after him. Not wanting to be left behind, he emptied his pockets, flung his flip-flops off, then followed right behind Hudson.

The water was warmer than he would've preferred, but it was nice. And more importantly, it was nice being here with Hudson rather than being alone, which was how he spent most of his time on the water. He knew that Cam, Dare, and Roan all believed Teague had a lot of friends and that he went out all the time. That wasn't entirely true. He didn't have *any* actual friends. No one he could call up when he had a problem or needed to talk. He had plenty of acquaintances and a couple of fuck-buddies, but again, those weren't the kinds of relationships where he would call someone up and ask if they wanted to go hang out on the water. Teague generally waited for Dare or Cam to invite him. Sometimes Roan.

The fact that he'd invited Hudson was a first. It felt right, though, so he wasn't going to spend any more time thinking about it.

Hudson popped up out of the water directly in front of where Teague was treading water to stay afloat. The smile on Hudson's face was contagious, and Teague found himself smiling back.

For a brief moment, he was actually glad Hudson couldn't speak, because Teague was enjoying the silence. And for the life of him, he had no idea what he would've said, anyway.

WHAT MADE YOU want to work at a marina?

Speechless

Hudson shot off the text once they'd made it back to the marina a few hours later. After docking the boat, Teague had mentioned that he was starving, so Hudson had steered him over to the restaurant, where they'd grabbed several premade sandwiches and bags of chips, then headed out onto the shaded patio to eat.

It was hot as hell, but the breeze was decent. They were predicting some storms tonight, which would hopefully lower the temperatures but wouldn't do a damn thing for the humidity.

Teague glanced at his phone between bites, then wiped his mouth and took a drink of his soda.

Hudson pretended he was simply making casual conversation, so he ate, staring out at the other boats still on the water while he waited for Teague to respond.

"It was an accident," Teague finally said.

Hudson heard the hesitancy in his tone, and he knew the kid wasn't fond of talking about himself. Cocking an eyebrow in interest, he encouraged Teague to continue.

"I had just turned sixteen and I wanted to buy a truck," Teague explained. "I didn't have any money and no way to get any without getting a job, so I started applying at every place I could walk to. I stumbled upon the marina and got to talking to Cam. Since I was fairly decent with an engine and was willing to do any of the odd jobs, he said he'd give me a shot."

Hudson actually knew this story because he'd heard it from Cam, but it was nice to hear it from Teague's point of view.

"I'm not sure I was the best employee. There was probably a whole slew of mechanics who had applied, but since Cam had given me a chance to prove myself, I wasn't about to let him down. I spent most of my time cleaning up, helping customers when they returned their boats. Shit like that. I showed up every day, rain or shine. It took me an hour to walk here from the place I was staying, but I didn't let that bother me."

The place he was staying? That was an odd way to phrase things. Did that mean Teague hadn't lived with his parents?

Not that he would ask, because it would be the best way to ruin a damn good afternoon.

However, Hudson hadn't known that Teague had been walking to work back at that time. He wondered if Cam even knew that.

"It took me eight months to save up for the piece of shit I still drive, but it was mine and that was all that mattered. I can definitely afford something nicer now, but since I rarely need it for anything more than getting me to the store—or to work before I moved here—I'm willing to deal with the quirks I've yet to figure out."

Hudson wanted to ask why Teague's parents hadn't driven him to the marina back then, but he didn't dare. He'd seen the kid's reaction firsthand when he tried to talk about family. Again, that would lead to an unnecessary argument.

So you're self-taught with engines?

Teague nodded after taking another bite of his sandwich.

Impressive. I would've thought you had some schooling. You're better than most mechanics I've worked with.

Speechless

He wasn't trying to make Teague blush, but it worked. He figured the kid didn't get a lot of compliments, but it was true. Hudson was ASE-certified and had a lot of schooling behind his trade. Teague was merely a natural. Not a lot of people could do that.

And they worked well as a team. Teague dealt with customers rather well, considering, and Hudson could handle dividing the workload and helping Teague when he needed assistance.

"Enough about me," Teague said, leaning back after pushing the empty basket away from him. "I think it's time to get a shower and hit the bed. I'm wiped."

Hudson smiled. Teague was twenty-five years old; it was only six thirty on a Saturday night... No way was he going to bed this early.

However, it was an interesting way for him to cut a conversation off.

Fifteen

Monday, July 18th

MONDAYS WERE BRUTAL.

At least ninety percent of the time, anyway, and today had definitely been one of those days. Sure, Teague was grateful the marina was so damn busy, but the heat was a surefire way to knock him on his ass. Thanks to two days' worth of rain, the humidity was ridiculous, and you couldn't walk outside without being drenched in sweat.

By the time he got home every night, Teague was too tired to keep his eyes open. And at that point, Hudson was either inviting him over or stopping by. It had been several days full of hand jobs and blow jobs, but still no intercourse, and Teague was beginning to think Hudson had no intention of fucking him.

Ever since his freak out when Hudson had his closest friends over—something he learned the following day when Hudson had texted him to clarify what Teague had so rudely interrupted—it seemed there was less friction between them.

Well, aside from the no-sex thing. That was causing friction all on its own.

Speechless

Yet Teague found himself craving the time he and Hudson did spend together. Hudson was still working the question game, but thankfully he'd started gearing them all toward sex, which made it a hell of a lot easier and lessened his anxiety significantly. Teague doubted Hudson would hold off on the personal ones indefinitely, but he held out hope.

As he made his way down the hall to his apartment, he smelled food and his stomach rumbled. He had no idea what he had in his refrigerator to eat, but he hoped there was something that hadn't passed its expiration date. Just as he was about to open his apartment door, Hudson's door opened. He turned to face him, noticing Hudson was wearing a pair of shorts and no shirt, similar attire to what he'd worn every night for the past week. And still he looked just as delicious as the first time Teague had seen him.

Hudson nodded what appeared to be an invitation for him to come over.

"Give me a little while," Teague told him with a sigh. "I'm starving. Need to eat, then I'll—"

He didn't get a chance to finish the sentence because Hudson grabbed his shoulders and steered him into his apartment, walking him right over to the small table in the kitchen. With a gentle shove, Hudson pushed him into one of the chairs, and there before him was a plate of spaghetti and meatballs. His stomach rumbled loudly, apparently impressed.

Hudson signed for him to eat. And yes, this time he understood him. He'd been studying for at least an hour, usually two, every night when he was alone. He hadn't told anyone about his extracurricular activity, and he was still a little nervous, but he was getting better. Deciding it was time to let Hudson know, he signed back: *okay.*

Hudson's eyes widened, his eyebrows darting down in a V, confusion etched across his rugged features. It made Teague smile that he'd gotten one over on the guy. It was usually the other way around.

As though testing him, Hudson signed back: *Tea or water?*

Teague was happy he knew that one, too. *Water.*

For a brief moment, he thought he saw some unnamed emotion flitter across Hudson's face, but he turned too quickly for Teague to be sure.

While Hudson got drinks, Teague stared down at the plate in front of him. He was tempted to dive in without waiting for Hudson, but he fought the urge. After all, he did have a few manners. He was starving and the meal looked so good—he wasn't sure when the last time someone had cooked for him was, but definitely not since high school. One of the last foster families he'd been with had tried hard to be nice to him. Unfortunately, by that point, Teague had grown tired of the system, tired of the rules, tired of everything. He'd countered their attempt at being kind with rebellion. By that point, it had been ingrained in him. And on the day he'd turned eighteen, one month into his senior year of high school, he'd packed up his one box of belongings and chosen to stay with friends or sleep in his truck. He'd had far more than he could handle at that point. If it hadn't been for Cam and Dare constantly nagging at him to finish high school, he would've dropped out and focused on working.

When Hudson took a seat across from him and nodded toward his plate, Teague grabbed his fork and dug in. They both ate in silence for a few minutes before Hudson stopped and picked up his phone. Knowing he was going to get a text, Teague pulled his from his pocket and set it on the table beside him, then resumed eating.

Who's been teaching you sign language?

Speechless

Teague continued to stuff his face while he read the message on his phone screen. After swallowing, he replied. "The woman on the Internet."

Hudson looked confused.

"I'm teaching myself. I found a website that has video clips. I can't talk to you in sentences yet and probably won't understand most of what you say, but I'm coming along. I recognize a few words at this point, and I can usually piece it together."

Hudson's smile overtook his entire face. He seemed incredibly pleased with that answer, and something in Teague's chest eased a little.

What made you want to learn?

Teague tilted his head to the side and repeated what he'd heard Dare say before. "I want to talk to you, not *at* you."

Hudson nodded and resumed eating.

Grinning, Teague added, "Plus, I figure if you wanna talk dirty to me, it'll help if I understand."

Hudson's smirk was dark and sexy, sending a tremor racing down Teague's spine.

Ignoring it because his stomach was still growling in protest, he once again focused on his food.

Teague noticed Hudson didn't look at him for several minutes, not until they had both cleared their plates. At that point, Hudson signed: *Want more?*

There was more? Oh, thank God.

Teague nodded, then laughed when Hudson brought the pot of spaghetti and the pan of sauce over to the table. Looked as though Hudson had made enough to feed a small army.

They both filled their plates one more time, and neither of them spoke until they had finished off everything that was left.

HUDSON KNEW THAT technically this could be considered a date. He seriously doubted that Teague realized that, and he had no intention of telling him. If he did, he risked sending Teague running for the hills, and Hudson had come to the realization earlier in the week that he was enjoying Teague's company far more than he'd expected to.

Sure, he figured they could eventually fuck like rabbits and never get enough, but since they hadn't yet had sex, he knew that there was something else at work here. Hand jobs and blow jobs would only go so far, they both knew that. But still, Hudson looked forward to seeing Teague every day, and he had every intention of holding out a little while longer.

Seriously, the kid had asked him to go out on the boat. That had been the shocker of a lifetime. No way in hell could he have refused Teague's invite, even if he'd had a meeting with the president. Hudson would've put off anything to make that happen, and he was glad that he had.

For the record, keeping his hands off Teague wasn't easy. His body craved Teague's. The intimacy they shared was more than he'd expected, but he knew it would only get better from here. He still had to contend with the fact that Teague would make a break for it once he got what he needed. Although Teague was tight-lipped when it came to his family and his life before the marina, Hudson had managed to confirm that Teague had no ties with anyone. On purpose. Hudson was not about to get his name added to the list of people Teague ran away from. Ending this thing between them would be inevitable, but Hudson hoped they could be friends afterward. It was more than they'd had in the beginning, so that was something.

Speechless

After they finished washing the dishes—something Teague had insisted on helping with—Hudson took their drinks over to the oversized sectional sofa and set them on the end table before pulling Teague down with him. He honestly had no intentions of doing anything tonight, but he did hope to have a conversation. He wanted to know more about Teague learning sign language. When the kid had signed his first response, Hudson had nearly fallen over. He'd been floored to learn that Teague was teaching himself so that they could communicate.

Luckily, he'd managed to mask the overwhelming response he'd had, not wanting to freak Teague out, but truth was, Hudson had been so touched he'd felt his heart swell inside his chest. Sure, Teague had attempted to play it off as though it were nothing, but it was so not nothing. It was ... everything.

"I really should go home," Teague mumbled when Hudson pulled him against his side. This was the first time they'd been on Hudson's couch together. Well, except for the time Teague had watched Hudson jack off, but he'd merely been an onlooker that night. This was different. Until now, Hudson had kept their playtime confined mostly to Teague's apartment, once on his desk in the office. Oh, and there was the brief time in his shower last night. One of those spur-of-the-moment things.

Stay, Hudson signed.

Teague nodded, then moved away, flopping down on the opposite end on his back, his legs hanging off the couch. It was as though he needed to keep his feet close to the floor in the event he had to make a run for it.

Propping himself up on pillows, Hudson retrieved his phone and tapped out a message: *Tell me something about you that no one else knows.*

As he'd learned to do, Hudson watched Teague's expression as he read the text. He had already learned to gauge Teague's reactions, which was why he was surprised when a small smile formed on Teague's face as he read the text.

Teague tilted his head, glancing over at Hudson.

"I had a dream about you," Teague began, his attention shifting to the ceiling rather than meeting Hudson's gaze. "I had a dream that you helped me back to my cabin when we were on the cruise. I kissed you…"

Hudson closed his eyes, taking a deep breath. He was right, Teague hadn't remembered that kiss. At least for the most part. He'd thought it was a dream.

"But then you walked out on me. In the dream. I remember waking up in the bed alone, willing myself to go back to sleep so the dream would pick up where it left off. I wasn't ready for it to be over. No matter how hard I tried, I couldn't go back to sleep, and it was over." Teague's head turned, his eyes meeting Hudson's. "That was when I knew this was inevitable."

Hudson swallowed hard. He looked away, then typed out a message.

That wasn't a dream.

Teague glanced at his phone, then back to Hudson. "It … it really happened?"

Hudson nodded, then typed some more. *I waited at the reception that night, watching you. I wasn't going to leave you there alone, so I waited until you decided you were finished. I helped you to your room. Before I could dump you on the bed, you kissed me.* Hudson swallowed hard, remembering that night. Remembering how hard it had been to walk away, to leave Teague alone. *I kissed you back. I'd wanted you so fucking bad, the only thing I could do was leave. If I hadn't, it would've fucked shit up between us.*

Speechless

Holding his breath, he waited to see what Teague would say. Knowing the kid, he waited for him to blast him, to call him an asshole or a pussy for not giving in.

When Teague sighed, Hudson frowned.

"Thanks for caring enough to get me back to my room."

That wasn't what he'd expected Teague to say, but he managed a nod when Teague peered up at him.

They sat there for a few minutes in silence while Hudson watched Teague. He noticed the moment Teague's eyes closed, and he didn't move, didn't try to keep him up. He could've kissed him, he could've stripped him naked and taken his dick in his mouth... It would've revived them both. Instead, he watched as the kid fell asleep on his couch. He observed him for the longest time before finally getting up and turning off the lights in the apartment. He grabbed a blanket off the back of the couch, then slipped back down beside Teague this time and covered them both up.

Teague never moved, never woke up. Not even when Hudson pulled him closer, wanting to feel his warmth. Teague even curled into Hudson's side, put his head on Hudson's shoulder, his arm over Hudson's chest.

And that's how they slept the entire night.

Sixteen

Tuesday, July 19ᵗʰ

TEAGUE WOKE UP the following morning to the sun shining in his eyes and a warm body pressed against him. It took a moment for him to figure out where he was and who he was with.

Then it hit him.

He had fallen asleep on Hudson's couch last night. He remembered them talking, remembered how tired he'd been.

Shit.

Doing his best not to wake Hudson, Teague untangled himself from the giant, warm body and slipped off the couch. He grabbed his phone and left the apartment, careful not to make any sound. By the time he opened his front door, directly across the hall, he was breathing hard. Something a hell of a lot like panic had taken control of his respiratory system in the last few seconds. He couldn't breathe and he didn't know why.

Closing the door, he leaned against it, inhaling deeply, exhaling slowly.

"Chill the fuck out," he commanded, talking to the empty room.

Speechless

He had slept on Hudson's couch. So what? It didn't mean a damn thing. He was still fully dressed, so obviously nothing had happened. And it wasn't like they'd been in Hudson's bed or anything.

"Fuck."

This was not a good feeling.

Teague tried to rationalize it all, but it wouldn't matter. He had promised himself he would never feel comfortable with someone enough to sleep with them—on a couch, a bed, the floor … it didn't matter. Up to this point in his life, he had never spent the night with a guy, and he'd never allowed one to spend the night with him. Hell, he'd never even had sex in someone's bed, or his own. Not one single time. And he knew that for a fact because he'd made a point not to.

"Shit." Teague bent over, trying to catch his breath. This had happened before—the full-on panic attack—and he knew he needed to relax, to get his mind on something else.

Nope, not one time had he been in some dude's bed. Sex standing up, sex in the shower, sex on the couch, sure. In a truck, car, on a boat, on a desk, in a fucking bathroom stall… He'd probably had sex in every conceivable place, but *never* on a bed.

As far as he was concerned, spending the night at their place was just as intimate as sex on the bed.

Stupid.

His legs gave out, and he slid down to the floor, holding his knees to his chest as he tried to calm down. There was nothing wrong with what he'd done. So what if he slept curled up against Hudson? That didn't mean a damn thing. He wasn't getting attached. Fuck, they hadn't even had sex yet.

Teague swallowed hard, dropping his head back against the door with a thud.

Hudson was his … friend.

That was the simplest way to explain it, even if the idea of actually having a friend scared the life out of him.

Regardless, that was all they were. Friends.

And Hudson had fed him. Teague had already been exhausted when he'd come home, and the food only exacerbated that. That was the only reason it had happened. There was nothing to worry about. He definitely wasn't getting attached to the guy.

"Nope. No way."

This was stupid. He was better than this. Stronger than this. He did not fall apart because of some stupid guy. He wasn't like his mother.

Forcing himself to his feet, Teague grabbed hold of the anger, latching on to it. He needed the reminder that he was meant to be alone in this world. Since it was clear Hudson had no intention of fucking him, Teague would have to move on. He was tired of the games, tired of the bullshit, tired of…

He wasn't going to allow himself to get any closer to Hudson. That wasn't the deal. He wasn't looking for a friend. He didn't need one.

What he needed was to get fucked. And since Hudson was clearly not interested, Teague would find someone who was willing.

And he'd do it tonight.

This shit with Hudson was over, as far as he was concerned. He didn't have time for the games anymore.

Speechless

HUDSON SPENT MOST of the day in the shop, working on an old engine that should've been tossed in the lake rather than fixed. If it hadn't been for the old man and his sentiment toward the old boat, Hudson would've told the guy as much—figuratively, anyway. Instead, he was a fucking softy, so he'd agreed to do what he could. Now, the damn thing was starting to piss him off.

Or maybe his irritation was due to the fact that Teague was ignoring him. Had been all damn day.

From the moment he'd seen Teague sneaking out of his apartment this morning, Hudson had known that last night had been a mistake. He hadn't known it at the time, but Teague hadn't been going home to get ready for work, he had been running from Hudson, running from whatever this was going on between them.

The kid was fit to be tied, grumbling and kicking shit all over the fucking shop. At one point, Hudson had made an attempt to talk to him and got called a giant fucking asshole for his efforts, so he'd given up. He didn't have time to play these bullshit games. If Teague wanted to be an idiot, if he wanted to act like an immature brat, Hudson would certainly let him.

The sound of a phone ringing had him lifting his head as he glanced across the shop to see Teague grabbing for his phone.

"Yeah, hey. Thanks for calling me back."

Hudson watched the kid, not bothering to pretend he wasn't. When Teague noticed, he turned around.

"I know. Sorry about that, by the way. He's just my neighbor. Thought I'd make it up to you tonight. You and Benny wanna meet at the club?"

Just his neighbor.

Fuck that shit.

Hudson swallowed the rage that threatened to consume him. One freak out and the kid was going back to his old ways. He should've expected as much.

"Yeah. Rain sounds perfect. I'll meet you there around nine, cool?"

Rain. That was a gay nightclub in Austin. Hudson had been there once a long time ago.

"Awesome. Can't wait. See you then."

Now the kid was just being a jackass.

Grabbing his phone, Hudson shot a text to AJ. *We're going to a club tonight. Meet me here at eight.*

His brother was quick to respond. *If you're making me go with you to a gay bar, I hope you know you're buying the drinks. And you're driving.*

Hudson answered with *Whatever*, then stuffed his phone back in his pocket. He wanted to confront Teague, but part of him wanted to see if the kid would actually go through with it. They had agreed that Teague could back out at any time, and it appeared he was waving the white flag already. Hudson simply wished he knew why.

Okay, he was fairly certain he knew why. Teague had slept at his place last night, wound tightly around him, and Hudson had woken up as Teague was leaving his apartment. Since they'd had a nice night, shared a good meal, even had decent conversation, he could only assume that Teague had freaked out about sleeping with him. Didn't matter that it'd been completely innocent.

There was no doubt about it, Teague didn't trust anyone. He didn't want anyone getting too close, and Hudson knew they were closing the gap between them. More importantly, they hadn't had sex yet, which was probably putting Teague on edge. Teague needed his get-out-of-jail-free card, and apparently he earned it by getting nailed to the wall, then walking away unscathed.

Speechless

If Teague wanted to go to the club tonight, fine. Hudson wouldn't stop him.

However, Teague might not have a problem walking away, but Hudson had a big problem with it. He couldn't stand the thought of another man touching Teague in any way, and if it meant he had to interfere to keep that from happening, so be it.

Hudson suspected Teague had never had anyone fight for him. But it was time he learned that there were people willing to do just that.

And Hudson was at the top of that list.

Although half the time he had no fucking clue why that was.

Seventeen

TEAGUE STROLLED INTO the club around nine thirty. Although he'd told Jason to meet him there at nine, everyone knew you had to be fashionably late, otherwise you'd be some guy's bitch because you looked too damn eager. Teague was no one's bitch.

He was eager, sure. He was fucking eager to forget about Hudson. He was also determined to put the past few weeks behind him, to move on with his life. He knew the guy had heard him talking on the phone, but Hudson had never brought it up at any point. He'd never once asked Teague what he was doing or why, and that only pissed him off more. And to top it all off, Hudson's brother had stopped by and they'd left in Hudson's truck a couple of hours ago, which only went to prove that he didn't give a shit what Teague did.

Hudson could go fuck himself. Teague didn't need him.

"Hey, baby, you're looking mighty damn fine tonight."

Teague turned around to see Benny smiling like a loon. His eyes were glassy, and it was clear he'd been drinking for a while. His shirt was partially unbuttoned... No, wait. It was off a button, which meant he'd probably already gotten felt up (and probably fucked) by someone at the club.

Great.

Speechless

"Can I buy you a drink?" Benny offered. "Something to loosen you up for later?"

Teague was tempted, but he opted to hold off for now, so he purposely changed the subject. "Where's Jason?"

Benny's white teeth flashed as he grinned. "He couldn't wait for you any longer. He slipped into the bathroom to get a BJ to take the edge off."

Teague nodded, briefly wondering why he'd chosen to come here tonight. Usually it wouldn't bother him that Jason was sword fighting with other guys at the club, but for some reason, he had thought Jason would've been able to wait long enough for Teague to show. That's what this was supposed to be, right? A hookup?

"Come on, sexy. Let's dance."

Benny took Teague's arm and jerked him toward the dance floor. He didn't resist, hoping that the music would put him in a better mood. It wasn't long before Benny's attention was caught by a good-looking black dude wearing a sheer shirt and too-tight jeans. Teague pretended not to notice the way the two of them were grinding against one another, or the fact that he didn't really give a shit.

He shouldn't have come here. He should've stayed home and...

And what? Watched television? Learned a little more sign language? Waited for Hudson to summon him over so he'd get a hand job to hold him over until...

A warm body pressed up against Teague's back, the hard ridge of an erection grinding against his ass. Normally, that type of behavior wouldn't bother him. In fact, he would usually welcome it, driving his ass backward, encouraging whomever it was to give him what he needed. But tonight just wasn't working for him. Before he could turn around and let the guy down gently, he found himself jerked up against a hard chest, strong arms banding around him.

A familiar scent teased his nostrils, but there was no way that was...

"Dude, I'm here with someone." Teague tried to pull away. "Chill, man. Can I at least—"

Strong hands gripped his shoulders, spinning him around until he was chest to chest with...

Teague peered up into furious green eyes. He ignored the slight twinge of relief that released some of the tension in his chest.

"What the fuck are you doing here?" he yelled, remembering he was pissed at Hudson, he didn't want to be anywhere near him.

Hudson grabbed Teague's hand and yanked him off the dance floor and over to the back wall, where there were less people. Not wanting to cause a scene, Teague stumbled along after him, gearing up for the fight of the century.

Teague found himself pressed up against the wall, the giant fucking asshole pinning him in place with his knee between Teague's thighs and his hands firmly cupping Teague's face. He couldn't look away from the angry man staring down at him, no matter how hard he tried. And he certainly tried.

Hudson held him in place for what felt like forever, until finally Teague felt the fight drain right out of him. He stood there, taking deep breaths, trying to calm his pounding heart. The anger was still there, simmering, but he couldn't bring himself to fight.

"You shouldn't be here," Teague told him, loud enough to be heard over the music.

Hudson merely cocked his head and held him in place with his eyes. It was a look that told Teague he felt the same way. The fact that Teague could read Hudson's expressions wasn't something he wanted to think about.

"I'm here with some friends," he explained, desperate to get away from him. "I'd appreciate if you would let me go."

Hudson shook his head.

"No?" Teague felt the anger bubbling back up. "What? Do you think you can keep me here all fucking night?"

Hudson shook his head again, but Teague had no idea what that meant.

"I'm not playing this game with you anymore. It's clear you're toying with me and..." Teague hated the emotion that churned in his chest. He refused to acknowledge it. "I'm not interested anymore, Hudson. That's all there is to it."

Hudson's hands were still on his face, firm but gentle. It was a tender touch, and Teague wanted to hate it, but he didn't. When Hudson's thumb brushed over his lips, he bit back the urge to suck it into his mouth, attempt to make this about sex, which it should've been about in the first fucking place.

He was done with this shit. He wanted Hudson to go away, to leave him alone.

When Hudson leaned down, his lips a hairsbreadth way, Teague fought to breathe. It wasn't a lack of oxygen that caused his chest to constrict, it was the need that coursed through him.

He told himself it was because he hadn't been fucked in too long. Hudson had teased him for weeks, but never had he given him what he needed. Teague was no longer interested. He was ready to move on.

Unfortunately, as he continued to breathe in slowly, he realized, just like everything else he'd told himself tonight ... that was also a lie.

HUDSON HAD BEEN lurking in the shadows when he'd seen Teague walk in the club doors a short while ago. He'd noticed plenty of heads turned when the kid strutted in as though he owned the place. With his distressed jeans and navy blue button-down, he was casual and cool and so fucking hot Hudson's dick had immediately perked up. People watched—guys, girls, gay, straight, didn't matter—eager to get a lingering glimpse of the sexiest man in the room.

He had fully intended to watch from the sidelines, to keep an eye on Teague for a while. He had even gone so far as to decide he would leave when Teague bought his first drink. That had never happened, though, which had caused a measure of relief to flood him. Still, he'd had a hard time staying in one place, wanting to get to Teague before anyone else could.

But then he'd seen Teague talking to the little punk bitch who had been at Teague's apartment that first night. Benny, he thought his name was. At that point, he couldn't take anymore. He'd had to intervene, no matter the outcome.

And that was how he'd landed himself right here, cupping Teague's chin, desperate to kiss him, to let him know that he couldn't handle him being with anyone but him. He was damn near ready to give Teague whatever he wanted, but Hudson knew that wasn't how this would go. Even if he didn't have the overwhelming desire to dominate Teague, to show him that a quick fuck wasn't what it was all about, he knew that fucking the kid would take them right back where they'd started.

Hudson wasn't willing to go back there.

But he wasn't willing to stay here, either.

Speechless

Pressing a gentle kiss to Teague's lips, Hudson pulled back, dropping his forehead to Teague's. They were both breathing hard, both ready to come apart at the seams. Whether it was anger, frustration, or simple lust, they had to tamp it down. Hudson couldn't allow himself to get out of control. He'd been down that road before, and it never benefited anyone. Over the years, he'd learned how to temper his frustration, to channel it into other ways. He prided himself on that self-control, and he wasn't going to allow Teague to strip him of it yet.

He grabbed his phone, needing to communicate with Teague with words. He didn't move away, not giving Teague enough room to bolt while Hudson typed up a message.

I'm leaving. You have two choices. Come with me and give this another chance. Or stay here and run away like you've been running your whole fucking life.

A flash of anger ignited in Teague's eyes as he read the text, but Hudson didn't care. It was the truth. Regardless of what had happened in Teague's life to make him the way that he was, he was still running from it. From himself. Hudson needed him to stop running. When shit got tough, when emotions were involved, running wasn't the answer.

Teague's reply wasn't what Hudson expected.

"What do you want me to do?"

Hudson wanted to tell Teague that it wasn't up to him. It would've been the smart answer. On the other hand, he knew Teague needed to feel needed right now, so he went with the truth, sending it via text message so there was no miscommunication.

I want you to come home with me.

"Why?"

Hudson lifted an eyebrow, needing Teague to elaborate.

"Why do you care so much?"

That was easy. He typed his response quickly. *Because you're worth caring about.*

After reading the message, Teague nodded, and for the first time, Hudson realized Teague was fisting his shirt with his free hand. Teague gently tugged on it, as though the words gave him what he needed. Forcing himself to back away, Hudson separated their bodies.

"My truck's here," Teague called out to him.

Hudson texted him: *Let's give your keys to my brother. He'll take your truck. We'll take mine.*

It probably would've been fine to let Teague drive himself home, but Hudson didn't want to be away from him for that long. He didn't want to give Teague time to think about all the shit again, to get himself worked up and pissed off. If he wanted to hash it out, he could do so with Hudson beside him.

Ten minutes later, after finding AJ standing by the door, ready to bolt, Hudson was behind the wheel of his truck with Teague in the passenger seat. AJ had reluctantly agreed to take Teague's truck back to his place tonight and to bring it to the marina before work tomorrow.

Surprisingly, Teague didn't say a word during the thirty-minute drive back to the marina. He didn't play on his phone, didn't mess with the radio station. He sat and stared out the window, a deafening silence filling the truck's interior.

Once they made it back, Hudson parked and hopped out of the truck at the same time Teague did. He didn't try to stop Teague when he made a beeline for his apartment; rather, he followed Teague inside before the door could get shut in his face.

Hudson moved over to the arm of the couch and sat, making sure Teague saw that he wasn't getting comfortable. He didn't plan to stay for long, but he did want to make sure Teague was okay.

Speechless

Teague paced the floor, passing by once, twice... On his third time, he stopped and looked at Hudson, his brows furrowed as though he was deep in thought.

"What caused you to be mute?"

That was a question that had been a long time coming, but not one he would've predicted for tonight. For some reason, none of the Pier 70 guys had ever asked him that. Then again, a lot of people avoided it. And since it was what it was, Hudson rarely thought much about it.

Hudson signed: *Born this way.*

Teague nodded.

Did he understand what Hudson had said? His next question confirmed he had.

"So, you've never been able to speak at all?"

Hudson shook his head.

"What caused it?"

Admittedly, most people accepted Hudson's initial response that he was born this way. Rarely did someone—who was not a medical professional—want to know the reason behind it. Knowing it would be too much to sign, Hudson pulled out his phone.

My vocal cords didn't develop appropriately, nor did my voice box. I've been told that it was simply a gene mutation.

Teague leaned against the wall, his attention bouncing between the phone screen and Hudson's face.

"So they couldn't do anything to fix it?"

Hudson shrugged. *There've been cases where the vocal cords are repaired and there is successful sound produced to a degree. From what I know, what I remember, my mother never was concerned about it. I communicated via sign language, and since it wasn't affecting me physically—no issues breathing, etc.—she left it at that.*

"I've never heard you cough or groan, either."

He again used his hands to explain: *No sound.*

"And you don't mouth the words, either," Teague mused aloud.

No, he didn't. He shook his head, agreeing. For whatever reason, he had never tried to pronounce the words. Most people—unless they were deaf or hearing impaired in some way—didn't read lips, so it never made sense for him to do so. It wasn't something he'd ever given much thought to, actually.

Teague nodded, then looked at Hudson again. "I was looking it up. Curious, I guess. One article said a doctor was able to refashion a voice box and vocal cords from one little boy's own tissue."

Hudson smiled. He liked that Teague had been interested enough to do research. The only other person Hudson knew who had cared that much was AJ.

There have been tremendous advances in medicine. But I'm thirty-five, Teague. The advancements weren't all there back then.

"Wait." Teague's eyes widened after he read the text message. "What? You're thirty-five? Then why the fuck did Cam have thirty-one put on your birthday cake this year?"

Hudson shrugged and smiled. He had asked himself the same question.

Eighteen

TEAGUE HAD NO idea why he'd become Chatty Kathy all of a sudden. During the drive back to the marina, he had told himself he would make an effort to be cordial to Hudson. By asking questions, he felt as though he was doing that. Only the questions he was asking, he honestly wanted the answers to. He was curious.

And of all the things Hudson had told him about his mutism, the only thing he latched on to was Hudson's age. Thirty-five. That made the guy almost a full decade older than Teague. It should've made a difference, but for some reason it didn't. Perhaps it would have if Teague hadn't been around Hudson all this time. Or if Cam, Roan, and Dare weren't all several years older than him. He was used to being the youngest guy in the room, and it looked like he still was, only now there was a bit more of a gap.

A gap that honestly didn't matter.

Some might say they had nothing in common because of that, but Teague knew better. He'd been around Hudson… They had quite a bit more in common than he'd thought they would.

"Do you and your parents get along?" Teague inquired.

Something passed in Hudson's eyes and Teague knew he shouldn't have gone there. But now he wanted to know, so he waited patiently. It was hypocritical, sure. He had no intention of talking about his own mother, but he couldn't help but wonder about Hudson's family.

My father left when I was two. Haven't seen him since.

"And your mother?"

Hudson signed, but Teague couldn't make out what it was. Nothing other than *mother*.

Hudson turned to his phone, tapped something out, and then Teague's phone vibrated. *My mother took her own life when I was sixteen. She suffered from depression.*

Teague desperately tried to hide his shock. Seriously, what were the odds that they'd both lost their mothers to...? He decided it was time to drop the subject. No way was he going to talk about...

He didn't know when Hudson had gotten up, but Teague looked up to see the big man staring down at him. He wished he could read Hudson's mind. He wanted to know what he was thinking, wanted to understand how he was coping with his mother's suicide, but at the same time, he didn't.

Teague didn't move when Hudson curled his finger beneath his chin and tilted his head more. He let out a low moan when Hudson's mouth came over his. The kiss was soft, sweet. He shouldn't have liked it, but he did. He allowed himself to get lost in Hudson's kiss, wrapping his arms around him, digging his fingertips into the tense muscles of Hudson's back while Hudson worked his tongue. He didn't want it to end, but that decision was taken from him when Hudson pulled back.

Hudson signed: *Good night.*

Speechless

Teague nodded, then signed good night back to him, stepping out of the way and allowing Hudson to leave. He watched the door for long minutes, wondering how he'd gone from angry to confused in the matter of a few hours.

Glancing at the clock, he realized it was already after midnight, and he would have to be at work early because he was once again helping with the tours. After stripping off his clothes and crawling into bed, Teague stared at the ceiling for a long time, thinking about what Hudson had said about his mother.

Looked as though they had more in common than he'd thought. Aside from the fact that they were both good with engines and they both enjoyed being out on the water ... they both had mothers who had taken their own lives.

What were the odds?

More importantly, Teague wondered how Hudson had been able to so calmly relay that information. The guy had said he was sixteen when his mother killed herself. Maybe that was the reason. Maybe he felt as though he'd had enough time with her.

Teague doubted that was the case. Hudson should've been more attached to her. Hell, his own mother died when he was three and Teague still didn't forgive her for what she'd done to him. In fact, he hated her for it. Hated that she'd been so selfish.

He remembered Hudson's comment: *She suffered from depression.*

Admittedly, Teague had done research on depression over the years, his curiosity getting the best of him. Depression was always the answer he was given when he tried to ask why his mother had taken her own life. Not that he was on board with that assessment, but that was everyone's reason. They said it as though it made sense. A lot like: that's the sky, the color is blue. She had depression, she took her own life. Like the two went hand in hand.

That was stupid.

He had wanted to know how his mother could've been so selfish, so caught up in herself that she would take her own life because some stupid asshole broke her heart. Teague wanted to know how she could've left him the way she had.

Rolling over, he clutched his pillow, frowning. Why did it seem that Hudson had come to terms with his mother's suicide? It was as though Hudson didn't blame her, rather blamed the mental illness. The *depression*. Did he honestly believe that some mental problem had caused her to end her life?

Closing his eyes, Teague tried to push it all away. He hated thinking about his past. Hated thinking about how his mother had abandoned him, how the world had given him the middle finger.

He'd been dealt a shitty fucking hand, that was all there was to it. And he was doing the best he could. So what if he would never be truly happy?

At least he was still breathing.

For now.

Speechless

HUDSON STAYED AWAKE for a long time after he'd left Teague's apartment. He hadn't bothered getting into bed; his brain was running full throttle, so it wouldn't have done any good.

After popping a frozen pizza into the oven, Hudson shot a text to AJ. *I assume you made it home okay?*

His phone buzzed almost immediately. *I got out of there as soon as you did. Not my scene, no matter how good the music is. Guess you're home safe and sound, too?*

All good here. Talk to you tomorrow.

He wasn't surprised that AJ had left when they had. The bars—gay or otherwise—had never been a place he or AJ frequented. They were more the outdoor types. When they were younger, the way to spend a weekend was a camping trip, usually just the two of them, sometimes a couple of their friends would come along. A tent, fishing pole, and time away from people was their idea of a good time. Damn sure not dancing or mingling in bars.

For Hudson, his reasons were simple. Communication was difficult, no matter what social situation he found himself in. It was rare he would meet a random guy who knew sign language, which meant he usually had to have a wingman along for the ride. And first dates … those were nonexistent for Hudson. He'd been on a couple, but having a conversation via text message with someone you didn't know while attempting to share a meal…

In a word: awkward.

However, he had met a couple of guys on the Internet years back. He'd even had one serious relationship in his early twenties. The guy's sister had been deaf, so he knew sign language, which was probably the only reason it'd progressed. And by that, Hudson meant it had lasted more than two months, but three was his max. Long term had never really been his thing.

Relationships were difficult for him. It wasn't easy getting close to people, and he had a hard time trusting. He'd spent too much of his life being ridiculed for his lack of speech, and then when his mother had taken her own life, he was mocked about that. One group of bullies had tried to tell him that it was his fault she had died. According to them, his own mother couldn't handle the fact that he was the way he was.

Kids were cruel.

It had been easier to keep his relationships limited to a couple of really good friends and his brother. He'd been lucky to befriend Calvin and Shawn. Neither of them had ever looked at Hudson as though he were a freak of nature. In fact, they'd seen him as no different than they were. It'd probably helped that Calvin's mother was a special education teacher. At a young age, Calvin had learned to sign the alphabet, and he'd picked up quite a bit of sign language from his mother. When they'd become friends, she was the one who had helped Calvin and Shawn learn to communicate with him.

All in all, Hudson knew that AJ, Calvin, and Shawn had his back. He'd learned over the years that those three people were all he could truly depend on. For the past few years, AJ had been focused on his career, which took him to California a lot, usually for weeks at a time. He owned a place about ten minutes from the marina, but he was rarely there. It was only recently that he'd started being around more. He'd mentioned they had assigned him a big account located in Austin, but Hudson was fairly certain AJ had manipulated that so that he could be closer to Hudson.

But when AJ wasn't around, Hudson's interactions with people were limited. In a sense, it seemed he and Teague had the trust issues in common as well.

Speechless

After taking a shower, eating his pizza, then plopping his ass down on the couch, Hudson stared at the front door for the longest time, reliving the conversation he'd had with Teague a short while ago. He wished he would've had the nerve to ask Teague about his mother. After sharing the details about his own, Hudson had seen something in Teague's eyes. A pain so deep he could only assume it was the root of Teague's anger.

And who are you? Dr. Phil?

He smiled at himself. Okay, fine. He shouldn't be attempting to figure Teague out. He should've been content that Teague had come home with him from the club and he hadn't had to knock any assholes out for touching the kid. But he wouldn't deny wishing that Teague was there with him. When he'd kissed Teague before telling him good night, he had been tempted to take things to the next level. Not wanting to get Teague spinning out of control again had been his only saving grace.

Now he wished he could go to sleep, let his mind rest for a little while. He wasn't sure how things would play out tomorrow. With Teague, it was always a gamble. The kid had drastic mood swings. Unlike anyone Hudson had ever known before. He was angry one minute, subdued the next.

He could only hope tomorrow would be one of Teague's good days.

Nineteen

Friday, July 22nd

BY THE TIME Friday night rolled around, Teague was a little less anxious than earlier in the week. It helped that Hudson was pretending that Teague hadn't gone off the rails the other night. In fact, Hudson was acting as though nothing had happened at all.

On Wednesday, Hudson had picked up sandwiches on his way back from the gym, and they had sat on Teague's couch, eating and watching baseball. On Thursday night, Hudson had ordered pizza and invited Teague down to the restaurant pier. They'd managed to hold conversations, but it all seemed to revolve around Hudson teaching Teague more sign language. He was getting better, although he wasn't anywhere near fluent. He could understand a lot of what Hudson said, but signing back was a little more difficult, but Hudson didn't seem to mind.

It had been at that point that Teague had realized Hudson was attempting to put Teague's mind at ease. He was ensuring that Teague wasn't worried that they'd end up falling asleep at Hudson's place again. By avoiding his apartment altogether, it had helped.

Speechless

Except tonight, Teague was in the mood for something a little less friend-like. Although he would secretly admit that he was enjoying the friendship aspect of this thing between him and Hudson, he was seriously getting worked up, and he was damn near ready to explode. Sure, he'd bitched about the hand jobs and blow jobs, but at this point, he would take either—he didn't have a preference—just as long as he got off.

However, when it came time to put his plan in motion, he found that Hudson wasn't home. While he sat staring at his phone, tempted to shoot Hudson a message, he felt his frustration level building. He hated sitting at home by himself. For the first couple of months it had been cool, but now he wanted to do something. He needed someone to talk to.

He blamed Hudson for that. He'd never craved that type of interaction, but since he'd had it, he found he wanted more.

Getting to his feet, he paced the floor, thrusting his hands through his hair. He couldn't go to a club, he couldn't call Jason and Benny, or any of the others from his long list of one-night fucks. It was too late to go out on the water, and Dare was no longer in the position to be Teague's wingman since he'd settled down. Cam, too. Of course, he could always call Roan, but he knew the guy was dealing with his own shit right now.

Which left him with absolutely no one.

His phone buzzed and he stopped pacing, staring down at it. He was tempted not to look because he knew it could only be one person. For weeks now, the only person who had texted him was Hudson. He really didn't like the fact that he was looking forward to spending time with the man.

With a shaky breath, he snatched up his phone and read the message.

Be home in ten. I'm bringing dinner. You will eat with me, so don't try to get out of it. But first, I need a shower, and that's where I expect you to be when I walk into my bathroom—naked. Probably smart to turn the water on soon so you don't freeze your ass off.

Teague's dick twitched. He had no control over it, thank you very much. It wasn't that he was excited for Hudson to summon him to his bathroom or anything like that. Except, he kind of was, and proof of that was the fact that he was already walking out his door and across the hall to Hudson's.

For the past few weeks, neither of them had been locking their apartments, rather only having the exit door of the building locked. It made it easier to come and go from each other's place on the rare occasions they did. Like now.

Hudson's apartment was the mirror image of his own. Well, except for the fact that Hudson's place was decorated more than Teague's and it actually had enough furniture to fill the space. Teague had a thrift-store couch, a cheap coffee table, a decent queen mattress set connected to an inexpensive metal headboard, and a wooden stand that held his alarm clock. Hudson's place was much nicer, as was the furniture. It was a studio, like Teague's—completely open, other than the bathroom, which contained a sink, a toilet, and a regular porcelain tub with a clear curtain hanging from a rod. Rather than turn on the water, Teague leaned against the sink and debated whether or not he wanted to go back to his place and pretend he hadn't received Hudson's text.

Then again, he couldn't do that because Hudson would probably show up, and if his door was locked, he would know something was up.

"Shit."

Speechless

Teague set his phone on the sink, then pushed away from the counter and went to turn on the shower. No sooner did he have the water on than he heard the apartment door open and close.

Fuck. There was no way that was ten minutes.

It took all of thirty seconds for him to strip out of his shorts and T-shirt, leaving them in a pile on the floor before he was hopping into the shower, swallowing a scream when the cold water pelted his skin. He gritted his teeth, waiting for the water to warm. It was just like at his place, the hot water taking forever to kick in. Had he done as Hudson instructed, he probably wouldn't have had to endure the ice shower.

Before he had time to flip-flop on his decision, the clear curtain was pulled back, and Hudson stepped in, completely, gloriously naked.

And when Hudson's giant body instantly backed Teague against the wall, the water temperature was suddenly the least of his worries.

HUDSON HAD NO idea what had come over him or why he'd been so adamant that Teague come over, but halfway through his workout, he'd had to stop. No matter what he did, he couldn't stop thinking about the kid. When he spent more time adjusting his semi-erect cock than lifting weights, working out became a wasted effort.

Nicole Edwards

For the last few days, he'd seen little of Teague while they were at work. The boys in the office were busy and had needed Teague's help out on the water, leaving Hudson on his own. He was used to that, so it wasn't the workload that had bothered him; it had been not seeing as much of Teague as he'd hoped to. That was the very reason he had insisted he have dinner with Teague during the week, but he'd made a conscious effort to keep his hands to himself.

Other than some boner-inducing groping last night as they stood in the hallway between their apartments, which had left his nuts aching when Teague finally had left him, Hudson had been the perfect gentleman.

Until right this moment.

Stepping into his shower to find Teague naked and waiting, just as he'd instructed, had him worked up more than ever. So horny, in fact, he hardly registered the tepid water that pelted his skin.

Without allowing Teague to say so much as hello, Hudson backed the kid against the tiled wall and inhaled him. Tonight wasn't about sweet kisses or teasing; he needed something more than that, and he suspected Teague did, as well. When Teague's tongue speared his, rough hands gripping Hudson's ass, he knew he was right.

"Fuck, Hudson," Teague groaned against his mouth. "Oh, fuck."

While Teague attempted to climb his body, Hudson continued to kiss him. He wasn't pretending to be gentle; he wanted Teague to know just what he did to him.

When Teague took Hudson's cock in his hand, he drove his hips forward, fucking Teague's fist. And when Teague aligned their dicks, the kid's slick hand gliding up and down both of them at the same time, their shafts sliding together … Hudson pulled his mouth away to watch. He was breathing hard, and he'd only been in there for a minute.

173

Speechless

"What brought this on?" Teague asked, his eyes glittering with heat.

Not caring whether Teague could understand him, he chose to sign since he had no other option. *Want to taste you.*

Teague watched his hands, then nodded.

Before he dropped to his knees, he signed again. *Do not come. This is only the beginning.*

Another nod from Teague had Hudson going to his knees. He didn't know if Teague understood or if he was simply saying yes to whatever Hudson wanted. Knowing Teague, it could go either way.

The porcelain tub bit into his knees, but Hudson ignored the pain when he was eye level with Teague's beautiful dick. He pinned Teague to the wall with his forearm across Teague's stomach. In order to keep from falling over, Teague widened his stance at the same time Hudson drew him into his mouth.

"Oh, fuck yes." Teague's hands rested on Hudson's forearm, gripping tightly. "I've missed your mouth so fucking much."

Unable to control his desire, Hudson bobbed up and down, slobbering all over Teague's cock, taking him deep, teasing the head, fisting him with his other hand. He worked him hard and fast, loving the way Teague panted and moaned, his stomach muscles flexing as he thrust his hips forward, attempting to drive deep into Hudson's throat.

Not wanting to push him over the edge, Hudson released Teague's dick from his mouth but resumed fisting him as he got to his feet, slowing things down a notch. Once more, he fastened his mouth onto Teague's smooth, warm lips, making love to him with his tongue. He was overwhelmed by sensation, but the urge to fuck was impairing his control, the need causing his heart to slam against his ribs. He wasn't sure he'd ever felt like this before, and he was a little shaken by it.

Taking a step back, Hudson reached for the body wash, dispensing some into his hand before rubbing it over his chest. He needed to take care of business so they could get out of here and have dinner. If he didn't, he risked fucking the kid right there against the wall.

Teague stepped forward, adding more body wash before he began rubbing his hands over Hudson's chest. It seemed the guy was on to him, knew he needed a minute, because his hands moved slowly, his fingertips kneading Hudson's tense muscles.

While Teague washed him, Hudson closed his eyes, relishing the sensation, enjoying the rubdown. It was intensely sensual, although Teague had successfully dropped the tension down a notch, for which Hudson was grateful. It wasn't like him to lose control like that, but there was no doubt he had. If Teague wasn't using those magic fingers on him, he would likely be ramming his dick into the guy's ass, sending them both over the edge.

I could let you do that all day.

"Good. Then relax a little more."

Okay, so apparently Teague did understand him.

Hudson gave him free rein, relaxing his muscles while Teague's soapy hands worked him from neck to toe, then back up.

"Turn around."

Speechless

Hudson turned, planting his palms on the wall. Teague continued his ministrations along his back, his ass, his quads and calves. When he worked his way back up, Hudson's heart slammed into his ribs again as slick fingers slid between his ass cheeks, rimming his hole.

Fuck, that felt good.

He didn't allow Teague to play for long, ready for a turn. While the water rinsed the soap from his body, Hudson kissed Teague again, keeping the pace languid this time. The urgency had dissipated, but the need was still great. He doubted he could resist Teague for much longer. It scared him to think about giving in, to give Teague what he'd wanted all along. The risk that the kid would turn away from him afterward was significant, but he knew he would have to cave eventually.

He wasn't sure he was ready to let go tonight, but on the other hand, he wasn't sure he had the willpower to resist.

Twenty

THAT WOULD GO down in the history books as the most innocent (although erotic) shower he'd ever taken when in the presence of a smoking-hot man. There for a minute, Teague had thought Hudson was going to lose control and bang the shit out of him right there against the tiled wall, but somehow the guy had recovered, and they'd washed up, dried off, and were now sitting at Hudson's kitchen table eating Chinese food.

He might've been irritated if it weren't for the fact that Hudson had only allowed him to put a towel around his hips. When Teague had started to dress, Hudson had informed him that it would be a waste of time. That little bit of information had arousal coursing through his veins, and his dick was tenting the towel.

However, it didn't have any impact on his appetite. He was starving.

They'd managed to make a decent dent in the food when Hudson signed to him before taking a drink of his tea.

Are you still working on sign language?

Teague nodded. "I'm trying. It's getting easier." He took another bite and chewed before continuing. "I talked to Dare the other day and he has a book he said I could borrow. He bought it when he took the class."

I can keep teaching you.

Speechless

He didn't want Hudson to know how much he would like that. Instead, after taking a drink, Teague grinned. "I'm sure there are quite a few things you can teach me."

And vice versa.

Hudson's eyes darkened with what looked to be restrained arousal, and the thought of pushing him until he snapped made Teague's dick twitch. It drove him crazy that the man had so much self-control. If Teague had a third of what Hudson had, he would be an entirely different person.

Finish eating.

Laughing at Hudson's discomfort, Teague dug back in and didn't stop until he had cleaned his plate. When he looked up, he saw Hudson was watching him.

Time for a movie.

A movie?

Okay, that wasn't what Teague had expected they'd be doing next, but he could go with it. For now.

"Let me do the dishes," he insisted.

Only if you lose the towel.

Teague felt his face go warm. He'd never been the type to strut around naked, but... "Okay."

He stood up and dropped the towel, watching Hudson's eyes as they slowly raked over him from head to toe, then back up. The guy made his skin heat a couple of degrees from the obvious approval that warmed his eyes. Teague got the feeling this was going to be a long night.

Somehow, Teague managed to clean the few dishes they'd used, but he felt Hudson's eyes on him as he worked. It didn't help that there wasn't a wall that separated the kitchen from the living room, so Hudson had gotten an unobstructed view of Teague's ass the entire time.

Once he was finished and he flipped off the kitchen light, Hudson urged him over to the couch, patting the spot directly beside him. The room was completely dark except for the glow from the television screen.

"If I have to be naked, I think it's only fair that you are, too," he told Hudson when he stopped in front of him.

Hudson's dark eyes paused on Teague's dick, which was standing up straight, begging for attention. After several seconds, they finally lifted to meet his.

Is that right?

Teague nodded. He was glad he'd spent so much time learning sign language. It was certainly easier to communicate this way than having to get his phone whenever Hudson wanted to talk. Granted, he didn't always understand everything but got the gist most of the time.

Hudson popped up from the couch, stripped off his shorts, then sat down again, grabbing Teague's arm and pulling him down beside him. He didn't even get a chance to ogle those long legs or his incredibly big dick. But when he brushed up against Hudson, he no longer cared. The warmth of the man's big body was welcoming as Teague leaned into him, his attention on the television.

Was that...?

"Porn?" He glanced over at Hudson, unable to hold in his laughter. "*That's* the movie you had in mind? Porn?"

Hudson's smile was wicked.

"Funny. I didn't think of you as a porn watcher."

What did you think I did in my spare time?

Suddenly, the only thing he could think about was Hudson sitting here on this couch, dick in hand, watching gay porn every night before he went to bed. Definitely a nice fantasy.

"Figured you were more of a reader." After all, there was a book on the coffee table.

Speechless

Hudson shrugged.

Teague remembered all the times Hudson had pushed his boundaries in the very beginning. He'd gotten somewhat used to not being fully satisfied, but he never knew what to expect during their encounters. It all seemed to be some sort of game for Hudson, which—provided there weren't any questions—Teague had actually come to enjoy.

Not to mention, it made the anticipation that much greater.

HUDSON COULDN'T GIVE less of a shit what they watched tonight or if the TV was even on, for that matter. He'd opted for porn because he figured Teague wouldn't think anything of it. If Hudson kept their interactions sexual, the guy wouldn't panic that things were getting too intimate.

Funny how Teague didn't shy away from the most intimate act of all—sex—but he freaked out after falling asleep on Hudson's couch. Not that it mattered now. Hudson was ready to settle in for the night, and he was going to let things play out however they were meant to. Whether he ended up giving in to his baser urges and claiming Teague in the most intimate way possible or he simply toyed with him for a while, Hudson intended for them both to come tonight.

Ten minutes later, it was clear that porn hadn't been a good idea. Hudson was still sitting up on the couch, and Teague had started teasing Hudson's dick with his hands. A gentle brush of his fingers at first, then Teague had covered Hudson's cock with his palm, fondling his balls with his fingertips. It wasn't long before Teague had spread out on the couch, his head on Hudson's thigh, and now Hudson's cock was tunneling in and out of Teague's fantastic fucking mouth with—as long as he leaned a little to the left—an unobstructed view.

He could sit here and watch this all fucking night.

While Teague blew him, Hudson let his hand trail down the smooth length of Teague's back. Since the kid was lying on his stomach, Hudson had to lean over, using his hands to knead the firm flesh of Teague's ass. The guy had a phenomenal ass.

Every time Teague released Hudson's cock, he squeezed Teague's ass, letting him know to keep going. He was a long way from coming tonight, but he wasn't going to bore Teague with those details. He would soon prove he had the stamina of a twenty-five-year-old.

Instead, he was going to work Teague into a frenzy, then…

Then what, he wasn't sure yet, but he wasn't putting any limits on the night. And if things continued in the direction they'd taken already, there was no doubt where they would end up.

Hudson slicked two of his fingers with his own saliva, then returned to playing with Teague's ass, only this time, he slid one finger down the crack, then two.

"Hudson…" Teague spread his legs wide, offering himself up to Hudson's searching fingers.

When he slid one finger into the puckered hole, Teague's ass clamped down on the digit.

Speechless

Fuck, he was tight. Hudson's dick pulsed and throbbed at the idea of sliding into the warm depths of Teague's body. He realized he was breathing harder than before, but so was Teague.

While he tried to focus on the television, he leisurely fucked Teague's asshole with one finger. In, out, in, out. Every now and then he would add another. Since Teague had ceased his oral ministrations, rather laying his head on Hudson's thigh, there wasn't a risk of Hudson blowing any time soon, so he enjoyed the buildup.

Hudson pushed in two fingers, curling them as he did. Teague moaned his name, gently pushing his hips back, trying to take more of Hudson's fingers inside him.

"That feels so fucking good," Teague groaned. "Don't stop."

He had no intention of stopping.

It didn't take long before Teague's moans had his body igniting, needing more. Freeing his fingers from Teague's ass, Hudson used his hands to jerk Teague's hips, urging him to turn over. When he moved, so did Hudson. He worked his way over Teague, straddling his head while his mouth hovered over the long, thick length of Teague's cock. When he teased the swollen crest with his tongue, Teague cried out, his hips jerking upward. Hudson took him all the way in his mouth, burying his nose in Teague's ball sac.

The kid smelled like Hudson's body wash, and he'd be damned if that didn't send a possessive spark shooting through him. The thought of Teague smelling like him... It made him want to claim him all the more.

"Oh, fuck... Oh, fuck..." Teague's hips began to pump erratically while Hudson sucked him, stroking the smooth, silky skin with his tongue. "Hudson... Oh, fuck..."

In an effort to take the edge off so Teague wouldn't come yet, Hudson got up onto his knees, staring down his body at Teague as he fed his own cock into his warm mouth. After showing Teague that he wanted him to return the favor, Hudson resumed his place over him and began sucking Teague's dick again. The warm suction on his cock made it difficult to focus on Teague's pleasure, but he tried. They remained like that—in the sixty-nine position—until Hudson couldn't take any more.

If he wanted this to last—which he absolutely did—then he was going to have to try a different tactic. One that involved him worshiping Teague's body for a little while, before sinking deep and losing himself for the rest of the night.

Twenty-One

BEFORE THE NIGHT was over, Teague was going to lose his fucking mind. And he knew that was Hudson's plan.

One second, he was deep throating Hudson's thick cock, the next, Hudson was kissing him senseless. He was so fucking hard it hurt, but the instant Hudson's mouth was on his, all of that faded away. He practically crawled up Hudson's body, straddling his lap as Hudson held his head, feasting on his lips. In an effort to relieve some of the tension in his balls, Teague ground his hips, sliding his cock against Hudson's. That lasted all of three seconds before Hudson stilled him by banding his other arm around him.

Teague briefly wondered whether or not he would survive tonight. Part of him hoped he didn't because ... holy fuck ... this was going to be one hell of a ride.

Teague found himself at the mercy of Hudson's mouth. He surrendered to the kiss, his fingers curling around Hudson's waist as he held on, letting Hudson deepen the kiss as he held him in place. The kissing thing was not quite so bad—not with Hudson at least. If he were honest, he would have to admit to liking it far more than he should. The way Hudson held him, tongue stroking tongue … there was actual *feeling* involved, although Teague pretended otherwise. He had no intention of going down that road, but if it would lead to Hudson screwing his brains out, he was willing to try just about anything.

A grunt escaped him when Hudson picked him up and flipped him over so that he was on his back, his ass hanging off the edge of the cushion. Hudson shoved the coffee table out of the way and knelt on the floor before him. Big, strong hands pushed his legs back, spreading them wide so that Teague's ass was open to Hudson's hungry gaze.

He watched, breath lodged in his chest as Hudson leaned down and licked him.

"Fuck!" The warmth of that tongue against his asshole had him trying to close his legs, but Hudson held him open while he licked him again.

The rimming was incredible. Although he was folded like a pretzel, his knees touching his shoulders, his head on the back cushion, spine bent, Teague couldn't think of anything except for the pleasure that slammed into him every time Hudson's tongue teased his sensitive flesh.

Needing more, Teague reached for his cock, but Hudson instantly stopped him, grabbing his wrist, then reaching for the other, effectively pinning his hands and his legs to the cushion.

"Oh, God," he groaned when Hudson speared him with his tongue.

Speechless

Chills raced over his skin because the pleasure was so intense, searing him from the inside out. Hudson continued to look at him while he ate his ass, licking, fucking, driving him out of his mind with his wicked tongue. He stopped only long enough to draw Teague's throbbing dick into his mouth, sucking roughly before licking over his balls and stabbing Teague's ass with his tongue again. Hudson repeated the steps over and over, sucking Teague's cock, laving his balls, licking his ass… Teague was slowly blinded by the pleasure.

He'd never had anyone focus this much on him. Sure, he'd had blow jobs galore, but never had a man focused so much attention on rimming him, on bringing him to the brink by licking him so perfectly. He never wanted Hudson to stop, but if he didn't, Teague was going to come. He didn't want to, but it'd been so long since his ass had been pleasured like this.

As though he could read Teague's thoughts, Hudson eased up, licking him gently, ratcheting up his desire another notch, then another. When Hudson released Teague's hands, their eyes met, and he could see the command in the emerald depths. He was not supposed to move.

Gripping the cushion tightly, Teague focused on Hudson, watching as he lifted up, his hands trailing down the backs of Teague's thighs, teasing him with the lightest brush of his fingers. Those hands roamed down to his balls, tugging, squeezing, making Teague cry out from the ecstasy that threatened to consume him.

He groaned when Hudson moved away, reaching over toward the side table closest to the kitchen. When Hudson returned, he was holding a bottle of lubricant, squirting some onto his fingers, then more onto Teague's ass. The liquid was cold against his overheated skin, but it felt good. It felt even better when Hudson's fingers slid over his hole, doing a slippery slide as he teased, pushing the very tip of his finger into Teague's ass.

"Oh, fuck … Hudson…" Teague met Hudson's gaze. "Need more. Give me more."

Anyone else would've fucked him by now, putting them both out of their misery, but it was clear Hudson was on a mission.

And once again, Teague had to wonder whether he would make it through unscathed.

HUDSON WAS WILLING to do this all night if he could look into those stormy blue eyes and see the lust that shined there. Teague was hanging by a thread, and Hudson wasn't even close to finished with him.

He continued to watch Teague's face while he penetrated his ass with one slick finger. Teague's mouth opened in a silent cry as Hudson pushed in deep, angling for his prostate. He massaged gently while Teague's body shook. He was folded damn near in half, his legs spread wide, his hands holding his ankles now as though he was scared he would try to touch himself otherwise. Hudson wasn't ready for Teague to join in. He wanted him to see how good it was when it wasn't about instant gratification.

Leaning forward, Hudson drew Teague's cock into his mouth once more while he added another finger into his ass, pushing in, retreating. He fingered Teague's asshole slowly, loving the groans that echoed through the apartment. Teague was so fucking beautiful like this, so damn vulnerable. Hell, watching him could probably get Hudson off if he wanted.

But he didn't.

He fully intended to be buried deep inside Teague's beautiful ass when the time came.

Speechless

Hudson continued to probe Teague's ass, fucking him with two fingers, scissoring them, working Teague open so he'd be ready for Hudson's cock. When Teague closed his eyes, Hudson smacked his ass. The kid's eyes flew open. Hudson narrowed his eyes and Teague nodded. He did not want Teague to close his eyes. He wanted him right there with him the entire time.

When Teague began begging him to let him come, Hudson stopped. He got to his feet and pulled Teague up to a sitting position. Twining his fingers into Teague's silky hair, he pushed his cock past those kiss-swollen lips. Heat coiled in his gut as he face-fucked Teague, allowing the sensations to consume him. Adrenaline surged through his body. His muscles were tense, heat coiling in his gut. He was doing his damnedest to hold back... Fuck, it wasn't easy.

When he was close, Hudson pulled out of Teague's mouth, urged Teague to turn over.

While Teague got into position, kneeling and holding on to the back of the couch, Hudson retrieved a condom, rolled it on, then grabbed more lube. While using one slick finger to fuck into Teague's eager ass, he coated his cock with his free hand.

"Need to feel you," Teague moaned. "Want you inside me."

Yeah, well. Hudson had every intention of filling Teague's ass. He was trying to do this Teague's way. If he were doing it his way, they would've moved this to the bed and Teague wouldn't be allowed to look away from him. But that was all in due time.

Placing his hand in the center of Teague's back, Hudson forced him forward, then gripped Teague's hips and pulled his ass back.

Fuck.

He planted his knees on the edge of the couch, pressed the head of his dick against the tight ring of muscle, and pushed into Teague slowly. The muscles in Teague's back tensed. Hudson did not want to hurt him, so he went slowly. Once he was in enough to let go, he gripped Teague's hips and ran his thumbs over the smooth skin of Teague's lower back, never looking away as his dick sank deeper and deeper.

The pleasure was intense; Teague's body strangled his dick with its warmth.

Oh, fuck.

Hudson bit his lip, trying to keep from slamming his hips forward.

"Please..." Teague's voice was raw with his lust. "Hudson..."

Teague's hand came back and gripped Hudson's thigh, his fingertips digging into the muscle.

"Feels so good... Need more... Please."

Hudson pushed in deeper, then retreated a little, pushed in again. He continued to work his dick into Teague, inch by inch, until he was balls deep and breathing roughly. Keeping his eyes locked on the place where they were joined, Hudson held on to Teague's hips and began pumping his hips forward, pulling back. His eyes threatened to close because the intensity was so great, the feeling exquisite. That, mixed with the grunts and groans coming from Teague, the way he begged and pleaded, asking for more, harder, faster...

Hudson's control snapped.

He slammed into Teague, pounding him harder, faster, giving him everything they both wanted and needed. It was a brutal mating, sexy and so goddamn hot. He never wanted it to end.

Shifting, Hudson put one foot on the couch, forcing Teague lower so that he could drill down into him, nailing him harder and harder.

Speechless

"Oh, fuck, yes... Hudson... Fuck me. Just like that. Don't stop. God, don't stop."

He couldn't stop. Thrust after thrust, he pounded Teague's ass, gripping his hips forcefully, sweat dripping down his temples. His heart was racing, his breaths slamming in and out of his lungs in time with the pounding he was giving Teague.

"Need more," Teague said. "Need to jack my dick. Let me, Hudson. Let me..."

Hudson smacked Teague's ass, signaling for him to do what he needed to do. It was that or Hudson was going to come, and he wanted to watch Teague come undone first.

Teague's arm disappeared beneath his body, and Hudson could feel the vibrations as Teague pulled and tugged on his dick, stroking faster, keeping pace with the punishing thrust of Hudson's hips. He dug his fingertips into Teague's flesh, letting him know he was close.

"Yes ... yes... Oh, fuck, yes... Gonna come... Oh, fuck, I'm gonna come."

Hudson released Teague's hips and leaned over him, wrapping one arm around him while he put the other on the back of the couch. He buried himself deep, driving his hips forward again and again until Teague screamed his name, his body jerking beneath him.

Only then did Hudson let go, his hips stilling as he covered Teague with his body. His dick pulsed as he filled the condom. He didn't want to let Teague go, but he knew he was holding him too tight. He couldn't help it. Although he'd given in tonight, Hudson feared this would freak the guy out, send him running for the hills. That was the last damn thing Hudson wanted, but he knew, no matter what, it was no longer up to him.

So, he took a deep breath, kissed Teague's back, and forced himself upright. He went to the bathroom to dispose of the condom and clean up. After brushing his teeth and washing his face—wasting far more time than he should have—Hudson took a deep breath and decided he had to go back out there.

He only prayed that he didn't step out of the bathroom to find Teague gone.

Twenty-Two

WHEN HUDSON DISAPPEARED into the bathroom, Teague collapsed on the couch, trying to act as though he hadn't been fucked within an inch of his life. More so than he'd ever been before.

Fuck.

Hudson was a damn stallion.

Holy shit. That had been incredible.

As he lay there sweating on the leather sofa, trying to catch his breath, Teague watched the closed bathroom door. After a couple of minutes, he started getting worried. What was taking Hudson so long? Was that Teague's cue to leave?

He wasn't sure how this was supposed to go, but he knew that Hudson had been holding back for a reason. It would've been fucked up if Teague simply walked out right after.

Right?

Or maybe that was what Hudson expected.

Shit.

Teague managed to sit up, brushing his hair back off his face as he debated what to do next. There was a bit of discomfort in his ass, so he eased over a little, the memories of that fucking flashing in his head. God, he hoped they got to do that again.

But not now.

Not tonight.

No, he really needed to go.

Or stay.

Shit. He wasn't sure what he was supposed to do.

Before he could make a decision, the bathroom door opened and Hudson stepped into the room. A look of sheer relief passed over his obscenely handsome face but quickly disappeared.

So Hudson hadn't wanted him to leave.

Which meant Teague had made the right decision.

That was possibly a first.

Unsure what to say, Teague watched as Hudson went to the refrigerator and grabbed a bottle of water before coming over to the couch. He snatched a hand towel on his way and tossed it toward Teague.

Smiling, Teague managed to clean up the mess he'd made. Thankfully, the couch was leather.

Surprisingly, Hudson didn't sit; instead, he crawled toward him, forcing Teague to fall backward again. Then he was staring up into Hudson's beautiful face looming over him.

"I take it you didn't want me to leave?"

Hudson shook his head, then leaned down and kissed him. It started out as a simple grazing of lips, but Teague wrapped his arms around Hudson's neck and pulled him closer, taking the weight of Hudson's big body, along with the warmth, on top of him. He had no idea what had come over him or why he was seeking some sort of intimate connection, but he needed it. Obviously, Hudson had knocked him for a loop during that thorough fucking. That was his only excuse.

But he was going to let it last for as long as it could.

Teague had no intention of staying the night, but there was no reason he couldn't bask in the glow of an incredible orgasm for a little while.

Speechless

When Hudson pulled back, Teague took the water bottle and forced Hudson to roll off him.

"So what now?" he asked before taking a long drink.

Hudson shrugged.

"I'd say we could watch a movie, but your selection is rather limited." Teague noticed the pornographic movie was over.

Hudson grinned, then took the bottle from Teague's hand and set it on the table. The next thing Teague knew, he was being pulled against Hudson once more. Another blistering-hot kiss consumed him, and he gave in to it. This time, though, he felt his panic setting in.

He'd been wondering where it was. Although he hated the feeling, he was familiar with it. It was as reassuring as it was disturbing. It meant he wasn't doing something stupid, like getting attached to Hudson.

As much as he was enjoying this, he knew he couldn't get too caught up in it. Sex was one thing… This—whatever this was—couldn't happen. It was too intimate, and no matter what, Teague did not do intimate. As it was, he'd already let this go on for too long.

He couldn't stay much longer or he'd give Hudson the wrong impression. The last thing either of them needed was for this to get complicated.

Sex was sex, period.

Two bodies coming together for the sake of pleasure. Emotions shouldn't be involved. People got hurt when that happened.

People did stupid shit when that happened.

Teague had no intention of ever becoming one of those stupid people.

HUDSON FELT THE shift in the air around them.

He realized the moment that Teague had disconnected. One minute they were kissing; the next Teague's body went rigid, his hands pressed against Hudson's chest, signaling he was trying to get away.

Sure, he'd been expecting it, but it bothered him just the same. He had hoped that Teague wouldn't freak, but unfortunately, that was getting ready to happen.

When Teague tried to pull away, Hudson held on for a second longer, then released his hold. Rather than push him for more, he managed to let Teague go, then dropped back on the couch and took a breath. When Teague got up and headed for the bathroom—to evidently get his clothes—Hudson didn't flinch. He was actually surprised Teague had made it this long. Hell, it was a miracle that Teague had been there when Hudson came out of the bathroom. If he had to guess, Teague was used to shouting a "thanks for the orgasm" as he headed out the door, not sticking around for cuddling afterward.

Hudson should've been grateful that he'd stuck around as long as he had.

But he wasn't.

And despite the fact that he didn't want Teague to leave yet, he had to admit they were making progress. If Teague thought this was a one-time thing, he would be sorely mistaken, that was for sure. But Hudson would gladly show him the error of his ways tomorrow when he took him again. Because he would definitely be claiming him again. No way was he going to let this end now.

Just as he expected, Teague returned from the bathroom completely dressed. He never met Hudson's eyes as he moved toward the front door. It looked as though the kid wanted to say something, but he never did.

Speechless

Hudson didn't try to stop him, either. It wouldn't have made a difference.

Once Teague was gone, Hudson forced himself up from the couch, turned off the lights, and made his way over to his bed. He fell face first onto the mattress and closed his eyes.

His body was sated, his mind not so much. It'd been an emotional day for him, and he hoped tomorrow would be better. Now that he'd fucked Teague, things should get easier. He wouldn't be spending all of his time thinking about it, that was for sure.

Then again, Teague could fall back to his old routine of running, pushing Hudson away.

Whatever.

Rolling over onto his back, he put his arm over his eyes.

He couldn't help but wonder how Teague was going to react tomorrow. It was always a surprise when it came to him. He could be mellow or pissy, but he was always unpredictable.

Sometimes he wondered whether or not Teague suffered from attention-deficit/hyperactivity disorder. He'd read up on it years ago when someone accused him of having it. Turned out the asshole had merely been being an asshole. Hudson had never exhibited signs. Then again, Teague had an uncanny attention to detail when it came to working on engines, so he doubted that was the case.

Was it something else? The mood swings made him think there was some underlying reason.

Not that he was putting on a psychiatrist hat, but he had to wonder.

Releasing a breath, Hudson relaxed his body and his mind. There was nothing he could do about Teague and his mood swings now, and tomorrow would be a new day. He'd figure it out then.

One way or the other.

Twenty-Three

Saturday, July 23rd

BY THE TIME the afternoon rolled around, Teague was hyper. He wasn't sure what had caused it, whether it was spending the morning on a boat with a small group of people from one of the local churches, forced to do nothing but sit there, or if it was due to assisting Dare with a couple of the Jet Skis. They'd gotten caught up, racing on the water and being carefree for a little while, and damn did it feel good to let go like that. It'd been a rush Teague had been looking for.

Unfortunately, it hadn't lasted nearly long enough.

Whatever it was, he couldn't seem to sit still.

Which was the reason he was headed to the repair shop. He had a couple of hours left in the day, so he figured he could help Hudson. The guy usually cut out early on Saturday in the event he did work, and since he was still there, Teague figured he had a lot to do.

For the first time in what felt like forever, Teague wasn't running the other direction. After last night … after Hudson had fucked him into oblivion, Teague hadn't been sure how he was going to feel this morning. Sure, he'd slipped out rather quickly, but he'd needed that time to get his head on straight.

When he'd woken up, he'd lain in his bed for a few minutes reliving the memory of last night. The panic had abated, reassuring him that he'd made the right decision by leaving. They'd agreed on sex and that was exactly what they'd done. Thankfully he'd come to his senses before he did something stupid like spend the night with Hudson.

But now, he wanted to get fucked again.

Only he wasn't about to tell Hudson that.

When he stepped into the shadows of the building, he heard someone talking. He went toward the small office, where he found Hudson and Dare standing just outside of it, while Dare rambled endlessly at Hudson. For a moment, Teague contemplated turning around and letting them chat, but then Hudson's eyes slid over to him, and he knew he couldn't slip out unnoticed.

"What's up, man?" Dare greeted cheerfully, fist bumping him when Teague joined them.

For some reason, Teague had a difficult time looking at Hudson, so he kept his focus on Dare.

Dare kept right on talking as though nothing seemed odd. "I stopped by to see if Hudson would be willing to help out with our move. Think you'd be game?"

"Of course," Teague told him. He didn't even need to know when, because he had absolutely no plans for the foreseeable future.

"Thanks, bro. I'm hoping to get the majority of our stuff moved all in one day while Noah's at the station. All his shit's in storage right now, so that'll make it easy."

Moving was never easy, but Teague kept that to himself.

"Just tell me when and I'm there." Teague still couldn't look at Hudson, but he could feel the heat of his stare on him.

Speechless

Dare must've sensed the tension, because he glanced between the two of them briefly, a slight crease marring his forehead, as though he was trying to determine if something was different. It was clear he was trying to figure out what—if anything—was going on between them. Considering Teague usually made an effort to avoid Hudson, Dare should've been used to it by now.

Luckily, Dare didn't say anything about it, instead jumping right back on topic. "All right. The plan is to move the stuff on August fourth. It's a Thursday, but it's also the first day we can move in. I talked my landlord into giving me a few days, but that's about all he's willing to offer. Keith and Holly agreed to handle the front office so Cam and Roan can help, as well."

Teague nodded.

Once again Dare studied him and Hudson, making Teague even more nervous.

"Oh," Dare said, snapping his finger. "I brought that book with me today. It's in the main office under the counter if you wanna grab it."

"Yeah, thanks." Teague felt his face heat. He'd already told Hudson that Dare had offered to lend him the sign language book, but still it made him feel awkward.

"Alrighty then. August fourth. We'll knock it out in one day." Dare's hazel gaze jumped between the two of them again.

Okay, so this was getting really weird. It was as though Dare was keeping up a running monologue to ease the strain. In case he hadn't noticed, it wasn't working.

"Cool." Dare started backing away. "I'll just let the two of you get back to it."

Teague watched as Dare's eyes went to Hudson's hands. Unable to help himself, Teague looked over.

Close the bay door on your way out.

Dare nodded, then grinned, a knowing gleam in his eyes. "Yeah. Sure. No problem."

With that, Dare turned and left, hitting the button to lower the door on his way out.

That left Teague and Hudson and the awkwardly strained silence hovering between them.

He was trying to come up with something to say, but before he could form words on his tongue, Teague was stumbling back as Hudson grabbed him and pushed him toward the wall. He didn't have time to react or even to take a breath when Hudson's mouth was on his, hot and fierce. The kiss obliterated all the tension, and Teague found himself grabbing for Hudson, holding the back of his head, keeping him in place while the man fucked his mouth with his tongue.

His dick instantly went hard.

Although he'd given some thought as to how their first encounter after last night would go, not once had he thought it would be like this. For one, he figured Hudson would space things out, make Teague wait for a while. And two, they were at work, out in the open, where anyone could walk in at any time.

Then again, he damn sure wasn't complaining.

FROM THE SECOND Teague walked through the door a short while ago, Hudson had been ready to jump on him. He couldn't pinpoint why that was, but he'd been counting down the seconds before he could kick Dare out and do exactly what he was doing now.

Speechless

Holding Teague in place against the wall, using his own body, Hudson devoured him. All day he'd thought about kissing him, stripping him naked, and fucking him into oblivion, and now he had that opportunity.

Admittedly, he'd been trying to home in on Teague's emotional state as soon as the kid had walked in. Hudson hadn't seen him all day, but he knew immediately that Teague hadn't been avoiding him on purpose like he'd originally thought.

Thank fuck.

"Hudson…" Teague groaned into his mouth, his fingers tugging on Hudson's hair as he tried to get closer.

Sliding his hand into Teague's shorts, Hudson fisted his cock, stroking roughly while Teague continued to moan in his mouth. He hadn't had a plan for what he would do when he got his hands on Teague again, so he was winging it here.

Teague's hands slid beneath Hudson's shirt, roaming over his chest, then around to his back. The kid was eager, there was no doubt about it. But then again, so was Hudson. He needed to be inside Teague, and he suddenly didn't give a fuck that they were in the repair shop. Anyone could walk in at any time, but since it was close to the end of the day, he knew the chances of that were slim.

Regardless, he didn't fucking care.

Pulling back from Teague's mouth, Hudson then released Teague's cock. He worked the buttons on his shorts, then pulled out his own dick and nodded for Teague to get on his knees. Without hesitation, Teague went to the floor, sucking Hudson into his mouth with fervor. The vibrations from Teague's strangled moans made his dick throb.

Fuck, it felt good. The warm, wet suction of Teague's mouth… Ahh, fuck, yes… He could get used to this. He took his time, teasing Teague's lips with the head of his dick, brushing it over Teague's tongue, before sliding inside again, letting the warm suction consume him.

Damn, Teague was good at this.

Teague wasn't trying to rush, his hands flattened on Hudson's thighs while Hudson controlled the pace, pushing in, sliding back. After another minute, Hudson pulled out of Teague's mouth, not ready for this to be over yet, then moved back so that he could rest his ass on one of the shorter tool carts. He motioned for Teague to come over, which he did, again without hesitancy.

Before Teague put his mouth back on Hudson's cock, he signed for the kid to take off his clothes. It was a risk, getting Teague naked in the shop, but he didn't give a shit. He was too worked up to care.

While he watched Teague, Hudson pulled out his wallet, snagged the condom and small packet of lube he'd stashed there that morning, and set them down beside him. Teague kicked off his flip-flops, then shoved his shorts down to the floor, stepping out of them. Since he'd already been shirtless, that was one less article of clothing they had to worry about.

Hudson pointed to his dick, and Teague understood him, coming back to take him in his mouth. For a few minutes, Hudson relished the way Teague moaned and sucked, bobbing his head and taking Hudson as far down as he could. Sliding his hands into Teague's silky blond hair, he helped control the pace by guiding Teague's head.

Fuck yes. So damn good.

Speechless

With his other hand, Hudson worked his palm down Teague's smooth, warm back, then reached for his ass, squeezing one of his cheeks hard. Teague didn't lose his rhythm, continuing to blow Hudson in the best way possible. Using his own saliva, Hudson slicked his finger, then returned his attention to Teague's ass, sliding inside up to his first knuckle.

Teague groaned, pushing his hips back to take more of Hudson's finger. He gave him what he needed, pushing in deep, massaging Teague's prostate while the kid moaned, sucking exuberantly on his dick.

Hudson needed to be lodged inside Teague now.

Pulling his finger out and freeing his cock from Teague's mouth, he kept his eyes on Teague while he ripped open the condom and rolled it down his throbbing length. The lube came next, and he coated his cock and generously lubed one finger before signing for Teague to turn around.

When Teague spun around and presented his ass to Hudson, his breath lodged in his chest. Fuck. He'd been thinking about this all damn day, eager and aching to bury himself inside Teague's tight ass.

With the slick digit, Hudson worked Teague's ass with one finger, then two, fucking into him while Teague gripped on to the toolbox across from him, using it to keep him from moving. When Teague's ass was loose enough, Hudson gripped his hips and pulled Teague back, sinking his dick into the guy's welcoming body.

"Oh, fuck yes," Teague hissed.

Hudson slowed his movements, watching as he pulled Teague back onto him, then pushed him off, his eyes locked on his dick as it eased into Teague's beautiful ass. He took his time, fucking him slow and easy, loving the way Teague groaned and begged for more. Hudson wasn't ready to give him more; he wanted to enjoy this for a while. The way the tight ring of muscle clamped down on his shaft, the way Teague moaned louder when Hudson bottomed out inside him… It was fucking phenomenal.

But he could only take so much before his balls started drawing up tight to his body and the telltale tingle in his spine warned him of his impending release.

Fuck.

Gripping Teague's hips tightly, Hudson stood and rammed in deep, fucking Teague faster, harder … so fucking deep. He was brutal, and the way Teague begged and pleaded for more only ratcheted up his need. He dug his fingers into Teague's hips as his release barreled down on him. He couldn't hold back, slamming home, retreating, slamming home again. Over and over, he impaled Teague, watching where their bodies were joined until he couldn't take any more.

With one final punishing thrust, Hudson came hard. The breath rushed out of his lungs as his dick pulsed inside Teague's ass. He could've stood there like that until his heart rate slowed, but Teague hadn't come yet, and Hudson fully intended to make that happen.

Pulling out, he dropped to his knees and turned Teague around. Without preamble, he took Teague's dick into his mouth and stared up at him.

Teague's eyes widened, his hands sliding into Hudson's hair.

Yes, he was handing over control and Teague understood that.

Speechless

"Oh, fuck," Teague muttered low, his fingers linking into Hudson's hair as he drove his cock past Hudson's lips. "Holy ... fucking ... hell."

Teague began pumping his hips, fucking Hudson's face while Hudson kept his eyes on Teague. He watched all the emotions flitter across his features as he chased his release. It didn't take long, but Hudson hadn't expected it to.

"Gonna come..." Teague whispered, meeting Hudson's eyes. "Gonna come in your mouth, Hudson. Oh ... shit..."

Hudson sucked hard when Teague pushed in as far as he could, his dick pulsing, spurting against Hudson's tongue. He worked him until Teague's fingers loosened in his hair, then released him and got to his feet. Grabbing Teague's head, he cupped the back and pulled him in for a kiss that stole both their breath. He wasn't sure what was going on here, but he got the feeling it was a whole hell of a lot more than simply sex.

But Hudson knew that no matter what might be playing out between them, this was all it ever could be. Unfortunately, he was smart enough to know that was all Teague would ever be willing to give.

Twenty-Four

Friday, July 29th

"OH, COME ON, Gannon!" Milly yelled. "It's just a little water. It's not gonna hurt you."

Gannon shook his head and Teague chuckled. Cam and Milly had been trying for nearly half an hour to get Gannon into the water; the guy had never moved from his seat on the deck of the boat. Not once.

"You don't know that," Gannon called back.

Milly grinned, kicking one dainty foot in the water and making a splash. She was perched in an inner tube floating carelessly near the boat. She looked happy. They hadn't seen much of her since the cruise, but Cam's last-minute idea for an afternoon on the water had apparently been right up her alley.

Cam, Gannon, Milly, Dare, Noah, Hudson, and Roan were all out there with Teague, all enjoying a bit of the waning afternoon sun. Clearly Cam had a burr in his butt, because he'd been insistent that they needed a little down time and they needed to do it out on the water. Today.

Speechless

Not that Teague minded. He was enjoying himself, but he wasn't in the water. Nor was Hudson or Gannon. As for why Gannon wouldn't leave the boat, Teague understood. He had no clue about Hudson.

His phone vibrated in his pocket and he pulled it out.

When we get back to shore, meet me at the private alcove.

Heat swarmed him, and he didn't think it had anything to do with the afternoon sun. Only once since last Saturday had he and Hudson gotten together for sex. And yes, Teague assumed that message was the equivalent of a booty call.

He wanted to call out that they should be heading back to shore, but he knew better. They'd been out there a little more than an hour now, and he needed to give it a little more time than that. Plus, everyone would want to know why he was so eager to head back in. It wasn't like he had any plans for the night. Well, he hadn't right up until that text.

"You good?" Roan asked when he climbed aboard, water dripping from him.

"Sure. Why?"

"You looked a little lost in thought."

Teague felt his face heat. Good thing Roan couldn't read his mind. If he could, hell, he would probably blush. The things Teague thought about when it came to Hudson ... probably best if no one else knew about that.

"How's your sister?" Gannon asked, effectively taking Roan's attention off him.

"Not so hot." Roan took a seat beside Teague, leaning his elbows on his knees as he dried his hair with the towel.

"She planning to go into another rehab?"

Roan shook his head, looking dejected. "Nope. She said she's done with them."

"Sorry to hear that. She still using?"

"Unfortunately. I'm trying to make it as hard for her as I can, but she's doing it when I'm not there. Since I can't be with her twenty-four/seven..."

Teague was surprised that Roan was sharing so much information about himself. Then again, he and Gannon had gotten pretty tight as far as friendships went. Teague knew that Roan was helping out with video games and shit, so that made sense.

"Well, if there's anything Cam or I can do, let us know."

Roan nodded, then turned his attention to Hudson. "I'm surprised your brother's not here today."

Hudson glanced at Roan, then used his hands to respond. *He's in California for work.*

"He spends a lot of time out there, huh?"

Hudson nodded.

Gannon turned to look out at the water. "Hey, Mill. You heard from AJ lately?"

That question had Hudson looking over at the woman floating in the water.

"Not since the cruise, no," she said, but it sure sounded like a lie, and Teague didn't even know her all that well.

"Really? He said he left you a couple of messages, but you never returned his call."

"Huh. I didn't get any messages."

And now she was definitely lying. Teague didn't claim to know her all that well, but he'd been around the woman enough that he knew she rarely answered a question or responded to something in only a few words. The woman talked incessantly.

Which would likely mean that Milly had a thing with AJ. Interesting.

Speechless

Not that Teague gave a shit, but at least it kept his mind off of what Hudson planned to do with him in a little while.

Great.

Now he was thinking about it again.

MILLY SHOULD'VE KNOWN the topic would turn to AJ.

Then again, the only reason she was there was because AJ wasn't. She knew he was in California because he had left her a message last week, trying to get her to call him back. He'd mentioned he would be out of town for a couple of weeks and had hoped to see her before he left.

She knew she was being a bitch by not calling him back, but she couldn't. What they'd shared on the cruise... Milly knew that had been one of those vacation romances that wouldn't stand a chance back in the real world. She worked too much and AJ was always gone... The last thing she wanted was a long-distance relationship.

Yes, she liked AJ.

A lot, actually.

He was a stand-up guy, far better than any guy she'd dated as of late, which only meant that they weren't meant to be. Based on her experience, it wouldn't take AJ long before he grew tired of her. Or he would want to change her, and that wasn't something she could deal with, either. She'd made it this far in life without ever settling down, so she didn't see the point in doing so now.

Looking up, she noticed Gannon watching her. She knew he had caught her in a lie. Rarely did she ever lie to him. Not only because he was her boss but also because he was her best friend, and she loved him for that. But she absolutely did not want to talk about AJ. The more distance she put between them, the better off they would both be.

Didn't mean she didn't think about him all the time, because she did. A woman had the right to fantasize, but a woman also had the right to know when not to get too close.

The last thing she wanted was another broken heart.

BY THE TIME they made it back to shore, the sun was beginning to set, which happened to be perfect for what Hudson had in mind. After helping get the boat tied up, he headed toward the repair shop so everyone would think he had some work to take care of. It helped that he had to go inside to grab something he'd stashed in his drawer earlier. He tucked it into the pocket of his cargo shorts.

What he was really doing was heading down to the alcove by slipping around the outer edges of the lake. Figuring Teague would come in from the other direction to avoid being seen with him, it seemed like the logical thing to do.

It took roughly fifteen minutes to trek through the trees and down to the water's edge. The spot wasn't exactly a secret since Cam, Dare, and Roan all knew about it, but Hudson knew that it was rarely used these days. Since Cam and Dare were both dealing with their own relationships, they didn't need to sneak down to the lake to make out. Or maybe they did; who really knew with them.

Speechless

However, he doubted they were coming down here tonight.

So, this was perfect.

The sound of a twig snapping had Hudson turning to see Teague nearing.

"Did you plan to get in the water?" Teague asked as he joined him.

Hudson signed: *No.*

"Okay, then what's the plan?"

Hudson grinned. The kid was apparently in a hurry.

Take your clothes off.

Clearly Teague understood the instruction, because he took a step back and lifted the hem of his shirt, pulling the dark fabric up and over his head. As he continued to watch Teague undress, Hudson backed over to one of the large, smooth boulders and perched on the edge.

He never took his eyes off Teague, enjoying the striptease. The guy was all corded muscle, sleek and lean. Hudson had been hoping to see him out in the water today, but the kid had opted to hang on the boat for whatever reason instead.

But he would get his fill now.

"Now what?" Teague stood gloriously naked a few feet away, while Hudson was still fully dressed.

Touch yourself.

"Touch myself? Like, jack off?"

Hudson cocked an eyebrow but left it at that. Teague would get with the program soon enough.

It only took a few seconds before Teague took his dick in his hand, slowly stroking while he continued to maintain eye contact with Hudson. He looked confused, which was cute. He liked keeping Teague guessing, and so far it seemed to be working.

Hudson didn't move for several minutes, fixated on the way Teague was stroking himself. He wasn't in a hurry, but he could see the way Teague's muscles tightened. He needed more than he could give himself right now, and Hudson wanted to oblige him, but he was enjoying the show.

"So, what? Are you going to sit there and watch me the whole time?"

Hudson shrugged. *What do you want me to do?*

"Something. Fuck," Teague huffed, never stopping the movement of his hand.

Tell me.

"I thought you were the bossy one," Teague mumbled.

Hudson grinned.

"Fine. I'll jack off, but you have to finger my ass."

Crooking his finger, he signaled Teague to come over to him. When he was within reach, Hudson jerked him closer, nipping Teague's chest with his teeth before flicking his tongue over Teague's nipple.

Teague hissed, his chest pushing forward, closer to Hudson's mouth.

Hudson nipped, licked, and sucked until the little brown disc was hardened against his tongue, then he switched to the opposite side. He reached between them and guided Teague's hand back to his dick, helping him stroke it. While he did, Hudson pulled Teague's head down, pressing his mouth to Teague's.

Smooth and soft, Teague's lips melded against his, a breathy moan escaping him. He wasn't sure if Teague realized he did that damn near every time Hudson kissed him. When he pulled back, he refocused his attention on working Teague's dick, closing his fingers over Teague's fist.

"Why do you like toying with me?"

Speechless

Hudson didn't need to answer that. The kid already knew. He wasn't sure he would ever get enough of Teague. Ever since the first time they'd had sex, Hudson had been trying to control himself. It wasn't easy, but the last thing he wanted was to hurt the kid. If he could, he would've already been slamming his dick deep into Teague's warm body. But he wanted to keep Teague off-kilter for a while. He didn't want to become predictable, because he knew that wouldn't hold Teague's interest for long.

And though he had originally intended for this to be a short-term thing, Hudson already knew that he wanted a hell of a lot more than that. But the key to getting it was to keep Teague coming back for more.

Twenty-Five

HUDSON'S MOUTH FELT so good. The way he sucked and bit Teague's nipple, adding that little sting of pain... Teague wanted him to keep doing that all fucking night.

Then again, if he kept that up, no way would Hudson finger Teague's ass, and he was already clenching in anticipation. Hudson's hands landed on Teague's hips, and he guided him back a step, so Teague complied. When Hudson released him, it was to pull out his wallet, which ratcheted Teague's eagerness by a million. However, Hudson didn't retrieve the condom Teague had seen; rather, he pulled out one of those small packets of lube he seemed to carry around with him.

Hudson stood up, then motioned for Teague to move over to the boulder. Confused, he looked at Hudson. The guy was smiling as he twirled his finger, signaling for Teague to turn around and face away from him.

Well, that made a hell of a lot more sense. Planting one hand on the rock, Teague leaned over and continued to tug on his dick. He was hard, but he needed more than his own hand if Hudson expected him to come. At this point, Teague wasn't even sure that was what Hudson wanted, but if it meant a possible release, Teague was more than willing to play the game.

Speechless

Cool fingers glided down his crack, but then Hudson repositioned Teague so that one foot was propped up onto the lower part of the boulder, opening him wide. If there was anyone out there on the lake, they would definitely be able to see them. The sun was still out, although it was low in the sky. Probably another forty-five minutes before it would be completely dark.

Plenty of time.

He hoped.

"Oh, fuck," Teague groaned when Hudson pushed two slick fingers inside his ass.

He clenched around them but then forced himself to relax.

Hudson took on a fairly slow pace and the pleasure was exquisite. The way he pumped those two fingers inside him, brushing his prostate every so often, massaging it other times... Teague's dick was leaking pre-cum, hoping for more.

He was so lost in the sensation, it took a second to realize that Hudson's fingers had been replaced by ... something harder. He pushed his ass back against the intrusion, and that's when the vibration started.

He held his breath as he realized Hudson was fucking him with a prostate massager. It was longer and thinner than Hudson's fingers, which wasn't at all unpleasant. And the vibration made his balls draw up.

"You're gonna make me come," he said by way of warning. He wasn't sure if this was how Hudson wanted things to go, so he figured he'd give him a heads-up. Although he didn't want to come. He wanted to enjoy the sensation for a while.

Gripping the base of his dick, Teague squeezed to hold off his release. He continued to rock back, taking the toy deeper.

"Fuck... Hudson... Feels so good." Better than good.

Hudson never picked up the pace, only continued to fuck him with the toy, even when Teague leaned forward and rested both arms on the boulder. His body was trembling from the impending orgasm, and he could do little more than hold himself up. When Hudson's big, warm hand gripped his dick, Teague knew he was in for it.

Unable to help himself, he thrust into Hudson's hands, then pushed back against the toy. He continued the motion, not caring that he was out in public or that anyone could happen upon them at any time. He needed to come more than he needed air, so he had to consider his priorities.

"Oh … fuck…" His body trembled; his ass gripped the toy while Hudson continued to bring him closer and closer to the edge of bliss. He couldn't hold back any longer, and Hudson must've realized that, because he jerked Teague's dick more firmly, but never did he change the ass-fucking motion.

Teague closed his eyes and gave himself over to his release. He cried out as he came, his dick jerking in Hudson's hand as he came so hard it knocked the air from his lungs. By the time he was able to catch his breath, Hudson had removed the toy and disposed of it somewhere, Teague didn't know where.

Nor did he care.

At the moment, he only cared about being able to walk back to his apartment. The way his legs were still shaking, he wasn't sure that was going to happen.

Speechless

THE ONLY WAY to explain it … Hudson was a saint. Otherwise, he wouldn't have been able to stand watching Teague come apart like that without burying himself inside the man. But he had.

And now his balls were aching and his dick was ready to break his fucking zipper.

Considering he'd been back at his apartment for nearly an hour now, it was safe to say he was a fucking saint. Except he had no intention of going to sleep tonight without enjoying Teague's body one more time. And this time, he intended to lose himself for a little while. Although earlier had been just as enjoyable. It wasn't always about him; sometimes, he simply wanted to make Teague lose it, and boy had he. It'd been beautiful.

He'd given Teague plenty of time to recuperate. Now it was time to start the party again.

After showering and downing a bowl of canned stew, Hudson planted his ass on his couch, grabbed his cell phone, and shot Teague a text.

You want me to come to you? Or you want to come here?

He smiled when he received a response. *To do what?*

For me to do you.

His door opened in less than thirty seconds, and he grinned like an idiot. Teague was evidently right there with him, which wasn't a total surprise. Seemed the guy was insatiable.

"Do you want me naked?" Teague asked, the eagerness evident in his tone.

Hudson nodded.

While Teague stripped, Hudson pulled off his shorts and sat down on his couch in the buff.

"Nice." The appreciative tone made Hudson's dick harden more as Teague's eyes did a slow roll over his body.

Spreading his legs, he signaled for Teague to kneel before him.

Once Teague was there, Hudson reached for Teague's head with one hand, cupping the back, while gripping his dick with the other. He brushed the swollen head across Teague's lips a few times, then pushed forward. Teague took the hint, opening his mouth and allowing Hudson to sink into the warm cavern of his mouth.

Fucking heaven. That's what this was.

In an effort to keep things from being over too quickly, Hudson allowed Teague to work his dick at his own pace, enjoying the suction, the warmth. His eyes threatened to close from the brutal pleasure that assaulted him, but he managed to keep them open, not wanting to miss a second.

When he knew he was getting close to no return, he pulled out of Teague's mouth. He retrieved the condom and the lube he'd stashed beside him and handed them to Teague to do the honors.

Apparently Teague was trying to kill him with pleasure. It took longer than necessary for him to roll the condom on, then lube him up. By the time he was finished, Hudson was damn near at his breaking point.

He signed for Teague to stand, and when he did, he urged him to turn around by putting one hand on his hips and guiding him. Hudson helped Teague to lower onto his dick, swallowing hard as the heat of Teague's body consumed him. There had been no foreplay for Teague—unless earlier counted—so he tried to be easy, working his shaft in slowly, pulling back, then working his way deeper.

When Teague was sitting on his lap, Hudson's dick buried deep inside, he took a deep breath and then gave Teague the reins.

Speechless

The kid fucked him by lifting and lowering on his dick, slowly at first, then bouncing more enthusiastically. Teague started out with his feet on the floor but soon put them on the couch on either side of Hudson's thighs, continuing to lift up and lower onto Hudson's dick.

"So fucking good," Teague moaned. "I could do this all damn night."

Hudson would let him, too, except he hadn't come earlier, which meant his release was far closer than Teague's probably was. Not wanting to leave Teague hanging, Hudson smacked Teague on the side of his leg to get him to stop. When he did, Hudson signed for him to turn around.

When Teague was facing him, Hudson once again lodged himself in Teague's ass, then pulled his head down and thrust his tongue into Teague's mouth. He allowed Teague to do all the work for several minutes, content with plundering his mouth with his tongue while Teague impaled himself on Hudson's dick.

Fuck.

So good.

He was going to come any second, and he wanted Teague to be right there with him. Reluctantly, he pulled back, releasing Teague's mouth. He gripped Teague's hips, stilling his movements, then took over, bucking his hips up off the couch and fucking Teague from underneath. Hudson gripped Teague's dick with one hand, stroking him in rhythm to his thrusting, while still holding his hip with the other. When that became too much, he allowed Teague to take over the hand job while he focused solely on fucking Teague until they both couldn't see from the pleasure of it.

"Yes … yes … yes…" Teague chanted, his eyes locked with Hudson's.

There was a connection there that neither of them could deny, but Hudson knew he was the only one who would acknowledge it.

Hudson signed: *Come for me.*

"You don't do that often," Teague panted. "I like it. A lot."

Hudson wasn't sure what Teague was referring to, and clearly Teague read that in his expression.

"Telling me what to do. With your hands."

Something shattered in Hudson's chest, and he didn't know what it was. A warm feeling consumed him. He continued fucking Teague, driving them both higher and higher until…

"Fuck yes!" Teague hissed, his hand stilling on his dick.

As he came, cum shooting onto Hudson's chest, Hudson let go, coming hard, lodged deep inside of Teague.

Never once did he break eye contact.

But neither did Teague.

Twenty-Six

Saturday, July 30ᵗʰ

THE FOLLOWING MORNING, Teague showed up for work early. He hadn't slept for shit last night. He had tossed and turned, thinking about Hudson, wishing for the first time in his life that he was in bed with him. The crazy thoughts had pissed him off, so he had gotten up before the sun and made his way down to the shop to work on one of the engines he'd been dealing with for the past few days.

At eight o'clock, he received a text from Hudson letting him know that he was taking the day off.

Teague wanted to ask him why but decided against it. It wasn't his business what Hudson did. They might've been fucking, but that was all they were doing. This wasn't a relationship, no matter how stupid his thoughts had become.

And they were stupid. Epically stupid.

Like, he found himself thinking about Hudson for absolutely no reason. Not how he was going to get fucked by Hudson, more along the lines of whether or not Hudson wanted to have dinner together.

Stupid.

And that shit lasted all night and through most of the damn day.

By the time the afternoon rolled around, he was more irritable than he'd been in days. Several times he had considered texting Hudson to tell him that they needed to call this thing off. It was getting too complicated. Teague was beginning to crave more than just the sex, and that would only lead to other things.

He didn't want those other things.

Yet with Hudson, they seemed unavoidable.

Every time they were together, something happened between them. Something Teague damn sure didn't understand and certainly wouldn't be trying to figure out. So what if they ate dinner together from time to time? Over the four years he'd been at the marina, he'd had din—no, lunch—with Cam or Dare or Roan countless times. They'd gone out to the clubs on occasion, out on the water, sat on the pier and drank beer… That was no different than what he and Hudson were doing.

Well, except for the fucking part.

But still.

Teague wasn't looking for all the extras. He preferred his sex without the bells and fucking whistles.

"Hey, Teague!" Roan called out from the other side of the shop.

"'Sup?" he hollered back, getting to his feet in time to see Roan turning back out of Hudson's office.

"Hudson's not here today?"

Teague shook his head, wiping his hand on a towel. "He said he was taking the day off."

"Oh, shit, that's right. He said he needed to spend some time at the gym."

The gym? All day?

What the hell did that mean? Who spent the entire day at the gym?

Teague shook off the thought. "Something I can help you with?"

Roan shook his head. "No big deal. He was telling me about a rehab center he'd heard about. Wanted to get more information from him. I'll catch up with him later."

"Why the hell would Hudson know about rehab centers?" *Oops.* Teague hadn't meant to say that out loud.

Roan seemed oblivious to Teague's outburst. "His mother was an alcoholic, and at one point, he thought AJ was having issues with alcohol, so he started looking into them. From what he says, his mother suffered from depression and was known for her destructive behavior. He still goes to group sessions for people who lost someone to suicide. I think he's interested because he doesn't want to see it happen to anyone else."

Well, that explained Hudson's no drinking rule. But what about—

"Anyway. I'll catch up with him later." Roan glanced around. "You need any help? I'm not good with engines, but I'm willing to try if you need me."

"Nah. I'm good."

Teague's mind was still processing what Roan had said about Hudson. His mother was an alcoholic and she had killed herself. Roan had mentioned destructive behavior. Was that why he'd interfered with Teague's life? Was this pity? Was Hudson worried he would do something stupid?

Some people might've been happy to know someone was looking out for them, but Teague didn't need Hudson's pity. Or anyone else's, for that matter. If Hudson was simply doing this because he thought Teague was going to do something stupid...

Fuck Hudson.

"HOLY SHIT, MAN. You're gonna kill me," Calvin grumbled after the second set.

They still had one more to go.

Don't be a pussy.

Calvin barked a laugh, glaring at Hudson, which made Hudson smile. They'd been at it for about four hours, taking a few breaks in between. Hudson had woken up that morning in desperate need of a good workout. One that would push him further than he'd ever pushed before.

In simple terms, he had needed something to take his mind off Teague for a little while.

"I hope you know you're buying me lunch after this."

Hudson smirked. *Last one. Make it count.*

Calvin shook out his arms and followed Hudson back over to the weight bench. They'd spent the majority of their time on chest today, but Hudson had worked in a few leg workouts in between. No doubt they'd be sore tomorrow, but Hudson welcomed the burn. He welcomed anything that would give him a reprieve from all the crazy nonsense circling in his head.

What the fuck had Teague done to him?

Lying on the bench, Hudson waited until Calvin got into position to spot him. He worked his hands onto the bar, getting them in position before hefting it off the rack and lowering it to his chest.

He ticked off the reps in his mind.

One.

Why couldn't he stop thinking about Teague?

Two.

When had this gotten so damn complicated?

Speechless

Three.

How the fuck was he going to tell Teague…

Four.

That he'd gone and fallen in love with him?

Five.

Worse. What would Teague say?

Six.

Or would he simply run? Leaving Hudson with nothing but a broken heart?

Seven.

Calvin grabbed the bar and helped Hudson put it back on the rack. His muscles screamed, but it did little to keep his mind from wandering back to places it shouldn't. He forced himself up, stretching his chest, shaking off the pain, then went to stand where Calvin had been so he could spot his buddy.

Once Calvin was done, he dramatically fell onto the floor, causing people around them to look their way.

You're an idiot.

"And you're a slave driver."

Maybe so. *I'm sure you'll live.*

"I don't know about that. I probably won't be able to pick anything up for a fucking week."

The mental image of his buddy trying to lift his toothbrush and not being able to do it made him grin.

Calvin pushed himself back to his feet and followed Hudson into the locker room so he could grab his stuff. While he spun the numbers for the combination, he felt Calvin staring at him.

"So, what brought this on, anyway? You still having trouble with the kid?"

Hudson hadn't talked to Calvin about Teague, but he'd wanted to. He had considered talking to AJ, but he knew what AJ would tell him. His older brother would tell him to go for it, let love win this time. Hudson wasn't sure that was the advice he wanted to hear.

Calvin was a bit more hardened. He wasn't as free with love as Hudson's brother.

Hudson yanked the lock open, pulled it off, grabbed his stuff, and shoved it in his pockets before turning to Calvin.

I'll tell you about it over lunch.

"Sounds like a plan. Where're you taking me?"

Half an hour later, Hudson was sitting across from Calvin at Thundercloud Subs. The place was his absolute favorite, and he generally ate there at least twice a week. Sometimes three.

"All right," Calvin prompted. "Lay it on me. What's the deal with you and Teague?"

Hudson went on to explain with his hands. He told Calvin about Teague's destructive behavior, about catching the kid at his place with two guys, about having to chase after him to the club. He told his best friend damn near everything, leaving out the sexual encounters because he wasn't willing to share all the intimate details. What happened between him and Teague in those moments was between them. He wanted it to remain that way.

"If I didn't know you better, I'd think you went and fell in love with the kid."

Hudson met Calvin's dark eyes.

"Oh, fuck," Calvin choked out, grabbing for his drink. "You did. You bastard. You went and fell in love with that kid."

He's not a kid.

227

Speechless

No one got to call Teague that but him. And he would never actually call Teague a kid to his face. He merely referred to him as one.

"Yep. You did it. You fell in love with him. Gettin' all defensive and shit." Calvin's grin widened. "So what's the problem?"

He's not looking for love.

"Hell, is anybody? Seriously. How long have y'all been doing this?"

Doing what?

"This little dance y'all do. I've seen the way you look at him and how he looks at you. It's been going on for a long damn time. And this arrangement you've got with him. When did that start?"

About a month ago.

"And you see him every damn day. No wonder you fell for him. How does he feel about you?"

Hudson took a bite of his sandwich, trying to deflect for a minute. He didn't want to answer that because, honestly, he didn't know. Teague was different now than he had been. Sure, he still had some abrupt mood swings, and Hudson never knew when he would possibly set the kid off, but he was more social, less destructive.

Or maybe that was what Hudson wanted to see. Maybe Teague hadn't changed at all, and this was only about sex for him. Not that Hudson blamed him. The sex was a-*fucking*-mazing. Never had Hudson experienced anything like it. Hell, just thinking about fucking Teague made his dick come to life.

"You're thinking way too hard over there," Calvin noted, wadding up the paper when he was finished with his first sandwich.

Hudson shrugged.

I'm not sure Teague's capable of loving someone.

"Everyone's capable. With the right person."

Hudson opened his second sandwich and stared down at it.

Was he the right person?

Or was this all in his head?

Twenty-Seven

TEAGUE HAD PURPOSELY slipped out of his apartment when Hudson had come home a short time ago. He'd even left his phone inside, so he wouldn't be tempted to answer it should the man choose to summon him. That disappearing act Hudson had pulled rubbed Teague the wrong way, and he didn't trust himself around the guy right now.

There were a million things on his mind, all of which were better left unsaid, so rather than risk running into Hudson, he decided to spend some time by himself.

And here he was, sitting on the deck of the marina's boat, his feet dangling off the edge as he watched the water rippling beneath his feet. It was nice out tonight. Still humid, but the breeze had taken the bite out of the afternoon heat. The marina had long ago closed, the dock and pier locked up for the night. Anyone who wanted to come out on the lake would have to do so on the opposite side, which left Teague completely alone.

He didn't mind it so much right now. Some days he hated the feeling, others he welcomed it.

The sound of footsteps had him turning his attention to the dock. He made out the silhouette of the man moving his way long before he made it to the boat.

So much for trying to get away from the guy.

Teague turned back to face the water as Hudson boarded. When a couple of minutes passed and Hudson didn't come over, he turned to see Hudson sitting in one of the chairs. He was leaned back, hands behind his head as he stared out at the night sky.

He didn't need to ask Hudson why he was there. From the look on his face, he hadn't come to find Teague. He'd probably come out here to be alone, the same way Teague had.

Figuring he could give him that time, Teague got to his feet and headed back into the boat so he could move to the dock. As he passed by Hudson, he expected the man to ignore him. When Hudson's arm snaked out and grabbed his wrist, Teague stopped and stared down at him.

"What?"

Hudson's eyes locked with his, but he didn't make a move to sign anything. Teague didn't know what to think about that. Hudson's eyes were heated, but there was something else there. Something Teague wasn't used to seeing, but he didn't know what it was.

When Hudson tugged on his arm, urging him closer, Teague resisted. He was still pissed at Hudson for disappearing the way that he had. Maybe he didn't have a right to be, but that didn't change the fact that he was.

Hudson tugged again and this time Teague wavered, stepping closer.

They never broke eye contact as Hudson got to his feet, pulling Teague against him.

Hudson's mouth claimed his softly, gently. It wasn't one of those dominating, controlling kisses, yet it affected Teague the same as if it had been. Teague wasn't sure what to do, so he kissed Hudson back, keeping his hands at his sides. He wanted to wrap them around Hudson, to pull him close, to feel the man's body, but he didn't dare.

Speechless

Then when Hudson's hands trailed down and unbuttoned Teague's shorts, he started to pull away, but Hudson's arm slipped around him, holding him close. Unable to resist thanks to the undeniable force pulling them together, Teague relented once more. The kiss continued until Hudson had managed to strip them both.

Teague straddled Hudson's legs when Hudson sat back down, pulling Teague with him while continuing to gently thrust his tongue inside Teague's mouth.

He should've argued, he should've turned and walked away when he'd had the chance, but it was too late now. Hudson finally pulled his mouth away, and Teague stared into those mesmerizing green eyes while he tried to catch his breath.

Hudson took Teague's hand, then pressed a condom and lube packet into his palm before releasing him. Once again, Hudson leaned back and put his hands behind his head, staring back at Teague. It was clear he was giving Teague the choice as to whether or not they moved forward from here. Since they were naked, it only made sense.

Or that was his excuse, anyway.

Swallowing hard and resigning himself to giving in to this man—even though he wished he was strong enough to resist—Teague eased backward on Hudson's legs so that he could reach the thick, throbbing cock that was waiting for him, teasing him.

Rolling the condom down, then greasing Hudson's dick, Teague continued to stare at Hudson's face, never breaking the eye contact. He wanted Hudson to see the frustration he felt, see that he wasn't happy about this.

Only he realized he wasn't as frustrated as before.

This wasn't terrible. They were outside, under the stars. Hudson wasn't trying to ask questions or talk, which was a plus.

In fact, it looked as though Hudson was giving himself to Teague.

If Hudson wanted to offer up his body for Teague to use, who was he to argue?

HUDSON HAD INITIALLY come down to the boat for some peace and quiet. He had wanted to spend some time thinking before going to Teague's place. His intention wasn't to find Teague out here, nor had he planned to strip them both, but it'd happened, and Hudson wasn't going to change the direction they were headed now.

Especially not after Teague suited him up, slathered his dick with lube, then lifted himself up and lowered right onto Hudson.

Hudson's hands immediately went to Teague's thighs as the kid's ass choked his dick.

Ahh, fuck. It was so good.

After the mental war he'd had with himself today, Hudson was all tapped out. He wanted nothing more than to sit here and watch Teague ride his dick until he came. He didn't even care if he got off, but he did care that Teague did.

But it felt so good. He closed his eyes while Teague rocked forward and back, taking Hudson's cock deeper and deeper.

"So good," Teague moaned softly. "Open your eyes, Hudson."

Hudson forced his eyes open, meeting Teague's gaze. It was dark, but not too dark that Hudson couldn't see every expression on the man's face. He looked both angry and content, which made no sense at all.

Speechless

"Is this what you want me for?" Teague asked, increasing his pace.

Hudson couldn't tell the kid the truth. He couldn't tell Teague that he wanted so much more from him. It wouldn't matter. Teague wouldn't want to hear it. If Hudson thought they could solve this by talking, he would've told Teague exactly how he felt. But he knew better.

So he would settle for this.

Sitting up straight, Hudson wrapped his arms around Teague's waist and pressed his face into Teague's chest, holding on while Teague continued to ride him. Hudson never wanted this to end. He wanted to spend the rest of the night lodged deep within Teague. It felt so good, the way Teague's ass clenched around him when he lowered back down.

Hudson was surprised when Teague wrapped his arms around Hudson's head, holding him in place while he continued to shift and move, fucking himself on Hudson's cock. Minutes passed as they remained just like that, lost in the pleasure.

"Need more," Teague mumbled.

Hudson reluctantly released him, sitting back to give Teague more room. When Teague stilled, Hudson met his gaze head on. He could see the determination there and he understood it. Whatever this was, Teague was denying it. It was evident that he knew something was at work, something far stronger than sex, but he wasn't willing to accept it.

Exactly how Hudson had expected it to be.

His own frustration bubbled up inside him. He didn't want the kid to fight this, but he had known this going in. Hudson had known that sex was all Teague was willing to offer, so he had to make do with that.

Wrapping his arms around Teague once more, Hudson surged to his feet, holding Teague on his dick. He moved over to the controls, propping Teague on the edge before he began slamming his hips forward, driving into Teague deep and hard while Teague's fingers dug into Hudson's shoulders as he tried to hold on.

Hudson pummeled him hard, fucking him deeper, faster… He wanted to send Teague over the edge, wanted to make him cry out his name. Not once had Teague moaned the way he usually did. He'd been verbal, but only when he wanted something else.

This wasn't how it was supposed to be. Teague was clearly pulling away, and Hudson didn't want that. He wanted to bring Teague closer.

"Fuck me," Teague bit out. "Fucking make me come."

Hudson drove his hips faster, sweat coating his entire body as his muscles strained.

Gripping Teague's hips, Hudson jerked him down with every upward thrust, going deeper. When Teague took his cock in hand, Hudson watched as his hand blurred, he was jacking himself that fast.

"Hell yeah…"

Hudson kept his eyes riveted on Teague's dick while he continued to thrust into Teague. When he saw the first spurt of cum shooting out, he let himself go, filling the condom while Teague came all over them both.

It sucked that it had to be this way, but Hudson knew he was willing to take what he could get from Teague. Which meant keeping his feelings to himself was critical.

Otherwise, this was going to be over long before Hudson was ready for it to be.

Twenty-Eight

Thursday, August 4th

IT'D BEEN ALMOST two weeks since the first time Teague had been gloriously fucked by Hudson, and over the course of that time, it'd been a daily occurrence. Especially since the night on the boat when things had been a little weird.

Since then, Hudson seemed primed and ready at all times.

With the exception of the last … day and a half.

To be honest, Teague's ass had been sore from all the fucking—something he'd never experienced in his life—so Hudson had given him a break. But now, as he helped Hudson carry in Dare's long leather sofa—well, technically it was Noah's—Teague's anticipation was beginning to grow. He was ready for Hudson again.

He wasn't sure how he hadn't grown tired of sex, but it helped that Hudson was so fucking creative. The guy rarely did the same thing twice. On Sunday night, Hudson had spent a solid hour massaging Teague's entire body on his couch before crawling over him, then sliding his dick right into Teague's ass. It had been fantastic.

Then on Monday, Hudson had invited him to run to the store to pick up a few things so Hudson could make dinner. It'd been at night. And yes, Teague had given in to truck sex, riding Hudson's dick in the parking lot of the marina when they returned. Needless to say, it was a good thing they hadn't bought ice cream.

Oh, and then on Tuesday, when Teague had come home from work after Hudson... Before he could get into his place, Hudson had met him at his door, then fucked him right there against the wall in the hallway between their apartments.

Again, wicked awesome.

And then nothing since.

Only now, Teague's anticipation was getting the best of him. It'd been almost two full days, and he continued to watch Hudson like a hawk. He was trying to predict what the man was thinking, but he'd learned that was damn near impossible.

However, it was making for an interesting day.

Hell, it was making for an interesting day every damn day.

The best part about it ... this was all about sex.

Sex, sex, and more sex.

Things seemed to be going great between them. The weirdness he'd felt the day Hudson had spent the day at the gym had subsided, and they were back to normal. He and Hudson had established an easy friendship with benefits, and Teague wasn't feeling the anxiety as much anymore. The fact that Hudson wasn't pressuring him for anything made it easy, as well. He didn't have to worry about spending the night at Hudson's, or vice versa. Most of the time, they were having sex in random locations away from their apartments, which was perfect.

Speechless

Teague couldn't have asked for anything more. He didn't have to worry about those pesky emotions interfering, and for that he was grateful. He certainly wasn't looking for a relationship, and Hudson clearly wasn't, either.

All the stupid shit that'd been going through his head was long gone. He'd moved on. The moment of insanity had passed, and he could accept this for what it was. Fucking for the sake of fucking.

"What's the smile for?" Roan asked when Teague set his end of the sofa down in the middle of the living room.

Teague instantly wiped the smile off his face. He hadn't realized he'd been smiling. Or that anyone had been watching him.

His first instinct was to look at Hudson, but he fought that urge. The last thing he wanted was for Roan or any of the others to become wise to what was happening between them. When other people knew that shit, they instinctively pushed for a happy ever after. Teague didn't want a happy ever after. He was quite content with a happy ending, which meant he would come at some point in the day.

Roan chuckled. "Never mind. I must've imagined it."

That made Teague laugh and his eyes cut to Hudson, who was also smiling.

Shit.

He sobered immediately. It was as though Hudson knew what he'd been thinking about, and the smug smirk only pissed Teague off.

Turning around, he headed back out to the moving truck to find something else he could carry inside. The faster they got this over with, the sooner he could get home and possibly get laid. When he'd signed up for this, he hadn't expected to have the scrutiny of so many eyes on him, but clearly Roan was looking to bust his balls, which turned his fairly decent mood sour all of a sudden.

Strong fingers landed on his shoulders, and Teague spun around to see Hudson standing behind him. "Don't touch me," he hissed, glancing around to make sure no one else saw.

Hudson frowned.

"The last thing I need is someone giving me shit because we're fucking." He knew he sounded like an asshole, but he couldn't help it. Why the fuck would Hudson touch him now? When there were too many eyes around to see?

As he was turning back to the truck, Teague fell off-balance when Hudson grabbed his arm and jerked him around to the other side, out of the line of sight from the house.

The man was still frowning and Teague didn't need to ask him why.

Hudson started signing, and Teague did his best to follow along.

Don't freak out. So what if they find out?

"So what?" Okay, and now he sounded a little hysterical. "I don't *want* them to find out. I don't want *anyone* to find out."

Why?

"Because it's none of their fucking business, that's why."

Hudson didn't say anything more, he simply nodded his head and turned away. Teague was pretty sure he saw disappointment flash in those green eyes, but he could've imagined it.

Shit. He had to have imagined it. No way could he and Hudson continue on like this if the guy was going to make this public. No one could know about this. That was the last damn thing Teague needed.

Speechless

ONE MINUTE TEAGUE was cool, the next he was a fucking mess.

Go figure.

Hudson grabbed one of the small end tables from the truck and carried it into the house, doing his best to ignore the little scene Teague had made. He didn't actually know what had happened, so it wasn't that difficult. He only knew that the second Roan had razzed him about smiling, Teague had freaked out.

Which meant Teague was thinking about him. Had to be. That was one of his hot buttons, and based on the fact he evidently didn't want anyone to know that they were fucking, Teague wasn't interested in doing much more than that.

It kind of sucked. They'd had a good couple of weeks, and the last few days had been the easiest. Ever since Hudson had decided to go with the flow and ignore the fact that he'd started having feelings for the kid, things had been easier between them.

The sex was off the fucking charts, that was for damn sure. It seemed that no matter what Hudson asked of Teague, the kid was willing. Well, to a degree, anyway. They had yet to have sex in an actual bed, but Hudson had planned it that way. After Teague's panic attack the time he'd fallen asleep at Hudson's, he knew that would only be asking for disaster.

So he had steered clear of it, hoping to work up to that point.

Based on the frown that marred Teague's forehead right now, it looked as though they might've taken several steps back, which wasn't at all surprising. In fact, Hudson had been waiting for it.

He wished he could say he wasn't disappointed, but he was. He'd thought they were making progress. And yes, he knew it shouldn't matter, because this was only supposed to be sex, but still. He was. Disappointed. Greatly.

Somewhere along the way, Hudson had started to enjoy Teague's company. Far more than he'd ever thought possible. They shared meals together, they worked side by side, and yes, they fucked. The past two weeks had been ... enjoyable.

Only now, Hudson was wondering how the fuck he'd allowed it to get that far. When he'd made the offer to Teague, he'd fully intended to keep it all about sex. He wasn't looking for anything more.

Well, technically he hadn't been, but it would seem he'd started to at some point.

And that was just fucking stupid. Teague didn't have anything more to give. Hudson knew that. He did. Teague was nothing if not completely forthcoming with that information. He had been clear from the beginning.

"Hey, man. You okay?"

Hudson looked up to see Roan studying him intently.

He nodded, brushing off his emotions. He didn't give a fuck whether Teague wanted anyone to know. It was better that they didn't. This thing wasn't going to last long, anyway. Hudson would get his fill soon enough, and they'd have no choice but to go their separate ways. That was how he'd planned it.

No, what Hudson needed to do was take a step back from Teague. Put some distance between them. Maybe he should stay at AJ's this weekend. Make sure he wasn't tempted.

Speechless

As he headed back to the moving truck to get another piece of furniture, Hudson pulled out his phone and shot a text to AJ. *Mind if I stop by this weekend? We can hang for a while.*

Hudson shoved his phone back in his pocket. He would wait for his brother to text him back, and he'd figure out what to do at that point. Whatever happened this weekend, he needed to hit the gym, work off some of the pent up frustration.

Hopefully, by giving Teague a few days to figure shit out, they could get back to normal on Monday.

The question was whether or not it would still involve sex. Or if they would simply move on.

At the moment, Hudson wasn't even sure which way he would prefer.

Twenty-Nine

TEAGUE WAS ITCHING for a fight. That was the only way to explain the rage burning in his veins. He'd spent the past two weeks mellowed out, and today Hudson had pissed him off. At one point, he had tried to look at it rationally, but then he'd said fuck it.

Except now he was in the shower, debating on what he wanted to do tonight. He had his choice. He could probably call Jason and Benny, hang out with them. Only that didn't sound as exciting as it once had.

But he needed to do something.

He heard his apartment door open and close, and he stopped washing his body. The only person who could be there was Hudson, so he didn't freak out. Anyone else wouldn't be able to get past the lock on the outside door from the parking lot. Only he and Hudson knew that code.

What the hell could he want?

Probably wanted to come over and talk about what had happened earlier at Dare's. Likely give Teague a lecture about—

The shower curtain was yanked back, and Hudson's big, naked body stood less than a foot away from him. Teague swallowed the startled scream that tried to break free as he took a step back when Hudson joined him in the shower.

"What the fuck do you—"

Speechless

His words were cut off when Hudson cupped his jaw and slammed his mouth down on his. Teague wanted to fight; he was tempted to bite Hudson, but the kiss stole his thoughts. Hudson wasn't gentle when he thrust his tongue into Teague's mouth. And fuck if it wasn't exactly what Teague needed.

However, it ended way too soon for his liking.

Hudson turned off the water, grabbed Teague's hand, and pulled him out of the bathroom. Teague had no choice but to follow. When he saw Hudson moving toward his bed, he tried to pull back, but Hudson simply lifted him off his feet and dumped him onto the bed, coming down over him instantly.

Before he could argue, Hudson's mouth was on his once more. It was as though Hudson knew exactly how to calm his racing heart, because it didn't take long for the panic to diffuse and for lust to take over. Teague wrapped his arms around Hudson and jerked him closer, taking his weight on top of him.

He moaned into Hudson's mouth, trying to touch every inch of him at once.

Then Hudson changed things up again, pulling back and flipping around so that he was kneeling over Teague's head, pushing his cock into Teague's face. He wasn't gentle, but neither was Teague.

As he attempted to figure out which way was up, Hudson's mouth slid right down over his shaft, and Teague bucked his hips upward.

"Fuck. Oh, God." Hudson sucked him hard at the same time he pushed his hips down, rubbing his cock against Teague's face.

And yes, he could take a hint.

Using his hands, he pushed Hudson up so that he could take his cock into his mouth, mirroring what Hudson was doing to him. Again, Hudson wasn't gentle as he pushed his hips down, fucking Teague's mouth, pushing his cock deep into Teague's throat. He could do little to stop him, but that was all right because he didn't want Hudson to stop.

This was exactly what he wanted from Hudson. Sex.

Nothing else.

No public relationship.

No dinners together.

No watching movies.

Okay, so maybe he liked some of those things, but he wasn't going to admit to it. He didn't want Hudson to know that he'd come to enjoy the time they spent together. Looked forward to it even. He needed to remind himself that the only thing he'd signed up for was the fucking part.

And Lord, was Hudson good at that.

Hudson's cock slid out of his mouth and the bed shifted. Then Hudson was once again above him, kneeling over his chest and pushing his dick into Teague's mouth. Teague welcomed it, swallowing him, licking, laving, sucking him while he stared up Hudson's impressive body. The man really was gorgeous.

Hudson's hands lifted and Teague followed them with his eyes.

Suck me.

Teague wasn't sure why he found that hot, but he did. Maybe it was because Hudson couldn't speak, but he could use his hands to relay what he wanted. Teague hadn't expected it, and maybe that was why it turned him on so much. He figured if Hudson could talk, he'd be extremely dominant and verbally demanding. Hell, he was already dominant, and that was relayed in every movement of his body.

Speechless

When Hudson pulled back, Teague took deep breaths, watching him as he rolled on a condom—*where the hell had he hidden that?*—then lubed his dick and his fingers. Without an ounce of tenderness, Hudson folded Teague in half, pushing his knees up damn near to his ears.

When Hudson pulled his hands back, Teague didn't let his legs fall. He watched as Hudson's hands began to move.

Hold on to your ankles.

Teague grabbed his ankles, holding himself open as Hudson slipped one finger into his ass. He groaned at first, the initial bite of pain stealing his thoughts. When a second finger joined the first, Teague managed to relax, allowing Hudson to finger-fuck him, working his ass open. He tried not to look into Hudson's eyes, not wanting to see what he was feeling. After their encounter today, he didn't want to see that same disappointment on Hudson's face.

Figuring he couldn't be too disappointed if he was getting ready to plow his ass, Teague decided to forget everything for a little while.

Forget it all and enjoy the ride.

HONESTLY, HUDSON HAD been expecting much more of a fight from Teague about having sex in his bed. At first, he'd thought Teague was going to tell him to go fuck himself, but Hudson had managed to maintain control of the situation.

Now, as he knelt on the mattress, staring down at Teague holding his ankles as he'd been instructed, Hudson wasn't sure Teague knew why he wasn't willing to have sex in a bed in the first place. Not that he wanted him thinking about that.

No, Hudson wanted to fuck the defiance right out of Teague. He wanted to claim him, to show him that he couldn't run from this. Regardless of how they'd intended for this to go, at some point it had gone sideways.

Very, very sideways.

"Fuck me," Teague pleaded as Hudson lined his dick up with Teague's hole.

He brushed the head against Teague's sphincter, pushing in, forcing his way inside, inch by glorious inch. Hudson watched as Teague's face contorted from the pressure, but then he relaxed when Hudson had pushed as deep as he could.

Only then did Hudson lean over Teague, planting his hands on each side of Teague's head, keeping the kid's body folded in half while he began pumping his hips, fucking Teague nice and slow. It wasn't what Teague wanted, he knew that much, but that was what Hudson was going to give him. This was the first time they'd been in a bed, the first time Teague had probably ever had a man fuck him like this ... and Hudson was going to show him just how good it could be.

Leaning down, he pressed his lips to Teague's, sliding his tongue along the seam while he continued to push his hips forward, then withdraw. He worked his tongue into Teague's mouth, kissing him the way he'd come to love. Slow and easy, the same way he was making love to him.

Speechless

Not that he would tell Teague this was making love. No way would he believe him, even if he did. The kid was in denial. He was unhinged. Which was the very reason Hudson was here and not at AJ's watching baseball. He hadn't wanted to risk Teague running down to a club, spending time with those assholes he used to fuck. Shit, the mere thought of someone else's hands on Teague made Hudson's blood boil.

Like it or not, Teague belonged to him.

Only Teague would never be on board with that, so Hudson was going to keep things the way they were now.

This.

Fucking.

Pulling his mouth from Teague's, he stared down into those stormy blue eyes, seeing everything the kid was thinking. Teague wasn't good at hiding his emotions, nor was he good at processing them. The more time they spent together, the more sides of Teague that Hudson saw, the more he noticed it was the little things that set Teague off. Like today.

"Harder, Hudson."

Teague was still holding on to his ankles, so Hudson pushed back, planting his hands on the back of Teague's thighs as he drilled down into him. He slammed his hips forward, giving Teague what he wanted, but still maintaining a slow pace.

"Oh, yes... Fuck, yes..." Teague moaned, continuing a running monolog with every violent thrust of Hudson's hips.

Still, Hudson kept his eyes locked on Teague's face. When Teague tried to look away, Hudson stopped moving. When Teague met his gaze again, Hudson held his stare and began pounding Teague hard and fast, fucking him deeper.

He crushed Teague beneath him, their faces so close, still staring at each other while Hudson drove them both to climax. He never stopped, loving the way Teague begged for more.

"Don't stop! Don't stop!" Teague's hands dropped to the blanket, fisting it tightly. "God, yes. Harder, Hudson. Fuck. Me. Harder."

He continued to give everything he had until Teague cried out his release, then Hudson followed.

Before Teague could jump out of bed, Hudson fell to his side, wrapped his arms around Teague, and pulled him against him, Hudson's chest to Teague's back. He held him there while they both caught their breath. The sheets were drenched because neither of them had dried off, but that didn't matter. For these few minutes, he was going to hold Teague.

And he wasn't going to apologize for doing so, either.

Thirty

Tuesday, August 9ᵗʰ

TEAGUE WAS STILL pissed at Hudson. Ever since the night Hudson had screwed him in his own damn bed, Teague hadn't been able to look at the guy. Well, he could look at him, but he didn't want to. Hudson had agreed to the rule about not fucking in a bed. Teague had specifically laid that out there, yet Hudson had somehow made it happen despite Teague's feelings that it was far too intimate.

Granted, Teague had jacked off at least twice to the memory of that night. It had been incredible, even in light of the fact that they'd been in his goddamn bed. Hudson wasn't supposed to break the rules like that, and Teague was going to hang on to his anger for as long as he could. It was only fair.

His phone buzzed in his pocket and he stopped what he was doing to fish it out.

Dinner at my place tonight?

Why the fuck did Hudson have to go and do that? Didn't he see how pissed Teague was?

He typed up a response: *No.*

The reply he got back was not what he expected.

Please.

Teague sighed, then turned to see Hudson standing in the doorway to his office, holding his phone. "Fine," he called out. "But know that it's under duress."

His phone buzzed.

Noted.

Teague did not want to like Hudson, but it seemed the more time they spent together, the more he did. He tried to convince himself that it was only due to the phenomenal sex. Seriously, what other reason would Teague have to like the guy?

Okay, maybe Hudson was a good cook, as well.

And he was nice to look at.

And maybe he wasn't too bad to talk to, either.

And he smelled so fucking good.

Shit.

Teague didn't want to like him, damn it.

Rather than dwell on how their neat little arrangement had somehow unraveled, Teague got back to work.

By six o'clock, Teague had showered and was standing at Hudson's door. Rather than barge in like he normally did, he knocked. They'd already gone too far, ignoring the rules; he needed to back things up a bit.

Hudson opened the door and there was a smirk on his mouth.

Fucker.

"I'm not having sex with you," Teague announced when he walked into Hudson's apartment. It was a lie. It would take very little for Teague to give in to Hudson, but Hudson probably knew that already.

Fucker.

Speechless

Hudson motioned for Teague to head over to the kitchen. His stomach growled in response as he passed the couch and the television and went over to the small table that held two place settings and a pan of...

"Is that Hamburger Helper?"

Hudson nodded.

"Cheeseburger macaroni?"

Another nod.

Teague wouldn't tell Hudson that it was one of his favorite meals. One of the foster families he'd stayed with during his junior year in high school had always made Hamburger Helper. All different varieties, probably close to twice a week. He wasn't sure he'd had it since.

When Hudson took a seat, so did Teague.

When Hudson started to eat, so did Teague.

This wasn't too bad.

Hudson put down his fork after a couple of bites, and Teague looked up at him. He watched Hudson's hands.

Tell me about your family.

Teague frowned, pretending not to understand. He took another bite as he shook his head.

Hudson cocked an eyebrow and grabbed his phone, which was sitting beside him on the table.

Shit.

There was no way he was going to get out of this.

A text came through, saying exactly what Hudson had signed.

"I don't have family," he said, shrugging it off.

Where are your parents?

Teague put down his fork and glared at Hudson. He did not have any interest in playing twenty questions with this man. He'd already told him way too much during the time they'd spent together.

I'm not going to stop asking.

"Well, thanks for dinner." Teague pushed back his chair and started to get up.

Hudson pointed to the chair as though Teague were a child who needed to be reprimanded.

"No, fuck you," he stated, his tone belligerent. "I didn't come over here to tell you about my family. It's none of your goddamn business. Just because we're fucking doesn't mean I have any plans to open up and share my life story with you."

Hudson didn't move from his chair and Teague refused to sit back down.

"Thanks for dinner, but I've gotta run."

Hudson signed: *Take it with you.*

"What?"

Hudson nodded toward the plate.

"Thanks, but I damn sure don't need your charity."

With that parting shot, Teague walked right out of Hudson's apartment and had absolutely no intention of ever going back.

HUDSON FINISHED HIS meal, glancing up at his apartment door every so often.

Teague was acting like a fucking brat, and he hated that he wanted to go after him. The kid was proving to be bad for his self-control. For years, he'd honed the ability to stay calm and cool, in every situation. But especially when it came to sex.

Speechless

Although he wasn't into the lifestyle, Hudson saw himself as a dominant lover. He enjoyed that aspect of his interactions. And with Teague, it was something he craved. He wanted to dominate the guy in every way possible. Every fucking time Teague pulled a stunt like he had tonight, Hudson wanted nothing more than to restrain him and force him to talk. Well, that or sink oh-so-deeply into him and convince Teague to open up more than just his body to Hudson.

There were so few things he knew about the kid, and that frustrated him. There was no denying he knew Teague's body. He knew what Teague enjoyed, even understood what he didn't. But there was more to this than simply sex, although Teague obviously wouldn't admit to that. Which was the reason Hudson had wanted to know more.

It had been a risk he'd debated on for quite some time.

He'd taken it.

He'd failed.

From where he sat, it looked as though he really had two options.

One, forget about the emotional aspect and the fact that he was being pulled into Teague's orbit in a way he hadn't anticipated and focus solely on sex. For the record, he'd been doing that already, and it wasn't working out for him. Or two, confront Teague about his feelings and see where that got him.

The first option—even if he only pretended that it worked—would get him laid for the foreseeable future. The second would get him booted to the curb, so to speak.

However, neither would get him what he wanted from Teague most.

He wasn't interested in option two; however, he wasn't sure how much longer he could endure this only being about sex. It wasn't as easy to fight his feelings as he had hoped it would be. Telling himself to do one thing didn't necessarily mean he could follow through.

Hudson grabbed his phone and tapped out a message: *Come back over here and finish your dinner. BUT, remove your clothes before you get here. I've got a new toy to try out on you.*

He sent the text and sat there, wondering whether or not Teague was pissed enough to resist.

Ten minutes passed and Hudson figured the kid was going to ignore him.

Only this time, he wasn't going to go after him. Teague had made the decision to walk out rather than man up and have a conversation. For that reason, Hudson wasn't going to chase him down and force him. If he wanted something more, he—

His front door opened and Teague stepped into the room. He was still dressed, which was not what Hudson had instructed, but Hudson had to give the kid credit for coming back. While he carried his own plate to the sink, he grabbed Teague's and put it in the microwave for a few seconds. When it was done, he put it back on the table and signed for Teague to sit down and eat.

Not surprisingly, Teague didn't say a word, but he did sit down and eat. The kid had a really healthy appetite, that was for sure. It didn't take long for Teague to finish his meal, and he carried his plate to the sink and washed it. Hudson watched him while he opened the new toy he'd purchased, put batteries into it and the remote that came with it, and then grabbed the bottle of lube.

Speechless

He felt Teague's eyes on him as he flipped on the television, pretending this was a casual encounter. It would be anything but casual should Teague choose to join him. But that was all on Teague at this point.

Hudson didn't bother hiding the toy, not caring whether or not Teague saw it. He'd picked out this one specifically for Teague. It wasn't big because that wasn't the point of it.

While Teague stood and watched, Hudson lubed the toy, his gaze drifting to the television every so often.

"What do you want me to do?"

Placing the toy on his leg, he signed: *Strip like I instructed.*

Teague kicked off his flip-flops, then shoved his shorts and underwear down. Hudson's gaze slid over to him, watching Teague's cock bobbing up and down, already hard.

Yep, safe to say the kid wasn't intimidated, which was a good thing.

Teague's shirt followed and he stood naked a few feet away from Hudson.

Spreading his legs wide, Hudson signed for Teague to come over to him and lie across his lap.

"What?" Teague didn't look amused.

Hudson lifted an eyebrow, held Teague's stare, and waited.

A solid minute passed before Teague huffed and stomped toward him. The guy was a natural submissive, even if he didn't realize it. It was hot as fuck.

After Hudson moved the toy, Teague got into position across Hudson's lap, moving when Hudson pushed him so that his ass was directly over Hudson's legs. Since Teague couldn't see him, there would be no communication, but that was okay. He was interested in pleasuring Teague at the moment, and that would be all the conversation they needed.

Thirty-One

TEAGUE HAD NO fucking idea what freaky shit Hudson had planned, but his curiosity won out. He had debated on simply walking right back out the door, but watching Hudson lube up the butt plug had been more than he could handle.

Granted, lying across Hudson's lap wasn't exactly a position he was fond of. At least not when he was completely naked and Hudson was fully dressed. It felt too … submissive. Yes, that was the word. Although Teague thoroughly enjoyed Hudson's dominant side, this was something new for him.

However, he was now committed, so he figured he might as well enjoy it. Laying his head on the couch cushion, he watched the television, smiling when he realized what was on.

"You sure do watch a lot of porn."

Hudson's hands glided over Teague's ass, and he instinctively clenched his butt cheeks. For several minutes, Hudson continued doing that, running his palms up and down Teague's legs, over his ass, back down again. The sensation was relaxing.

But it didn't last long.

When Hudson's finger slid down his crack, Teague sucked in a breath. That finger probed his anus, pushing in a little, then a little more. It felt good. Teague had always enjoyed getting his ass fingered. Especially when the person doing the fingering was so skilled at it.

While he watched the movie, Hudson began gently finger-fucking him, slow and easy. One finger. In. Out. In. Out. The rhythm was driving him crazy, the pleasure oddly intense for such limited movement.

Again, that didn't last long.

With one hand, Hudson separated Teague's ass cheeks, then Teague felt something cool and firm against his hole. He knew it was the butt plug, so he forced himself to remain relaxed, focusing on the movie. On the television, a hot brunette was on his knees, getting his face fucked by the bigger blond guy. He had no idea what the premise of the movie was—though he doubted it was all that deep—but he was enjoying it.

He felt the butt plug being pushed inside. It wasn't even remotely close to the size of Hudson's dick, so it wasn't difficult for Teague's body to take. He wasn't sure what the point of it was if it wasn't going to stretch him, but he kept that to himself.

It slipped in rather easily and Teague managed to relax again.

Right up until Hudson smacked his ass hard.

Teague bolted up, kneeling beside Hudson, glaring at him. "What the fuck was that for?"

Hudson smiled, then got to his feet. Within seconds, he had stripped off his shirt, dropped his shorts to the floor, and moved down to the opposite end of the couch. He still eyed Teague while he got comfortable.

Suck my dick.

Speechless

As though that said it all, Teague watched as Hudson spread his arms wide across the cushions of the couch.

Yes, Teague understood what he was saying.

"Fuck you."

After you suck my dick.

Damn it.

Teague knew he shouldn't be enjoying this, but he'd be damned if he wasn't.

With his ass still stinging from the slap, he reluctantly lay out on the couch again and rested his head on Hudson's lap. Hudson shifted so that Teague could get comfortable—as comfortable as was possible in this position—and Teague gladly began working Hudson's dick. The faster they got through the foreplay, the sooner Teague could get fucked and the quicker he could go home.

Hudson was encouraging him with one hand in his hair, massaging his scalp, while the other tapped the end of the plug every so often. As was usual, Teague got so caught up in sucking Hudson, attempting to give the man as much pleasure as possible, that he didn't notice the subtle vibration in his ass. Not until it intensified, anyway.

He groaned with Hudson's dick all the way in his mouth.

This was another first for him. He'd had plugs before and he'd had vibrators. Never had he experienced a vibrating plug, though. He focused on the tremor, realizing he liked it. Maybe more than he should. He got so caught up he apparently stopped sucking Hudson because he was once again guided back down onto Hudson's dick.

The vibration intensified again.

Teague spit Hudson's dick out and moaned loudly. "Oh, fuck…" He liked that so fucking much.

The vibration stopped, and Teague had been playing this game long enough to know that Hudson wanted something in return. Every time Teague stopped sucking, so did the glorious sensation in his ass, so he wrapped his fist around Hudson's shaft and drew him into his mouth once again. The vibration was back, and he continued to moan, grinding his hips into the couch, seeking friction on his dick.

He knew he was leaking pre-cum all over the fucking couch, and if Hudson wasn't careful, Teague was going to blow in the very near future. He wouldn't be able to help it. He got off on this shit. The majority of his sexual experience consisted of blow jobs, hand jobs, and a quick fuck. Never had he been with a guy who wanted to drive him crazy like this. He briefly worried he could get addicted to this shit. Or maybe he already had.

"Fuck... Hudson..." Teague groaned around Hudson's swollen shaft. "Feels good. Need to come... Fuck, I need to come."

The vibration intensified once more; this time the buzzing in his ass skyrocketed him into the ether. He couldn't take any more, and he couldn't stop his orgasm as it crashed into him, his dick jerking beneath him, spraying his stomach as he succumbed to the pleasure.

SON OF A BITCH. Teague was so fucking beautiful when he came. The way his body tensed, his muscles going rigid, the sweet cries that came out of his mouth... Hudson loved making him come. Only now, his dick was in desperate need of attention, but he wasn't through with Teague yet.

Speechless

Had Teague been more patient, Hudson could've done that for hours. The foreplay was always his favorite thing. And it'd been a long damn time since he'd had anyone he could use toys on. Apparently it'd been a long time for Teague, as well. Then again, Hudson should've known after he had used the prostate massager on Teague not too long ago.

Using the remote to turn off the plug, Hudson shifted on the couch, planting his feet on the cushion, pressing his back against the armrest and spreading his knees wide. Teague obviously knew what he wanted, because he got up on his knees, moved closer, and once again took Hudson's dick in his mouth while remaining on all fours. The warm suction made his body tense. Teague had been doing a half-ass job so far, but Hudson didn't hold it against him. With the plug vibrating in his ass, clearly the man wasn't capable of focusing.

One thing he'd learned about Teague, he enjoyed having his ass played with.

Which was hot.

Hudson reached down and flipped the plug back on, smiling when Teague's body jerked slightly. If he was lucky, Teague would come again from that alone.

Gripping Teague's hair in his fists, Hudson guided his head up and down, forcing him to take all of him while he pumped his hips upward. What he wanted to do was to plant his mouth on Teague's, to kiss him and fondle him until Teague couldn't take any more, and then he would lodge himself in Teague's ass for the rest of the damn night.

Except he was trying to keep this as unemotional as he could because Teague was already on edge. It sucked, but Hudson was willing to compromise if it kept Teague from doing something stupid.

Reaching down once more, he turned up the vibration, and Teague began humming on Hudson's dick, which made him see stars. He gripped Teague's head and began fucking his face while Teague reached between his legs and jerked himself.

Fuck. Yes.

Hudson was close. He wished he could cry out so Teague knew. He wanted the kid to lift his head and meet his eyes while they both came together, but he knew that wasn't going to happen. So, he pushed the thought away, gripped Teague's hair more forcefully, and drove himself to completion.

What shocked him most was the way Teague cried out, coming again at the same time Hudson did. Clearly he got off on Hudson finding his release, which told him that Teague wasn't in it for personal satisfaction alone.

When Teague fell onto his side, Hudson forced his weary body up from the couch, moved down, and removed the toy from the limp man before him. He then disappeared into the bathroom to clean up.

It wasn't a surprise to find Teague had disappeared by the time he returned. He glanced at the couch and saw that Teague had cleaned up, which, again, told him more about the kid than Teague was probably aware of.

Hudson knew that he couldn't keep this charade up forever. He wanted nothing more than to curl up in bed, wrapped around Teague's body, and hold him while they slept. It was becoming harder and harder to ignore that desire. Every time he saw Teague, he fell deeper and deeper.

He simply didn't know what he was going to do about that.

If anything.

Speechless

As he sat on his couch, staring at his phone, he tried to convince himself to leave it alone. Letting Teague go tonight was the only way this would work.

Except Hudson didn't want the night to be over. He ached to hold Teague, to have him there in his arms when he woke up in the morning. A solid month and a half of this and Hudson was slowly going insane with the need to move things forward.

Didn't matter that he had agreed to no strings, his heart hadn't quite understood that specific detail.

Grabbing his phone, he pulled up Teague's contact information and typed up a text.

I know it's not part of the deal, but I'd give anything if you'd come back over here and stay the night. I want to wake up with you in the morning.

Before he could talk himself out of it, Hudson hit send.

And for twenty solid minutes, he cast eager glances at his door and his phone. Back and forth, back and forth.

Unfortunately, Teague never returned. Nor did he respond to the text.

Thirty-Two

Thursday, August 11ᵗʰ

IT HAD BEEN two days since Teague had let Hudson use the toy on him.

Two fucking days.

During that time, Hudson hadn't paid much attention to him, and he had no idea why that was.

Okay, maybe he did. It could've been one of three things.

One, Hudson was pissed about the way Teague had reacted to his questions about Teague's family. But then Hudson had summoned him back over for sex, so didn't that mean Hudson was over it?

Maybe not.

Or Hudson could've been angry that Teague had slipped out while he'd been in the bathroom. Surely he had the right to go home afterward. Hudson shouldn't be such a big fucking baby about it.

But those were the lame excuses Teague had come up with. If he was completely honest with himself, Hudson was probably pissed that Teague hadn't responded to that fucking text.

Speechless

When he closed his eyes, Teague could still see the words so clearly: *I know it's not part of the deal, but I'd give anything if you'd come back over here and stay the night. I want to wake up with you in the morning.*

The minute his phone had chimed, he'd grabbed it and read the words. Then he'd read them again and again. Over and over he'd read them, and for hours on end that night, Teague had tried to figure out how the fuck things had gotten so fucked up.

He did not want to like Hudson. And he damn sure didn't want to care about the man. But that text... He'd felt something crack in his chest and he'd refused to acknowledge it then. Or now.

And he didn't even give a shit if Hudson was mad.

Not about not answering his probing questions, not about leaving, and certainly not about ignoring his admission of something that never should've been said between them.

That wasn't part of their deal. None of it was.

Teague never planned to share the fucked-up story of his life with anyone. Not even Hudson, and truth be told, Teague was closer to Hudson than he'd ever been to anyone in his life. So close that it really fucking scared him.

Once upon a time, Teague had been in a relationship. At seventeen.

Yep, he had been seventeen at the time and the guy's name was John. Teague had met John right before his senior year when Teague had moved in with a family in Westlake. Oh, how he had thought he'd hit the jackpot. John was the next-door neighbor, and he'd been eighteen, smoking-hot, and a football player to boot. They would've been in the same grade that year, and for once, the new foster family wasn't all that bad because he got to spend time with John.

Yeah. That lasted all of two fucking weeks. He had learned his lesson in fourteen short days. Thank God that wasn't enough time to actually really like someone, much less love them. Teague had been prepared but shocked all the same.

John was a football player and apparently it wasn't cool to be seen with Teague. Unfortunately, Teague had learned that the hard way. Football practice had started before the school year had, and one day, for the hell of it, Teague had showed up to watch the practice. He was bored, so what the fuck else was he going to do?

When John had caught sight of him in the stands, Teague had nodded a hello. No, he hadn't waved or jumped up and down like some sort of pussy. A simple nod had set things in motion.

Some of the other guys had started giving John shit about it. Turned out, John wasn't out of the closet, although he had bragged to Teague that he was.

However, Teague had showed John. When he and his buddies had decided to gang up on Teague that afternoon on his way home from practice, they had learned that it would take a hell of a lot more than three of them to jump him. He'd been fighting since first grade, remember? Breaking the one guy's jaw would've likely landed him in some deep shit except for the fact that all three of those guys were eighteen and Teague was still only seventeen.

It hadn't been love by any means, but it sure had been another life lesson that had put Teague on this path.

Speechless

Those were the types of things he didn't intend to share with Hudson. He also didn't plan to tell Hudson about his mother or the life he'd spent bouncing around from one house to another. Teague actually wanted to forget about that. He wanted to make his past disappear completely. Every time he thought about it, he got angry. Sure, the anger felt good sometimes. It was better than the bleakness that frequently consumed him.

However, talking wasn't his thing. One of his high school counselors had tried that once. Teague had ended up getting expelled from school for fighting. He'd done it on purpose. They'd tried to force him to share his feelings; he'd chosen the alternate route.

The sound of metal hitting a can caught his attention, and Teague looked up to see Hudson standing in the doorway of his office. He signed: *Cam is looking for you. Said he needed you up front.*

Teague nodded, then grabbed a towel and wiped the grease from his hands. He had no idea what that was about, but he didn't want to keep Cam waiting. Tossing the rag to the floor, Teague grabbed his sunglasses, shoved them on his face, and headed for the Pier 70 office.

When he got there, Cam was leaning on the counter, staring at the appointment book in front of him.

"What's up?" Teague walked right up and casually leaned in front of Cam.

"Since Hudson's not gonna be here for a few days, I wanted to make sure you were going to be able to handle the workload. We're booked solid for the next couple of weeks, and I might even need you to help out with some of the appointments."

Hudson wasn't going to be there? When the hell had that happened? And why the fuck hadn't Hudson relayed that information to him?

Cam lifted his head, and Teague masked his expression, not wanting Cam to know that this was the first he'd heard of it.

"I'll be fine. And yeah, I can handle a couple of appointments, no problem."

"It'll just be tomorrow, maybe Saturday morning," Cam explained. "Thankfully, Hudson'll be back on Monday."

Roan appeared out of nowhere. "I heard you say Hudson's goin' somewhere?"

Teague glanced down at the appointment book and pretended to be looking at it.

"He said he needed a few days off to clear his head. He's gonna spend some time with his brother, but he'll be back on Monday."

"Guy deserves a break," Roan noted, glancing at Teague. "Y'all work too damn hard out there."

That was the damn truth, but not once had Teague taken time off like that. And to think, Hudson was the one who said Teague ran from his problems.

Who the fuck was running now?

IT WAS A chickenshit move, no two ways about it.

The minute Teague headed up to the main office, Hudson grabbed the bag he'd packed and headed for his truck. Two nights ago, after Teague hadn't responded to his text, he'd come to the conclusion that he needed to put a little distance between him and Teague. As it was, Hudson wanted to spend all his time fucking Teague senseless, and that wasn't getting him where he needed to go.

Speechless

Sure, it fucking rocked, but for some reason, Hudson wanted more and Teague didn't.

So, this morning, he'd talked to Cam and let him know he'd be taking a long weekend, starting today. He had purposely avoided telling Teague, though, and now he had some doubt. However, he had told Cam all the details, so Teague simply had to ask to find out. Or—something he doubted would happen—Teague could text him and Hudson would let him know.

Honestly, he was hoping that a little space would allow Teague to realize that this was as much for him as it was for Hudson. Not that he'd be that lucky, but if Teague could admit to himself that there was a connection between them that wasn't entirely hedonistic, maybe they could move forward.

"You look like shit," AJ said by way of greeting when Hudson walked in his front door ten minutes later.

Hudson dropped his bag and gave his brother the finger.

AJ chuckled.

"So, this is new. The running away thing. I thought that the kid was the one doing that, not you."

Hudson headed for the kitchen and grabbed a bottle of water from the refrigerator before joining AJ in the living room. He flopped onto the couch, put his feet up on the ottoman, and took a deep breath. After taking a sip, he set the bottle down and peered over at AJ, who was still watching him closely.

I'm not running, he signed.

"Oh, you're definitely running. But I assume you've got a good reason for it."

He had a good reason, all right. He'd gone and fallen for Teague, and now he couldn't get him off his mind. He had even opened himself up, and Teague had given him the cold shoulder. He wanted more than fucking five or six solid hours with Teague a week. He wanted Teague in his bed all night long, close enough for Hudson to breathe him in.

"You love him, huh?" AJ asked, his tone not at all teasing.

Hudson took another deep breath and nodded.

"I knew it would happen. You thought you could keep this on the physical level. That shit never works out."

Sounds like you know from experience.

AJ's smile was sad. "Milly refuses to return my calls."

Well, damn. Hudson hated to hear that, and he had no idea what had happened between AJ and Milly other than they'd spent most of their time together on the cruise. Obviously they'd stayed the night together, but honestly, Hudson had never seen his brother like this.

That sucks.

"Have you told the kid how you feel?"

In a way, yes. The text he'd sent Teague the other night was as open as he could be. Not that he would tell AJ that. Instead, Hudson gave his brother a *get real* look.

"What? You're the one who's always talking about communicating. I find it ironic that you're going back on that now. Considering all the lectures you've given me over the years."

Whatever.

"I'm serious. Ever since Mom died, you've been on me to be open about how I feel. Said it'll only cause problems to keep it bottled up. And here you are, damn near ready to combust because you're not talking to Teague. He deserves to know."

He doesn't want to know.

Speechless

"Are you sure about that?"

Yes. Positive. He's looking for casual sex, nothing more. He refuses to get close to anyone.

"Tell me how you can spend the past month screwing someone stupid and still not see that he's already gotten close to you. I always said you were as dumb as you look."

That made Hudson laugh, albeit silently.

"Yep." AJ took a sip of his beer and turned his attention back to the television. "We're a couple of sad cases, you know that?"

Yep, he knew. He definitely knew.

"So what do we do now?"

Hudson shrugged. *Baseball and pizza sounds like a plan.*

"I like where your head's at." AJ reached for his cell phone. "Double meat?"

Hudson nodded.

"I'm on it. Pizza, beer, and baseball. One hell of a way to spend a weekend."

One hell of a way.

Not the way Hudson had hoped his weekend would go, but he didn't have much of a choice.

And now the only thing he could do was sit back and wait. Either Teague would move on and Hudson would be left trying to heal the pain he'd caused himself, or Teague would accept that this was something more and he'd finally give in.

Hudson hoped like hell it was the latter. He wasn't sure he could handle the former.

Thirty-Three

Saturday, August 13th

"GIANT FUCKING ASSHOLE!" Teague threw the book across the room, watching as it slammed into the wall and crashed to the floor. "Fuck this shit."

Getting to his feet, he paced the floor, trying to relax. For the past two hours, he'd been attempting to teach himself sign language right up until he'd realized it was futile. Why the fuck did he need to learn that shit? He didn't have a damn person to talk to out loud, much less using his hands.

This was bullshit. Sitting around the fucking apartment like some lame motherfucker.

He needed to do something. Something that didn't involve sitting on his ass. Alone.

Fuck.

He was slowly going insane. This was the very reason he spent his time at the clubs, drinking, hanging with people who gave a shit. Or at least they pretended to for a little while. This sitting at home thing sucked. Big-time.

Speechless

Thrusting his hands into his hair, Teague grabbed his head, pulling it down and into his chest as he took a deep breath. He needed to chill the fuck out. This was simply a panic attack brought on from being alone. It would pass. It always did.

"Arrgghh! This is such bullshit!"

It was Saturday fucking night. Why the hell was he sitting here alone? And where the fuck was Hudson? The giant fucking asshole had been gone since Thursday afternoon right after the stupid asshole had snuck out of there when Teague had been talking to Cam and Roan. Cam had said Hudson was going to hang with his brother, not spend all his fucking time with him. The giant fucking asshole had left without saying a goddamn word, proof that he was another one who pretended to give a shit when it was beneficial to him.

For the past month, Hudson had been beckoning Teague when it appealed to him. They'd spent damn near all their time together and all of a sudden … boom! Hudson's gone.

The fucker.

What the hell could Teague have possibly done to make Hudson tuck his tail between his legs and run away? Was he that difficult to be around?

Teague reached for the glass of water sitting on the counter. He took a sip, then glanced at the door. Next thing he knew, he was throwing it, glass shattering, spraying back toward him. Rather than clean that shit up, he grabbed his truck keys and stormed out of his apartment. He needed something a hell of a lot stronger than water, and he didn't give a shit about Hudson's goddamn rules anymore.

Fuck Hudson.

Fuck him and his stupid arrangement.

Fuck him to hell and back.

Teague was done.

It was time he got back to what he was good at. Losing himself in whiskey would be a fine way to jumpstart that.

Stomping down the outside stairs that led to the parking lot, he nearly jumped out of his skin when he rounded the corner, damn near plowing into Roan.

"Bro, you all right?"

Teague met Roan's eyes and nodded. "Fucking fantastic."

"I heard something crash. You okay?"

"Just fucking perfect."

Glancing down at his hand, Teague realized he was shaking. The last damn thing he needed was Roan getting all motherly. He damn sure didn't need that shit on top of everything else he was dealing with. Hell, he hadn't needed a mother his whole fucking life, no reason to start now.

"I just need to get out of here." *Forever.* He would keep that last bit to himself.

Roan didn't look convinced, but Teague didn't give a shit. He sidestepped him and made a beeline for his truck, ignoring Roan when he called out to him.

He'd spent the past month and a half being the good little boy that Hudson wanted him to be. And where the fuck did that get him?

No-goddamn-where. That's where.

And it was way past time that he fixed that.

Starting right now.

Speechless

ROAN STARED AFTER Teague as his truck tore out of the parking lot, spraying gravel against the side of the building. A couple of pieces hit his shins but he ignored it. Instead, he snagged his cell phone from his pocket, then tried calling Teague.

No answer.

Damn it.

He then pulled up his contacts and added Cam, Dare, and Hudson to one text message.

Something's wrong with Teague. He just left and he doesn't look good. We need to get him back here before he does something stupid.

Fuck.

Roan stared out at the highway in front of the marina. Headlights flew by with the passing vehicles. He didn't even know which direction Teague had gone because he hadn't paid any attention.

Shit. He should've grabbed Teague and tied his ass up to keep him here. Instead, he had let him walk away, and he wasn't lying when he'd said he didn't look good. Something was definitely bothering Teague, but Roan had no clue what that could possibly be.

However, he had a good idea that Hudson knew what this was all about. Perhaps that was the reason Hudson had taken a few days off.

His phone rang and he hit the talk button.

"What happened?" Cam asked, concern in his tone.

"No fucking clue. I was in the office working on some paperwork and I heard something crash upstairs. Next thing I know, he's barreling down the stairs, fit to be tied."

"Shit."

"Exactly." Roan sighed. "I don't know what's been going on this past month, but the kid's been different."

"Different how?"

"A little less … chaotic, I guess you could say. Or so it seemed to me. If I had to guess, he and Hudson have been…" He didn't want to have to spell it out.

"Really? Where the fuck have I been?"

"Married," Roan said simply, chuckling.

"So, if he's been less chaotic, what's his problem now?"

"No idea," Roan told him. "Maybe it's all bottled up. Shit, I don't know."

"Damn it. Hold on a minute."

Roan could hear Cam explaining the situation to someone, most likely Gannon.

"I'm gonna head up there. Don't leave. Have you heard from Dare or Hudson?"

"Not yet."

"Okay. See you in a few."

Roan hung up the phone as a text message was coming in.

Hudson.

What's wrong with Teague?

It would've been easier to explain verbally, however, since Hudson wasn't there, he had no choice but to spell it out via text.

Not sure. He looked really pissed. Something going on with you two?

Not surprisingly, Hudson didn't answer his question; however, he did text back advising that he and AJ were headed to the marina.

Roan went back into the building and waited. He didn't know what he was supposed to do, but he knew they had to do something. He'd known Teague long enough to figure out that whatever mood he was in was dangerous. He'd seen him pissed before, but not quite like that. Quite frankly, it scared him.

Speechless

Letting Teague run off had been stupid, and now that he had, he simply had to find Teague, drag his ass back here, and find out why he'd gone off the rails.

He could only hope he wasn't too late. Teague was nothing if not volatile, and from what Roan could tell, his fuse had been lit.

"WHAT'S GOING ON with him?" AJ questioned as they headed for their trucks.

Hudson shrugged.

He honestly had no clue. He had purposely given the kid some space so that he didn't feel suffocated. They'd spent the better part of the last month together. He should've seen this coming after Teague's freak out at Dare's place when they were moving, and again last Tuesday when Hudson had invited him over for dinner. Hudson had known a storm was brewing, but he'd honestly thought a little space would've done the kid some good.

Now he was beginning to wonder whether he'd made the right choice.

"I'll see you there," AJ called out, climbing into his truck.

Since Hudson was parked behind him, AJ had to wait until he backed out of the driveway.

It wasn't like he'd been doing anything important. Rather than sit at his own apartment and watch television, he had opted to hang with AJ for the weekend. They'd been chilling on the couch, watching baseball, when Roan had texted him.

The instant the words had registered, Hudson's heart had slammed against his ribs. He couldn't deny he felt a bit of panic knowing that Teague had stormed out of there. He had no clue what was going through the kid's head, but he could only imagine.

Fifteen minutes later, Hudson was pulling into the marina parking lot, which was full of vehicles—all belonging to people who worked there.

Cam, Gannon, Dare, Noah, Roan, as well as Cam's father and Cam's brother-in-law were all standing in a huddle.

Hudson pulled his truck alongside Noah's, put it in park, and climbed out.

All eyes moved to him as he walked up.

"You have any idea what's wrong with Teague?" Cam asked bluntly.

Hudson shook his head.

"Something going on with you two?" Roan's question held a hint of accusation in it. Hudson had managed to dodge it in the text a little while ago, but face-to-face, it wasn't that easy.

Cocking his head slightly, he stared Roan down. He did not want to go into what was going on between him and Teague. Especially not with so many people looking at him skeptically. It wasn't their business.

However, it might be now that they were worried about Teague. Although Teague wouldn't believe it, Hudson knew that every damn person standing there thought of him as family.

Sure, Hudson understood why they wanted to know. Only, he didn't feel like sharing what was going on between them, so instead, Hudson grabbed his phone and quickly tapped out a text to Teague.

Where are you?

Speechless

After the text went, Hudson put his phone back in his pocket and turned his attention to Roan, using his hands to speak: *Where did he go?*

Roan shrugged. "He didn't say. But he was pissed. More so than I've ever seen him."

AJ stepped up. "Does he have any family? Maybe he went there."

Cam shook his head. "Not that we know of."

"Did he put an emergency contact down on his application when you hired him?" AJ inquired.

Cam grinned. "Yeah. 9-1-1."

That figured.

"Well, that doesn't help." AJ looked as confused as Hudson felt.

He had no clue how they were going to find Teague. They could scour the bars, but hell, he could be anywhere.

His phone vibrated in his pocket. He yanked it out.

Pulling up the message, he shook his head. Teague sent two pictures. One of a bottle of Crown, the other of him flipping Hudson off.

Roan glanced over and Hudson showed him the screen. No sense in hiding it now. They had to find Teague before he did something stupid.

More importantly, Hudson had to find Teague because, oddly enough, he felt responsible for Teague going off like this. Add to that the fact that he believed Teague was suffering from depression of some sort, and it brought back horrible memories for him.

Memories he didn't want to have to live through again.

Thirty-Four

TEAGUE WAS DEFINITELY feeling no pain.

Over the course of two hours, he had downed the entire bottle of whiskey, which was a feat in and of itself. Then again, once he'd gotten started, he hadn't been able to stop. The numbness had embraced him. And now he was working on another bottle, sitting on the pier staring down at the black liquid abyss before him. His feet were dangling in the water, but he had yet to jump in, although he was seriously contemplating it. Something was holding him back, but he didn't know what, nor was he giving it much thought.

He was at the lake, although he didn't know where he was exactly, but he wasn't at the marina. He knew better—even in his inebriated state—than to go there. For the past two hours, his phone had buzzed endlessly with text after text, people wanting to know where he was and if he was okay.

Screw them.

They didn't give a shit about him. No one did.

It took him getting pissed off before anyone even acknowledged he was alive.

That was how the cards had been dealt for him.

The only person he'd had in his life had killed herself, purposely leaving him all alone, and that was how it was meant to be.

Speechless

"Bitch," he mumbled aloud, although simply thinking about his mother made his chest ache. He didn't remember anything about her, so missing her seemed stupid, yet he did. He briefly wondered whether or not he'd ever get to see her again.

His lips were numb and it felt fucking fantastic.

Teague thought about Hudson and how easily he had explained his mother taking her own life. The guy was a fucking moron. No one could sit there and tell him that shit was due to some fucked-up illness. His mother had been selfish, just like Hudson's. They weren't thinking about anyone else when they'd offed themselves. Otherwise, they would still fucking be here.

At least that was what he believed. He didn't give a shit if Hudson claimed it was some mental problem that had caused it.

Seriously. He knew because he felt the same damn way right this minute.

Teague was only thinking about himself as he sat here and contemplated slipping into the warm water and ending it all. If he drank enough, that'd be doable, no doubt. As it was, he couldn't walk because he couldn't feel his legs. It was a wonder he could even lift the bottle to his lips anymore. Swimming would be damn near impossible.

That was the plan.

And that was selfish.

But it made him feel better. Knowing that tomorrow he wouldn't have to wake up and feel the ache of loneliness deep inside... Yep, selfish.

"Depression. Pfft." That was bullshit, too. One of his counselors in high school had tried to tell him he suffered from depression—major depression or some shit—and that was likely compounded by post-traumatic stress disorder due to the fact that he'd found his mother's cold, lifeless body.

Seriously.

Fucking.

Bullshit.

It was all bullshit.

He stared into the dark water.

What would happen if he slipped into it and allowed it to swallow him up? Would anyone grieve for him? Would they go to his funeral? Would there *be* a funeral? Or would he merely be put in a box and tossed in the ground? After all, no one would be there to take care of that shit. Would anyone shed a tear that he was gone?

"Nope." That answer was easy.

No one would fucking care.

Well, maybe Cam, Roan, and Dare. Maybe. Although he doubted they'd think about it for long. They were too busy with their own lives to give two shits about him. Hell, if Roan hadn't been at the office, no one would've known where Teague was or what he was doing. No one.

Not until Monday morning when he didn't show up for work.

Even then, he doubted anyone would give it a second thought until maybe Tuesday.

Bullshit.

Teague inched closer to the edge of the wooden pier, slipping his feet farther into the water. It was warm and soothing. It'd probably feel good to slide all the way in and sit on the bottom. He'd be free of all the pain, the anger, the ... bullshit.

Free from all of it.

Grabbing the bottle, he took another long swig, then another before tossing the bottle into the water.

He sat there for a few minutes, staring up at the sky. His arms were heavy, his head, too. He was so tired. Mentally, physically, emotionally...

Speechless

He didn't want to do this anymore. Didn't want to deal with the sadness, the anger, the … pain. He wanted to feel nothing.

He was done.

"Fuck. This. Shit!" he screamed into the night. Then he lowered his voice to a whisper, "Good-bye, world. Not that anyone gives a fuck."

And with that parting shot, Teague gave himself over to what would become his liquid grave.

HUDSON WAS RUNNING full out when he heard someone yell. He didn't know who it was or what they'd said, but he put on another burst of speed. It was a long way to the water from where he had parked his truck at the curb.

He could hear AJ behind him, but he wasn't waiting for his brother. He'd been out driving around this part of the lake for the past hour, while the others had split up in search of Teague. Gannon had taken on the task of going into Austin to meet Milly, who had offered to start searching downtown clubs. Everyone else went looking in every nook locally to see if anyone had seen the kid. They knew he had to be somewhere.

Thankfully, Cam had asked his father for help—a former police officer—and Mr. Strickland had reached out to a couple of his old cop buddies, asking that they give him a heads-up if someone reported Teague somewhere.

And they had.

The call had come in from an elderly woman about ten minutes ago about a blond guy sitting down on her private pier. The woman hadn't attempted to confront Teague, but Hudson knew it was him. Considering the bottle of alcohol he'd texted a picture of, Hudson also knew that this wouldn't be good.

And that was the reason he was running past the woman's house, through her backyard, and down to the water. His legs were screaming, his chest burning. He was out of breath when he reached the pier, realizing Teague wasn't there.

Fuck.

There was a ripple in the water not far from the end of the pier, which meant…

No.

Fuck no.

Tossing his cell phone to the ground behind him, Hudson sucked air into his lungs and took the plunge. The water was inky black and he couldn't see a damn thing. Using his hands and feet, he flailed around, searching blindly. Time seemed to stand completely still. He swam a few inches to his left. Nothing. A few inches to the right. He propelled himself deeper into the water, still flailing his arms, hoping like hell he felt Teague's body.

Son of a bitch.

Where was he?

He moved farther away from the bank, reaching, searching. His hand brushed something and he grasped for it. It was cloth. Grabbing hold, he pulled it toward himself, but it didn't move easily.

Oh, fuck.

Teague.

What have you done?

Speechless

Hudson had to use all his strength to move Teague's lifeless body. His lungs burned from lack of oxygen, and his heart slammed against his ribs as he wrapped his arms around Teague and kicked toward the surface. The water wasn't deep where he was, so it didn't take long. Thankfully, by the time he broke the surface, AJ was kneeling there, waiting for him.

AJ managed to drag Teague up onto the pier while Hudson hefted himself out of the water.

Everything seemed to be moving in slow motion as he watched Teague's motionless body lying there, the moon providing just enough light to see him. He was pale, his eyes closed, mouth slightly open.

AJ put two fingers against Teague's neck, looked at Hudson, and nodded. "Fuck. I don't know CPR," AJ said frantically.

No, but Hudson did.

He knelt beside Teague, leaned down to listen to whether or not Teague was breathing. As he suspected, he wasn't. Hudson then clasped one hand in the other, situated them on Teague's chest appropriately, and began chest compressions.

"Yes, we need an ambulance," AJ said frantically, obviously talking into his phone.

Hudson tuned him out, focusing on Teague.

Come on, damn it.

This could not be happening. Why the fuck had he left Teague alone? He should've been there, should've stayed and tried to work it out with him. Should've talked to him like AJ said.

While he leaned down and breathed oxygen into Teague's airway, a slideshow ran through his brain … all the times they'd spent together over the past month. Teague's smile, his laugh.

Fuck.

Don't you fucking leave me, Teague.

If he could've shouted it to the world, he would have.

I'm not gonna lose you now, goddammit. We've come too damn far.

Hudson resumed chest compressions, but now he was starting to panic. Teague still wasn't breathing. There was no telling how long he'd been down there, but it couldn't have been too long based on the ripple in the water. At least that was what he was telling himself.

Motherfucker. Don't you leave me, Teague. God, don't fucking leave me. I can't lose you, too.

As though he heard him, Teague gasped for air, coughing up water, and Hudson felt the relief all the way to his toes. He pushed him over onto his side as Teague vomited up more water. The next thing Hudson knew, the EMTs were there, taking over, pushing Hudson out of the way. He gave them room to work, his heart slamming against his ribs.

Cam, Roan, Dare, and Noah all arrived as they were loading Teague into the ambulance. Cam was on the phone with Gannon, telling him to come back.

Hudson was shaking. He was soaking wet, but it was August, so the tremors racing through him had nothing to do with the temperature and everything to do with the fear that still trickled through his system. What if he'd been a few minutes later? Teague would've drowned. He would've been … gone.

Hudson couldn't bear the thought of that. His life without Teague…

More pain constricted his chest.

He turned to Cam and Dare, the two people who knew Teague better than anyone else. Using his hands, he said what he felt needed to be said.

Speechless

He needs help. Hudson nodded toward the water. *Professional help. He tried to kill himself. I don't know about you, but I am not willing to lose him.*

"I agree," Cam said softly, his eyes searching Hudson's face.

Hudson didn't care if Cam saw the emotion. He couldn't hide it. He didn't want to hide it.

"Think he'll listen?" Dare chimed in.

"Don't think he'll have much of a choice," Roan added somberly.

Hudson signed: *I'm going home to change, then I'm going to the hospital.*

"We'll meet you there and we'll talk more about this then. But I think we're all on the same page. He tried to take his own life. Next time, we might not be there to save him."

Hudson didn't even want to think about that. As it was, his heart was fractured from the pain he felt. The pain he knew Teague was feeling.

Despite what anyone thought, Hudson fully believed that suicide was a last resort. He didn't think his mother would've taken her own life if she hadn't felt as though it was her only option.

Hudson didn't want that to be Teague's only option.

Thirty-Five

Sunday, August 14th

TEAGUE FELT LIKE dog shit.

Not only had he almost died, but now he had the mother of all hangovers.

Somehow he'd managed to sleep most of the night, likely the effects of the alcohol. They'd kept him in the hospital for observation from the near-drowning, as they called it. And now, the sun was up, and he'd been sitting in the hospital bed for the past few hours staring at the wall. Thankfully, most of the alcohol was flushed out of his system thanks to a hell of a lot of vomiting and the stupid IV in his arm. He was dehydrated, they'd said.

He'd specifically told the nurse that he didn't want anyone to visit, although he didn't suspect anyone would. It made him feel better to think he was keeping them out, not them ignoring him altogether. Knowing Cam, he was probably super-pissed right about now. Teague didn't need anyone telling him he was stupid or that he should've come to them. Blah, blah, fucking blah. He damn sure didn't need a lecture.

Speechless

Why the fuck had Hudson pulled him out of the goddamn lake, anyway? If he had left him alone the way he wanted, Teague wouldn't be dealing with this shit right now.

He didn't remember a hell of a lot about last night, but he remembered Hudson's hands on his face when Teague had come to. He remembered vomiting his guts up while Hudson hovered over him. Teague had been so damn angry at the time. Hudson had ruined everything.

A knock sounded on the glass door of the tiny room he was in a second before it slid open and a nurse walked in.

"Can I get some aspirin?" he asked as soon as she cleared the doorway. His head was pounding.

"I'm sure I can come up with something," she replied kindly.

"When can I leave?"

The frown on her face told him he was not going to like the answer. "The doctor has opted to keep you for a little while."

"What's a little while?" It was obvious she was being vague.

"Seventy-two hours."

"Why?"

"For observation."

Yeah, that was bullshit.

The only thing that kept Teague from launching up out of the bed was Hudson appearing in the doorway.

"I don't want to talk to you," Teague blurted, glaring at the big man who filled the entrance to the room.

Hudson signed: *Too bad. I need to talk to you.*

Teague hated that he was willing to give in, but he knew he wouldn't be getting out of here if he was belligerent. He'd seen enough TV shows to know that. So when the nurse turned her attention on him, Teague nodded, staring down at the blanket covering his legs.

290

The nurse left them alone, and Hudson closed the door behind her, then came to stand at the end of the bed. Teague hesitantly looked up.

Where is your phone?

"Probably on the bottom of the lake." He had no idea where any of his stuff was. When he'd come to, he was wearing a stupid hospital gown and all of his shit was gone.

Hudson typed something out on his phone, but Teague had no idea what.

A minute later, that question was answered because Dare appeared at the door, then stepped into the room to join them.

"Hey," Dare greeted softly. "You doin' all right?"

Teague gave him a *what do you think* look. He had a blinding headache, and they were keeping him against his will, so no, he wasn't fucking all right.

Hudson signed again, but this time, Teague didn't pay any attention. He leaned his head back against the pillow and stared at the ceiling.

"Hudson wants me to translate for him," Dare announced.

"Whatever." Teague didn't bother to look at either of them.

"We want you to get some help. Psychiatric help, Teague."

"I don't need help."

Dare huffed. "I think you and I both know that's bullshit, and that's not Hudson talking." His voice lowered. "You tried to kill yourself."

Yeah, well. If he'd succeeded, he wouldn't be here listening to this shit.

"We care about you, Teague. We want you to get some help."

Speechless

"Well, they're keeping me for three days, so looks like you get your wish."

"That's not the help we mean. Three days isn't nearly enough."

Teague closed his eyes. "Are you going to fire me?"

"Of course not," Dare snapped.

"Then I think I'll be fine. I just need to get back to work."

"No."

Lifting his head, he glanced at Dare. The finality in that one word told him that it wouldn't be that easy. "Why the hell not?"

"Because we're not willing to sit back and watch you hurt like this. We can't go through this again." Dare cleared his throat. "I got this. You might not believe this, but we care about you. You're a hell of a lot more than a damn employee, Teague. You're fucking family. And we're not willing to lose you. You're hurting and you don't have to."

Teague realized Hudson was no longer signing and Dare wasn't repeating what Hudson wanted him to. He was speaking what was on his mind. Looking at Dare once more, Teague said, "Can I borrow your phone? That way I can talk to Hudson and then he can be on his way."

Without question, Dare tossed his phone over, then stepped out of the room. He didn't look happy, but he'd said what he'd needed to say. Teague didn't need a lecture.

A text came in immediately.

I want you to get help, Teague. You don't have to suffer like this.

"Oh, so now you're gonna tell me I'm mentally ill? Is that it?" He should've known Hudson would feed him that bullshit. "I'm fine. I lived, didn't I?"

This time.

Teague didn't bother responding. Hudson had a point.

Have you ever attempted suicide before?

Teague shook his head, staring down at his legs. Admittedly, he was embarrassed by what he'd done. He'd always thought he was stronger than that. He'd *thought* about taking his own life, sure, but it'd never gotten that far. He wanted to be better than his mother.

The phone buzzed.

Where are your parents?

He glared up at Hudson after reading the text. "That's none of your business."

Hudson signed: *It is now.*

Teague's teeth clamped together as anger surged inside him. "My mother killed herself, is that what you want to hear?" The words flew out of his mouth before he even thought about what he was saying. "I was three years old. I don't remember her, but she killed herself and left me all alone. I don't have any other family. None. So now you can tell me all about how mental illness made her kill herself while her three-year-old son was in the next room, right?"

Hudson took a step closer, and Teague continued to glare at him.

You have me.

Okay, that's not what he thought he'd say.

Teague snorted. "Do I? Is that why you abandoned me? Is that why you ran off?"

Hudson's eyes narrowed. *I was trying to give you space.*

"Yeah, right."

Hudson started in on his phone again.

You said you didn't want anyone to know. I thought by staying with my brother, you'd get some time to think things through.

Speechless

"What does that even mean?" Was he supposed to change his mind because Hudson had sent him that text? Or did Hudson want Teague to end this between them?

I thought you would realize that what we have is more than sex. I don't want this to only be about sex anymore, Teague. I want more. I want all of you.

Teague was floored. He stared open-mouthed at the phone, rereading the message over and over again. He was still staring when another text came through.

Roan knows of a good psychiatric hospital that we can get you into. They can get you the treatment you need.

"Get me into? What? Like you want me to *stay* there? No fucking way."

They have outpatient care, but you would have to do everything they say.

Teague frowned. "And you trust me to do that?" That didn't sound like Hudson. Or anyone he knew, for that matter.

We'll all be with you. So, yes, I trust you. We knew you wouldn't want to be holed up in the hospital, so we checked into outpatient treatment. It involves intensive counseling and there will be medication. But I'll be right there beside you. I'm not walking away from you. I'm all in at this point, Teague. All in.

Was that Hudson's way of saying … he loved him? Could that really be true?

"And you think they can fix me?" For the first time in a long time, Teague felt hopeful. He'd been dealing with this for most of his life. He was smart enough to know something was wrong, but he didn't know what. But if there was—

Depression isn't curable. But it is treatable. They'll have to diagnose you, Teague. At that point, they can figure out a way to treat it. Medication will help.

Well, that wasn't what he wanted to hear. Fuck.

"Why do you even care?" Teague blurted. "That's the one thing I really don't get. Why the fuck do you care?"

HUDSON HADN'T FIGURED Teague would be willing to be admitted to a hospital, but he was hopeful that Teague was going to agree to outpatient therapy. Or he had been right up until Teague had asked that question. He debated on how to answer it, but he opted to go for the truth.

He wasn't going to say it in text, though, so he put his phone down and signed: *Because I care about you.*

Teague snorted. "Right. You care about *fucking* me."

Okay, enough of this shit.

Hudson picked up his phone and shoved it in his pocket and moved closer to the bed. He sat on the edge of the thin mattress next to Teague. Cupping Teague's face, he stared into Teague's eyes. Emotion swamped him, consumed him from the inside out.

He'd been a mess ever since he'd pulled Teague out of the lake. His hands still shook as he held Teague's head. There was no way Teague didn't feel that.

While Teague was being treated, Hudson had been sitting alone in the waiting room, keeping his distance from the others because he needed time to pull himself together. After going home and showering off the lake water—he might've actually cried for a solid ten minutes on top of that—he had raced to the hospital only to find out that no one was being allowed to see Teague. The only thing he'd wanted was to be with him.

Speechless

That was hours ago. They'd all stayed in the waiting room overnight, waiting until they could get in to see him. He doubted Teague would believe him, but everyone, including Milly, AJ, Keith, Holly, and even Mr. Strickland, was still out there. He doubted they were going to leave until some decisions were made about what Teague would do when he left here.

There were a lot of people who cared about Teague, even if the kid was too stubborn to believe it.

However, Hudson loved him. Not only did he care about his well-being, he loved him. Heart, body, and soul. He wasn't sure he could live without Teague, and he didn't want to imagine a world without him in it.

Admittedly, Hudson had never felt like this before. It was hard to breathe at times. The thought of losing Teague … it was more than he could bear. At first, when he had initially wondered whether or not he'd gone and fallen in love with the kid, he had talked himself out of that only to realize it was true.

He loved Teague.

Sometime during the last month and a half, he had fallen in love with Teague, and the idea of spending the rest of his life without him in this world was something Hudson couldn't comprehend.

Staring into Teague's eyes, Hudson noticed a sheen of moisture there.

He brushed his thumb over Teague's cheek again.

"I'm scared," Teague whispered.

That admission leveled him, and Hudson pulled Teague against him, cupping the back of his head while he fought the tears that formed. He couldn't imagine the pain Teague was in. The ER doctor had called in a psychiatrist to evaluate Teague because of the attempted suicide. Cam and the others had shared what they could with the doctor, knowing Teague would likely keep it all bottled up. There was no doubt he suffered from depression, but the severity was unknown. Since no one knew about his past, there was no way for them to determine anything more than that. The fact that he'd attempted to take his own life said that he was suffering significantly. They had to get him help.

Hudson kissed the side of Teague's head, holding him there for another minute before pulling back enough that he could kiss Teague's mouth. He didn't linger, but he needed him to know that he wasn't running from this and he wasn't going to allow Teague to run, either.

When he pulled back, he lowered his hands and signed: *I really do care about you.*

Again, Teague didn't look convinced, so Hudson decided to go for broke.

I love you.

Teague obviously understood what he'd said because his eyes widened as they darted up to meet Hudson's. For the longest time, Teague didn't say a word, he simply stared. Hudson wasn't sure what he wanted the kid to say, but when he opened his mouth, his hope returned.

"Will it help?" Teague asked, sounding so vulnerable, so lost. "The therapy? The medication?"

Speechless

Hudson nodded. He truly believed that it would. After his mother had taken her own life, he had devoured information on mental illness. There were entire organizations devoted to getting the information out there, making people aware, eliminating the stigma. It didn't only affect a few people. It affected millions.

And it had affected his mother. She'd been diagnosed with severe depression years before, and it had ended up killing her. Hudson would not sit back and allow that to happen to Teague.

"Okay," Teague muttered softly. "I'll do it."

The relief was overwhelming. He signed: *Sleep for a little while. I need to talk to the others. I'll be back. I won't let you do this alone.*

Teague nodded, then leaned back against the pillow, watching Hudson closely. He had no idea what was going through the kid's head, but the fact that he was willing to get help was a good sign.

Once he was out in the waiting room with the others, Hudson relayed his conversation with Teague. Well, most of it, anyway. He left out the admission of love, of course.

He saw the relief on their faces when he told them that Teague was willing to get help.

"Inpatient or outpatient?" Roan asked.

Hudson signed: *He says outpatient, but we'll let him make that decision when he gets there.*

"Agreed. They have a partial inpatient program also," Cam said. "I've already contacted them, and they'll gladly take him as a patient, either way. He'll need to be evaluated by their doctors."

Hudson nodded. He understood that.

Now, the hardest part was going to be the transition. Then the waiting.

But he knew, in the end, if it meant Teague could get some help to deal with his depression, it would be worth it.

And he would be right by Teague's side the entire time. No matter how hard things got.

Thirty-Six

Monday, August 22nd

HUDSON SAT AT his desk, staring at his laptop before pulling up the search engine and typing in the name of the place he'd seen on the brochure.

It'd been a little more than a week since Teague had admitted himself to the inpatient program at the hospital they'd suggested. Hudson had driven Teague there himself, sat with him while he talked to the administrator, and even waited while he was evaluated by one of their physicians. When they were explaining Teague's options, Hudson had sat beside him and nearly cried when Teague had reached over and taken his hand.

Honestly, he'd never been prouder of Teague than he was that day.

When the doctor had explained that his best chance for success was their inpatient program, followed by their extensive outpatient care, Teague had said he was interested. Hudson had been shocked but so fucking happy. Teague had said he was following Hudson's lead. He was all in. Another shock to Hudson's system came when Teague had requested that he get a therapist who knew sign language. When they mentioned family sessions, Teague said that he would want Hudson there and they would need to know ASL to communicate. Hudson had nearly sobbed.

Admittedly, the marina wasn't the same without Teague there, though. The workload was manageable, but Hudson spent most of his time thinking about Teague regardless of what he was doing. After Hudson had kissed Teague one last time and they had taken Teague back, Hudson had asked to talk to the doctor alone. Since the doctor didn't know sign language, he had asked his questions via text. Mostly, Hudson wanted to know what he could do to help Teague. Was there counseling that he could attend to help him understand more about what Teague was dealing with? Or would he simply be expected to adapt to Teague's mood swings and try to figure out how to help him on his own? He'd been serious when he told Teague he wasn't going to have to do this alone. Hudson was going to do whatever he possibly could.

The doctor had been happy to tell him all about how Hudson could encourage Teague to continue treatment, about giving positive reinforcement, helping to create a low-stress environment. All of the things Hudson had already read up on. When he specified about family therapy sessions, the doctor gave him some information on local organizations that would offer help to them both once Teague was back in the real world full time.

Speechless

And when Hudson got home, he did as he had always done. He looked into that information, then started searching on his own. He was willing to do whatever it took to be there for Teague, to help him to cope with what they were calling major depressive disorder. As far as he was concerned, it was no different than any other medical condition. He needed to know what to do in order to help Teague adapt to it.

Right now, the doctors were in the process of getting Teague's medication adjusted, and Hudson had been looking into that, as well. Of course there were side effects with every drug, and he felt he should know what they were. Some of that shit scared him, but he trusted the doctors would monitor him.

As it was, he was also talking to Teague every day. Because Hudson couldn't actually *talk* on the phone, the hospital had agreed that Teague would be allowed to text message for a few minutes every day. It made Hudson feel a little better. Teague didn't seem exactly happy, but he wasn't as angry as Hudson had expected him to be, either. It was an adjustment; they all knew that.

"Did you find more information?" Cam asked, drawing Hudson's attention from the computer screen.

He looked up as Cam stepped into Hudson's office.

Hudson turned the laptop so Cam could see the place he'd been looking into.

Cam's smile was wide. "Awesome. I think that's a great idea, by the way. I know how Teague is with Lulu." Cam propped himself on the edge of the desk. "I honestly had no clue that they had service animals for that type of stuff."

Hudson had been going through all the information the hospital had given him and stumbled across a place that trained dogs to be emotional support and psychiatric service support for patients who could benefit from them. He had mentioned it to Cam one afternoon when they'd been having lunch at the marina restaurant, and Cam had convinced him to go for it. Because of the price of the animals, Cam, Dare, and Roan had all three offered to go in together with Hudson to purchase one. Hudson could've and would've easily spared the expense to help Teague, but he wanted to show Teague that his friends truly cared about him.

"So, are you going to tell Teague about it?"

No. Thought I'd surprise him.

"I think that'll be a good surprise for him." Cam stood. "Let me know if you need anything else from me or if we can help in any way."

Will do.

Now, Hudson only needed to reach out to the people and get the ball rolling.

Which he was going to do right now.

Thirty-Seven

Wednesday, September 7th

HUDSON WASN'T SURE what to expect when he arrived at the hospital to attend one of Teague's counseling sessions with him. When Teague had asked, there had been absolutely no hesitation on Hudson's part. He was genuinely thrilled that Teague wanted to include him. It meant so much that the man would want Hudson by his side.

Teague had officially been in the program for twenty-five days, and things seemed to be looking up. However, Hudson still didn't know how the session would go. He wasn't sure if there was something specific Teague wanted to hash out, or if this would be more about Hudson. Whatever it was, he was ready to embrace it.

After signing in and then being taken back to the room where the counseling session would occur, Hudson sat patiently. The room wasn't anything special. The walls were a muted tan color, the carpet blue and a little worn in spots, there were a couple of high-back upholstered chairs that sat across from a tan-and-blue loveseat, along with a few framed prints on the wall, all in various shades of blue. Hudson was sensing a theme here. In one corner, a tall plant sat near a window, providing the only color other than tan or blue in the entire space.

Maybe it was supposed to be calming or something.

When Teague stepped into the room a short while later, Hudson's heart stopped momentarily.

God, he looked good.

So good.

The lines around his mouth had softened, and there wasn't as much strain around his eyes. Clearly he was feeling better. Then again, Teague had already told him he was.

"Thanks for coming," Teague said, leaning down and kissing Hudson gently on the mouth. "I can't promise how this will go, but I wanted you here."

I'm glad you invited me. I missed you.

Teague's smile was slow and genuine. "I missed you, too."

It'd been a little more than three weeks since Teague had admitted himself into the hospital. For Hudson, that sometimes felt like three years.

They weren't there long before the doctor stepped into the room.

She smiled kindly when she turned to greet him. "You must be Hudson. It's very nice to meet you. I'm Dr. Ashby."

Speechless

Dr. Angela Ashby was a short, stout woman with strawberry-blond hair and gentle, light green eyes. She looked professional but somewhat casual in her black slacks and emerald-green shirt. Not at all intimidating as he had expected.

Hudson nodded in greeting.

"So, it's my understanding that you can hear, but you can't speak, correct?"

Hudson signed. They had promised they would assign Teague a counselor who knew ASL, so he assumed she would be able to understand. *That's correct.*

"Okay, then would you prefer that I do everything verbally and you sign your answer when necessary? Or would you prefer that I sign, as well?"

You don't need to sign.

"Good. Just wanted to get that out of the way." Dr. Ashby turned to look at Teague. "You look good this morning. They told me that you've been spending some time in the gym. How are you feeling?"

Teague was leaning back on the sofa beside Hudson, one ankle crossed over the opposite knee, his hands in his lap. "Better. They finally got my meds worked out, which made a huge difference. And yes, I've been utilizing the treadmill, though I can tell you, it's really not my thing."

That made Hudson smile. He figured Teague was finding ways to pass the time.

"So, you can feel the difference from the medication adjustment, then?"

"I can, actually. I honestly didn't think they'd make a difference, but they do."

"Do you think you're ready to go home yet?"

Teague instantly shook his head. "No. Not yet." Teague surprised Hudson when he turned and looked at him. "I miss home and I miss Hudson"—he turned back to the doctor—"but I'm not willing to go home until I feel capable of dealing with everything on my own."

Hudson wanted to tell Teague that he would be there for him, but he knew what Teague meant. Although Teague had a solid support team, it was important that Teague could function on his own without needing them every minute of every day.

"I have to agree with you," Dr. Ashby noted. "I like that you're committed. I think you're doing remarkably well. Not nearly as rebellious as the beginning." She smiled. "So, we'll keep moving forward until you're ready."

Teague took a deep breath while the doctor glanced down at a yellow legal pad she held in front of her.

"I noted that you wanted Hudson to attend your next session." She looked up at Teague. "Now that he's here, what would you like to talk about?"

Hudson turned to look at Teague. He could see the lines in his mouth forming. Whatever he wanted to talk about wasn't going to be easy.

"I want to talk about my mother." Teague looked back at Dr. Ashby. "I'm not interested in telling this story over and over, so I thought it'd be best if he was here for it."

Something loosened in Hudson's chest. The fact that Teague wanted to open up—something he had avoided doing for as long as Hudson had known him—was a huge step forward.

"Okay, then. Why don't you tell us about your mother, then."

"Mind if I move around?" Teague asked.

Dr. Ashby simply motioned for him to do what he needed to do.

Speechless

Teague was up on his feet, pacing slowly across the room. Several minutes passed, and Hudson watched as Teague seemed to be gathering his thoughts. When he finally began to speak, Hudson focused solely on him.

"From what I've heard, I was three years old when my mother committed suicide. My birth certificate didn't have a father's name, and I don't have any recollection of ever meeting him. My mother had no family; her parents died when she was younger according to their death certificates. She was an only child. I found all of that out when I was a teenager. I only learned more because I looked into the details since they hadn't been shared with me.

"I was told that my mother worked for a grocery store, and her manager, a man she was intimately involved with, came to check on her a few days after she didn't show up for work. According to the police report, he said they'd had a fight and broken up a couple of days before that. I assumed she had offed herself because of him."

There was absolutely no emotion in Teague's tone. He relayed the story as though it were something he'd heard on the news.

Teague's eyes met Hudson's. "He came to check on her when she didn't show up for work on the second day. That's when they found me and her body. Since I had no one else, I was taken into foster care."

Hudson swallowed hard, never taking his eyes off Teague.

"From then on, I recall being bounced around from one family to the next. I can't say I was the easiest kid to get along with. I've been giving the world the middle finger since I was old enough to realize my mother had left me like that. I always blamed her. I always believed she selfishly took her own life because of that guy." Teague's eyes met Hudson's again. "It wasn't until you told me that your mother suffered from depression and that was why she took her own life that I thought perhaps it hadn't been a man she had killed herself over. I honestly never believed that shit was real, though."

Hudson didn't interrupt, not wanting to stop Teague from sharing. There was a hint of emotion in his voice now, and Hudson knew this wasn't easy for him to talk about.

"Anyway…" Teague looked away, continuing to pace the floor again. "I've never been close to anyone in my life, and I did that on purpose. I didn't want to be left again. I wasn't going to invite someone into my world and let them leave me. So, I kept myself distanced on purpose. Sex was a simple act. It had no emotional value. And that's the truth. I didn't use sex to get close to people."

Hudson noticed the way Teague stated that in past tense.

Teague turned to look at Hudson directly, which only made his heart pound more.

"Then you came along."

His chest swelled, and he felt a wealth of emotion consume him as Teague once again held his gaze.

"You never thought when you made that offer that I'd go and fall in love with you, did you?"

Oxygen was now scarce, and Hudson could hear his own heart pounding in his ears. Teague loved him?

Speechless

"I didn't know what I was feeling when you sent me that text. It scared the shit out of me that it affected me so much, I think. And then I panicked when you went to your brother's," Teague continued, looking right at him. "The loneliness consumed me because I let it. I'd been fighting what I felt for you, and I felt abandoned."

Hudson did sign then: *I shouldn't have left you.*

Teague shook his head. "It's not your fault. That's definitely not what I'm saying. If it wasn't then, it could've been a month from now. A year. Who knows. I've contemplated suicide before, Hudson. Nothing you did or didn't do could've pushed me that direction. I might be confused about a lot of things, but not once have I blamed you. I did it because I felt that was my only option. Now, I know that it's not. I know that these feelings I have, the constant sadness, the anger, the bleakness … there's a reason for them. And I'm learning how to cope."

I want to help you cope.

Teague smiled. "I'd definitely welcome that."

And those were quite possibly the sweetest words Hudson had ever heard.

Thirty-Eight

Monday, September 12ᵗʰ

"IS TEAGUE STILL scheduled to come home on Friday?" Roan asked as the four of them sat on the pier at the end of the day.

Although it was after Labor Day and the summer was officially coming to an end, the lake had been unusually busy today, so they'd decided to relax for a bit once the marina closed. Hudson didn't mind, because if he wasn't there, he would be in his apartment pacing the floor, wondering about Teague.

Hudson nodded. *That's the plan. When I talked to him yesterday, he said everything was still a go. He sounds so much better.*

"That's great to hear, man," Dare chimed in.

Hudson knew something was up when Dare turned to look at him more fully.

"So, what's the deal between you and Teague? Y'all serious now?"

Speechless

Hudson shook his head in disbelief. He should've known Dare would call him out like this. In fact, he was surprised it hadn't happened sooner. For the past four weeks, he'd been waiting for one of them to bust his balls about his relationship with Teague. Which was why he'd talked to Teague about whether he wanted them to know. When Teague told him he didn't care if Hudson told them, he'd been elated.

We're serious.

"Well, fuck me stupid. That's fantastic," Dare announced. "Any wedding bells in the near future?"

Cam interrupted. "Wedding bells? We're still waiting for you to announce *your* wedding date."

A round of laughter ensued.

"What? We're getting there."

"Well, I suggest you don't go pushing other people to the altar before you make that trip down the aisle."

"Fine." Dare glanced at Hudson again. "So, y'all gonna move in together?"

We're gonna take things slow.

Dare nodded as though he understood.

Hudson could've told them that he was hoping to move in with Teague. That he was scared to leave Teague alone. That he never wanted to spend another night away from him, but he didn't. He had to take this at Teague's pace. He wasn't sure how things would go when he got out on Friday. They still had another month of intensive outpatient care, which involved Teague spending several hours a week at the hospital to undergo therapy. After that, they would have to seek counseling on their own. They weren't out of the woods yet, and Hudson damn sure wasn't going to push himself on Teague.

He'd learned what happened the last time he'd tried to manipulate the situation to get what he wanted.

It had backfired in the worst possible way.

"Well, the good thing is, y'all live across the hall. Just leave the doors open and it's like you're sharing a place," Dare mused, staring out at the water.

"You seem awfully worried about Hudson and Teague all of a sudden. Something we should know about?" Roan inquired.

Dare smirked. "Unless you want to hear about all the slap and tickle Noah and I are engaging in, no, probably not."

"Spare us the details of that," Roan snorted.

"Speaking of Noah," Cam inserted. "Where is he?"

"At home. Probably waiting for me. Naked."

Hudson laughed with the others. That was Dare for you.

"What about Gannon?" Dare countered. "Where is he?"

"He's having dinner with Milly," Cam said, his tone less playful. "Something's going on with her."

Is she okay? Hudson signed.

"Yeah. She said she needed to talk, so he took her to dinner." Cam lifted an eyebrow as he focused on Hudson. "Do you know if AJ's talked to her?"

Last he'd heard from his brother, AJ had given up on trying to get in touch with Milly. They had talked briefly at the hospital when Teague had his incident, but according to AJ, it hadn't been good. He said he couldn't be that guy who spent all his time chasing after a woman who didn't want him. Rather than tell Cam all that, Hudson shook his head.

"What about you?" Dare asked Roan, clearly not finished being nosy. "How's your sister?"

Roan frowned, then looked out at the water. "I really don't want to talk about it."

"Y'all have another fight?" Cam questioned, clearly not taking the hint.

Speechless

"Yeah. Big one this time. She's gone off the deep end again."

When Roan looked back, Hudson signed: *You really need to get her admitted.*

"It's not that easy. If she's not willing to do it, they won't take her. And she's definitely not willing."

Hudson hated to hear that. From what he'd heard Roan say lately, his sister was on a downhill slide. Considering she was already at rock bottom, he knew that couldn't be good at all.

"Well," Dare announced, standing up and stretching, "I think I'm gonna head home. Got a man waiting naked for me."

Hudson shook his head again.

"I'll see y'all in the mornin', yeah?"

"We'll be here," Roan replied.

Hudson watched Dare trot off toward the parking lot. He envied the man getting to go home to Noah. It made him think of Teague. He couldn't wait for him to come home on Friday. Although he was excited, he was also terrified. He wasn't sure how this would work, and the last thing he wanted to do was make it worse. Everyone kept telling him to treat Teague the same as before, only to keep an eye open for signs of problems.

Now that he knew how bad things could get, he would certainly be doing that.

As for treating him the same…

Fuck, he hoped the kid was up for some serious fucking, because it'd been thirty-two days (yes, he'd counted) since he'd had his hands on Teague, and Hudson's balls were about to shrivel up and die.

Thirty-Nine

Friday, September 16th

"WHERE ARE WE going?" Teague asked Hudson as they were leaving the hospital.

Technically, *he* was leaving the hospital and Hudson was his ride.

And holy fuck, he was glad to be out of there. Sure, they might've helped him, and he knew he would be going back for a while, but spending every day and night in that place for weeks on end... It'd been a whole lot harder than Teague had anticipated.

Which only made today that much sweeter.

Teague had checked himself into the inpatient care program after being assessed by one of their doctors. It wasn't necessarily because he'd wanted to, but he had seen the look on his friends' faces when they'd come to see him in the emergency room, and he'd known he had to do something. He'd put them through hell, and Teague had trusted that Hudson knew what he was talking about when he'd said the doctors could help him cope with his depression.

Almost five weeks later, he would have to agree.

Not that it had been easy. Nor was he anywhere close to being done.

Speechless

Hell, it had been a nightmare in the beginning, but he had decided to go all in. The medication they'd started him on had fucked him up, and it'd taken nearly a week before they'd gotten him settled. The therapy sessions were the worst because talking about himself was not something he opted to do. Being that he could share the information confidentially, it wasn't so bad. He'd attended group therapy sessions, but he kept his mouth shut during those. They might've helped him focus and to understand what was wrong with him, but they couldn't change the fact that he didn't want to share the details of his life with complete strangers.

But it wasn't over, and they'd made sure to remind him that as his release date neared. Due to the headway he'd made, he and his doctor had decided he could progress to the intensive outpatient program. He would still be going to the hospital three days a week for four hours a day, but it was better than being there all the time.

For one, he was horny as fuck. And watching as Hudson steered the truck out of the parking lot, the muscles in his arms bulging from the movement ... well, it wasn't helping at all. He needed to get laid. And there was only one person he wanted to be with. The same guy driving the truck in the opposite direction of the marina.

"You didn't answer my question," Teague told him.

Hudson merely smirked.

Asshole.

Hudson signed: *Detour.*

Well, okay then.

Rather than ask a million questions, Teague relaxed. Or tried to. He could smell Hudson's cologne, and it was making his dick harder by the second. Although he didn't quite know where he and Hudson stood with their arrangement—or with a relationship, which they seemed to have veered into— Teague hoped like hell they could get back on course.

And soon.

They passed a huge sign with an arrow, but Teague didn't catch the name. It wouldn't have seemed important, except Hudson steered off the main road and down a winding dirt drive that dipped and swerved through a thick grouping of trees.

Hudson parked the truck in front of what appeared to be a log cabin with a huge front porch. There was a big white rocking chair on one end and a dog bed on the other. The front door was painted red and had a glass insert that was covered with what looked like blinds.

When Hudson got out of the truck, Teague had no choice but to follow. When they walked to the door, Teague noticed there was an open sign on it. Clearly a business, then.

Hudson turned the knob and pushed it open, waiting for Teague to go in first. He was leery, but he stepped inside. An older woman with gray hair pulled back in a sloppy ponytail came out from somewhere in the back, alerted by either the barking dog or the bell chiming.

"Hudson," she greeted kindly, a warm smile on her face. "So glad to see you again. And you must be Teague. My name is Tina."

Teague nodded, shaking the woman's hand when she held it out.

"We're all ready for you," Tina said kindly, peering past Teague to Hudson again.

Speechless

Hudson nudged Teague forward when the woman pivoted and walked away.

Over his shoulder, Teague muttered, "What are we doing here?"

"Teague, we'd like you to meet Charger," Tina called from around the corner.

Teague turned in time to see a yellow Labrador mix staring back at him from across a small room. The dog didn't move from where he sat, but his tail instantly started thumping on the wood floor.

"Why do I need to meet him?" Teague asked, glancing from Tina to Hudson, then back.

Tina smiled widely. "Because Hudson picked him out for you."

Okay, now he was thoroughly confused, and apparently Tina picked up on it. She glanced to Hudson and Teague noticed when he nodded.

"Charger is a trained psychiatric service dog," she explained, and it was clearly something she'd done often. "Our dogs, which are all rescues, are trained to perform highly specialized tasks for people who suffer from psychiatric illnesses such as depression and PTSD."

Okay, Teague really wasn't liking where this was headed. Hudson had out-and-out told this woman that Teague had a mental problem?

"Now before you get upset," Tina said, obviously interpreting his expression correctly, "which Hudson warned us you might do, I want you to know, he has provided me with limited details about you. We needed to know in order to accurately pair you with the right animal. But before we get too far into it, please greet Charger. He's anxious to meet you."

Hesitantly, Teague turned around and stepped into the room with the dog. Charger was sitting still, staring up at him as though waiting for a command. And okay, maybe he was cute.

"We're going to give you a few minutes," Tina called out before pulling the door shut. Evidently, she wasn't giving Teague a choice in the matter.

He turned his attention back to the dog.

"Charger, huh?"

Without an audience, it was easier for Teague to greet the dog. And it only took a few minutes for him to completely fall in love. Hudson must've known this would happen. Then again, everyone knew how Teague felt about Lulu, the marina's retriever who resided with Dare most of the time.

"So, you're gonna take care of me, huh?" Teague asked, kneeling down in front of Charger. "I guess that means I'm gonna take care of you, too? I hope you know how that's gonna work, 'cause I haven't done this before."

He had never had an animal of his own. Oddly enough, he liked the idea of having someone with him all the time even if it was a four-legged someone. Then it dawned on him that was the reason Hudson had done this. So Teague wouldn't have to be alone.

A smile tugged at the corners of his mouth and he couldn't fight it.

He knew the guy was a great big softy underneath all that sexy dominance.

"What d'ya say, Charger? You wanna hang with me?"

Charger licked Teague's face and something loosened in his chest. He wasn't sure what it was—if anything—but he felt a little less anxious than when he'd left the hospital a short while ago.

But he couldn't help but think that Hudson had done this for him.

Speechless

Hudson.

Big, bad, sexy, tattooed Hudson Ballard.

The man Teague had evidently gone and fallen in love with.

It was clear Hudson cared.

Teague wasn't sure what to think about that. He'd never had someone want to take care of him like this. Sure, he'd had foster parents who had graciously offered up their homes. They'd been generous, but he'd seen it differently. But now, his eyes were wide open.

And he knew that this sort of kindness came from love.

Hudson loved him.

Sometimes, even after all he'd been through, that was still hard to wrap his head around. But he was certainly trying.

HUDSON HADN'T KNOWN what to expect when he brought Teague here. He had talked to Cam, Dare, and Roan, and they'd all tried to come up with the best way for this to play out. Since nothing they'd come up with sounded easy, Hudson had opted for his original plan. He would surprise Teague by bringing him to meet Charger straight from the hospital.

Thankfully, it had worked out in his favor, and almost forty-five minutes later, after Tina had reviewed with Teague all of the commands that Charger knew, and after receiving all the paperwork on the service animal that they'd purchased to help Teague, they were piling in his truck and heading back to the marina. Charger had followed every single one of Teague's instructions, including getting into the backseat of the truck, where he would be safe for the ride home.

"I'm not sure if I should be mad or happy right now," Teague said when they pulled out on the main road. Hudson noticed that Teague continuously glanced into the backseat to ensure Charger was good. "It's uncool that you told someone about my problems, but I think I understand why."

In the past few weeks, Teague had made tremendous progress. The doctor had diagnosed him with major depressive disorder, and the team of clinicians and psychiatrists had worked to develop a treatment plan. Strangely, Teague had seemed committed to the program the entire way through. Not that that was a bad thing, it was simply unexpected, but Hudson knew that Teague was often extremely unpredictable.

Like now.

He was rattling on, which was very unlike him.

However, Hudson knew that the animal would be a good idea. After he'd contacted the place, they had put him in touch with some of their other clients. He had then had Cam contact them to seek input on how well the animals were working out for each of them. They'd received nothing but positive feedback, which confirmed they were making the right decision. On top of that, Hudson had brought it up with Teague's psychiatrist at the hospital, and she had agreed that service dogs were being used to help with mental illness. And in Teague's case, the fact that being alone was the hardest part for him … well, it definitely made sense.

Speechless

The place Hudson had contacted would've preferred that Teague be there in person to interact with Charger during the training process, but Hudson had explained that it was impossible and he didn't want to wait to bring Charger home. Or rather for Teague to bring him home.

Although Hudson wasn't sure how that was going to work at the moment.

The mere thought of leaving Teague alone by himself … it didn't sit well, although the kid had clearly made some progress.

The thing about depression, it wasn't curable. Even with the medication, there would still be times when Teague would be down. Hudson had to learn to cope with that and to help Teague through it without being overbearing or freaking out. He understood that. Didn't mean he knew how it would play out.

"So, think you might fuck me when we get back to your place?"

Hudson's head snapped over to Teague and he saw the kid smirking.

He turned his attention back to the road and tried to think of the fastest way home.

As excited as he'd been to bring Teague to meet Charger, he was certainly more excited about the prospect of sinking inside Teague's body again. It had been a little over five weeks now, and his dick still remembered the feeling, his body still craved Teague's closeness.

"I take the fact that your foot's practically on the floor to mean that's a yes." Teague chuckled. "We could always pull off somewhere."

Hudson shook his head in disbelief. That wasn't a bad idea, but he needed a hell of a lot more room than the front seat of his truck. All the pent up sexual energy needed more than this small space could offer.

And if he was lucky, they wouldn't leave the apartment until they had to be at work on Monday morning.

Forty

TEAGUE FELT LIKE a circus act. The kind where everyone was staring, trying to figure out what was going on and what would happen next.

Christ.

He wasn't broken, so he didn't know why everyone was looking at him as though he might shatter into dust and blow away on a stiff breeze.

Okay, sure, this was a conversation he'd had with his therapist. He'd been expecting this, so he wasn't totally caught off guard. He was merely frustrated that Cam, Dare, and Roan were treating him with kid gloves.

The only person who didn't seem to be was Hudson, but he was being a little distant. Hopefully, they'd change that as soon as they made it up to their apartments. He had honestly hoped they'd have been there by now, but they had detoured into the main office when Cam had come out to greet them in the parking lot. Everyone, including Lulu, was officially introduced to Charger.

"What d'ya think of Charger?" Dare asked, bending down to pet the dog currently sitting at Teague's feet.

"He's great," Teague said fondly. He was enjoying having Charger, and they'd only known each other a short time. Having a pet would be an adjustment, but Teague welcomed it. He was looking forward to spending time with Charger just as soon as he got to spend a little time with Hudson.

"Hudson knew you'd like him," Dare noted, looking up at Teague.

Yeah, well, Hudson knew Teague pretty well.

Why don't we let Teague settle back in for a bit?

Teague loved that idea and he was glad Hudson suggested it.

"Absolutely. We're probably gonna head out in a few. No appointments for the afternoon, so we're gonna shut it down early," Cam explained.

Good to know. It meant that Teague and Hudson could be as loud as they wanted to be.

The thought made him smile.

"Come on, Charger," Teague called to his dog. "Let's go check out your new digs."

Waving off his friends, Teague made a beeline out the door and around the side of the building to the stairs that led to the second floor. Once he made it past the outside door, he felt a little more relaxed. Even more so when he stepped into his apartment.

When he opened the door, he gave the okay for Charger to go inside, but the dog remained right beside him. This was going to be interesting.

"Relax," Teague told Charger, and instantly, he was at ease. He honestly hadn't expected it to be that easy.

Speechless

For a moment, Teague took it all in while Charger sniffed from one corner to the next. It looked the same as it had when he'd left, minus the glass shattered on the floor. Someone had cleaned that up, and if he had to guess, Hudson had done so. On the floor in the kitchen was a small metal bowl with water in it and another with dog food.

Teague turned to look at Hudson, who was standing in the doorway, leaning against the jamb.

"You thought of everything, huh?"

Hudson's hands came up. *I thought of little else except you.*

Teague felt the words all the way to his soul. For the past thirty-four days, Teague had thought about Hudson. When he was in therapy, he'd thought of Hudson. When he was eating any of his meals, he'd thought of Hudson. When he'd lain down to go to sleep at night, he'd thought of Hudson. There hadn't been a single day that had gone by when he hadn't thought about Hudson.

And now the man was right there, close enough for him to touch.

Teague backed up a step and leaned against the couch, crossing his arms over his chest. "Remember what you told me when I was in the emergency room?"

Hudson nodded, as though he knew exactly what Teague was referring to. Maybe he did.

"Is it still true?" He felt incredibly vulnerable asking that question, but he couldn't help himself.

Watching Hudson closely, Teague didn't move when Hudson pushed off the wall and stepped toward him, stopping less than a foot away. Warm hands embraced his face as Hudson tilted Teague's head up so that he was looking him in the eye.

Hudson nodded, dropping his hands. *It's definitely still true. Now more than ever.*

"Tell me again," Teague pleaded, meeting Hudson's eyes once more before glancing back at Hudson's hands.

I love you.

Unable to stop himself, Teague lunged for Hudson, throwing his arms around him and pulling Hudson's head down so that he could meet his mouth.

A light whimper sounded from closer to the floor, forcing them both apart. Teague couldn't help but laugh. Charger was sitting there, staring up at them. Glancing over at the couch, he then looked back at Charger.

"Sit," Teague said, patting the couch.

Charger bounded up onto it.

"Lay," he ordered softly.

Charger dropped to his belly.

"Stay."

This time Charger lowered his head to the cushion, seemingly satisfied with his new bed.

"Where were we?" Teague asked, turning back to Hudson, who was now grinning from ear to ear.

Without hesitation, Hudson pulled Teague to him roughly and kissed him. The warmth of Hudson's lips felt better than anything he'd ever known. The strength in Hudson's arms when they wrapped around him grounded Teague, made him believe that everything might be okay.

He knew he had fucked up. Trying to take his own life had been stupid. At the time, he'd thought he had no other choice. Except he knew better because he had Hudson. Hudson had been there for him day and night for weeks on end, and Teague had never accepted what was really going on between them. Neither of them were good at communicating—something he'd learned thanks to all the damn counseling sessions—but they would have to work on that.

Speechless

"I love you, too," Teague whispered against Hudson's lips. "God, I've never said those words to anyone. I thought it'd feel weird to say them, but…" Teague pressed his lips to Hudson's once more, allowing Hudson to thrust his tongue into Teague's mouth.

The kiss reminded him of everything he'd nearly given up. Sure, he knew there was a long road ahead of them, but they could make this work. Teague was finally open to the idea of something more than sex. He'd never thought he'd get to that point, but he had to admit, he'd been there before things had gone south. He'd simply been too stubborn to admit it.

"I want to feel you, Hudson. I want to feel you inside me."

Hudson pulled back, his breaths rushing in and out of his lungs as he stared at Teague. The desire flashed in those brilliant emerald eyes, and Teague knew Hudson wanted him, too.

It was all still there. Everything had changed, yet in many ways, nothing had changed. And for that, he was thankful.

Then again, he'd be even more thankful if Hudson would lose the damn clothes.

HEARING THOSE WORDS from Teague's mouth … Hudson's knees nearly gave out on him.

All morning, he'd been mentally rehearsing how this day would go. He hadn't been sure what to expect from Teague. They'd shared texts for the past five weeks, and Hudson had attended the one counseling session, but other than that, Hudson hadn't seen him. The moment he'd set eyes on Teague at the hospital, he'd felt the air rush out of his lungs. The kid looked so damn good. Healthy. Strong.

And if Hudson had been worried about how to handle him, he'd been reassured when he saw the way Cam, Dare, and Roan had made Teague uncomfortable. Admittedly, Hudson had seen the way they'd treated Teague. As though he were fragile, as though he might break.

Teague Carter was anything but fragile. He was strong. He was a fighter.

And he was his.

Unable to refrain any longer, Hudson jerked Teague against him roughly, grabbing for the hem of Teague's shirt. In a fumble of arms, they managed to strip down to bare skin before Teague—yes, *Teague*—led Hudson toward his bed.

Hudson pretended it didn't have any significance that they were about to make love right there in the one place Teague had never wanted to be. It actually meant everything in the world to Hudson, but he knew Teague wouldn't appreciate having it called out.

Instead, he wrapped one arm around Teague's back, then lowered him down to the bed, crawling over him, their mouths fused together, tongues thrusting, searching, desperate for more.

"Oh, God, I've missed you," Teague moaned into his mouth.

Speechless

Hudson ground his hips forward, sliding his rock-hard dick against Teague's. He needed to feel the sweet suction of his mouth on him. It felt like an eternity had passed since the last time Hudson had felt like this. So overwhelmed by everything. He was on sensory overload and he craved more.

When Hudson pulled back, Teague lay back on the bed, staring up at him with so much heat glittering in his eyes it was mesmerizing. Working his way up Teague's body, Hudson kneeled over Teague's chest, his legs holding Teague's arms down by his sides.

"Glad to see I'm not the only one who's eager."

Hudson smirked. He grabbed a pillow and tucked it beneath Teague's head, bringing that sexy fucking mouth closer to his dick.

"Let me feel you in my mouth," Teague groaned as Hudson brushed the head of his cock against Teague's smooth lips.

Teague opened his mouth, and Hudson tucked the head just inside, the gentle swipe of Teague's tongue making the hair on his arms stand on end. The pleasure was intense. Vibrations shot through his shaft when Teague closed his lips around him and hummed.

Nice and slow, Hudson signed.

Teague winked, then took more of Hudson in his mouth. Hudson couldn't look away, loving the sight of Teague beneath him, sucking, licking, taking as much of him as he could. Hudson could've done this all day, except he wanted to give pleasure to Teague, as well. After a few minutes, he managed to scoot back down Teague's body, lying on top of him, feasting on Teague's mouth once more. He lingered there for long minutes before trailing his lips over Teague's skin. He started with his jaw, then worked his way down his neck, his collarbone, then lower. Hudson paused to torment Teague's nipples, using his lips and his teeth, drawing those sexy moans from him.

While he worshipped Teague's body with his mouth, Teague's hands roamed over Hudson's head, his shoulders, his back. He never tried to hold Hudson in place, but the touching was enough. He loved the way the kid's hands felt on him.

When Hudson made his way past Teague's stomach, he settled between his legs, pushing them wider, forcing his knees back so that he could work him the way he knew Teague needed.

"You know if you put my dick in your mouth, I'm gonna come." It wasn't a warning, simply a statement.

The way Teague's cock pulsed as Hudson brushed his lips down the length told him Teague was serious. Wanting to draw this out as much as possible, Hudson didn't take Teague's dick in his mouth. He nipped the inside of Teague's thighs, brushed his nose against Teague's balls, slid his tongue along the sensitive spot beneath, making Teague buck and moan some more.

"Hudson... Oh, God, yes... I'm not gonna last... Fuck... That feels so damn good... It's been too long."

Speechless

Torn between wanting to be inside Teague and simply wanting to make him come apart, Hudson opted for the latter. For now. He would give Teague whatever he needed, whenever he needed it. And right now, it was evident the man needed to come.

Rising up, Hudson planted his hands on each side of Teague's hips, then lowered his mouth over Teague's cock. He sucked him inside, taking him to the back of his throat. Another breathy moan tore from Teague, which spurred Hudson on. He bobbed up and down, working Teague's dick with his mouth. He didn't stop until Teague was panting, begging, practically pleading for Hudson to send him over. When Teague began bucking his hips, Hudson held still, allowing Teague to fuck his mouth from beneath.

"Oh, fuck … oh, fuck … oh, fuck… Yes! That's it! Almost… Suck me, Hudson. Suck hard." Teague took a breath as his back bowed. "Fuck! Fuck!"

Hudson sucked and swallowed as Teague came, watching the way Teague's fingers curled around Hudson's wrists, holding on to him as he splintered into pieces.

It was so goddamn beautiful … Hudson could hardly contain the emotion churning inside him. Although they'd done plenty of things since the beginning of this arrangement, not once had Teague been so invested. The little touches, the way he looked at Hudson … it was more than he expected.

And he fully intended to do more…

Just as soon as they both caught their breath.

Forty-One

BEST BLOW JOB in the history of blow jobs.

Teague pulled Hudson closer as he tried to draw air into his lungs. He wasn't sure he'd ever come that hard before. Then again, it'd been more than a month since he'd had Hudson's mouth on him; maybe he was simply overwhelmed.

Whatever it was, he damn sure hoped they did that again in the near future.

Like, really near future.

Like, now.

When Hudson relaxed onto his back, Teague got up and straddled Hudson's hips, smiling down at him.

Hudson's hands started moving. *What are you thinking about?*

"Wouldn't you like to know?" Teague chuckled, then leaned over and grabbed the bottle of lubricant sitting behind his alarm clock.

With that in hand, he scooted backward, moving down Hudson's legs until his giant cock was in view. The man's dick was a work of art. So long, so thick … so hard that the veins bulged beneath the silky-smooth skin. A masterpiece that Teague wanted to worship for hours on end.

"I wasn't lying when I said I missed you," Teague told him, meeting Hudson's gaze briefly, "but I think I might've missed this guy more."

Speechless

Hudson put his hands behind his head, the muscles in his chest flexing beautifully as he did.

Teague got comfortable, sitting on Hudson's shins while he pumped the lubricant into his hand. He watched Hudson's face as he reached out and wrapped his fist around Hudson's thick cock, stroking up and down slowly, making the skin glisten from the lube. Hudson's stomach muscles contracted—which was so damn sexy—as he squirmed beneath Teague's touch.

Hudson pulled his hands from behind his head long enough to sign: *Keep that up and you won't be getting fucked.*

Teague chuckled, but he didn't stop.

Hudson got comfortable again as he continued to watch. Teague was glad that this wasn't awkward between them. He hadn't been sure how things would play out when he got back home. He'd hashed it out a million times in his head, wondering if Hudson would be scared to touch him, to do all the wicked things he'd done to him before. He was damn glad that wasn't the case.

For the most part, Teague didn't feel any different aside from the fact that there seemed to be less chaos in his head. He wanted more than anything to be normal, and he intended to be—he merely had to figure out what normal was for him, which would probably take some time.

But this was certainly helping.

Hudson's head tipped back, the strong column of his neck stretching as he swallowed hard. Teague continued to stroke him, driving him higher and higher. He slowed his movements until Hudson relaxed once more. Then he grabbed the bottle of lube and added a generous amount to his hand, slathering it on Hudson's dick before moving into position.

Straddling Hudson's hips once more, Teague reached around behind him and guided Hudson's cock against his hole. He took a breath and eased down, forcing the blunt head inside.

He groaned with the first bite of pain. It only took a second for him to relax. When Hudson was seated fully inside him, Teague leaned closer to Hudson, noticing how wide Hudson's eyes were. It was as though he wanted to say something but he couldn't. And not merely because he couldn't speak, but perhaps because he couldn't figure out how to express it.

Teague knew just how he felt.

After all, this was the first time in Teague's life that he'd taken a man inside him…

A man he loved.

Without a condom.

And holy fucking hell was it worth the wait.

HUDSON COULDN'T BREATHE. He couldn't swallow. Hell, he could hardly keep his eyes open as the pleasure slammed into him.

He was lodged to the hilt inside Teague and the feeling was … exquisite.

Without the latex barrier, the sensation was so much better, so much hotter, so much … everything.

"Feels good?" Teague whispered, leaning down and brushing his lips to Hudson's.

Hudson nodded.

"It'll feel so much better"—Teague peppered his mouth with kisses—"if you fuck me."

His control snapped, and Hudson reached for Teague, grabbing his hips and pulling him down as he thrust his hips upward.

Blinding.

Holy fuck, the pleasure made him see stars. Teague's ass squeezed him in the most exceptional way.

Taking a deep breath, he began fucking Teague, driving into him from beneath, over and over.

"Fuck, yes," Teague moaned, planting his hands beside Hudson's head. "Exactly what I've been waiting for."

There wasn't nearly enough friction for his peace of mind, so Hudson lifted up, forcing Teague up and then onto his back while Hudson moved with him, never dislodging from Teague's body. When he was over him, Hudson rocked his hips forward, back, forward, back. He drove deeper and deeper every time.

"So much better without the condom," Teague moaned, his hands curled around Hudson's sides. "So fucking much better."

Yeah. What he said.

Hudson tried to focus on Teague, tried to focus on giving him what he needed, but it was too much. All of his senses were focused between his legs where he was connected with Teague. The heated grip of Teague's body was too much.

"Don't stop now," Teague encouraged. "Fuck me, Hudson. Fuck me hard."

Hudson met Teague's gaze, pulling himself out of his stupor. He began pumping his hips steadily as he pushed Teague's legs back, allowing him to angle in deeper.

"Oh, yes…" Teague hissed. "Just like that… Fuck yes."

Hudson watched Teague's face contort with the same pleasure hurtling through him. He wanted this to last forever, but there was no way that was happening. Not this time. Maybe they could take a break and try again later. Then Hudson would fuck Teague for hours. But right now… This…

It was … overwhelming.

Teague pulled Hudson's head down until their lips connected. Hudson went with it, allowing Teague to kiss him, to obliterate what was left of his mind while he slammed his hips forward, retreating, slamming forward again. He never stopped. He was dripping sweat by the time he felt the electrical charge ignite inside him, triggering his orgasm.

"Ahh, yes," Teague growled, holding Hudson's head tightly, his mouth pressed against Hudson's ear. "Come for me. Come inside me. Fill me up, Hudson."

That did it. Teague's roughly mumbled words sent him barreling over the edge. He slammed forward as his dick pulsed. He came, the intense pleasure bordering on pain.

Before Teague could say anything more, Hudson slammed his mouth over his, sucking his tongue in deep as he let his orgasm wash through him. It was an experience he hadn't expected. Condoms were status quo for him, and he'd never really thought much past it. Having never experienced sex without one, he hadn't realized what he'd been missing.

And holy fuck … he'd been missing, that was for damn sure.

Then again, perhaps it was Teague that he'd been missing all this time.

Still lodged inside him, Hudson opened his eyes and stared down into the stormy blue ones looking back at him. Teague was smiling, which in turn made Hudson smile.

Speechless

"I'm thinking we'll have to do that again soon. Only next time, maybe you can hold out a little longer, yeah?" Teague laughed, a deep rumble erupting from his chest. His ass squeezed around Hudson's dick, strangling the last of his seed from him.

Sitting up, Hudson smacked the side of Teague's ass for being a smartass. That only made Teague laugh more, and Hudson decided he truly loved the sound of Teague's laugh. More than he loved anything else.

"What d'ya say we clean up, then we take Charger for a walk, maybe grab some food, then come back here and try that again. I think there's room for improvement. And if not, what the hell. Practice never hurt anyone."

Hudson grinned and he felt the smile in his chest. This man had stolen something from him a long time ago, something he'd been holding on to, something he hadn't been sure he could ever give. He was damn glad he'd never given it to anyone else, too.

Because this kind of love ... it was only meant for one person.

And Teague was it for him.

Forty-Two

TEAGUE OPTED TO take a shower after they returned from taking Charger for a walk and then grabbing burgers at the marina restaurant. He was tired, both mentally and physically. The first day back in the real world had been better than he'd expected, but he was tired just the same.

Before he went to wash up, he put more water down for Charger, then put a blanket on the couch, showing Charger it was all right for him to get up there. He briefly wondered if he would regret that later but decided he didn't care. Charger seemed content, which was all Teague worried about at the moment.

"Okay, man, I'm gonna shower. When I'm done, we'll watch some TV before bed."

It only took fifteen minutes for him to shave and shower, and when he was finished, he was still tired, but at least he was clean.

This was the first time since Hudson had picked him up from the hospital that he'd been alone.

Oddly enough, it didn't bother him as much as he'd thought it would.

Then again, something else was on his mind entirely.

Hudson.

More accurately, spending the night with Hudson.

Speechless

During dinner, Teague had thought about bringing the subject up but decided against it. He didn't want to look as though he was trying to rush things. Really, he wasn't. Instead, he was doing what felt right.

It had taken weeks of therapy for Teague to realize that he'd spent his entire life rebelling against what felt right. He had allowed the feeling of abandonment to control his life. It wasn't until he'd understood more about depression and the effect it had on people that he'd realized his mother hadn't left him by choice. She had been sick and the illness had stolen her from this world. No different than any other medical condition, from his perspective.

His *new* perspective.

Teague remembered his first therapy session. It was a wonder he and his therapist had made it through that in one piece. To say he'd been belligerent was probably an understatement.

"So, what do you want me to talk about?" Teague questioned the woman sitting across from him. For the past few minutes, she'd been jotting something down in a notebook, making him incredibly nervous.

"What do you want to talk about?"

Teague narrowed his eyes at her. "I thought that was for you to decide."

"I'm open to anything," she said, as though this was simple, casual conversation.

He was in a mental hospital, for fuck's sake. Shouldn't she have a clue what they needed to be chatting about?

"I tried to kill myself," he told her, hoping she would come up with something.

"So I heard."

Not helpful. Not helpful at all.

"That doesn't bother you?" he questioned.

"Does it bother you?"

What the fuck kind of question was that?

"If it didn't, I wouldn't be here."

"Why are you here, Teague?"

Was she serious?

Staring at her, he realized she was really interested in his answer.

"Because I tried to kill myself," he repeated. God, she was dense.

"Have you ever sought medical help before when you felt like you wanted to take your own life?"

He shook his head. "I never felt that way before." It was mostly the truth.

"What way?"

"So ... defeated. Out of options. Abandoned."

"So, this was the first time you've ever contemplated taking your own life?"

"No. But it's the first time I attempted."

"Did something push you? Have you been having problems at work? With your family?"

"I don't have any family," he blurted. "And work's just fine."

"So what is it then?"

It was in that moment that Teague thought about Hudson. About the pain he'd seen on Hudson's face. Attempting to kill himself had hurt the man, and Teague would do anything to take that pain back. He couldn't promise he would never do it again since he had no fucking clue what had pushed him in the first place, but that was the reason he was here. For this woman and these doctors to help him.

For the first time in his life, Teague opened his mouth and spit out everything that came to mind. He wasn't gentle about it, either. It needed to be said.

Speechless

It'd been an ugly session. Emotions—namely his—had run high, but in the end, though he'd been mentally drained, he had felt better. Even in a strange place, Teague had slept that first night. Better than he ever had. He wasn't sure if that was because he'd reached his breaking point or if simply sharing what was on his mind had helped.

He might not ever know, but he was glad that he'd sought help. He only wished he hadn't been so stubborn beforehand, because he had allowed things to get completely out of control.

Charger put his head in Teague's lap, and he wondered if the dog sensed the change in his mood.

"It's cool, man. I'm good. So much better than before." Teague looked up at the door. "But you know what would make me even better?" Smiling down at Charger, he nodded toward the door, then got to his feet.

Only one thing could make this day better.

Only one man, actually.

AFTER TAKING A quick shower, Hudson crawled into bed. He wasn't exactly tired, but it was the only way to keep from going over to Teague's to check on him. Since Teague was a grown man, he didn't need Hudson hovering over him. They'd had a good day. A fantastic day, actually, and the kid was probably out cold.

Too bad he wasn't there with him.

Hudson had wanted to ask Teague to stay the night, but he remembered that the doctor had told him that Teague needed to get back to normal as soon as possible. They couldn't harp on the fact that this had happened, but rather they needed to learn to adapt to Teague's mental state.

Hudson wasn't good at adapting, but for Teague, he would do whatever it took.

With the lights off, he stared up at the ceiling. There was only a sliver of moon out tonight, so not much to see by, but he could make out the shadows of his curtains.

He wasn't sure how long he'd been lying there when he heard his door open. He lifted his head to see Teague and Charger coming in, the light from the hallway illuminating them.

He sat up abruptly.

"I'm fine, Hudson," Teague said softly, clearly reading his mind.

Hudson heard Teague pat the couch, then Charger hop up on it, followed by Teague's soft command for Charger to stay. That made Hudson smile. The guy had already gotten attached to the dog.

His heart did a rapid thump-thump in his chest when he felt the blankets being pulled back before Teague crawled into bed with him.

Hudson couldn't see Teague's face, couldn't sign anything because he knew Teague couldn't see him, either. He wanted to ask a million things, but he couldn't.

"Mind if I sleep here tonight? Not because I'm scared of my own bed," Teague said with a soft chuckle. "But I'm just not ready to let go of you yet." Teague shifted. "Of course, if you don't want me to, I—"

Hudson grabbed Teague and pulled him closer, effectively silencing him. He wanted Teague there more than he wanted anything else in the world.

Speechless

Teague curled up against his side, his arm slung over Hudson's chest, his head resting on Hudson's shoulder. They both let out a deep breath at the same time, which made Hudson grin like a fool.

"I really did miss you." Teague's voice was soft. "I should've done this a long time ago."

Curling his arm around Teague's head, Hudson held him close, pressing his lips to Teague's forehead. God, he loved this man. Loved him with all that he was. To think that only a month ago, he'd nearly lost him…

What was worse was the fact that Teague had been suffering from something Hudson was all too familiar with. Instead of recognizing the depression, instead of trying to get Teague treatment, Hudson had thought he was capable of handling things his way. He knew what depression could do because he'd seen what it had done to his mother. He had watched her suffer in silence, then he'd been riddled with guilt when she had taken her own life, succumbing to the disease. He'd spent years telling himself he should've done more, he should've been there for her, should've encouraged her to get help.

Hudson sent up a silent prayer of thanks. Thanks that his path had crossed with Teague's, thanks that they'd had the opportunity to build what they had now, and most of all, thanks that they had this opportunity. Who knew where it would go or how things would end up, but Hudson was in it for the long haul. He was committed to this man.

And he would make damn sure Teague knew just what he meant to him for the rest of his life.

Forty-Three

Monday, September 19th

MILLY KNEW SHE should've called first.

But no.

She'd been so freaked out she'd hopped in her car and sped out to the lake, heading right for Cam and Gannon's. Experience told her she should've given them a heads-up so that she didn't end up finding the two of them in the throes of … whatever. Unfortunately, her brain was too mixed up for her to think clearly.

The door opened and Gannon stared back at her with a frown marring his forehead. "Milly? What's going on? Are you all right?"

As soon as her best friend opened the door, allowing her to enter, Milly burst into tears.

Not dainty little tears but the huge, crocodile ones that came along with sobs so horrific she sounded like a horse with a cough choking on an apple.

Gannon led her through the foyer and into the living room while she blubbered like an idiot.

Cam peeked around the corner, his eyes widening when he saw her.

Speechless

"You know what?" he said quickly, his gaze slamming into Gannon. "I just remembered I need to head back to the marina. I've got a … something. Shit."

Gannon had warned her that Cam wasn't good with crying women. Since she'd never been a blubbering mess like this before, this was the first time she'd seen it with her own eyes.

"You don't have to go," she said on a sob.

"Oh, I definitely do."

Milly eased onto the sofa while Cam kissed Gannon quickly, then disappeared out the door.

"Okay, honey, calm down." Gannon dropped to the cushion beside her. "What's going on?"

"I know I should've called, but I … I didn't know what to say, and what I have to tell you shouldn't be said over the phone, anyway. I tried to tell you the other night at dinner, but I chickened out. And now I didn't have anyone else to talk to. Noah's so caught up in Dare I didn't want to bother him, and heaven forbid I call my dad because he would freak out. I—"

Gannon put his hand over her mouth.

She looked at him with wide eyes.

"Tell me what's wrong."

Sucking in a deep breath, Milly swallowed hard. "I'm… Oh, God, Gannon! I'm pregnant." And there went the waterworks again. She couldn't seem to stop them. Even when she looked up to see Gannon's mouth hanging wide open, his eyes huge behind his glasses.

Knowing he was as stunned as she had been when she'd first learned of the news, Milly nodded. And then she couldn't stop. It was as though her neck was a bungee cord. Up, down, up, down. Her head wouldn't stop moving.

"Take a deep breath, Mill. It's gonna be all right."

It was her jaw's turn to come unhinged. She stared back at her best friend in disbelief. "All right? How in the world do you think everything's gonna be all right? Oh, my God, Gannon, did you hear what I said? I'm pregnant."

"Yes, I heard you the first time. That's the only reason I haven't offered wine."

That made her cry again. Wine. She would miss her wine. She would be off wine for at least six more months.

Flopping back on the couch, Milly blew her bangs out of her face and tried to relax. It didn't work. She sat up again and put her head in her hands.

"Why don't you start at the beginning?" Gannon prompted.

Lifting her head, she looked at him. "Well, it all started because your dumb ass wanted to get married."

"Me?" Gannon looked affronted. "What the hell do I have to do with this?"

"Well, for starters, if we hadn't gone on that stupid cruise, I wouldn't be in this predicament."

Gannon didn't respond.

"I slept with AJ. Hudson's brother. You know, the guy—"

"I know who AJ is," he interrupted. "So, it's safe to assume he's the father?"

Milly huffed. She was the one affronted now. "Of course he's the father. I haven't been with anyone else since that stupid cruise, and I hadn't been with anyone in six or seven months before that because I was too busy trying to put together your stupid wedding. I slept with him, and yes, before you give me the talk about safe sex, we used a condom, but he's pierced and I've always heard that—"

"I don't need specifics, Mill."

"You asked," she blurted.

Speechless

"I assume this is the hormones talking?" Gannon's smile was mischievous. He was teasing her.

"I don't know what this is." Milly sighed. "I haven't been feeling well, as you know. I finally gave in and went to the doctor last Tuesday. Since he said he couldn't find anything wrong with me and he didn't think it was a virus, the doctor ran a blood test. He called on Thursday to let me know I needed to make an appointment with an obstetrician. Of course, I did. I needed to be sure." She forced a smile. "I'm sure."

"Holy shit."

Milly cocked her head to the side. "Really? That's all you've got?"

"What do you want me to say? I don't even know what your plans are."

"My plans?"

"Have you told AJ?"

Milly shook her head. She wanted to call him, but she figured sharing the news that the man was going to be a father probably wasn't the greatest thing to do over the phone. She thought about texting him, but that seemed worse.

"Well, I think it's safe to say you should probably start there."

"You think?" This wasn't going the way she had hoped it would. Granted, she didn't have a clue what she'd thought Gannon could do for her in the first place. Sitting up straight, she tried to compose herself. "I haven't talked to him since the night when Teague was in the emergency room. He called a few times and left messages before that, but I never returned his call. I wasn't all that kind to him at the hospital, either."

"You two have a falling out or something?"

Or something. Kind of. "I really liked him," she admitted. "But I know myself. He's a nice guy, he's got a good job, he's got a place of his own and a truck that's paid for…"

Gannon chuckled. "Completely understand. Totally not your type."

"Exactly. I always go for the bad boy. And I'm not talking in the sexy, romantic sense, either. I'm talking no job, musician types who live in their mother's basements and hitch rides with their friends anywhere they want to go."

"Yep, that about sums up your last ten boyfriends."

"This is not helping," she said, smiling for the first time since she'd stepped foot in his home.

Gannon's voice lowered when he lifted her chin and forced her to meet his eyes. "Do you want to keep the baby?"

Milly nodded. She wasn't sure if that was selfish or not, but she so totally wanted to keep this baby. Never in her life had she expected to be a mother—her plan had involved falling in love first, but since she knew that wasn't in the stars, she had all but given up hope.

"Then I suggest you meet with AJ. If you got pregnant on the cruise, that means you're what…?"

"About three months." According to the book she'd been reading, she would probably start showing in a few weeks.

"How did you not know you were pregnant?"

Milly glared at him. "It's not like the baby stuck its hand out of my vagina and waved. How would I have known?"

Gannon's look told her she was being ridiculous. "I'm assuming you missed a couple of periods."

She waved him off. "That's normal for me. I have a screwed up menstrual cycle. Always have."

"I still think you should go see AJ as soon as possible. He's a good guy, Milly."

Speechless

"I know. That's the problem. What in the world would he want with me?" It was a rhetorical question. Gannon would likely go on and on about her qualities, but she didn't want to hear them. "But you're right. I have to tell him."

"Do you want me to go with you?"

Milly huffed. "Are you crazy? Good Lord. It's gonna be hard enough as it is."

Gannon chuckled and Milly realized she actually did feel a little better.

She just wondered how long that would last once she got to AJ's.

Forty-Four

Tuesday, September 20^{*th*}

TEAGUE'S PHONE BUZZED and he grabbed it from where it sat on his toolbox.

Glancing at the screen, he smiled to himself.

Wanted to see if you and Charger want to go over to AJ's with me. He said he needs to talk.

This was the first time Hudson had invited him to go to his brother's house. Granted, Hudson hadn't been over there since Teague had gotten out of the hospital five days ago. They'd spent most of their time around the marina, getting Charger familiar with everything. They'd even gone out on the water yesterday afternoon for a couple of hours. Charger was a natural when it came to the lake. But that had been the extent of their outings. Well, except when Teague had gotten a peek at Hudson's gym on Sunday. The crazy bastard had invited him to go work out.

Right.

Working out?

Not Teague's thing.

Speechless

Hell, just watching Hudson work out made him tired. He told Hudson from now on, the only working out he was willing to do required them both to be naked. Hudson hadn't complained when Teague had showed him what he meant as soon as they got home.

Teague texted Hudson back. *You sure he doesn't want to talk to you alone?*

Hudson's response was almost immediate. *Let me rephrase that. I would like you to go to my brother's with me. Will you?*

Teague laughed, looking up to see Hudson standing at his office door, staring back at him with a huge grin on his handsome face.

"Of course I will. What time?"

Hudson signed: *Six.*

"I just need to take Charger for a walk after work, then I'll be good to go." Charger was two years old, which was practically a puppy. His energy levels were high, which Teague had learned the first night he'd stayed with Hudson. They'd been woken up by a very rambunctious dog pouncing in an attempt to get their attention. Turned out he had needed to go out. That was easy enough to satisfy, but after that, Charger wasn't interested in sleep, which meant their day had started at six. In the morning.

Since then, Charger had gone everywhere with Teague. Everywhere. Even to work, where he wandered around the shop or napped in Hudson's air-conditioned office when he got tired. They'd all three settled into a fantastic rhythm, as though they'd been doing this forever.

Hudson nodded.

Teague wondered if AJ's need to talk had anything to do with whatever was going down with Milly. He'd overheard Cam on the phone with Gannon last night when Cam had showed back up at the marina unexpectedly. Teague had gotten into a conversation with him when Cam's phone had rung. The guy had been rambling on and on and then bam! Not a peep out of him. Teague had glanced over to make sure he was all right, and Cam's eyeballs had been the size of spaceships.

Whatever it was, Teague was more than happy to go with Hudson.

He was just getting back to work when his phone buzzed again.

Oh, and afterwards, when we get back, I plan to spend the rest of the night lodged somewhere in your body. Mouth. Ass. Your choice.

Warmth consumed him as he read the message.

Then after that, I hope you'll spend the night again.

Hudson's last comment made Teague's chest swell. The first night Teague had made the first move, sneaking into Hudson's apartment and crawling into bed with him. Then on Saturday night, Teague had stayed at his own place. On Sunday, Hudson had snuck into his bed. Last night, Teague had again slept alone. He found he preferred going to sleep and waking up next to Hudson.

Who would've thought?

I'll be more than happy to stay the night. Just remember, Charger's gonna wake us up early.

Teague knew better than to put his phone away, so he waited for Hudson's reply.

Not a problem. Maybe I'll be nice and even let you sleep while I take him out. After all, I do plan to wear you out.

Speechless

Teague chuckled, then shoved his phone in his pocket and got back to work. The sooner he got this done, the sooner the day would be over. They could go to AJ's and come home. He was certainly looking forward to the last part.

TEAGUE LET OUT a long, low whistle while Hudson stared at AJ slack-jawed.

Hudson wasn't sure he'd heard right.

Pregnant?

AJ nodded.

Hudson couldn't believe what his brother was telling him.

Milly was pregnant.

"Dude, they make these things called condoms…" Teague supplied unhelpfully.

AJ smirked, continuing to scratch Charger's head while the dog sat on the floor between Teague's legs and AJ's. "We used a condom. But when your dick is pierced…"

"Got it. Don't need details." Teague turned to look at Hudson. "You gonna say something to your brother?"

Hudson shrugged. What the hell was he supposed to say?

For one, he couldn't tell if AJ was happy about it or not. He sounded entirely too calm, which meant either he was okay with the news or he was going to go postal at some point. With AJ, it wasn't easy to predict.

"When's the baby due?" Teague asked, managing to carry the conversation without Hudson's input.

"Her due date is March sixth."

Hudson managed to get with the program.

How do you feel about this?

"How am I supposed to feel?" AJ asked, but Hudson could tell it was rhetorical. "Here's this woman who I had a fan-fucking-tastic time with for nearly a week, the same woman who ignored me as soon as we got back to dry land … and we're now gonna have a baby together."

"So, you're still on the fence?" Teague muttered sarcastically.

Surprisingly, AJ laughed.

"I'm thirty-seven years old. I guess I never gave much thought to having kids. Since I've never been married."

Are you going to marry her?

AJ barked out a laugh. "This ain't the old days, Hudson. I don't have to marry her to have a baby with her."

"True," Teague noted.

Hudson glared at Teague, which made Teague laugh. This was a weird conversation for two reasons. One, AJ seemed oddly at ease with the news that he was going to be a father, and two, Teague seemed pretty relaxed. Maybe Hudson needed to chill the fuck out.

So, what is the next step?

"I invited her to go out to dinner," AJ admitted.

"Kinda late for the romancin' stuff, don't you think?" Teague teased.

Hudson shook his head in disbelief, staring over at Teague.

"What? It's true."

"I like the woman," AJ added. "Since we got back from the cruise, I've been trying to get her to go out with me. I gave up a while ago because I'm not one to chase women."

"Looks like there's a bigger plan for you, man," Teague said, still smiling.

"Looks like it."

Are you going to be part of the kid's life?

"Of course. I told Milly I wanted to do everything I could to help her. Both during the pregnancy and when the baby is born."

So she agreed to go out with you?

"Finally," AJ said with a huff. "It took some work, but she finally caved."

"If you're half as demanding as this one, I can totally see why she did."

Unable to resist, Hudson put his arm around Teague's shoulder and pulled him in for a kiss. He wasn't sure how the kid would react with AJ sitting right there, but he took the chance anyway. Luckily, Teague didn't seem to mind, because he kissed Hudson back, albeit chastely.

Hudson turned his attention back to AJ. *If you're happy, then I'm happy for you.*

"I'm happy. And thank you. We've got a long road. We both admitted that we're clueless when it comes to relationships and even more so when it comes to babies, but I think we'll figure it out."

Hudson didn't doubt that was the case. He knew AJ was a stand-up guy and he would do the right thing no matter what. Hudson only hoped he managed to find what he was looking for along the way.

Love didn't come along every day, and when it did, it didn't always smack you in the face to let you know it was there. So maybe there was a happy ending for AJ and Milly after all.

Hudson figured only time would tell.

Forty-Five

"PREGNANT," TEAGUE MUSED aloud as he walked into his apartment a short time later. "I never woulda seen that coming." Turning to look at Hudson, he grinned. "That means you're gonna be an uncle."

Hudson still looked a little out of sorts. Far more than AJ had, which was surprising.

Fully expecting Hudson to say something related to AJ's news, Teague was taken completely off guard by what came next.

I want to tie you up.

"What?" Surely Hudson hadn't said what he thought he had. "Repeat that."

Hudson moved closer, sidestepping Charger, who had flopped down on the floor near Teague's feet.

I want to tie you up.

"That looked a hell of a lot like 'I want to tie you up.' Tell me I'm a little rusty on my sign language."

Hudson took another step closer, shaking his head.

"You're shaking your head, which means no, I didn't read it right?"

The smirk that curled Hudson's perfect lips was wicked. Apparently, he hadn't misunderstood.

I want to tie you to your bed.

Speechless

Okay, that was not supposed to be hot. Teague knew he should've been freaking out about now. He had never let anyone tie him up. Never even considered it. It was a trust thing.

Trust me.

Apparently Hudson could read his mind.

And he really did trust Hudson. More so than he'd ever trusted anyone in his life. But did he trust Hudson enough to let him tie him up?

I won't hurt you.

"I know that." He did.

Hudson had stopped moving closer, and Teague knew he was waiting for an answer, although there really hadn't been a question.

"Will you fuck me?" Teague asked.

Hudson nodded.

"Okay."

Say it.

"Say what?" Teague was confused.

Tell me that you trust me.

"I do trust you," Teague admitted, his breath raspy.

Hudson's mouth came down over his, and Teague had no choice but to hold on for dear life. Somehow, while their lips were crushed together, Hudson managed to get Teague out of his clothes. Not that he minded, because the wicked look in Hudson's eyes when he pulled back and took Teague in from head to toe said he would not be disappointed with his answer.

On the bed.

Teague turned away, then slowly crawled onto the bed, giving Hudson his ass while he did. He peered over his shoulder to see Hudson grabbing his crotch, rubbing his cock through his shorts. Clearly he was enjoying the show.

Teague wasn't sure how this was going to work. Was Hudson going to make him spread out, tie his hands to the bars on each side of the headboard? He'd never done this before.

And what was he going to use? It wasn't like Teague kept spare rope around the house.

He flopped onto his back, then glanced at Hudson, who seemed to be contemplating the same thing.

Don't move.

"Where the hell are you going?"

Hudson didn't reply, he simply disappeared out the door while Teague lay naked on his bed. He looked over to see that Charger was paying him no attention. Good thing because that would've been awkward. He looked up at the ceiling again.

His palms began to sweat while he waited for Hudson to do whatever it was Hudson was doing.

Just when he was about to say never mind, Hudson reappeared, closing Teague's door behind him and coming to stand at the side of the bed.

Teague looked at what Hudson had in his hands.

"Are those ... socks?"

Hudson grinned, then signaled for Teague to put his hands above his head.

Well, this was different. He was being restrained to the bed by tube socks.

Somehow, Hudson managed to work the sock around Teague's wrists, then hook them by using a third sock to the metal bar on the headboard. Teague's arms were stretched above his head, but he would be able to turn over if he wanted. His arms would cross, but he'd be able to do it.

Peering back at his hands, he saw that he could probably get free if he needed to, as well. He wondered if Hudson had done that on purpose.

Speechless

He didn't get a chance to ask, because Hudson leaned over and kissed Teague's wrist, then his mouth began trailing down his arm. As he got closer to Teague's armpit, it began to tickle, but he pushed the thought away. Hudson's tongue trailed down the entire length of Teague's body, stopping at his knees, before he moved to the other side. The sensation was relaxing, and Teague found the tension in his body seeping out the longer Hudson teased him.

When Hudson's mouth found his, Teague turned his head, giving in to the kiss. He went to move his arms, and they tugged against the restraints. Surprisingly, he didn't panic.

And that was when he realized he did trust Hudson. He trusted him with his mind, body, and soul.

TEAGUE LOOKED SO damn good lying there on his bed, unable to do anything but take the pleasure that Hudson was insistent upon giving him. And he had every intention of pushing Teague as high as he could take him.

While he thrust his tongue into Teague's mouth, Hudson pulled a blindfold from his pocket, then worked it around Teague's head. Lifting up, he looked down at the beautiful man.

"Are you blindfolding me?"

Hudson nodded, fully intending to relent should Teague refuse. It was enough that Teague had agreed to be tied up, but he knew the sensations would be magnified if his eyes were covered.

"Okay."

Pulling the blindfold down over Teague's eyes, Hudson resumed kissing him.

Needing to remove his clothes, he pulled back but continuously put his hand on Teague somewhere as he undressed. He touched Teague's hip, his thigh, his knee, his chest. He wanted Teague to know that he was still there.

Once his clothes were off, Hudson climbed on the bed beside Teague, lying on his side and facing him. He trailed his hand from Teague's mouth, down his neck, then lower. He watched his hand move along Teague's smooth, bronzed skin. He went lower still, brushing one finger over the hardened length of Teague's shaft.

That earned him a groan.

Hudson continued doing that for several minutes, touching every inch of Teague with his fingertips, then proceeded to do the same thing with his tongue.

Once Teague was writhing and moaning beneath him, Hudson worked his mouth down between Teague's legs. He kissed the insides of Teague's thighs, slid his tongue along the part where Teague's leg met his hip. The entire time he teased, Teague tried to thrust upward.

"Hudson..."

Hudson grinned at the warning tone. Teague was completely at his mercy right now.

When Hudson did give in and glide his tongue along Teague's shaft, Teague cried out. It was a beautiful sound. Hudson continued that same motion, barely touching Teague, breathing against his skin while the kid begged and pleaded for Hudson to suck him.

"Oh, fuck!"

Teague's back bowed when Hudson pulled him into his mouth, taking him all the way down. He slowly worked his mouth off Teague's thick shaft, then did it again. He continued with only his mouth, keeping his hands on the bed rather than give Teague more than he could handle.

Speechless

For nearly a full half hour, Hudson teased and tormented the bound man, loving every second of it.

"Want you in my mouth," Teague pleaded, gasping for air when Hudson released him from his mouth.

Hudson had intended to flip Teague over and sink inside him, but if Teague wanted to suck him, he was more than willing to oblige.

He moved to the edge of the bed, then pulled Teague's head toward him, sliding his cock past Teague's smooth, warm lips.

Oh, yeah. Fuck.

Teague knew just how to suck him to make him see stars. The kid had a wicked mouth that no doubt would drive him wild for years to come.

Before Teague could send him over the edge, Hudson pulled his cock from between Teague's lips, grabbed the bottle of lube from the nightstand, then flipped Teague over onto his stomach before crawling up behind him.

After lubing himself up, he worked the head into Teague's ass slowly.

"Yes," Teague hissed. "I've been waiting for this all damn day."

Hudson pushed in another inch, Teague's ass clamping down on him. He smacked Teague's ass, warning him to relax, which he did.

Working his dick deep into Teague, Hudson then leaned over him, planting his forearms beside Teague's arms, which were still stretched out above his head. Hudson kept most of his weight off him, but he wanted Teague to feel his body, to know he was right there with him. He rocked forward and back, fucking Teague slow and easy for several long minutes. He pressed kisses to Teague's shoulder and neck, keeping him wrapped tightly beneath him.

"I could get used to this," Teague moaned. "You loving me like this."

Hudson's heart slammed into his ribs. Every time Teague mentioned love, the same emotions assaulted him. Sometimes it was hard to believe they'd come this far. He had no idea what the future held for them, and he wasn't in a hurry to find out, but he was looking forward to every single minute they spent together.

"Oh, yes," Teague groaned when Hudson shifted, changing the angle slightly. "Oh, yeah. Right there."

Hudson continued to pump his hips forward, back, sliding in deep, retreating, until they were both breathing hard. It didn't take long before Teague was begging him, and Hudson was more than willing to give him what he needed.

Lifting up, Hudson knelt between Teague's spread thighs, then pulled Teague's ass up. Teague had to move his knees underneath him because he was still bound to the headboard. Once he was in place, Hudson grabbed his hips and slammed home.

"Fuck! Yes!" Teague tried to push back against him. "Fuck me hard."

Hudson plowed into him, slamming home over and over. He never slowed his pace, even managed to reach around and grab Teague's dick while he continued to drive into him deeper. Wrapping his hand around Teague's steely length, Hudson jacked him in rhythm with his thrusts.

"I'm gonna come... It's too much, Hudson... Oh, yeah... Fuck yeah... Gonna..." Teague cried out. "Come!"

Watching Teague fly apart was utter perfection, causing Hudson to follow him right over.

Forty-Six

Saturday, September 24th

"WHERE ARE WE going?" Teague asked Hudson for what was probably the hundredth time.

The guy had been tight-lipped all damn day. Since the minute they'd woken up, Teague had known something was up. Hudson didn't usually act this weird.

"Are you taking me to dinner?"

Although Hudson had already given Teague a birthday card and one hell of a blow job, he got the impression that his birthday wasn't over yet. He merely wasn't in the loop on what Hudson's plans were.

Ten minutes later, he figured it out all on his own.

When they pulled into Cam and Gannon's driveway, he realized Hudson had made plans to have dinner with the other couple. Made sense because Cam had mentioned something earlier in the week about him and Hudson stopping by on Saturday. Teague hadn't bothered to mention it was his birthday, though.

"You know, dinner at home would've been just fine. I would've let you fuck me as soon as we were done."

Hudson grinned.

Oh, I plan for that to happen no matter what.

"Do you now?" Teague chuckled. "Maybe you should let me top since it is my birthday and all."

Hudson's eyes widened, making Teague double over in a fit of laughter.

"Kidding. I very much prefer having you nail me to the bed with that giant dick of yours." Teague grinned widely. "However, I do know a couple of tricks you might like. If you trust me, that is."

I definitely trust you.

"Enough to let me use my tongue and fingers?"

Hudson's eyes flashed hot and bright right before he shook his head as he normally did, as though he couldn't believe the shit coming out of Teague's mouth. Then he grinned widely and hopped out of the truck.

"Charger, why does the man not listen to me?" With a sigh, Teague got out of the truck and looked around at Cam's quiet neighborhood. It was one of those uppity areas that probably didn't let people park on the street overnight because there were hardly any cars anywhere.

Hudson was waiting at the front of the truck when Teague finally made his way around. Admittedly, he was taking his time just to pester Hudson.

After Hudson knocked on the door and they were waiting for Cam to answer, Teague leaned over, lowering his voice when he said, "Maybe we can slip out early and you can fuck me in the truck."

The door flew open and Teague jerked back in time to see Hudson's eyes go wide. He loved teasing the man. Although he had learned his lesson in the past couple of days. Hudson could only be pushed so far before Teague found himself with the man's dick in his mouth.

Again, not complaining.

"Hey," Cam greeted. "Glad y'all could make it. And perfect timing, too. Gannon's just pulling the steaks off the grill."

Teague followed Hudson and Charger into the house. The place was all fancy and clean. Far too formal for Teague's taste, but it seemed to work for Gannon and Cam. To each his own and all that.

"We set everything up outside since it's so nice out tonight."

Again, Teague followed them through the house, then out onto the back deck. It was already dark outside, but lights were twinkling from the patio cover, and the moon was shining off the water farther away.

"Surprise!"

Teague damn near swallowed his fucking tongue.

He jumped back, causing Charger to bark loudly as people started stepping out from whatever fucking hiding places they'd been in.

"What the hell?" he whispered, sucking air into his lungs.

"Happy birthday!" Milly said, walking right up to him and wrapping her arms around his neck. "Were you surprised?"

Teague nodded at the same time he said, "No."

Milly giggled. "Yeah! It worked. Your man had you pegged. He said you never would've expected this."

His man.

Teague liked the sound of that.

And Hudson had been right.

"Happy birthday," AJ said, coming to stand beside Milly. Teague noticed that he didn't stand too close.

Dare and Noah came up to him next. Dare bumped Teague's fist. "So, you old enough to drink yet, or what?"

Teague was about to flip Dare off when he noticed that Cam's sister, his brother-in-law, and their kids were there. Along with Mr. Strickland. Probably best to keep the hand gestures to himself.

Roan came over, grinning from ear to ear. "Looks like I lost the bet."

"What bet's that?" Teague questioned, knowing he shouldn't.

"I said you'd go all ninja and freak out if we surprised you." Roan nodded toward Hudson. "He said you'd pretend not to be affected."

Teague laughed. No way could they know whether he was pretending or not.

He was. They didn't need to know that, though.

HUDSON GRINNED AS he watched Teague. Honestly, he hadn't expected them to be able to pull off the surprise. When he'd gone to Cam, Dare, and Roan and suggested a surprise party, they'd all but convinced him it would never work.

Hence the bet. Hudson would have to remind Roan to pay up because it'd worked, all right.

The smile on Teague's face proved it.

"Come on, y'all! Let's eat. Seriously. Steaks are gonna get cold," Cam hollered.

While everyone else headed toward the tables where the food was being placed, Hudson remained where he was right beside Teague.

"I hope you know I'm gonna pay you back for this," Teague whispered.

Speechless

Promise?

"Absolutely."

I can't wait.

Teague smirked.

Hudson had no idea what Teague had in mind for him, but if he had to guess, it pertained to some sort of sexual activity. Since he was still trying to come up with creative ways to make Teague beg for more, he welcomed Teague shaking things up.

Then again...

He thought about Teague's comment in the truck. Did the kid seriously want to top him? He'd never considered it with Teague, but ... he was a little intrigued, he wouldn't lie.

He would definitely have to think more about that later.

However, he did have to keep his eyes open for what Teague had in store for him. Teague could be incredibly bratty when he wanted to be. That was something that hadn't changed—for which Hudson was grateful—and he knew the kid would give him a run for his money.

I'm going to go wash up.

"I'll come with you," Teague said.

Hudson grinned to himself as he led the way back into the house, then down the hall to the guest bathroom. When Teague followed him inside, Hudson pushed the door closed, then flipped the lock.

Teague shot him a sideways glance. "Don't you think one surprise is enough for the day?"

Turning Teague, Hudson pushed him up against the door, then went to his knees before him.

"What are you doing?" Teague questioned, his voice low.

Apologizing.

"Oh. Well, in that case…" Teague reached for the button on his shorts.

Hudson didn't even have to do the work; Teague took care of it all for him.

Happy birthday, baby.

Epilogue

Saturday, October 8th

"I NEVER WOULDA pegged you for a hockey fan," Teague told Hudson as they made their way out of the stands.

Gannon had managed to get them all tickets—fucking fantastic ones at that—for the first home game of the season for the Austin Arrows. Turned out Gannon had an in with the Arrows' owner, Phoenix Pierce.

Who doesn't like men on skates chasing pucks with sticks?

Teague chuckled. That certainly wasn't how he saw the game, but whatever.

"We really goin' to meet the players?" he asked, glancing over at Roan, who was walking along beside him.

Teague was pretty sure Roan had a stick lodged up his ass tonight. He'd been incredibly weird, and no one seemed to know why. Granted, Roan wasn't the most talkative all the time, but when he was having a good time, he could get carried away. That didn't seem to be the case tonight.

"Yep," Dare said. "We get to meet 'em all tonight. You probably don't remember, but a group of 'em came out to the lake back in June." Dare glanced over at Roan. "I remember that because you suddenly had something come up, and I got to hang with them for the afternoon. Definitely your loss."

Roan didn't even acknowledge Dare, which was interesting.

Teague followed the group, walking close to Hudson as he did. Although he liked the idea of meeting the players, he really wanted to get home. He missed Charger and hated leaving the little guy for too long while he was out. Granted, Charger probably enjoyed being alone for a little while, but still. Teague wasn't fond of it. Charger did have full run of both apartments since, as of last week, Teague had officially moved into Hudson's bed. He hadn't moved his things over, and they were still paying rent for both apartments above the marina, but he was sleeping like a baby right next to the big guy every single night. It was working out nicely for them just to utilize both places as they needed.

"Hey, guys," Phoenix greeted them when they made it to the corridor they'd been advised to go to. "Glad y'all could make it. Enjoy the game?"

"Immensely," Cam replied. "Your boys are lookin' good out there this year."

Everyone knew that the Austin Arrows had had a shit season last year. Like, totally fucked up. They'd gone from winning the Stanley Cup the year before to not even making the playoffs last year. In fact, Teague was pretty sure Cam had said they'd come in last place. First to last. It'd been brutal. Teague only knew because Roan and Cam were hockey fans and they'd talked about it.

"Not too shabby," Phoenix agreed. "A shutout is definitely the way to start a season. Come on, I'll introduce you to those that I can."

Speechless

Everyone followed behind Cam and Gannon, but Teague noticed that Roan was slowly working his way to the back of the group. Before he could slip past him, Teague elbowed him in the arm.

"Going somewhere? Looks to me like you're trying to hide from someone." Teague made a show of looking around, trying to see what, or who, Roan could possibly be running from.

"Shut the hell up," Roan muttered.

Teague chuckled. "Not all that fun to get your balls busted, huh?"

Phoenix spoke up. "Guys, I'm sure he doesn't need an introduction, but this is Spencer Kaufman, the Arrows captain."

Cam shook Spencer's hand, his face lighting up like this was Christmas or something.

"And that over there is Kingston Rush, the man in the net."

All eyes slid to where Kingston was currently talking to a reporter.

Phoenix started walking until he stopped at another group of men. He began rattling off names, introducing them to the players as his friends.

"And this right here is the man of the night," Phoenix noted. "Colton Seguine, defense. Colton, these are some friends of mine. They own a marina out on Lake Buchanan."

Something sparked in Colton's eyes as he looked from face to face. Teague was fascinated watching as he searched for … something. Rightfully so, because those eyes continued to roam until they suddenly stopped.

Right on Roan's face.

Well, son of a bitch.

There was definitely some recognition there.

Teague glanced over, noticing that Roan was staring at the floor, not making eye contact.

Definitely something going on between those two.

"Again, thanks for coming out tonight. Tickets for the games are yours whenever you want them," Phoenix said to the group. "I've gotta go catch up with my husband and wife. I'm sure they're looking for me."

Teague glanced at Hudson, trying to figure out if he'd heard Phoenix correctly.

Husband *and* wife. Damn. How crazy did you have to be to sign up for that shit?

Hudson shrugged as though reading Teague's mind. Teague looked at Hudson's hands when he signed: *You ready to head out now?*

Teague smiled, then signed back so that he could keep the conversation between the two of them. *The only thing I caught was head. Is that an offer?*

Be careful, kid. You don't want to taunt me too much.

"Oh, but I do," he said, still grinning up at his man. "I most certainly do."

And that was exactly what Teague did for the entire drive back to the marina.

He did it with a smile on his face, in fact.

Oh, and also with Hudson's dick in his mouth.

Not for the first time, they'd both been speechless.

In more ways than one.

Dear Reader,

This book touched on some very sensitive subjects, including suicide and depression, all of which should not be taken lightly.

If you or someone that you know suffers from depression or has thoughts of suicide, please, I encourage you to seek professional help.

If you are in crisis, call 1-800-273-TALK (8255)

National Suicide Prevention Lifeline

http://www.suicidepreventionlifeline.org

For more information or resources on suicide prevention:

American Foundation for Suicide Prevention

http://www.afsp.org

♥□□□□♥□□□□♥

I hope you enjoyed Hudson and Teague's story. Speechless is the third book in the Pier 70 series. I started writing their story shortly after I finished Fearless because I felt it needed to be told. It wasn't easy for me, but at the same time, it ended up being therapeutic during a particularly low point for me. You can read more about the sexy guys in charge of the marina by checking them out on my website.

Want to see some fun stuff related to the Pier 70 series, you can find extras on my website. Or how about what's coming next? I keep my website updated with the books I'm working on, including the writing progression of what's coming up for the Pier 70 series. www.NicoleEdwardsAuthor.com

If you're interested in keeping up to date on the Pier 70 crew as well as receiving updates on all that I'm working on, you can sign up for my monthly newsletter.

Want a simple, *fast* way to get updates on new releases? You can also sign up for text messaging. If you are in the U.S. simply text NICOLE to 64600 or sign up on my website. I promise not to spam your phone. This is just my way of letting you know what's happening because I know you're busy, but if you're anything like me, you always have your phone on you.

And last but certainly not least, if you want to see what's going on with me each week, sign up for my weekly Hot Sheet! It's a short, entertaining weekly update of things going on in my life and that of the team that supports me. We're a little crazy at times and this is a firsthand account of our antics.

Acknowledgments

I have to thank my family first, for putting up with my craziness. From my sudden outbursts when I think of something that needs to be added or when I question why one of the characters did what they did, to the strange hours that I keep and the days on end when I'm MIA because I'm under deadline or just engrossed in a story... Y'all are incredibly tolerant of me and for that, I am forever grateful. I love you with all that I am.

My street team – The Naughty & Nice Posse. Ladies, your daily pimping and support fills my heart with so much love. You are a blessing to me, each and every one of you.

My beta readers, Chancy and Denise. Ladies, I'm not sure thanks will ever be enough. However, not only are you the ones who catch the weird things and ask the bigger questions, you've both become my friends and you keep me going.

My copyeditor, Amy. Punctuation and grammar... well, that's not my strong suit. But it is yours and you are truly remarkable at what you do. You simply amaze me and I am so glad that I found you.

Nicole Nation 2.0 for the constant support and love. This group of ladies has kept me going for so long, I'm not sure I'd know what to do without them.

And, of course, YOU, the reader. Your emails, messages, posts, comments, tweets... they mean more to me than you can imagine. I thrive on hearing from you, knowing that my characters and my stories have touched you in some way keeps me going. I've been known to shed a tear or two when reading an email because you simply bring so much joy to my life with your support. I thank you for that.

♥••••♥••••♥

About Nicole

New York Times and *USA Today* bestselling author Nicole Edwards lives in Austin, Texas with her husband, their three kids, and four rambunctious dogs. When she's not writing about sexy alpha males, Nicole can often be found with her Kindle in hand or making an attempt to keep the dogs happy. You can find her hanging out on Facebook and interacting with her readers - even when she's supposed to be writing.

Nicole also writes contemporary/new adult romance as Timberlyn Scott.

Website
www.NicoleEdwardsAuthor.com

Facebook
www.facebook.com/Author.Nicole.Edwards

Twitter
@NicoleEAuthor

Also by Nicole Edwards

The Alluring Indulgence Series
Kaleb

Zane

Travis

Holidays with the Walker Brothers

Ethan

Braydon

Sawyer

Brendon

The Club Destiny Series
Conviction

Temptation

Addicted

Seduction

Infatuation

Captivated

Devotion

Perception

Entrusted

Adored

The Coyote Ridge Series
Curtis

The Dead Heat Ranch Series
Boots Optional

Betting on Grace

Overnight Love

.

Also by Nicole Edwards (cont.)

The Devil's Bend Series
Chasing Dreams

Vanishing Dreams

The Devil's Playground Series
Without Regret

The Pier 70 Series
Reckless

Fearless

Speechless

The Sniper 1 Security Series
Wait for Morning

Never Say Never

The Southern Boy Mafia Series
Beautifully Brutal

Beautifully Loyal

Standalone Novels
A Million Tiny Pieces

Inked on Paper

Writing as Timberlyn Scott
Unhinged

Unraveling

Chaos

Naughty Holiday Editions
2015

35064777R00213

Made in the USA
San Bernardino, CA
14 June 2016